An UNCERTAIN DREAM

Books by Judith Miller

FROM BETHANY HOUSE PUBLISHERS

BELLS OF LOWELL*

Daughter of the Loom

A Fragile Design

These Tangled Threads

Bells of Lowell (3 in 1)

LIGHTS OF LOWELL*

A Tapestry of Hope

A Love Woven True

The Pattern of Her Heart

FREEDOM'S PATH

First Dawn

Morning Sky

Daylight Comes

POSTCARDS FROM PULLMAN

In the Company of Secrets

Whispers Along the Rails

An Uncertain Dream

THE BROADMOOR LEGACY*

A Daughter's Inheritance

*with Tracie Peterson

POSTCARDS *from* PULLMAN ★ 3

An UNCERTAIN DREAM

JUDITH MILLER

BETHANY HOUSE
MINNEAPOLIS, MINNESOTA

An Uncertain Dream
Copyright © 2008
Judith Miller

Cover design by Koechel Peterson & Associates, Inc. Minneapolis, Minnesota

Scripture quotations are from the King James Version of the Bible.

Published by Bethany House Publishers
11400 Hampshire Avenue South
Bloomington, Minnesota 55438

Bethany House Publishers is a division of
Baker Publishing Group, Grand Rapids, Michigan.

Printed in the United States of America

Library of Congress Cataloging-in-Publication Data

Miller, Judith, date
    An uncertain dream / Judith Miller.
       p.   cm. — (Postcards from Pullman ; 3)
    ISBN 978-0-7642-0278-0 (pbk.)
    1. Pullman Strike, 1894—Fiction. 2. Strikes and lockouts—Fiction.
3. Railroads—Employees—Fiction. 4. Pullman (Chicago, Ill.)—Fiction. I. Title.
    PS3613.C3858U53   2008
    813'.6—dc22

                                               2008002529

To my daughter, Jenna,
for your laughter, enthusiasm, and tender heart

JUDITH MILLER is an award-winning author whose avid research and love for history are reflected in her novels, many of which have appeared on the CBA bestseller lists. Judy and her husband make their home in Topeka, Kansas.

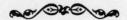

For my mouth shall speak truth;
and wickedness is an abomination to my lips.
—Proverbs 8:7

CHAPTER ONE

Pullman, Illinois
Friday, May 11, 1894

Angry shouts stopped Olivia Mott midstep. The brick and mortar walls of the Pullman Car Works muted the enraged voices outside the Administration Building. Certain something was amiss, Olivia cocked an ear toward the front door. Instinctively, she tightened her hold on the crystal vase cradled against her chest. The soles of her leather shoes clattered on the tile floor as she raced down the hallway and pushed open the heavy front door. The alarming sight of hundreds of men pushing and shoving their way toward the iron gates that surrounded the Pullman Car Works caused her to take a backward step.

The strike has begun! The thought ripped through her mind like a flash of lightning. In spite of the beautiful spring weather, beads of perspiration suddenly formed around the neckline of her white chef's jacket.

"Lower rents and livable wages! Lower rents and livable wages!" Again and again, the men chanted the words inscribed on the cardboard placards they waved over their heads.

Olivia hesitated only a moment before she sidled out of the doorway and edged her way toward the sidewalk. Instantly she was swept into the frenzied sea of humanity now moving away from the car works like a giant tidal wave. Why hadn't she protected the glass vase before leaving the building? She silently condemned her oversight and yanked the toque from her head. Using the white hat as a protective wrapping, she encased the crystal vase that was to become the centerpiece on the main dining table at today's luncheon and pushed her way back toward the doorway.

Workers clad in dark jackets hurled insults in the direction of the Administration Building, no doubt hoping their discontent would be heard by someone in authority. Olivia saw that a few of the men carried their personal tools and lunch pails. If their anger further escalated, those items could become dangerous weapons. She shuddered.

"You work in there?" one of the men approaching her shouted.

His fusty breath assailed her, and she took a sideways step. "No. I'm on my way to the hotel." She pointed to her jacket.

He glanced at the Hotel Florence emblem stitched on her jacket. "Mr. Howard in there?"

Her mouth felt as though it had been stuffed with cotton, but she forced her words around the dryness. "I don't know. I didn't see him." She hoped her response would appease the man.

He grunted and stared at her a moment before turning to join the crowd and continuing the chants: "Down with George Pullman! Down with George Pullman and his cruel treatment!"

Olivia waited until a less frenzied group of workers

approached and beckoned to one of them. "Do you know where I can locate Fred DeVault?"

"Check the park. That's where we're supposed to meet."

Unlike the boisterous men with signs and the worker who'd angrily questioned her, this man appeared numb. Olivia wanted to ask if he had been bullied into joining the strike, but she held her tongue. Her cousin Albert hadn't joined the union, and Olivia knew he had suffered the ire of his fellow workers. She wondered if he had walked out today with the strikers or if he'd remained behind to perform his duties.

Olivia joined the men, and quickly the momentum of the crowd moved her forward until she was again crushed in the throng of workers. A heavy boot unexpectedly came down on her foot. She squealed in pain, but her cry went unheeded in the din.

Still clutching the vase, Olivia pushed against the forward movement of the crowd, hoping somehow to remain out of harm's way. She edged her way toward the perimeter but soon lost her footing in the loose gravel surrounding the building. A beefy hand reached out to steady her.

"Thank you!" she hollered, but the man had already disappeared into the crush.

Inhaling a ragged breath, she moved to the far side of the building and rested against the wall. Her heart pumped at an alarming rate as the mass exodus continued. With each new surge of men, the call for fair treatment exploded into the late morning breeze. Still hoping to capture a glimpse of Fred, she stretched up on tiptoe and craned her neck. A quick look was enough to tell her she'd not have much luck. She should take the man's advice and seek Fred out in the park, but first she'd need to work her way through the horde and out the gates. If she waited a few minutes longer, perhaps the crowd would thin out. Olivia settled against the building. The coolness of the bricks seeped through her jacket as the workers continued their mass departure.

A wave of whoops and cheers rolled through the crowd as the men turned to look back toward the factory entrance. From her vantage point alongside the Administration Building, Olivia couldn't make out what had happened. After leaning forward for a better view, she clapped a hand to her mouth. The women from the Embroidery Department had filed out of their building. Not even Fred had believed the women would join the walkout. Riotous bellows of approval greeted the approaching women, many of whom waved their work aprons overhead like banners. Surprisingly, only a few appeared embarrassed by the attention.

The sight of the female workers was enough to move Olivia from her place of safety near the building. She wanted to know what had possessed the ladies to join the strike. These were the wives and mothers who had voiced deep concern when they'd first heard talk of a strike, fearing they'd be put out on the streets. Olivia noted that only some of the women joined in the chanting; others remained grim-faced and silent. The moment she spotted Lettie Meek, a woman she'd met in church, Olivia pushed her way through the group.

She grasped Lettie's arm. "What's happened?"

Lettie looked at Olivia as though she'd lost her senses. "It's a walkout—a strike."

"Yes, I understand, but I didn't think the women would ever agree to it."

Lettie shrugged her narrow shoulders. "We can't go on like this. The women took a vote this morning and decided they'd support the strike. Personally, I didn't vote to strike, but I'm going to support the majority. Maybe Mr. Pullman will come to his senses and lower our rent." She waved to her husband waiting near the iron fence. Her eyes shone with fear. "I'm scared we'll lose our housing, but our pleas to Mr. Pullman and the managers have gone unheeded. What else can we do? I pray this will get their attention and we'll return to work in a few days."

Swept forward in the surge of workers pushing toward the street, Olivia gasped for air. A group of young men shoved their way through the crowd, seeming to enjoy the upheaval. They jostled and pushed other workers aside while shouting boisterous, ugly remarks. She wondered if they truly worked in Pullman or had simply happened into town and joined the fracas.

One of the men grabbed Olivia's arm, and before she could say a word, the crystal vase crashed to the sidewalk and shattered. Her breath caught in her throat. While the crowd clamored around her, she knelt on the ground and stared at the shards of glass. *Broken.* Everything in Pullman seemed to be irretrievably broken on this beautiful spring day. Nothing would ever be the same—not the crystal vase, not the men and women who'd walked out on their jobs, and not the company that employed them. Olivia could feel it in her bones. Nothing would ever again be the same.

A man tripped over her stooped form and muttered an apology, but instead of offering to help, he stepped around her. The reverberating shouts continued with an intensity that forced Olivia back to her feet. She shook the shards of glass from her toque. No need to retrieve the broken pieces. She couldn't repair the vase. Now she could only hope that the vase wouldn't be foremost in Chef René's mind when she returned to the hotel kitchen. If so, she might be unemployed before morning.

Though she wanted to stay and find Fred, she dared not keep the chef waiting any longer. He would be looking for her to return and assist with today's luncheon. Most likely he was immersed in food preparation and oblivious to the day's happenings. But she must alert him that the strike had begun. Turning to the left, she skirted the crowd and raced along the path that led to the side of the hotel.

Breathless, she bounded up the steps and into the kitchen, causing a near collision with Chef René.

"Miss Mott! Where have you—"

"Come with me! Hurry!" She panted for breath while tugging him toward the door. "I don't think there will be any luncheon today."

He jerked away and stared at her, his dark eyes shining with anger. "Where is the vase, Miss Mott?"

She shook her head, and a dark curl escaped one of her hairpins. "You don't understand. The strike has begun! At least a thousand workers have walked out of the car works, and more continue to follow. I saw them with my own eyes. Please come!" Beneath her jacket, Olivia's heart pounded a ferocious beat.

"*Non!* Surely not," Chef René exclaimed, but he obviously sensed the urgency of her demand, for this time when she grasped his arm, he willingly followed. After they had circled the hotel and crossed the grassy expanse, he stared at the growing throng. "So *this* is why you were late."

"Yes. I was caught up in the crowd." Olivia watched for any sign of Fred as they wended their way through the gathering.

Chef René pointed toward a group of workers crossing the street. "I hope your Fred is not making a mistake with his union participation."

"*My* Fred, as you call him, made his decision to stand with the union long ago. I think he's prepared to go to almost any length to help the workers succeed." She waved toward the mass of workers. "Something must be done to help them."

"Have I not aided you in helping the workers through these past months? Unlike your Fred, one can lend assistance in a discreet manner." A group of men shoved their way through the crowd and inadvertently pushed the chef against a tree. "This chaos is not a good thing. I am better suited to the order I require in my kitchen."

She patted his arm. "Each of us is different. I've had to accept that Fred can no longer hide his union affiliation. When the men decided to join the American Railway Union in March, he prayed over his decision, just as I prayed over mine last November."

"*Oui.* But your decision permitted you to remain at my side in the kitchen. I fear that if your Fred is forced out of Pullman, he will take you along with him."

She shook her head while continuing to scan the sea of faces. "I think you're safe awhile longer. He's not yet declared his love."

"Then he is a fool!" The chef shouted to be heard over the deafening crowd. He bent close to her ear. "Stay and see if you can locate Fred and find out exactly what is happening." He gestured toward the hotel. "I am going back to the kitchen. Don't be gone too long. I may need your help."

"I promise." She sighed with relief, thankful he hadn't inquired further about the vase. A gust of wind whipped across the lawn and slapped at her skirts. Using her elbows when necessary, Olivia pushed her way through the mass of people. She stood on a nearby bench and finally spotted Fred near a large walnut tree, surrounded by a press of workers. Elbowing her way through the triumphant crowd, she stopped beside him.

His blue eyes flashed with jubilation. "Isn't this a magnificent sight? Except for a smattering of unskilled laborers, the men at the brickyards, and the members of management, all of the workers have pledged support." Fred scanned the crowd. "Nearly three thousand of us have walked out. More than enough proof to the company that we are serious about our need for higher wages and lower rents."

His enthusiasm was contagious; Olivia could feel her own excitement rising. "You've surely met with success. Has Mr. Pullman arrived to negotiate with you and the other local union delegates?"

Fred's wavy brown hair whipped in the breeze, and he brushed the errant strands from his forehead. "I don't expect it will go as easily as that, but we're hopeful he'll come and declare his intentions. We pray that he will agree to negotiate, but I doubt he'll do so."

The muscles of Fred's arm flexed beneath her fingers, providing a stark contrast to the softness of Chef René's arm as well as a reminder that she must return to the hotel kitchen. "Then I shall pray, also. We need to see an end to the inhumane conditions the workers and their families have been forced to endure."

Just then a nearby coal stoker raised his fist in the air and spewed out a curse. From the fetid odor that permeated the air, it seemed he'd been wearing the stained and sweaty shirt for more than a week. He swaggered past them, jostling Olivia into Fred's arm as he passed by.

Fred grabbed Olivia in a protective embrace. "God knows we'll need every prayer that is uttered."

Her gaze traveled toward the tower clock. "I must return to the kitchen or Chef René will regret having allowed me to visit with you. Please say you'll come by this evening and tell me all that happens."

"Our local union is holding meetings this afternoon. If all goes well, I'll see you later."

Fearful trouble would erupt at any moment, she said, "Promise me you'll remain safe."

"There's not going to be any violence. All union members have taken a pledge." He squeezed her hand and then surprised her with a fleeting kiss on the cheek. Warmth crept up her neck, and she turned before he could see her blush. It had taken these past six months to regain Fred's trust, but she'd have it no other way. Olivia wanted him to recognize that she was now the woman he'd thought her to be when she arrived in Pullman two years ago.

CHAPTER TWO

"Fred! I was hoping to locate you."

Fred whirled around to see Albert Mott, Olivia's cousin, pushing through the crowd. Albert grasped his hand in a firm handshake. "You know I didn't want to strike, but I had no choice once the entire Glass Etching Department voted to walk out. I hope you fellows know what you're doing."

"I wish I could relieve your worries, but none of us knows exactly where this will lead. We're going to have to place our trust in the Lord."

There was little doubt Albert's fear rose from the responsibilities incurred by his marriage. And now that Martha was expecting their first child, he didn't want to endanger his family's income. But all members of Albert's department had pledged their support to the union after hearing Joseph Jensen give his inflammatory speech. The men had listened intently while the man declared George Pullman and his board of directors unconscionable capitalists who cared nothing for their workers. After all, wage cuts and freezing houses had become the norm in the city of Pullman throughout the winter.

A single tear had rolled down Mr. Jensen's cheek when he told how his youngest son had frozen to death while waiting outside the woodshop for shavings to heat the family's flat. "I buried one son because I couldn't afford a bucket of coal, but I'll not lose another son without a fight," he'd declared. When he'd raised his fist overhead, the men had joined in a rousing cheer and pledged their loyalty to the union.

Albert doffed his cap and wiped his forehead. "I can't afford to be without work, Fred. Martha had to quit her position at the hotel a month ago, you know. With my wages barely covering the rent, we're going deeper into debt each day."

"That's been the case for most families throughout the winter. You've been more fortunate than most, what with Martha's wages."

"I know, I know. But that doesn't keep me from worrying about what this strike is going to do. How are we supposed to pay rent or buy food? How long do you think it will last?"

"No one can answer that question, Albert. Most of the men feel certain there will be a quick return to work. I'm not so sure—we'll have to wait and see." Fred clapped him on the shoulder. "If you'll excuse me, Thomas Heathcoate is signaling me."

"I hope when all is said and done, you won't be sorry for your part in this matter."

Fred pulled his hat low on his forehead. "Whatever happens, I believe I've made an honorable decision. I can live with that."

He didn't wait for Albert's response. Fred had weighed his decision with much thought and prayer and knew the risks. He strode toward Mr. Heathcoate, the man who had been elected chairman of the Strike Committee at last night's rally. The first action of the committee had been to form a rotating twenty-four-hour guard for the car works. The union members agreed this would prevent property damage and undue negative publicity. It would also establish a picket line to thwart the use of strikebreakers.

"Well, we've done it, Fred. I wondered if the men would maintain their courage when the hands of the clock settled on ten thirty this morning, but they proved they're men who abide by their word."

"And women," Fred commented while surveying the crowd. "We mustn't forget the ladies. They have proved staunch supporters."

Thomas nodded. "You're absolutely right. We must remain unified if we are to gain Mr. Pullman's attention." He reached inside his jacket and retrieved a piece of paper. He carefully ripped the page in half. "After going home last night, I made up a schedule for the guards. I would be most thankful if you'd inform these men." He handed Fred one of the pieces. "Tomorrow will tell us more. We'll see if Mr. Pullman arrives in his private railcar and agrees to talk. In the meantime let's continue our good work."

Fred headed off with his list in hand, and one by one he advised each man of his assigned time of duty. All remained optimistic. Fred hoped their optimism would continue if the strike should last for more than a week or two.

————

Chef René met Olivia at the kitchen door. "What did you discover? Do they plan to continue with the strike, or do they merely hope to frighten Mr. Pullman?"

"They appear determined," she replied, taking up one of the meat mallets. "They hope Mr. Pullman will soon arrive and enter into serious negotiations."

Chef René lifted his arm in an exaggerated motion and pinched his nose. "I hope they don't hold their breaths. They will die waiting. I have witnessed these walkouts in the past." He shook his head. "Never are they successful."

"But there's never been a strike of such magnitude. In the past it's been only one or two departments—not the entire car works." She waved the meat mallet toward the window. "Look out there. They are united."

"What do I know? Perhaps you are correct." He shrugged and his crisp white jacket lifted from his shoulders and then dropped back in place. "For now, we must complete the noonday preparations. The luncheon is going on as planned."

"Guests are no doubt enjoying the spectacle across the street." Olivia had noticed the hotel visitors gathered on the spacious hotel veranda. They would have quite a tale to tell when they returned to their homes. "With all this commotion, I'd think they would desert the place like mice fleeing a sinking ship."

"I have a feeling the hotel will be filled to capacity by tomorrow. Mr. Howard sent word that the board of directors will be dining with us tomorrow evening."

"And Mr. Pullman?" Olivia inquired.

"No mention was made of Mr. Pullman. To me, that means he will not be present. To you, that may mean something entirely different." He leaned over and peeked inside the oven. "What do you think? Shall I add a taste of mint to the potatoes?"

"Mint jelly for the lamb is sufficient. Too much mint will overpower the meal."

He laughed. "I have taught you well, Miss Mott."

She arched her brows. "That was a test?"

"But of course! Do you think I would truly add mint to *two* of my dishes?" He pursed his lips and closed his eyes while shaking his head. "Non. Never would I do such a thing." He nodded toward the dining room. "Did you put the vase in the dining room, Miss Mott?"

In all the commotion she'd completely forgotten. She averted her eyes. "No."

A deep V formed between his wide-set dark eyes. "Where is the vase?"

"Broken." Her response was a mere whisper.

He tilted his head toward her and cupped his hand behind his ear. "What did you say, Miss Mott? I *know* I didn't hear you correctly."

"A group of young men were shoving through the crowd." She swallowed the lump that had formed in her throat. "The vase shattered when one of them grabbed my arm."

The chef studied her. "Please say you are jesting."

Olivia shook her head. "I wish that were the case. You will find the shattered pieces on the brick walkway inside the gates."

The chef massaged his forehead with the tips of his fingers. "Who gave you the vase? Mr. Mahafferty or Mr. Howard?"

She didn't know what difference it made, but with her future hanging in the balance, she dared not ask. "Mr. Mahafferty."

"Good. Then perhaps we are safe. Mr. Mahafferty believes in using the duplicate vase."

"Duplicate? I thought the queen presented only one vase to Mr. Pullman."

"Oui. But Mr. Pullman had a copy made. He feared the original might be broken." The chef tapped his finger on the counter. "I want you to concentrate. Did you notice the royal insignia on the vase?"

Olivia tried to picture the vase. She truly hadn't taken a close look. However, while living in her homeland of England, she'd worked in the kitchens of Lanshire Hall and was familiar with the royal coat of arms. Surely she would have noticed it.

"I remember seeing only a Pullman car etched into the glass and a date. Perhaps some other words below. I don't believe it bore any insignia, but I can't be certain."

His frown eased but only by a slight degree. "I hope you are correct. Later this afternoon, I will go and speak with Mr. Mahafferty. Until then, you may want to offer up a prayer or two." The chef walked toward one of the open windows and surveyed the open expanse. "The workers appear to remain in high spirits. I wonder how long that will continue."

Even in the warmth of the kitchen, Olivia shivered. She wondered the same thing. The union leaders said they would prevail through sheer numbers and unity. But given the formidable power of Mr. Pullman and his board of directors, Olivia feared the accord of the workers would prove fruitless. From what she'd seen in the past, she doubted the workers could outmaneuver the likes of Mr. Pullman or even Mr. Howard, but she dared not give voice to her fears. Like the others, she wanted to believe the workers would triumph. Yet Chef René's comment that there had been no mention of Mr. Pullman's attending tomorrow's meeting seemed an indication that the company's owner had little interest in negotiations. She fervently hoped that was not the case.

———————

Olivia paced across the black and white kitchen tile. She hadn't expected Chef René would wait until so late in the day to see Mr. Mahafferty. After glancing at the clock for the fifth time in the past half hour, she decided to prepare the food baskets on her own. The rest of the staff had already left for the evening, and even though Olivia was eager to speak with Fred, she must await the chef's return. "No need to sit and idle the time away," she muttered.

With quick, precise cuts, she sliced the leftover loaves of bread, divided thin pieces of lamb from the noonday meal, and located extra fruit and pound cake. There appeared to be enough for six baskets. If more of the guests had departed as she'd expected, more baskets could have been filled.

Her palms grew damp when she looked up to see Chef René enter the kitchen. "Did you speak to Mr. Mahafferty?"

"I did. Your prayers have been answered. He didn't give you the original vase. However, you must pay to have the broken vase replaced."

"But I—" The chef's stern look was enough to halt her objection. "Thank you for speaking to Mr. Mahafferty. I will make arrangements to pay for the vase."

"No need. He will have it withheld from your pay." Without further discussion, the chef checked the baskets and gave a firm nod. "Let's go and deliver these."

"I had planned to meet with Fred."

"Then we must hurry. You deliver three and I will deliver three. I'm sure your Fred wouldn't want us to quit helping those in need merely because the strike has begun."

The chef was correct. How could she argue with such logic? Many of the families had come to depend upon the goodwill of the chef, and all recipients had been sworn to secrecy. Soon after the closing ceremonies of the Columbian Exposition, lay-offs at the car works had commenced. Shortly thereafter, a decrease in employee wages had taken effect throughout the company—except for supervisors and managers, of course. The affected families were now without adequate funds to purchase groceries. Yet fine dining had continued at Hotel Florence, where the wealthy remained unmoved by the depression plaguing the common man. Economic downturn or not, the capitalists and their families expected fine cuisine.

Several months earlier, during the preparation of some of those fine meals, Olivia and Chef René had devised a plan whereby each of them contributed a portion of their pay toward the purchase of food. With this method, they could prepare extra food and distribute the leftovers to families with hungry children each evening. Though what they offered was little in comparison to the need, Olivia had successfully developed a rotation plan to feed as many of the children as possible. At the end of the day, all of the luncheon and supper leftovers, along with any remaining baked goods, were divided and packed for individual families.

Balancing the food baskets on her arm, Olivia bid the chef good-night. The homes she would visit tonight were located nearby, so her deliveries shouldn't take too long. Apparently the union meeting had not yet ended, for she saw few signs of life in the park as she approached. Just a few women and children were out enjoying the evening. The town seemed far too quiet.

Olivia hurried to the end of the street and entered the alley behind the row of brick houses where the Barker family resided. She and Chef René never delivered to the front door. Too many prying eyes and loose lips might see and report their visits. Mrs. Barker welcomed Olivia with an effusive gratitude that embarrassed Olivia.

"I was praying you would come today, and God has answered my prayer," the woman said while ushering Olivia into the tiny kitchen. Mrs. Barker tucked a loose strand of hair behind one ear. "Do sit down."

Olivia settled the baskets on the wooden table. "I can't stay. I have other deliveries to make."

Marilee, the oldest of the Barkers' five children, leaned against the doorjamb. A tattered plaid dress hung from her thin frame. She offered a faint smile, but her hollow eyes reflected a sadness that caused Olivia to look away.

"This strike is going to provide the answer for us, don't you think?" Mrs. Barker asked while she unpacked the basket.

Olivia noticed the spark of hope in the woman's eyes. "I surely hope so, Mrs. Barker."

"Lamb! Look, Marilee. What a treat to have meat to feed the children. These baskets you bring contain the only fruit and meat the children get." She pulled an apple from the basket and rubbed it on her apron. Fear clouded the woman's eyes when she looked at Olivia. "With all the folks on strike, we're not going to be receiving the food baskets as often, are we?"

"You need not worry. I believe many others will come forward to help. You may receive more than the occasional basket Chef René and I deliver. I'm certain the union will make every attempt to locate resources to feed all those in need."

The older woman glanced at the open door. "I do wish Mr. Barker would return from the meeting. I want to know exactly what the union has planned. Everything has been such a secret up until now. Why, I didn't even know they were going to strike this morning, did you?"

Olivia shook her head. "No. I hadn't been told, either. I imagine the men decided secrecy was best because they didn't want members of management to know their plan ahead of time."

Mrs. Barker ruffled the blond curls of the young boy who entered the kitchen and hungrily eyed the apple in his mother's hand. "Let's pray Mr. Pullman will listen to reason and the men are soon back to work and earning a livable wage. Our rent continues to accumulate, and each day I wonder how I will feed these children." As tears began to form in her eyes, she swiped them away with the corner of her apron.

Two more gaunt children clattered into the kitchen and hurried toward the food on the table. Mrs. Barker held up her hand. "You must wait until I have finished speaking with Miss Mott."

Olivia gathered the empty basket together with those still requiring delivery. "I'll be on my way. I know you are all eager to have your supper, and I must complete my rounds."

Delivering the remaining two baskets proved just as heart-rending as the first. Both Mrs. Landers and Mrs. Wilson were grateful, but seeing their emaciated children made Olivia's effort seem futile. How many children in this town went to bed hungry every night? She prayed there would be much more left-over food tomorrow. They must fill more than six baskets each day.

When Olivia finally left the Wilsons' flat, she saw a group of men returning from the union hall in Kensington, the small town located a mile and a half outside of Pullman. Regulations forbade union meetings within the town of Pullman, but Kensington had welcomed the workers' presence—and their money—with open arms. Although the union leaders discouraged drinking, many of the men consumed liquor while in Kensington, yet another prohibition in the town of Pullman.

Olivia searched the crowd for Fred and soon found him in the park, surrounded by a group of workers and their wives. She approached the edge of the gathered residents and listened while he attempted to answer their many questions. Olivia could hear the fear in the women's voices as they inquired how they were expected to withstand the strike.

"We remain certain those who live in Pullman will not be evicted from their houses," he was telling them. "You've had near nothing to live on all winter. Though our wages have decreased, our rent has remained the same and Mr. Pullman continues to withhold it from our pay. However, we believe aid will be offered to us in our time of need, and we're hoping for swift negotiations."

Murmurs of assent filtered through the crowd. Then Fred signaled to Olivia. "If you'll excuse me, I've promised to escort Miss Mott to visit my mother." Fred edged his way through the group and offered his arm.

Taking hold, she offered him a smile. "It appears some of the wives are frightened by the prospect of the strike. I do hope their husbands discussed their intentions beforehand."

"I imagine some did, but after hearing a few wives' angry questions just now, it appears there are many who didn't." They turned the corner, and he rolled his fingers into a fist and poked his thumb back in the direction of where he'd been standing a few minutes earlier. "I wonder if some of those men now wish they were single—at least for a fleeting moment."

"So that's why you've never married. You're afraid you'll be no match for a wife!"

He suddenly grew serious. "I believe I could be a good match for you, Olivia."

Her breath caught in her throat. She hesitated, certain he would declare his love for her. Instead, he only mentioned a meeting that had been scheduled for later in the evening.

CHAPTER THREE

With a sigh, Olivia rested her back against the trunk of a large oak that offered her shade during the morning respite. As promised, she had arrived earlier than usual, but the many breakfast orders had kept her on the run from the instant she had entered the kitchen. She had hoped for a moment to visit with Fred during the morning, though she hadn't yet spotted him among the group of men assembled in the park. The striking workers were playing baseball and lawn tennis as though they were on holiday. She wondered if their carefree attitude would disappear once they learned Mr. Pullman had fled the city for one of his summer homes far from Chicago. At least that's what Mr. Howard had told Chef René earlier that morning.

Her attention settled upon a man walking with a determined stride toward the entrance of the car works. She couldn't distinguish his features, yet there was something familiar about him. While he stood in front of the building reading the sign that had been posted the previous night, she continued to study him. He turned in her direction. She shielded her eyes from the sun and watched him rake his fingers through his sandy brown hair. Was that—could it be Matthew Clayborn? When he waved his hat, she knew he'd spotted her and she'd been correct. He loped across the street and came to a halt directly in front of her.

"Olivia! I was hoping to see you or Fred. What a stroke of good fortune." He settled his hat on the back of his head. "I'm covering the strike for the Chicago *Herald,* and I want to get my story from the perspective of the employees rather than the managers or supervisors. My editor thought it would give our newspaper a distinctive slant and would set us apart from the other Chicago newspapers."

"I'm not one of those on strike, Matthew, but you'll likely have little difficulty locating Fred. If you don't find him among those men playing baseball, you can stop by his flat. I'm certain his mother can advise you of his whereabouts." She glanced over her shoulder toward the hotel.

"Worried you'll be seen fraternizing with the enemy and lose your job?"

She stiffened at the note of condemnation in his voice. "Though you may find it difficult to believe, I can be of more use to the cause if I continue my employment at the hotel—unless I'm seen talking to newspaper reporters."

He donned his hat and strode off without another word. It had been her contact with Matthew, back when she'd been riding the rails, that had led to her confrontation with Mr. Howard. She'd been placed in a precarious position during that time and had been forced to wrestle with a difficult decision. She had prayed long and hard when Mr. Howard had issued his ultimatum last November.

Although Olivia was confident Mr. Howard never believed

she had given Matthew Clayborn any of her notes regarding the treatment of the Pullman porters or the dining car staff, nevertheless he had threatened to fire her.

That is, until she had countered with knowledge of his unethical practice of hiring unqualified employees whenever enough money would cross his palm. Money that had been placed in Mr. Howard's pocket without Mr. Pullman's knowledge, and hiring practices that the company owner would have known to be detrimental to his car works.

Once she'd revealed knowledge of his wrongdoing, Mr. Howard had offered a bargain. If she remained silent, he wouldn't fire her. After much prayer, she'd returned with a counteroffer. She would remain silent if he would immediately cease the unethical hiring practice and would make restitution to Mr. Pullman or to those who had paid for their positions. She believed her offer provided an opportunity to put an end to Mr. Howard's shoddy dealings. She had no way of knowing if he'd ever complied with her repayment provision, but the unethical hiring practice had ceased. Even now, she harbored doubt whether she'd heard God whisper His answer or if she'd merely listened to her own heart. Knowing the difference had proved to be an unexpected conundrum. She had questioned several believers regarding that particular issue, but they'd all said the same thing: continue to meditate on God's Word and spend time in prayer. Day after day she had done that very thing, but when she'd made her agreement with Mr. Howard, God's answer hadn't been entirely clear.

"Are you planning to spend the entire day lounging against this tree, Miss Mott?"

Olivia startled at the sound of Chef René's voice. "No, no. Of course not. Have I kept you waiting?" She jumped to attention and brushed an invisible wrinkle from her jacket. "You are ready to begin the noonday preparations?"

"I have already begun, and I am waiting for you to assist me." He stretched his arms outward. "I have only two hands. Can I stir all of the pots myself?" Without waiting for her response, he lumbered toward the kitchen, waving her onward.

Olivia laughed. "You have kitchen boys and scullery maids who can stir your pots."

"You are correct, but I have only one Miss Mott to prepare fine gravies and sauces. Come along. We don't want to keep the board of directors waiting when their meeting ends." He held the kitchen door open and then followed her inside.

The gravies and sauces would be ruined if she prepared them this early, and she wondered exactly why Chef René had hurried her indoors. She glanced about the kitchen. "It appears everything is well cared for."

"Everything except your behavior. Did you consider that someone might see you speaking with that newspaper reporter? What if Mr. Howard thinks you are sharing disparaging information with Mr. Clayborn? Do you so quickly forget what happened the last time that man wrote an article about the Pullman employees?"

"I haven't forgotten." She patted his arm. "And in spite of my friendship with Mr. Clayborn, I still remain an employee of the hotel. God has taken care of me, Chef René. I pray He will continue to do so."

"Perhaps God expects people to use their good sense, also. Non?" He shooed one of the kitchen boys out of his path as he trundled across the room toward the stove.

"So you *do* believe in God. If I've accomplished nothing else, I've managed to gain that much information today."

"I never said I didn't believe in God, Miss Mott. I said I had no use for attending church. There is a difference. And I believe you had better accomplish more than that if you wish to maintain your employment. Please go and see that the dining room is in order. I am told we are short of staff."

The chef's brusque instructions didn't dampen Olivia's spirits. His mention of a belief in God had given her hope. He didn't know it, but she'd been praying for him ever since he'd suffered from heart problems. Rather than circle outside the kitchen, Olivia cut through the carving room. Angry voices emanated from the meeting room where the board of directors were gathered, and she stopped short outside the door.

Flattening herself against the wall, she strained to listen. She couldn't distinguish the voices, but there was little doubt the men were unhappy with Mr. Pullman.

"The least George could have done was meet with us before he ran off to avoid the press. He'll have to return and face them eventually, for I suspect there'll be little progress made in the next three months. Who knows? It could go on longer. If the workers have prepared in advance, it's going to take more than a couple weeks to wear down their resistance."

"The shops must remain closed until we can break the union," someone else commented. "The board need only follow the same path we have in the past: do nothing until their ability to resist has crumbled. After all, the financial power of the company far surpasses the workers' limited means."

Shouts of "Hear, hear!" were followed by a smattering of applause.

"Mr. Pullman has specifically cautioned against interviews. All requests for information may be directed to me." Olivia recognized Mr. Howard's voice.

"And what statement will you give them, Samuel?"

"That the union is solely responsible and the company is indifferent as to length of the strike. Mr. Pullman hopes to minimize any adverse publicity by keeping our comments to a minimum."

A platter crashed in the kitchen, and Olivia jumped away from the wall with a start. After a quick glance over her shoulder, she hurried to the dining room. If she didn't soon return to the kitchen, Chef René would come looking for her.

———————

The appearance of Matthew Clayborn in the park came as no surprise to Fred. In fact, Fred had expected him to arrive the previous evening. No doubt Matthew's editor hadn't given him permission to come to Pullman until this morning. And Matthew would have competition for his story, for a number of other Chicago newsmen had already arrived.

"Good to see you. I hoped you'd be assigned to cover the strike." Fred clapped him on the shoulder. "We want reporters we can depend upon to tell our story accurately."

Matthew nodded. "I can tell you there is sympathy for your cause, but many believe the present business conditions are going to prove the strike a foolish mistake—that you are bound for failure."

Fred stiffened at the assessment. "Would they have us continue to sit here and do nothing? Most families haven't enough money for food, and they go deeper into debt each month. We've tried to convince Mr. Pullman that the rents should be lowered to correspond with the decrease in wages the company has instituted, but he'll hear nothing of it and says the car works and the town company are independent of one another.

He fails to mention he owns both. The man gives with one hand and takes with the other."

The two men dropped to the grass, and Matthew jotted notes while Fred related the plight of journeyman mechanics in the Freight-Car Construction Department. "In the past year, their wages have decreased from fifty-three dollars a month to a little less than fourteen dollars, yet the rent on a single-family house remains the same—nearly sixteen dollars. Money for their rent is withheld from their pay, so they have nothing left, and their debt increases each month." Fred doubled one hand into a fist and jammed it into the palm of the other. "The whole thing makes my blood boil. If they are two different companies, how can he withhold wages paid by the car works for rent owed to the town company?"

"You make a valid point. But knowing George Pullman, I'm sure there's something written in your employment agreement or rental contract whereby you grant permission for the rent to be deducted." Matthew nodded toward the folks who had gathered to listen to the Pullman band playing a rousing tune in Arcade Park. "At least there's still a bit of enjoyment to be had in all of this. A model strike in Mr. Pullman's model town, wouldn't you say?"

Fred grinned. "We've discouraged any form of property damage or violence by the workers."

"I think that's wise. For now, the newspapers and the public appear to consider Pullman the rogue. However, there is growing sentiment that the unions are becoming too demanding." Matthew shifted positions and rested against the tree. "Was it Mr. Ashton who advised the workers to ally with the American Railway Union?"

"Yes. He said the union was strong, and Mr. Debs explained

that all workers, no matter their occupation, qualified for membership since the company operates over twenty miles of rails in the town."

Matthew tucked his notebook into his pocket. "I imagine I'm going to be spending a good deal of time here in Pullman. I'm glad it will give us an opportunity to see each other again, but I wish it were under more pleasant circumstances." He glanced toward the hotel. "What's become of you and Olivia? The last I spoke with Ellen Ashton, she said the two of you had made amends."

Fred laughed. Matthew made it sound as though they'd reached a formal agreement to settle their differences. Then again, in some respects he supposed they had. Not anything formal, of course, but he and Olivia had promised there would be no more lies between them.

"Through all our difficulties, I've never stopped caring for Olivia, but there have been problems we've had to overcome. I imagine that's true for most couples."

Matthew arched his brows. "Sounds as though you're preparing for a serious commitment."

"One day, but now isn't the time. There's too much upheaval at the moment."

"Don't wait too long or someone may steal her away from you, my friend."

Fred clenched his jaw. "Does that mean you're interested in Olivia? Because if it does—"

With his palm turned toward Fred, Matthew stretched his arm forward. "Whoa! I wasn't speaking for myself, although I'd be among the first to admit Olivia is a lovely young woman." He chuckled when Fred inched closer. "I am pleased for both of you. But I'm not sure this strike should be a reason for determining the course of your future with Olivia. In fact, she's one of the few who remains gainfully employed."

"Exactly!"

"Ah. I sense a bit of pride welling in your chest, Fred." Matthew pulled a blade of grass and tucked it in the corner of his mouth. "There will be many who wish for a wife who can help support their families in the months to come."

"Months?" Fred shook his head. "We're hoping the company will capitulate before then."

"And the company is confident the workers will capitulate long before it must give in. It's the same with every strike. Unfortunately, history predicts the workers will lose their battle."

"Not this time, Matthew. I believe we're better prepared than those who have gone before us." He spoke with bravado even though his words were filled with a degree of puffery. The winter had been too long and hard, the paychecks too small, or nonexistent, for any of them to be prepared for a long siege. Perhaps his pride had taken hold of him in more ways than one.

A young woman rushed toward the park, frantically waving her handkerchief overhead. "The Arcade stores are no longer giving credit!" she hollered while running toward her husband with wild abandon. "What will we do? How shall we survive?"

"How *will* all of you survive, Fred?" Matthew pulled the blade of grass from between his lips.

Fred tilted his head. "I believe we'll have to seek aid from any charitable group willing to come to our rescue."

"I'll mention your need for help in my news article." Matthew pushed himself to his feet. "Speaking of my work, I must return to Chicago."

Fred could rely upon Matthew to write the truth, and if

An Uncertain Dream

Matthew's article should be slanted in one direction or the other, he would steadfastly align with the striking men. The residents of Pullman were going to need all the support they could muster.

CHAPTER FOUR

London, England
Sunday, May 13, 1894

Lady Charlotte clapped her hands and extended her arms toward her son. "Come here, Morgan." The toddler giggled and ran to her, his chubby legs carrying him across the nursery in zigzag fashion. His clear blue eyes sparkled with undeniable childish delight.

"You have become such a fine big boy, haven't you? In three months, we shall celebrate your second birthday with a proper party."

He nodded his head, and his blond curls bobbed in wild abandon. "Paree," he repeated.

She laughed at his attempt to mimic her. "No. Par*tee*."

Rather than participate in a lesson in pronunciation, he picked up his ball and tossed it in the air. All who saw him said young Morgan's eyes were a near match to her own. Yet Charlotte knew her eyes revealed neither sparkle nor delight, for she had experienced little happiness since her return to London, except for the reunion with Morgan and her parents, of course.

An Uncertain Dream

Her father lay dying in his bedchamber, and her mother remained unwilling to accept the doctor's recent declaration that the Earl of Lanshire didn't have long for this world. Since her return to England, it seemed Charlotte and her mother had exchanged places within the family. The daughter, once considered headstrong and undisciplined, had gently eased into her role as Morgan's mother and had been forced into the role of mistress of Lanshire Hall. The servants looked to Lady Charlotte for instruction regarding the care of her father as well as the day-to-day management of the household, while the Countess of Lanshire spent her afternoons visiting with friends or on holiday at their country estates. Rather than concerning herself with the impending death of her husband, the countess worried where the family would vacation during the upcoming summer months.

To make matters worse, Ludie, the servant who had acted as Lady Charlotte's personal maid from the time she was a young girl, had resigned her post at Lanshire Hall several months before Charlotte's return to England. Other than one or two of the servants who had remained on staff after Charlotte's hasty departure to Pullman, Illinois, in 1892, the mansion was now filled with strangers.

Her mother's sour-faced maid had been assigned to assist Charlotte as well as perform her usual duties for the countess. The woman's resentment had quickly become evident, and Charlotte soon released the woman from providing her with any further service. Instead, Beatrice, the young girl who helped with Morgan's care, offered to aid Lady Charlotte with her toilette each day, which seemed rather silly now. Charlotte had, after all, cared for herself during her time at Priddle House, a fact her mother hadn't believed until she had recently observed Charlotte fashion her own hair.

The countess stepped into the nursery, carrying a light brocade parasol embellished with a flounce of silk, lace, and ribbons. "I'm off to Hargrove for a visit with the marchioness. Do look in on your father. He appears to be improving quite nicely this morning. I believe he'll be able to discuss our summer plans by this evening."

"Father misses you when you're off on your daily visits to the country. I wish you'd remain at home with us."

"And I wish you'd cease your daily attempts to oppress me with guilt. We both know that he sleeps most of the day. What am I to do? Sit beside his bed and read or embroider?" Her mother slapped her gloves on the carved walnut side table. "I think not! I cannot believe how you have changed, Charlotte. Living among those religious zealots in Chicago has changed you. And not for the better, I might add."

"Mrs. Priddle isn't a religious zealot. She helped me discover what it means to accept Jesus as my Savior and how to lead a Christian life. We studied the same Bible that sits on your bedside table." Charlotte gathered Morgan onto her lap. "And how can you say I'm not a better person? I have returned to accept responsibility for my child, and I do my best to help you and Father at every turn."

Her mother sighed. "That much is true. And I am most thankful you have returned to England." She leaned forward and tousled Morgan's curls. "I haven't time to continue this discussion. I'm going to be treacherously late." She blew Morgan a kiss and left the room.

Much to Charlotte's delight, the child mimicked his grandmother. Charlotte kissed his chubby fingers and then released him to play with his ball. She prayed her son would become an honorable man, unlike his father, and that he would never toy with the affections of a woman who loved him.

Her return to Lanshire Hall had renewed Charlotte's memories of her brief affair with Randolph Morgan. One of George Pullman's associates, Randolph had visited Lanshire Hall to discuss Mr. Pullman's business. During the day, Randolph had charmed her father into purchasing stock in George Pullman's company; during the night, he had charmed Charlotte into his bed. Her subsequent pregnancy had been the reason she had forced Olivia to travel with her to Pullman. How cruel Charlotte had been to the former scullery maid.

"Yet look how far Olivia has come since leaving this place," Charlotte murmured. Using a letter of recommendation forged by Charlotte, Olivia had succeeded in securing a position at Hotel Florence as an assistant chef. When Charlotte discovered Randolph Morgan already had a wife and children, her dreams of a future with him had collapsed around her, and she thought her life had ended. "What heartache and pain I caused with my foolhardy conduct," she muttered.

A tap on the nursery door interrupted Charlotte's musings. "Enter," she called.

Beatrice opened the door and peeked inside. "I've brought tea, ma'am."

Charlotte nodded and waved the maid into the room. "I'm certain Morgan will be pleased to have a biscuit or two before his nap, and I should very much enjoy a cup of tea."

Beatrice scanned the room as she arranged the tray atop the nearby table. "Your mother has departed for the day?"

"Yes. I doubt she'll return until this evening." Charlotte poured a cup of tea while Beatrice held up one of the biscuits.

The moment Morgan spied the treat, he toddled toward the maid with his fingers outstretched.

Why her mother preferred to spend time with the marchioness rather than with members of her own family was beyond Charlotte's comprehension. For her, the tiresome behavior of English nobility had become increasingly difficult to bear. She attempted to overlook the stares and whispered conversations that took place each time she attended a social event. But much to her dismay, the behavior of the upper class had caused her to react in a less than Christian manner.

Though none of the *ladies* would say to her face what they whispered behind their hand-painted silk fans, their words hadn't failed to reach Charlotte's ears, for the servants were more than willing to pass along gossip from house to house. The maids and cooks heard as much tittle-tattle as did their employers, and they took pleasure in passing along the tidbits as much as did the members of the noble class, if such a thing were possible.

When her parents had returned from America with an infant in tow, all of London's nobility immediately assumed the boy to be Charlotte's illegitimate child. And upon Charlotte's return to England, they twittered that their assumptions had surely been correct. The child could belong to no other. Eligible men fawned over her. When she refused their advances, they reminded her that she'd already wandered down the path of impropriety. She was, after all, considered to be a tarnished woman and surely knew what men expected of such a woman. At first she had coyly overlooked their remarks, but none would be deterred.

They'd prepared in advance their outrageous speeches, quick to point out the fact that young Morgan bore a remarkable resemblance to her. With his distinctive blue eyes and pouting lips, how could Lady Charlotte possibly expect anyone to believe the child was not her own? The preposterous story her parents had told of finding an abandoned child while traveling abroad hadn't been believed by anyone with a whit of sense. At least that's what the eager young men alleged.

After abiding several such encounters, Charlotte had refused all further social invitations. Remaining at Lanshire Hall with her son gave her much greater pleasure.

————————

"Your ladyship, please come quickly. It's your father." The servant who had been assigned to sit at her father's bedside waved Charlotte toward the door before hastening back to her post.

"I'll not be gone long, Beatrice. Please remain with Morgan until I return." She called the command over her shoulder and raced down the hallway.

Fear gripped her heart. Hadn't her mother reported an improvement in her father's health only hours ago? She tried to calm herself with that thought as she entered the bedchamber. The nurse had propped her father upright on his pillows, and he forced a smile as she came to an abrupt halt near his bedside.

She clutched a hand to her bodice. "When Wilda came to fetch me, I thought your health had taken a downward turn." Sighing, she dropped to the chair beside his bed. "I'm pleased to see you wish to visit."

He signed for the servant to leave the room and then waited for the familiar click of the door. "Move your chair closer so I need not exert myself while speaking to you, child."

She did as he bid and then settled back in the chair. "When you're feeling well enough, I shall bring Morgan for a brief visit. Would you like that?"

"I should enjoy seeing him, my dear, but you and your mother must accept the fact that my health is not going to improve." His voice faltered. "I need someone in whom I can confide. It should be your mother, but she has suddenly taken to acting like a foolish young woman. I fear my news will send her plummeting into one of her bouts of hysteria." He glanced at the coffered ceiling. "And perhaps I couldn't blame her."

Charlotte gently grasped her father's hand, once again surprised to feel how frail the fingers were that nestled within her own. "What is it? Surely nothing can be as difficult as you're thinking."

A tuft of white hair drooped across his forehead. "I fear it's worse than either you or your mother could imagine, my dear."

Charlotte steeled herself for what she might hear. "Please don't withhold anything from me, Father. I promise I can withstand whatever it is you need tell me."

He gave her hand a feeble squeeze. "We are financially ruined, Charlotte. There is no easy way to divulge this, but I cannot die without making you or your mother aware of the consequences you will face upon my death."

Her jaw went slack. How could this be true? Her father must be hallucinating.

He tightened his hold on her hand. "I can see your disbelief, but what I'm telling you is true. Even Lanshire Hall will be lost. I've borrowed against it, and there's no possibility of repayment. Those who hold outstanding notes against me will come calling soon after my death. It won't take long for them to discover there isn't enough to cover what I owe."

"But how is that possible?"

His brows furrowed above his rheumy eyes; he shook his head. "Foolish investments and even more foolish wagers. I had hoped to recoup my investment losses at the gaming tables. I didn't succeed."

He broke into a raspy cough. Turning to the bedside table, Charlotte poured him a glass of water. "Here. Let me help you." After slipping her arm behind his back, she lifted the glass to his lips. "You must concentrate your efforts upon regaining your strength. You need not fret about Mother and me. We will find some way to manage."

He pushed away the glass and settled back against the pillows. "The best thing would be for both of you to take young Morgan and throw yourselves upon the mercy of Lord and Lady Chesterfield. They have an obligation to take you in. After all, Lady Chesterfield is your mother's half sister."

Charlotte grimaced. The thought of living with Lord and Lady Chesterfield at Briarwood was enough to cause beads of perspiration to form along her forehead. She retrieved an embroidered handkerchief from the pocket of her dark blue skirt. Since keeping to the grounds of Lanshire Hall, she'd begun to dress in her most basic attire, the plain clothing she'd worn while performing her duties at Marshall Field and Company when she had lived in Chicago. Even the narrowly folded satin rows of trim seemed somehow overindulgent.

"Oh, Father, I don't think—"

He held up his hand to silence her. "It is your only choice. You have every right to rail against me. I know your mother will do so when she hears this ugly piece of news."

Charlotte lifted his hand to her lips and kissed the paper-thin skin. "The past is behind us. Neither of us can change it, so we must look to the future. I fear you have given up on life."

"Not at all, my dear. Life has given up on me. If I live beyond the week, we will both be surprised. You may speak to the doctor. He will confirm what I've said."

A single tear slid down his cheek, and Charlotte hastened to wipe it with her handkerchief.

"I've let you down where young Morgan is concerned. That wasn't my plan, you know. I had hoped to rear him as my heir, to leave this estate to him and allow him every advantage. Instead, he will be destined to a life of poverty. Your uncle Henry will likely force the boy to work in the stables. You must not permit that to occur."

Charlotte shook her head. "You need not worry on that account, Father. When the time comes, I believe I'll find another alternative for Morgan and me. And Mother, too, if she'll hear of it."

"What alternative have you thought of that I've overlooked? Do you have some wealthy suitor you've not told me about?"

"No. But if things turn out to be as dire as you indicate, I will arrange passage and return to America. I would rather earn my own way than be reliant upon our reluctant relatives for handouts. We both know how that sort of arrangement turns out." She shook her head. "In America Morgan will have the same chance as the next man to succeed in life. He won't have that opportunity if we remain in England."

"That's true enough, yet I worry that your mother wouldn't adapt to the American way of life. She'll be forlorn if she's forced to give up at least the pretense of nobility. There are wealthy men who would be delighted to marry you. Of course, you'd be required to never divulge that Morgan is your son."

Charlotte wouldn't tell him that the gossipmongers had

already declared her Morgan's mother. Her father would be devastated to learn that no member of nobility would consider asking for her hand in marriage. "Please, Father, you must quit worrying yourself and instead concentrate on regaining your strength."

He shifted in his bed. "If you locate a kind suitor, he might be willing to accept responsibility for the boy. You could say your mother isn't up to the task of rearing the young fellow. That much is certainly true." He wheezed the final words.

"You're taxing yourself unduly with all this talk. You must rest. We will visit tomorrow."

He clutched her hand. "Upon my death, you must immediately contact my solicitor for advice." He removed an envelope from beneath his pillow and held it out to her. "I've enclosed instructions for you. If any of my creditors contact you, send them directly to my solicitor."

Charlotte longed to ask how she would compensate a solicitor for his services, but this was not the time. Perhaps she would find the answers to her questions inside the envelope. If not, she would pen a list of questions and speak to her father in the morning.

After she had removed the extra pillows from behind her father's back, Charlotte remained at his bedside until the wheezing subsided, then tiptoed to the door.

She signaled to the servant. "My father is asleep. I'm going to return to the nursery. Maintain a close watch, for his breathing is shallow."

"Yes, your ladyship." Wilda hesitated and then pointed her forefinger in the air. "I nearly forgot. Beatrice asked that I inform you she has taken the young master to the south lawn for his playtime."

"Thank you. I'll join them there. Do keep a close watch on my father and call me if his condition worsens."

The servant dipped into a curtsy and proceeded to her post.

While strolling across the grounds toward the south lawn, Charlotte decided that a talk with her mother must take place as soon as possible. Charlotte could only imagine what the gossips were saying behind her mother's back. After all, the rumormongers were keenly aware of the earl's illness. The cream of London society surely thought it unseemly that the countess was absent from Lanshire Hall so frequently. And they would take pleasure in discussing her mother's conduct at every opportunity. She prayed her mother wouldn't later regret her decisions—especially if her father's predictions concerning his imminent death proved correct.

A smile tugged at her lips as she watched Morgan run toward her beneath a sky streaked with shades of amethyst. A prayer of thanks for the child forced away the gloom that had surrounded her only moments earlier.

———

When her mother didn't return home for supper, Charlotte could only assume the older woman had decided to remain at Hargrove for the night. It wouldn't be the first time. She told herself it was her mother's way of dealing with a difficult situation and then instructed the staff she would dine in the nursery with her son.

After they had eaten and Morgan was tucked into bed, Charlotte strode down the hall for a brief visit with her father before retiring for the night.

The earl's wheezing snores lifted toward the heavens in a strained blend of disharmony. She wished she could inhale a clear breath for him. Merely listening to the belabored sounds made her own breathing difficult.

She stepped closer and Wilda looked up from her embroidery. "He'll sleep the rest of the night, Lady Charlotte. I gave him his laudanum."

Charlotte folded down the coverlet and brushed a kiss on her father's cheek. She turned toward the servant. "I'll stop in before breakfast in the morning," she whispered.

Wilda bobbed her head. The woman had already picked up her needle. If Charlotte's father didn't soon recover, Wilda would complete enough items for a bride's trousseau. But nobody in Lanshire Hall would be in need of a trousseau. Instead, they'd require mourning clothes. Charlotte hugged one arm around her waist at the chilling thought. She dreaded her mother's reaction to her husband's death and to the discovery of their financial woes. No doubt there would be excessive histrionics.

Once she'd settled in bed, Charlotte turned to the bedside table and picked up the envelope her father had given her. She slid her finger beneath the seal and carefully removed the contents: several pages of carefully listed creditors, along with a solicitor's business card. She scanned the pages, amazed by the list of debts her father had incurred. Except for the fact that there would be no charge for the solicitor's services—due to a debt he owed the Earl of Lanshire—there was little encouragement to be found in the letter.

When she finally drifted off to sleep, she dreamed of angry creditors pounding on the doors of Lanshire Hall. They appeared as men in tall hats with angry eyes and twisted mouths and insisted upon the family's immediate eviction from the premises.

"Lady Charlotte, wake up!" The words filtered into her dreams, but it was the insistent jostling of her shoulder that finally roused her to attention. She brushed back a strand of hair. "What is it, Wilda?"

Light from the small lamp cast dancing shadows across the servant's face, but the fear illuminated in her eyes was evident. "It's your father, ma'am. I've sent for the doctor. I fear the earl isn't long for this world. I need to hurry back to his room."

"Go on! I'll follow in a moment." Charlotte tossed back the light coverlet and sat up. After pushing her feet into her slippers, she snatched her dressing gown from the bed. Still shoving her arms into the sleeves, Charlotte raced through the silent hallway. In the eerie nighttime quiet, even her soft slippers beat an echoed cadence.

Panting for breath, she raced into her father's bedchamber and came to a halt. The hush of death cloaked the room, and she dropped to the chair by his bedside. She stared across the bed at Wilda. "The doctor?"

"He hasn't arrived, but there's no longer any—"

Charlotte nodded. "I know. I'll stay here. Send one of the servants to fetch my mother."

"But it's the middle of the night, your ladyship. Shouldn't we wait until morning?"

"No! Fetch her immediately—she *must* return home!" The urgency in Charlotte's voice sent the servant scampering from the room. Her mother's return before daylight would help stave off unwelcome rumors. There would be enough gossip once her father was in the ground.

CHAPTER FIVE

Pullman, Illinois
Saturday, May 19, 1894

The clanging pans and Chef René's angry commands were enough to alert Olivia that something had gone amiss prior to her arrival at the hotel kitchen. She approached the door with foreboding. A cloud would hover over the kitchen until the problem was resolved.

She straightened her shoulders and assumed a carefree attitude as she entered the door. "Good morning to all of you." Her greeting fell on deaf ears, or so it seemed. No one responded. Ignoring the silence, she shoved her arms into her white chef's jacket.

"You are late!" The chef's words reverberated through the air like a clanging bell.

Olivia glanced at the clock. "I am exactly on time." She donned her toque and stepped to the counter.

"Non! You should be in the kitchen prepared to commence work at least five minutes in advance. Otherwise you are considered to be late!" He slammed a skillet atop the stove.

"When did that rule take effect?"

He ignored her question and pointed toward the baking kitchen located downstairs. "Do you see any light or hear any activity from down there?"

Olivia leaned forward and peeked around him. "No. Where are Edna and Fanny?"

"Both gone!" The angry words exploded from his lips.

"Well, you must tell me more than that. Gone where? And when shall they return?"

"How should I know where they have gone, but I know they will not return. Do you think I would give them another position in my kitchen when they would leave me like this? With the hotel filled to capacity?"

She had hoped to calm the chef before his anger escalated and caused him chest pains. "I will go downstairs and begin the baking. I can quickly prepare muffins and biscuits. Tell the waiters they are to offer only those two bread choices this morning. I feel sure the diners will survive."

Her words seemed to soothe the chef, for the redness began to fade from his cheeks. "Now, tell me why Edna and Fanny quit."

Olivia knew the two women well. They wouldn't have left without any explanation. Married to the Thompson brothers, both Edna and Fanny had been working in the hotel kitchen for more than five years. Unlike many of the wives, both of them had been supportive of their husbands' participation in the union as well as the strike. Fred counted on them when he needed trustworthy help.

"They said a relative promised work to both of their husbands in Pennsylvania. This relative also assured them there would be work for Edna and Fanny. Since no one seems to know how long this strike will last, they decided it would be best to eat the bird in their hand."

Olivia grinned. *"What?"*

"Something about a bird in the hand and another one in a bush. Words that made no sense to me and had nothing to do with baking bread and pastries. I did not care to hear such nonsense." He turned and glared at the kitchen boy after a pot clattered to the floor. "We must find at least one replacement today. Go down and begin mixing your muffins and think of someone I can hire. Someone who knows what must be done in a pastry kitchen."

Olivia descended the stairs and set to work. She measured and stirred the muffin ingredients while she considered who might be capable of handling the position to Chef René's satisfaction. His first priority would be an excellent baker; his second requirement would be an employee he could rely upon. *Mrs. DeVault!* The older woman would be absolutely perfect. And the added income would be an answer to Mrs. DeVault's prayers. She and Fred had opened their home to Paul and Suzanne Quinter and their three children when Paul was dismissed from his position as a steamfitter back in January. Now without Fred's income, Mrs. DeVault worried how she would feed so many mouths.

Olivia could barely contain her excitement. She rang for one of the kitchen boys to come down and help carry the muffins and biscuits into the hot closet off the dining room. Once she checked that everything was properly stored upstairs, she returned to the kitchen and remained in the background while Chef René issued serving orders to the staff.

"Let's hope there are no complaints. I saw Mr. Howard enter the dining room, and you know he prefers toast with his breakfast." Chef René wiped the beads of perspiration from his forehead.

Olivia caught sight of a young boy passing by the hotel door with sunken cheeks and little flesh on his bones. "If he complains, you can tell him there are hungry children who would be happy to have the muffins and biscuits. I'll be certain there's apple butter on the table for his biscuits." She grinned. They both knew Chef René dared not speak to the company agent in such a manner, but her words appeared to relieve the fretting chef.

"I have thought of someone to work in the bake kitchen."

He stared at her for what seemed an eternity. "Well? Are you going to tell me or must I guess?"

"Mrs. DeVault," she announced with pride.

He sat down on a nearby stool. "The mother of your Fred?"

She muffled a chuckle. "Yes. She is an excellent cook and baker, dependable, she has no husband or small children who will need her at home, and the wages will be of great help, of course. What do you think?"

"If she is all that you say, you must go and fetch her while we have a free moment. Tell her we need her to begin immediately." As if to rush her along, he waved toward the door.

She hadn't thought he would respond with such immediacy. "I'll see if she wants to accept the position and if she is willing to begin right away."

He arched his brows. "You *said* she needed the wages."

Olivia turned on her heel. There was no use in arguing over the matter. She yanked the toque from her head and hung it on the chair spindle. Chef René's admonition to hurry followed her across the lawn. Without looking back, she waved her hand overhead and picked up her pace. She didn't intend to run down the streets like a child at play.

The two older Quinter children had scratched out squares and were playing hopscotch on the front sidewalk when she arrived. "Good morning, girls. Are you having a fine Saturday?"

They bid her good morning. "Except Lydia cheats," Hannah said.

"Do not!"

"Do too!"

Olivia stopped beside the front steps. "You know, I would have been delighted to have had a sister to play games with me when I was young. You girls are very fortunate to have each other."

Hannah wrinkled her nose. "You can have Lydia for your sister, if you like. I can get along without her."

Olivia laughed. Her words had obviously had little impact. She walked up the steps and knocked on the front door.

"You can go on in," Lydia said, following her to the door. She grasped Olivia by the hand and pulled her inside. "Mrs. DeVault!" For a young girl, she certainly had a loud voice. "Miss Olivia's here to see you."

Fred's mother peered around the kitchen door at the end of the hall. "Olivia! What a surprise. Shouldn't you be at the hotel?" She squinted as Olivia drew near. "Are you ill?" Without waiting for a reply, the older woman turned toward the stove. "I can make some tea."

"I haven't time for tea, and I'm not ill. I've come to offer you a position as a baker at the hotel—that is, Chef René would like to discuss that possibility with you. Actually, he'd like you to come over right away."

The woman's work dress was covered by a worn apron. Proper attire for cleaning, but not the clothing that ladies wore when walking about town. She brushed her hand down the front of the apron and tucked a loose strand of hair behind her ear. "Look at me. I couldn't possibly go anywhere at the moment."

"But you are interested in the position?" Olivia bobbed her

head while asking the question. She hoped her affirmative nods would influence the woman's reply.

"Yes, of course. We need the money. And I am told I excel in the kitchen. I'm sure Suzanne would be willing to take charge of the entire house." There was a growing enthusiasm in Mrs. DeVault's voice. "I'll be there in an hour. Will that suffice?"

Olivia tightened her lips. "If you could come more quickly, I know Chef René would be grateful. We have many guests to feed, and with—"

"I understand. I will hurry." Mrs. DeVault removed her apron in one swift movement and hung it beside the kitchen door.

After bidding the two Quinter girls good-bye, Olivia retraced her steps to the hotel. Since the first day of the strike, the outward charm of Pullman hadn't changed. The strike hadn't interrupted the sense of decorum and sensibility that had always defined the community. However, the small groups of men who now gathered to visit in the park or play lawn tennis were a marked reminder that nothing was as it seemed at first blush. Since the strike, much had changed. The Chicago newspaper reporters continued to visit each day and write their reports. Mostly, they continued to favor the workingmen and their plight while chastising Mr. Pullman for fleeing to his island retreat in the St. Lawrence River to escape the chaos now swirling within his own company.

"He's simply attempting to starve you out," Matthew Clayborn had commented when he'd spoken to Fred and Olivia two days past. "He's followed this same pattern each time there's been a walkout or talk of a strike. I fear your strike is going to produce little if you don't gain additional leverage."

Fred had agreed that such a pronouncement would discourage the men, and while they'd continued to discuss the future of the strike, Olivia had taken her leave. She didn't want to hear their plans. A fear rested in her heart that she might slip and accidentally repeat something she heard.

She waved at her cousin Albert. Since the strike he'd been frequenting the park near the hotel. "How is Martha faring?" she called.

He jumped up from the bench and ran toward her. "She's uncomfortable and anxious for the child's birth. You should come by and visit her. She's lonely."

His request shamed her. On several recent occasions, she'd considered a visit but had put her own needs before those of her cousin's wife. "Fred and I will stop for a visit tomorrow afternoon." Olivia had hoped to spend Sunday afternoon picnicking by the lake with Fred, but a visit with Martha was more important. A robin chirped nearby and filled the silence between them. Albert's eyes had shifted away from her at the mention of Fred's name.

"If you come alone, I can go and play a game of lawn tennis and permit the two of you time for a private chat."

Olivia didn't argue. She expected to see Chef René appear on the hotel lawn if she didn't soon return. There was little doubt Martha would want to hear the latest news from the hotel, but that wasn't reason enough to exclude Fred from the visit.

The kitchen door banged behind her, and Chef René glanced over his shoulder. "I thought perhaps you had joined the men in their strike."

She ignored the sarcasm and donned her tall white hat. "My cousin stopped me to ask that I visit Martha. I could hardly ignore him."

"The potatoes await a cream sauce. There is fresh parsley from the garden. Use it for seasoning." He continued to braise the lamb chops. "Have you nothing to say about Mrs. DeVault, or have you so soon forgotten why you were gone?"

The man could test the patience of a saint. "She said she would be pleased to interview for the position, but she needed time to prepare."

"What is to prepare except the food in this kitchen? Did you not tell her I need help at this very moment?"

"Yes, but she was in the midst of performing her household chores. She needed time to—"

The chef tipped his head and looked heavenward. "She does not need fine clothes or perfectly arranged hair to work in my kitchen. A baker needs strong hands for kneading the bread and rolling the piecrusts." He shook his head. "I will never understand women."

Olivia chuckled. "Then perhaps you should become better acquainted with a few ladies so that you will learn more about our ways."

He ignored her retort, but Olivia knew his irritation was simmering like a chicken stewing in one of his large cooking pots. She had best say no more or he would boil over. She continued with her assigned duties and paid no heed to his behavior. Both of them moved about the kitchen like a well-oiled machine while the kitchen boys and scullery maids jumped forward to assist at their signals.

A mere half hour had passed when Mrs. DeVault tapped on the screened kitchen door. Her speedy arrival ensured she had passed Chef René's first test. He wiped his hands on a nearby towel while he formally introduced himself. Olivia watched his earlier irritation disappear. Leading Mrs. DeVault through the kitchen, he presented each member of the staff and offered explanations regarding their duties. It seemed he had completely forgotten the lamb chops and creamed potatoes. He had become the epitome of chivalry.

"Perhaps you should give Mrs. DeVault a tour of the lower kitchen. If you are going to hire her, she might want to begin dessert preparations for the evening meal."

Chef René wagged his finger. "We must not neglect our good manners, Miss Mott."

What had happened to the impervious man who'd chided her for her dalliance only a short time ago? "Perhaps I should take over with the lamb chops."

"But of course. I shall leave you in charge while I escort Mrs. DeVault downstairs and explain her duties."

Explain her duties? No interview, no meeting with Mr. Howard? Olivia realized the chef was desperate for a bakery assistant, but she had expected him to at least question Mrs. DeVault regarding her abilities. Was he going to rely solely upon her recommendation of the older woman? If so, Chef René would hold her responsible if Mrs. DeVault proved to be a poor addition to their staff. And who could know if the older woman would hold up under the pressures of the daily baking and Chef René's expectations.

Perhaps she shouldn't have suggested Fred's mother for the position. If this work arrangement didn't prove successful, it could cause a strain between her and Fred. She whisked the cream sauce with renewed vigor and signaled for one of the kitchen boys.

"Ask the headwaiter to make certain the dining room is in readiness. I won't have time to discuss arrangements with him before the noonday meal."

The young man's chest swelled with pride. He squared his shoulders and hastened to do her bidding. Sounds of laughter drifted from the lower kitchen, and Olivia glanced toward the stairway. One of the kitchen boys ceased scrubbing the pots and pointed a dripping finger while several female dishwashers giggled in unison. Olivia waved them back to work and hurried to the top of the stairs.

"Once you've completed your instructions, I could use your help with the final preparations, Chef René."

A short time later the chef ambled toward her. "While I was ill, you managed this kitchen without any help. Now that I am well, you cannot manage for even a few minutes without me?"

"We could hear your laughter up here," she whispered. "I feared unseemly rumors might circulate."

He dipped his head near her ear. "I am a Frenchman, Miss Mott. I relish the thought that anyone thinks I am worthy of such talk." His hearty laughter caused the staff to turn and watch the two of them. "You see? Now I have given them something else to discuss."

Olivia had never before observed Chef René finish meal preparations in such a lighthearted manner. Even when one of the kitchen boys dropped a platter a few minutes later, he didn't shout or lose his temper. Once their duties were completed and the time had arrived for their afternoon respite, Olivia hurried downstairs to chat with Mrs. DeVault. The older woman had used the last several hours to advantage: one edge of the baking table was lined with her fruit pies.

During Olivia's first year of employment, she had been required to bake samples of all the pastries that would be served at one of Mrs. Pullman's teas. Before agreeing Olivia could adequately perform the task, Chef René had insisted upon tasting each one in advance. She now wondered if he had required the same test of Mrs. DeVault.

"I see you have been hard at work. Is there anything I can do to assist you?"

The heat from the ovens had caused a pink hue to rise in Mrs. DeVault's cheeks. "I believe it's going well. Chef René said he would check on me later this afternoon. I don't recall you ever mentioning his charm."

Olivia muffled a laugh. She considered the chef a fine friend and a marvelous chef, but charming? She'd never thought of him in that vein. Before she could respond, she heard footfalls on the stairs.

"Ah, Mrs. DeVault. I see you are attempting to make my mouth water with all these delectable fruit pies." His tone was as sweet as the sugar Mrs. DeVault had mixed into the baked goods. His smile faded when he caught sight of Olivia at the far end of the baking table. "I wanted to make certain all was going well for you, but I see Miss Mott has—"

"I'm pleased you came down, Chef René," Mrs. DeVault said. "I thought you might want to taste a piece and see if these meet the hotel's standards. I know you serve only the finest food." She beamed in his direction.

Olivia remained in the background, watching and listening to the two of them. If she didn't know better, she'd think they had been smitten by Cupid's arrow. Of course, she realized Chef René and Mrs. DeVault would never be interested in romance, especially with each other. They were complete opposites.

"I trust that anything you bake will be *magnifique*." As if to punctuate his approval, he gathered his fingertips into a tight knot and briefly touched them to his lips.

The color heightened in Mrs. DeVault's cheeks. "You are too kind. Do sit down and let me cut you a slice."

Mrs. DeVault was acting like a schoolgirl, giggling and

blushing at each exchange, and Chef René appeared to be captivated by her charms. A rush of inexplicable discomfort washed over Olivia. Though she'd arrived before Chef René, she felt like an unwelcome intruder.

She wished only to escape and return upstairs. "Don't let me interrupt the two of you. I believe I'll go outside for a breath of fresh air."

Mrs. DeVault turned and looked at Olivia as though she'd completely forgotten she was in the room. "Oh, I'm sorry, my dear. Would you like a piece of pie, too?"

"No, thank you." Olivia rounded the table and shook her head while moving toward the steps. "I'm pleased to see all is going well."

Olivia retreated up the stairs and wandered outside to a bench beneath the large oak. She plopped down and wondered at what she'd just observed. Why should she be surprised that the two older adults had been drawn to each other? A kind and generous woman, Mrs. DeVault also possessed an infectious cheerfulness. And by Mrs. DeVault's own account, Chef René could be quite charming. They were both alone, and certainly love could flourish under such circumstances. What would Fred think of such an idea? Once again, Olivia wondered if she'd made a mistake in recommending Mrs. DeVault. Lost in her thoughts, she watched some men playing ball with several young boys.

"Ah, here you are!"

Unsure how long she'd been daydreaming, Olivia jumped up at the sound of Chef René's voice.

"You have brought me an excellent baker, Miss Mott. Not only is Mrs. DeVault a fine cook, but also she is a most congenial woman. She is going to be a good addition to our staff."

Olivia thought the chef appeared several years younger than he had earlier in the morning—surely her imagination was playing tricks on her. "So you have hired her for a permanent position?"

He nodded. "Oui! I would be a fool to do otherwise."

"Answered prayer," Olivia whispered.

"What's this you say about prayer?"

"Mrs. DeVault has steadfastly prayed that Fred or Mr. Quinter would locate work during the strike so there would be funds enough to purchase food for the family. Her prayer has been answered."

"Not so, for it is Mrs. DeVault who has located the work, not your Fred or this Mr. Quinter."

"It makes little difference who earns the wages. They need money to purchase food. It is an answer to prayer."

He shrugged his broad shoulders and waved her toward the kitchen without further comment. Mrs. DeVault might easily win Chef René's heart, but Olivia wondered if the older woman would have as much success winning him to God.

CHAPTER SIX

Fred loped up the front steps of the local headquarters of the American Railway Union located on Howard Street in Kensington. He counted his small part in helping form the local union as one of his greatest achievements. Scattered throughout the country, the local unions were joined together under the national umbrella of the American Railway Union. The organization had ruled that the train tracks running through the Pullman Car Works entitled employees of the company to membership in the larger national union. As expected, the majority of the striking men had arrived for the meeting. Since most had little else with which to occupy their time, they'd trudge the mile and a half to Kensington and congregate at the union headquarters each day. In addition to passing the time, they were close at hand if any news developed. Fred called greetings to several small groups gathered nearby.

Thankfully, the prevailing attitude of the men had remained calm. Although they'd initially been disappointed by Mr. Pullman's departure from Chicago, the striking workers believed the ongoing meetings of the board of directors would soon lead to positive results. They had continued to abide by the union's call for order in the community, although many complained about their credit being suspended at the Market and Arcade stores.

"There's nothing the union can do in that regard," Fred had told them. *"The shopkeepers in the Arcade and Market rent their space from Mr. Pullman. They must abide by his rules whether they want to or not."* However, he understood their concern: their families needed food, and they had no money. The strikers had depended upon using credit at the local shops.

He didn't want trouble to develop between the strikers and those, like Olivia, who continued to work in the town. *"We must remember that we need the services offered by those people,"* he had emphasized. *"We don't want the men at the firehouse to walk away from their jobs. And those who work in the hotel and stores are sympathetic to our cause. Many have already furnished aid, and we must remember they are not embroiled in this strike. This strike includes only those who work inside those iron gates at the car works."*

Fred didn't know if the men had taken his message to heart, but the complaints had subsided, at least when he was present. He had directed the men to use their efforts toward requesting donations of food and clothing and suggested that the workers emphasize their difficult struggle to anyone who would listen to their plight and spread the word. He had pledged to do the same. Union officials on both the regional and national levels continued to stress that keeping the public on their side remained of paramount importance. The strike hadn't drawn much coverage from the national press, but the Chicago news-papers consistently reported the day-to-day activities in the town. Union officials didn't want to lose the momentum created by the sympathetic response of Chicago residents.

Once the men were seated and Thomas Heathcoate had called them to order, he signaled Fred to come forward and take charge of the meeting. "I have some good news to report," Fred said. The men leaned forward.

"We have received a substantial donation that will assist us in feeding needy families for a time."

A rallying cheer went up from the crowd after Fred announced they had received a large donation of flour, potatoes, and meat worth fifteen hundred dollars from Chicago Mayor Hopkins. The mayor, donating the food through his general store, had also pledged a thousand dollars in cash to assist the needy families.

Fred waved for silence. "The mayor has also approved the solicitations being made by the Southside policemen. He has taken the position that there is no legal objection to the police doing charitable work." Fred waited until the shouts of approval ended. "In addition, some doctors and nurses have pledged to volunteer their services, and for those in dire need, several drugstores have agreed to fill prescriptions at no cost. Also, a number of prominent Chicago ladies have been calling financial institutions, seeking donations."

While he realized the collected funds and donated food wouldn't last long, Fred marveled at the outpouring of generosity offered to the citizens of Pullman. Because the entire town was in need of help, the residents of Chicago and other nearby communities had banded together and responded as if the town had suffered a natural catastrophe—and in some respects, that is exactly what had occurred. Their pleas for help were being heard.

Occasionally rumors of a malaria outbreak in the town or

residents going insane from hunger were reported in the newspapers, but the local union officials made every attempt to quell
such stories as quickly as possible. While they wanted the newspapers to report their circumstances, they didn't want exaggerated or fictitious stories, especially those that could cause a
panic.

"One of our Kensington merchants has provided free stor-
age space for the food donations. Once we dismiss, the Relief
Committee will meet to make arrangements for delivery of the
goods from Chicago to Kensington. A notice will be posted on
the doors outside listing the times and dates for distribution."

Though there wasn't any news regarding negotiations, the
men departed the meeting in good spirits, and Fred was pleased
by their approval of the union's work on their behalf.

He walked home, eager to tell his mother and the Quinters
the latest news. Paul Quinter had made another journey to Chicago looking for work and hadn't been present for today's meeting. He would undoubtedly be pleased to hear of the food and
medical care that would be available for his family.

As he bounded up the front steps and entered the house,
Fred called out a greeting to his mother. He sailed his hat
toward the hall tree, pleased when it made a perfect landing on
one of the protruding hooks. Reaching the kitchen doorway, he
stopped short.

Mrs. Quinter stood at the stove with baby Arthur balanced
on her hip. "Your mother asked me to prepare supper," she said.

Fred glanced over his shoulder toward the stairway. "Is she
ill?"

"No." Mrs. Quinter dropped a handful of carrots into the
pot on the stove and returned to the table for more.

She would save time by placing them all in a bowl rather than making several trips back and forth, he thought, but didn't say anything. Instead, he awaited the woman's reply.

"She's at work."

Fred waited for her to furnish additional information. When it didn't appear she would, he urged her on. "Where is she working? I knew nothing of this."

Mrs. Quinter offered the few tidbits of information she possessed while she continued to prepare a stew that seemed to lack much in the way of meat. This dearth was a reminder of the news he'd delivered a short time ago at the union meeting, but before he could share the information, Paul Quinter shouted a greeting to his wife. Mrs. Quinter peeked around Fred and called for her husband to join them in the kitchen.

The frown on Paul's face reflected he'd had no luck finding work in Chicago. He'd taken to the dangerous practice of jumping freight cars for his daily treks into the city. But desperate circumstances caused men to take chances they might otherwise never consider. With so many men out of work now, even the occasional day jobs he'd located in the city had dried up— and so had his congenial attitude. His elder daughter, Lydia, followed behind him and stood leaning against the doorjamb.

He kicked a chair away from the table with the toe of his shoe and dropped onto the seat with a thud. "If this strike doesn't soon end, we're all going to starve to death."

Suzanne glanced at her daughter, whose eyes had instantly opened wide at the comment. "Do stop those remarks, Paul. The girls hear what you say, and they believe every word of it." She looked at her daughter. "Your father is exaggerating, dear. We're not going to starve to death."

Paul extended his arm, and Lydia ran to receive his embrace. "Don't listen to me, girl. I'm just angry because I can't take care of you children and your mother the way you deserve."

Lydia sat down on his lap. "Mrs. DeVault says God's watching over us and there's no need to worry, Daddy."

Paul patted his daughter's blond curls. "Sometimes that's hard to—"

His wife's stern look stopped him.

"Hard to *what*, Daddy?" Lydia's hazel eyes shone with expectation.

"Hard to remember God will take care of us. Sometimes, it's hard for your daddy to remember God cares about us."

The child stretched to kiss his cheek. "I'll remind you each day. Will that help you remember?"

"That will help. Thank you, Lydia. Now go and play with your sister. I'll call you when supper is ready."

Suzanne remained silent until the screen door slammed and then turned to face her husband. "I've told you over and over—"

Fred held up his hand to stave off what could escalate into a family argument. "I have some information to pass along from today's meeting."

The interruption halted Mrs. Quinter's angry invective. Fred's news regarding the distribution of donated food and cash brought an immediate smile to her face and an appreciative nod from her husband.

"So you'll be taking charge of the kitchen now that Mrs. DeVault has taken this new position?" Paul asked.

His wife nodded. "I'm pleased to help out, but don't expect my cooking to match Mrs. DeVault's."

"You'll do fine," he said with a wink.

A blush spread across Suzanne's cheeks, and she turned back toward the stove. "I imagine we should go ahead with supper. Before your mother left for the hotel, she said I should remain on our regular schedule and not worry about her."

Once Lydia had set the table and all of them had washed up, they gathered around the table for supper. After they joined hands, Fred offered a prayer for God's continued provision and thanks for the meal set before them.

"And for this strike to end soon," Paul added, with a final amen.

The stew was thin and lacked flavor, but the hot cross buns helped fill him up. Hannah was the only one who complained that their supper wasn't as good as usual. "No grumbling, young lady," her father admonished. "There are many who would be pleased to eat at this table tonight." At her father's reminder, eight-year-old Hannah wilted and offered an apology.

"I'm home!" The group turned in unison at the sound of Mrs. DeVault's greeting.

Fred pushed away from the table and met his mother in the hall. Bright color dotted her cheeks. He expected her to appear weary and haggard after her first day at work. Instead, she appeared several years younger.

He pecked a kiss on her cheek and stepped back. "You sound quite energetic for someone who has been hard at work all day."

She propped her hat on the hall tree and gently slapped his arm. "And what has changed? I have always worked hard each day. Who do you think has been keeping this house clean, cooking meals, washing and ironing your clothes, and—"

"I didn't mean to suggest that your household duties aren't taxing, but it's different working for someone else—having a supervisor watching your every move." He tipped his head to the side. "Don't you think?"

She laughed and nodded. "Well, I agree with most of what

you've said. I will admit that my feet ache and I'm eager to relax and enjoy a cup of coffee."

"Sit down and rest your weary bones," Suzanne said. "I'll pour you a cup; then you can tell us all about your day."

Mrs. DeVault didn't hesitate to accept the offer. She sat in her usual spot next to Fred. Once Suzanne had placed a steaming cup of coffee and a hot cross bun in front of her, she took a sip of coffee and then explained the details of her new position.

"Chef René is a wonderful supervisor. He came downstairs to the baking kitchen several times during the day to compliment me. He said he'd never had anyone accomplish so much in such a short period of time." She beamed and glanced from face to face.

For a moment, his mother reminded Fred of a young girl. Each time she spoke of Chef René, the color in her cheeks heightened and she became more animated. He watched her closely, uncertain what to think of her unusual behavior. She appeared somewhat smitten by the man—or was it merely the fact that someone other than family had acknowledged her talents? In the past Olivia had spoken highly of Chef René, but she'd also mentioned a few of his faults: a short temper, the need for perfection, and his lack of faith.

Fred squeezed his mother's arm as the girls excused themselves from the table. "I'm pleased he realized what a gem he's recruited for his kitchen. His gain is our loss." He quickly cleared his throat. "I'm sorry, Suzanne. I didn't mean to imply that your cooking isn't . . . ."

Suzanne laughed. "You don't need to apologize, Fred. We all know my food doesn't hold a candle to your mother's fine fare."

The older woman smiled. "Practice makes perfect, Suzanne. My new position will give you time to hone your skills. This will be a fine opportunity for all of us. God has answered our prayers."

"Let's hope God answers our prayers to end this strike," Paul said.

Mrs. DeVault nodded. "I understand your concerns, Paul. But for this one day why don't we simply thank Him for what He has given us."

"I need to practice what I preach to my daughters," Mr. Quinter said with a chuckle. He pushed away from the table. "I'll send the girls in to help you with the dishes, Suzanne."

Fred leaned close to his mother. "I hope you told Chef René that once the strike is over, you don't intend to continue working at the hotel."

She arched her brows. "I've done no such thing. Who knows what will happen over the next months? I may discover I'm well suited for this position." She tapped her son's chest with her index finger. "If I am able to support myself by working in Pullman, you may finally have the opportunity to leave and seek work in Chicago without fear of forcing me to move." His mother smiled broadly. "Now there's a possibility I don't think you've considered."

———

The following morning Fred stood outside Greenstone Church wearing his good suit and crisp white shirt. Olivia's heart thumped a quick staccato rhythm at the sight of him. Since mid-April he'd been threatening to attend Sunday services in Kensington, and each Sunday morning she rounded the corner and wondered if he'd be waiting for her. Fred had grown increasingly unhappy with the preacher. And Olivia understood Fred's disdain.

An Uncertain Dream

The preacher ought not be using the pulpit to promote his own views. However, since his arrival in Pullman back in January, Reverend Oggel had made his position clear: he supported management. And as winter had worn on and tensions continued to mount in town, the preacher had become increasingly anti-union. One of his mid-April sermons had been a tribute to George M. Pullman that recounted, in painstaking detail, the man's rise from poverty to a position of fame and fortune throughout the country. The discourse had set Fred on edge. For nearly forty minutes, the preacher had touted the model town as an experiment in contemplated beauty and harmony, as well as a place of health, comfort, and contentment for the residents. Never once did the preacher mention the suffering or current needs of his flock.

Since that time, the preacher hadn't been quite so flagrant with his remarks, but he never failed to include at least an oratorical "tip of the hat" to Mr. Pullman or members of management in his sermons. While most members of his congregation wore the white ribbons tied to their wrist that displayed unity with the strikers, the preacher's lapel continued to bear the small flag that signified his alignment with the company.

Olivia grasped Fred's arm and offered him a bright smile. "I'm pleased to see you. I had hoped to stop by last evening, but with the shortage of help in the kitchen, I worked late. By the time I left, I wanted nothing more than a soft bed."

"I thought my mother had been hired to fill the vacant position. Was there some misunderstanding on her part?"

She heard the concern in his voice. "There was no misunderstanding. Both of the bakers left, and though your mother is quite talented, she can't complete the work of two women. I stayed behind to restock items for her so she wouldn't be

75

overwhelmed come Monday morning."

Fred greeted several groups of men before the two of them ascended the steps and entered the vestibule. "I'd think there would be a number of women eager to apply for the other position."

"Indeed. But so far, Chef René hasn't received authority to hire anyone else. I don't think Mr. Howard was overly pleased when he discovered your mother had been hired without his approval." Olivia inched her way in front of a couple who refused to scoot to the center of the pew and sat down. "He may feel that Chef René needs to be taught a lesson for overstepping his bounds. Let's don't forget what happened last week when Mr. Billings hired a washwoman."

The closing of the laundry had presented Mr. Billings with a difficult situation: mountains of dirty hotel linens that must be laundered. Without Mr. Howard's permission, the hotel manager hired a washwoman. When Mr. Howard discovered the hotel manager had set up an independent laundry and usurped Mr. Howard's authority as company agent, a public argument ensued between the two men that permitted comic relief for both strikers and management alike.

The incident had led to a general agreement that no one would ever override Mr. Howard's authority in the future. But now it had happened again. And Chef René could well suffer the same dressing-down Mr. Billings had received.

Mrs. DeVault bustled into the church and entered their pew while the organist struck the opening chords of the hymn that signaled services would soon begin. "I thought I was going to be late," she whispered to the two of them.

Fred grinned at his mother. "You *are* late, but your secret is safe with us."

While the congregation stood, his mother touched a gloved hand to her lips in an effort to stifle a giggle. The hymn singing and Scripture reading continued without incident, but when Reverend Oggel stepped to the pulpit, he delivered an attack that condemned the strike and branded the union leaders as agitators. He sent the congregation home with his final words ringing in their ears—half a loaf was better than none.

Fred jumped up from the pew and grasped Olivia by the elbow. "Until that man has been replaced, I'll be attending church in Kensington. It's one thing to have an opinion about the strike, but it's quite another to use the pulpit to promote that agenda."

Olivia noted the look on Mr. Howard's face when he passed their pew. He'd obviously been quite pleased with the morning's sermon.

———

"You could smile," she said to Fred as they neared the flat her cousin Albert had rented shortly before he and Martha had wed.

"I was looking forward to spending time alone with you after church." He pushed his hat back on his head and sauntered a little more slowly. "I don't think I'm going to be welcome at Albert's home. I could meet you in the park at four o'clock."

"Don't be silly. I'm certain Albert and Martha will be pleased to visit with both of us. Albert tells me Martha has been quite lonely and misses her work at the hotel."

Fred nodded. "Now that the strike's begun, she has Albert to keep her company."

"Yes, but that's not the same as having others pay a call. I've been doing my best to remember all of the latest news from the hotel."

Fred grinned. "You mean gossip?"

"No! I mean *news*," she said, playfully slapping his arm.

They continued their banter until a short time later when they mounted the steps to the flat and Olivia knocked on the door. Albert offered a broad smile when he saw Olivia, but his eyes shone with concern when he caught sight of Fred standing beside her. He opened the door and motioned them inside while peering up and down the street.

"Are you expecting someone else?" Fred asked.

"No, I uh . . . well, I . . ." Albert shook his head. "No. We're not expecting anyone. Come in."

"Why don't we go and play a game of lawn tennis?" Fred suggested.

Albert instantly declined. "A bit too warm for me out there, but we could go into the kitchen and give the ladies time to visit alone, if you like."

Fred didn't argue. "The kitchen it is," he said.

"Come join me in the parlor, Olivia," Martha called.

As the men walked down the hallway, Olivia entered the parlor and leaned down to embrace Martha. "You look wonderful."

"Thank you." She patted the seat cushion beside her. "Sit down. I want to hear all the latest news."

With the men out of earshot, Olivia answered each of Martha's questions, adding as much detail as possible. "I do miss having you at the hotel," she said when Martha's inquiries finally ceased.

"And I miss being there, too, but I must admit I don't miss Mr. Billings and his snoopy ways."

Olivia chuckled. "He hasn't changed much. Are you certain you've been feeling well? Albert appeared concerned when I inquired about your health yesterday."

"I'm absolutely fine. He worries when there is no reason. The doctor assures me everything is progressing normally and on schedule. I admit the heat gets dreadfully difficult to bear at times, but overall we are both doing well." Martha glanced toward the kitchen. "When you come to visit again, it would be better if you didn't bring Fred along."

Olivia frowned. "Why not? We are all friends."

"Albert worries he won't be rehired if he associates too closely with those leading the strike." She grasped Olivia's hand. "It's because of me and the baby. He wants to be a good provider."

"All of the men in Pullman want to be good providers, Martha. That's why they've gone on strike—so they will receive a livable wage."

"I don't want to argue or cause strife between us, but I wanted you to know that Fred's presence causes Albert grave discomfort."

"Since Fred and I are frequently seen together, I would think my presence would cause him distress, too."

"Perhaps a little, but not so much as Fred's." Martha had just confirmed what Fred suspected. Her cousin planned to distance himself from anyone who fervently supported the union movement.

When the clock chimed, Olivia jumped to her feet. "I didn't realize the time. We should be on our way. I'll do my best to stop again when time permits. We're quite busy at the hotel, so I can't make any promises."

"Of course. I understand."

There was no need for further explanation. They both under-stood that until the strike ended, their visits would be rare.

————————

When a message arrived for Chef René to join Mr. Howard in his office on Monday morning, Olivia feared fireworks would result.

"Tell him I will come once the guests have all been served breakfast," he told the messenger.

Olivia signaled the kitchen boy to wait. She stepped to Chef René's side. "I think you should reconsider. If you anger him too much, he may fire Mrs. DeVault. You have no power to place her name on the payroll without his approval. Perhaps you should tread lightly this one time."

His toque drooped to one side when he offered a firm nod. "You are correct. This is not the time to put my importance to the test. However, we both know Mr. Howard would be required to close the kitchen without us. If we refuse to work unless Mrs. DeVault is placed on the payroll—"

"Are you advocating a strike of our own?"

"It is an exciting idea, non?" He chuckled. "I will take your advice and go to Mr. Howard. However, if he refuses my request to place Mrs. DeVault on the hotel payroll, then you and I must force his hand and stage our own walkout, Miss Mott."

"Let's hope it doesn't come to that." She gave him a fleeting smile. "Offer to prepare your stuffed pork chops if the situation becomes difficult."

"Miss Mott! Are you suggesting I stoop to bribery?" The chef's hearty laugh resonated as he walked down the hallway. She hoped he would follow her advice. Otherwise, all three of them could be unemployed before the day's end.

CHAPTER SEVEN

London, England

Charlotte selected a fan and a pair of gloves before she strode down the hallway to her mother's bedroom. She rapped on the heavy wooden door and waited. When there was no response, she waited a few moments and knocked once again.

"Mother! I know you're in there. Must I forgo all civility and enter without your permission?" Charlotte tapped her foot and silently counted. When she reached ten, she placed her hand on the doorknob. "Mother?"

"Oh, do cease your nattering and come in." Her mother, still in her dressing gown, sat in front of one of the windows that looked down upon the summer garden. With her arms tightly folded across her chest, she speared Charlotte with an angry gaze. "You know I dislike being disturbed so early in the morning."

"It is not early, and you're hiding simply to avoid me. The moment my carriage departs, you will flee to Hargrove Estates and trifle away the hours with the marchioness. You need to face the truth. For the final time, I beg you to come with me to Mr. Proctor's office."

"I have no intention of darkening the doorway of that man. If he had any respect for me or your deceased father, he would come to Lanshire Hall."

"He attempted to arrange a visit last week, and you banished him from the grounds with strict orders never again to step foot in Lanshire Hall."

Her mother shrugged. "He should have waited an appropriate period of time before requesting a meeting."

"You should be grateful Mr. Proctor concerns himself with our welfare rather than with stuffy English propriety. I admire his desire to do Father's bidding. I should think you would be most grateful. Instead, you are rude and treat him with disdain."

Her mother continued to stare out the window, seemingly unaffected by Charlotte's harsh comment. "He is a solicitor. They always bear bad tidings. And even more loathsome, they expect to have their pockets lined with sterling after delivering their unsavory news. I choose to ignore them."

"No good purpose will be served by your conduct, but if I cannot convince you to accompany me, then *I* shall attend to the matter." There was much to be accomplished this day, and Charlotte couldn't waste further time in tiresome discourse.

Once she'd settled inside the carriage, Charlotte ignored the discomfort of jostling over rutted roads and cobblestone streets. She had prepared a list of questions and prayed Mr. Proctor would have a measure of good news for her.

When she arrived, Mr. Proctor's clerk escorted Charlotte directly into the solicitor's office. "I appreciate the fact that you are prompt, sir," she said.

Mr. Proctor waited until Charlotte sat down; then he settled behind his massive mahogany desk. "I only wish I had a better report for you." He fidgeted with the sheaf of papers arranged before him. "I am thankful your father gave you warning of his financial condition prior to his death. I advised him to do so. Otherwise, I can't imagine being forced to deliver such news to you and your mother." He pushed several papers across the desk. "I had hoped your mother would join us today."

Charlotte glanced at the papers. They looked much like the ones she'd received from her father. "Mother says she's not up to unpleasant conversation, though she'll soon be forced to take stock of her financial condition."

The solicitor arched his bushy dark brows. "And why is that?"

"I plan to return to America. My mother is unwilling to leave England. I do understand her decision, but she will be required to deal with this awkward state of affairs."

Mr. Proctor rubbed his jaw and nodded. "A fine kettle of fish, I fear. You'll note that there is nothing but debt. Lanshire Hall will be lost, along with all the contents. I trust you will advise your mother to secure her jewels if she has hope of keeping them. Perhaps Lord Chesterfield could see to that matter for her?"

"I plan to visit Lord and Lady Chesterfield when we've finished our meeting. I will speak to him on my mother's behalf." She perused what seemed an endless list of debts and then met the solicitor's intense stare. "Am I to conclude that all is lost, then?"

"Nearly all. Your father did entrust me with a small sum of money to be divided between you and your mother upon his death. I would strongly advise you keep this our secret. Those to whom your father owed money will show you no mercy if they discover even this meager amount is available." He removed a small leather pouch from his desk drawer and handed it to her. "I trust you will use it wisely."

"Indeed, I will. Thank you for your service to my father. If my mother should be in need of—"

"I will do whatever possible. Your father was a dear friend for many years." Sadness clouded the solicitor's eyes as he walked her to the door and bid her farewell.

Charlotte longed to return to Lanshire Hall, but this final leg of her journey could not be postponed any longer. Leaning back in the carriage, she closed her eyes. Perhaps she could devise some simple method to broach the topic of her mother with Lord and Lady Chesterfield during the carriage ride to their estate.

When she arrived at Briarwood, Charlotte still hadn't decided upon a plan. The maid escorted her to one of the small sitting rooms while she went to fetch Lady Chesterfield. If Charlotte could speak to her mother's half sister alone, perhaps things would go more smoothly.

At the sound of voices, Charlotte glanced toward the door. Her spirits plunged when both Lord and Lady Chesterfield entered the room. Lady Chesterfield raised her brows until they disappeared beneath the fringe of curls on her forehead. "To what do we owe this *unexpected* visit?"

Charlotte had known that her unsolicited call would not be appreciated, but she possessed neither the time nor the energy to follow social protocol, especially with Lord and Lady Chesterfield. "Since we are family, I trust you will forgive my breach of etiquette."

Lady Chesterfield sighed and waved for Charlotte to sit on

one of the chairs while Lord Chesterfield frowned and stroked his chin.

"I do hope this won't take long. Lady Chesterfield and I have plans for the remainder of the day."

"Not long at all. I've just come from the solicitor's office, where I've gone over matters concerning my father's estate."

Those words were of enough interest for Lord Chesterfield, or Chessie, as everyone called him, to promptly sit down beside his wife. "There are rumors that your father was insolvent, you know." A man who had never been popular with other members of nobility, Lord Chesterfield had always resented those who were easily accepted. And Charlotte's father had been one of those men.

"Unfortunately, the rumors are valid." News that the Earl of Lanshire had squandered his holdings appeared to give Chessie a great deal of satisfaction. Had Charlotte not required their charity, she would have walked out without another word. Instead, she forced a wan smile. "It is for that very reason I've come here."

Lady Chesterfield leaned forward and patted Charlotte's hand. "How is my sister contending with this dreadful ordeal?"

"She avoids discussing it. However, I plan to return to America, and Mother refuses to accompany me. Lanshire Hall will soon be sold, and she is in need of a place to live. Since you are her only living relative . . ."

The older couple exchanged a guarded look. "I suppose you expect *me* to provide for her," Chessie said.

"I do believe it is your obligation, sir." Charlotte did her best to keep a civil tone, but she longed to tell him exactly what she thought of his pompous behavior. "I'm certain you're pleased you won't have the added burden of my son and me. I depart in two weeks."

"So soon?" Lady Chesterfield clasped her bodice. "You haven't given us much notice, Charlotte."

"I feared you might flee the country," she said, forcing a laugh. Although Lord and Lady Chesterfield joined in her laughter, Charlotte knew her statement contained more truth than fiction.

Two weeks later, Charlotte stood in front of the mirror and donned a hat of fancy straw adorned with a cluster of yellow roses that were an exact match to the accordion-pleated silk bodice of her summer gown. Her young son toddled across the room, dragging her lace and beribboned parasol, apparently anxious to depart. Charlotte smiled at the child. She hoped he would behave as pleasantly on their voyage.

"Are you prepared for our journey, Morgan?"

He turned away from her and pushed the parasol in front of him like a shovel. Once he reached the closed bedroom door, he shouted, "Ope!"

Charlotte laughed at his antics. "Ope-nn," she said, using her tongue and lips in an exaggerated movement to form the final letter.

Instead of repeating her, Morgan slapped the parasol handle on the wooden door. Charlotte hurried to his side and removed the sunshade from his hand. "I'll take that before you manage to hurt yourself."

"Or ruin your parasol," Beatrice added. "You're going to have your hands full once you're on board the ship. Are you certain you don't want me to accompany you?"

An Uncertain Dream

Charlotte could hear the pain in Beatrice's question. The nursemaid would have great difficulty adjusting to the departure of her young charge, and though Charlotte would welcome help on the voyage, Beatrice had been clear: she didn't want to remain in America. And Charlotte couldn't afford to use her meager funds on round-trip passage for the nursemaid. There were more pressing items for which she would need the money when she arrived in Chicago.

Beatrice scooped the child into her arms and nuzzled his neck with kisses. "I'm going to miss this fine little boy," she whispered into his neck.

Morgan giggled with delight and snatched the frilly white mobcap from her head. He tossed it in the air and then wriggled until Beatrice returned him to the floor, where he promptly retrieved the cap and pulled it over his blond curls. Both women laughed at his antics, and soon he joined in their laughter.

"It sounds as though there's a celebration taking place in here."

All three of them turned toward the door, but it was Charlotte who waved her mother into the room. "Come join us." She pointed toward Morgan. "Your grandson is entertaining us this morning."

The countess offered a brief smile and then motioned for Beatrice to take Morgan from the room. "I'd like to speak to my daughter privately." Her gaze remained fixed on Beatrice while she trundled Morgan from the room.

Once the door closed, the countess sat down and shifted her attention to Charlotte. "You know I dislike begging, but I've come to make one final plea. I don't know how I'm going to manage if you depart."

"I'll not be dissuaded at this late date, Mother. My ship sails this afternoon. We've already discussed this issue in detail." Charlotte crossed the room and sat down on the brocade settee beside her mother. "You will always be welcome to come to America. I don't know what accommodations I'll be able to offer you, but I would take pleasure in having you live with Morgan and me."

Charlotte's offer was sincere, although both of them knew it wouldn't be accepted. The countess would not permanently leave her homeland—she'd made her decision quite clear when Charlotte had initially suggested the move after the visit with Mr. Proctor.

Her mother dabbed the corner of a lace handkerchief to her eye. "I think the least you could do is remain for an appropriate bereavement period." She flipped her hankie in the air. "And you should be ashamed for wearing that yellow dress during mourning. In truth, I think you should remain here for at least six months, or even a year. I need you to help me through this difficult transition."

"The color of my dress may give the local dowagers gossip for their next social, but it doesn't denote the depth of my grief." Charlotte stood up. "There's no need for tears. We both know that my remaining in England would serve no useful purpose. I've done all that I can. Mr. Proctor has assured me that if you have any concerns, he will assist you."

"He can't do anything to halt the rumors that are on every gossip's tongue. I don't know how I'll ever survive. We're the laughingstock of London. Your father has done me a great disservice."

"I agree that his gambling was irresponsible, but he didn't set out to hurt either of us intentionally. With each roll of the dice and each game of cards, he hoped he'd recoup his losses."

"Well, he didn't! Now I'm alone and penniless with a daughter who is running off to live in another country."

Arguing with her mother was pointless. They'd traversed this path numerous times since her father's death. Though she knew her mother had intended to wear her down until she agreed to remain in England, Charlotte had remained steadfast. And she certainly wouldn't change her mind now that the day of departure had arrived. There was little doubt that once she boarded the ship, her mother would settle into a routine at the estate of Lord and Lady Chesterfield. Indeed, she'd likely return to her previous habit of visiting the marchioness at Hargrove every day.

The mantel clock chimed the hour, and Charlotte gathered her gloves from the walnut dressing table. "We must depart or we'll miss our sailing. Do come downstairs and bid us farewell."

Her mother stood and nodded, seeming to accept the fact that she'd lost the battle. Though the countess had waged a valiant struggle to keep her daughter in England, Charlotte knew her mother would accept the loss graciously. Proper breeding dictated genteel behavior, even in the face of defeat.

———

Fred sauntered down the street, taking in the sights and sounds of Chicago. He never tired of the constant hubbub of the city. No matter the time of day, it seemed the streets and sidewalks always teemed with people in a hurry to get somewhere. A man pushed past him and then another. He wondered if he'd soon be spun around in a circle or knocked flat to the sidewalk. Deciding neither idea appealed to him, Fred picked up his pace.

He'd be early for his appointment with Mr. Ashton, but at least he could sit down without the concern of being mowed down. After he had continued for nearly another block, the clasp of a hand on his shoulder brought him to a halt.

With a sideward glance, Fred noted the fingers digging into his shoulder and tilted his head. "Matthew! Good to see you."

Matthew matched Fred's stride and grinned. "Where you heading in such a hurry?"

"I'm not in a hurry." He pointed his thumb toward the people behind him. "Just keeping pace with the crowd."

Matthew laughed. "You have time for a cup of coffee? My treat."

"In that case, I have all the time in the world."

Matthew grabbed Fred by the arm and pulled him toward a side street. "Great little place down here. Good food, cheap prices, and out of the way."

The words *Good Eats* had been painted in white block letters on the brick exterior of the building. If the chipped paint was any indication, the eatery had been there a long time.

Matthew greeted several customers and waved to a man behind the counter. "Two coffees, Hank." He turned to Fred. "Want a piece of pie? They've got great pie."

Fred shook his head. "Coffee's fine." He followed Matthew to the rear of the restaurant, where they sat down at a small round table. The man Matthew had greeted soon appeared with two cups of coffee and placed them on the table with a clank. "Got a good lunch special today—better come back in a couple hours."

Matthew nodded. "If I'm still in the neighborhood, you know I'll be here."

An Uncertain Dream

Hank grinned and returned to his station behind the counter.

Fred took a sip of the coffee and offered an appreciative nod. "Good coffee."

"Newspaper reporters always know where to get a cheap meal and a good cup of coffee." Matthew downed a gulp and returned the cup to the table. "My boss assigned me to the convention. I had to twist his arm a little, but he finally agreed I was the best man for the job. You going to be one of the delegates?"

Fred nodded. "We held elections last week, and I was picked as one of the representatives."

"Being elected as a delegate to the national convention is quite an honor, Fred. Of course, you'll be required to spend a great deal of time in Chicago attending all of the meetings, but I'm sure it will prove exciting, especially since one of the big items on the agenda will be whether the national membership should support the Pullman workers in their strike. Word has it that the American Railway Union claims over four hundred fifty local unions and fifteen thousand members nationally. Eugene Debs has proved himself to be a fine leader of the union, and he wants fair treatment for the workingman."

"I'm amazed to think I'll hear him speak and be asked to vote on the issues presented to the assembly. It's a humbling responsibility."

Matthew leaned across the table. "I think the entire country is going to see history in the making before this convention ends. We can only pray that real benefit will be afforded to all those who are suffering during this strike."

Fred downed the remainder of his coffee. "I couldn't agree more. And you've been doing your part to help, too. When word got out that the brickyard workers were going on strike, too, those news articles you wrote caused quite a stir."

When the Pullman workers went out on strike in May, the sizable group of unskilled immigrants from Italy and Bohemia who worked in the brickyards continued working, primarily because they'd not been invited to join the American Railway Union. But shortly after the strike began, they organized and demanded wage increases, and when their demands were refused, they, too, walked out.

Eager for a fresh story, reporters swarmed the town and made their way to the seldom seen frame homes adjacent to the Pullman brickyards to speak to the workers. Subsequent news articles reported unpaved streets lined with three-room hovels that lacked any indoor plumbing yet fetched eight dollars a month in rent. The reports brought unwanted attention to a section of Pullman that had been overlooked by the outside world and caused a good deal of embarrassment for the company, which pleased most residents of the town.

The waiter offered another cup of the steaming brew, but the men declined. "If you have no objection," Matthew said, "I'll walk along with you. Mr. Ashton may have some information that will give my article a different slant than some of the others. We're all scrambling for news until the convention actually begins on the ninth."

Fred nodded. "You'd think it was already in progress. Seems like there's a lot more folks in town than usual. The train station was brimming with people."

"The railway union has gained national attention. Reporters from the eastern press and national wire service have been arriving for days now. I believe it's going to prove beneficial to the Pullman employees that the annual convention was scheduled for this time and place."

"Some say it is the hand of God at work," Fred said.

"And you?" Matthew asked.

Fred shrugged. "I'm not certain. Either way, I know it's a good thing the convention will bring attention to our plight."

"Before this is over, the entire country will be interested in what's happening here," Matthew said as they entered Montrose Ashton's law office.

The white-haired attorney pointed his familiar unlit cigar in their direction. "Are you concocting another headline, Matthew?"

"No. I thought I'd have you do that for me. When Fred said he was coming to visit, I invited myself along. Thought you might have some insider information for me."

The older man flapped a newspaper in the air. "From what I'm reading in here, looks like those easterners think the nation's headed toward catastrophe."

While Mr. Ashton and Matthew bantered back and forth, Fred picked up the paper and perused the lengthy article about groups of men, former members of Coxey's Industrial Army, who were now roaming the countryside seeking assistance. He'd heard about Jacob Coxey. With so many out of work after the Panic of 1893, Coxey organized a march on Washington, D.C., to petition Congress for measures to help relieve unemployment. Numerous groups of men from across the country gathered to join Coxey's march. They had arrived in the nation's capital in late April this year, where Mr. Coxey had hoped to persuade Congress to issue federal bonds to build public roads and put the unemployed to work. Instead, he'd been arrested and Coxey's Army had disbanded.

"Do you believe this?" Fred asked while pointing to a comment in the article he'd been reading. "Jacob Coxey named his son Legal Tender Coxey."

Matthew glanced at the paper and nodded. "Hard to believe a man would go so far to prove he's not a socialist."

Fred shook his head in disbelief. "Poor kid. I won't ever complain about being named Frederick again."

Mr. Ashton dropped into his leather chair. "We had best get down to the business at hand. I want to discuss the impact you can have on this convention and the men in Pullman, Fred. You've gained their respect and proven you hold sway with them. Mr. Debs has asked me to find the right man to act as a liaison during the convention, someone who will keep the men in Pullman advised that we will need their ongoing support through this process. It may take longer than they anticipate."

"Wouldn't Thomas Heathcoate be the proper person for that? He's chairman of the Strike Committee."

"Heathcoate will be too busy here in Chicago during the convention. I doubt he'll have time to visit his family in Pullman, much less keep the strikers informed. Can Mr. Debs depend upon your help?"

The very idea that Mr. Debs had requested Fred's assistance boggled his mind. "Yes! Of course! You know I'm dedicated to helping the union succeed."

"Good! I'll inform Mr. Debs that we have our man." Mr. Ashton tapped the newspaper Fred had placed on his desk a short time ago. "Jacob Coxey and his army are old news. When the American Railway Union convention starts, you'll not be reading about Coxey or his son in the Chicago newspapers."

"Or in the newspapers of any other city, for that matter," Matthew agreed.

An Uncertain Dream

The conviction in Matthew's voice was enough to make Fred wonder if they'd soon meet with the same fate as Jacob Coxey. Although Fred possessed the courage of his convictions, he certainly didn't want to end up in jail.

CHAPTER EIGHT

Pullman, Illinois
Friday, June 8, 1894

Olivia rounded the corner of the hotel and inhaled the sweet scent of the early summer blooms. The roses that framed the garden near the hotel kitchen had begun to blossom in a profusion of color, and the bud-laden bushes promised a summer of beautiful flowers. The peonies and lilacs had already made their annual appearance, and it would be another year before their colorful blooms lined the park.

Mrs. DeVault and Chef René were enjoying an early morning cup of coffee when Olivia entered the kitchen. Instinctively she looked at the clock.

"You are not late, Miss Mott," Chef René said. "Mrs. DeVault and I happen to enjoy an early morning cup of coffee. It gives us an opportunity to visit before we begin our day."

Olivia eyed the two of them. If she overlooked Chef René's white work jacket and Mrs. DeVault's starched cook's apron, they could pass for any married couple enjoying a morning coffee. Chef René, with his dark brown eyes and sagging jowls, seemed to devour every word Mrs. DeVault uttered. And Mrs. DeVault's blue eyes sparkled at the undivided attention. A plain china vase filled with plump red roses had been placed on the table near their coffee cups.

Olivia pointed at the flowers. "Lovely roses."

A faint blush tinged Mrs. DeVault's cheeks. "René cut them for me this morning."

"How lovely of him." Olivia glanced at the chef, but his attention remained fixed upon Mrs. DeVault.

René? Mrs. DeVault was no longer addressing her supervisor as *Chef* René. When had that change occurred? Feeling like an interloper, Olivia picked up the menu and pretended to study the day's offerings while the older couple continued to converse quietly. What could the two of them possibly be discussing every morning? And when had this ritual begun? Though she'd noticed a spark of interest during Mrs. DeVault's first day at work, Olivia had observed nothing since then. Had she simply overlooked a relationship that had been taking wing before her very eyes? She inched a step closer.

"If you would like to join our conversation, you may pour a cup of coffee and sit with us, Miss Mott."

"Oh, I don't want to interrupt." With a fleeting smile, she flipped the menu card in the air. "We are having additional guests today?"

The chef nodded. "The board of directors will hold another meeting with Mr. Howard. He said to expect their arrival mid-morning."

"So we will need to prepare only the noonday and evening meals for them?"

He shrugged his shoulders. "Who can say? Mr. Howard said their meetings may not be concluded until tomorrow. I doubt any of them will remain until Monday."

Olivia frowned. "Unless they have a matter that requires their immediate attention. With the convention beginning tomorrow, I'm sure the board members are concerned."

Chef René wagged his plump index finger. "While in the kitchen, we are to concentrate on the food rather than the reason our guests have elected to stay at our lovely hotel."

Mrs. DeVault patted the chef's arm. "I'm going to go downstairs and begin my work. There's much to do before the noon meal."

He smiled and covered her hand with his own. "Oui. I will come downstairs once breakfast is completed."

From Olivia's vantage point, it appeared the chef had gently squeezed Mrs. DeVault's hand before releasing his hold. Olivia remained transfixed. Fred had revealed nothing about a relationship between his mother and Chef René. Yet, with the excitement of the convention about to begin, she doubted Fred would take notice of anything other than union activities. With the exception of discussing several new desserts she wanted to serve at the hotel, Mrs. DeVault hadn't broached the topic of work or Chef René with her. If time permitted, Olivia would pay the older woman a visit this evening.

"Something is wrong with my menu?" Chef René pushed away from the table.

"No, not at all. Why do you ask?" When Olivia turned, she noted the roses had disappeared. Mrs. DeVault had obviously carried them downstairs with her.

"You have studied the entrées for nearly ten minutes."

Olivia dropped the menu card onto the worktable and removed several bowls from the shelf. "I wanted to make certain there were no unfamiliar dishes being offered." She began to crack eggs into the pale gray crock.

The chef rounded the counter and rested his forearms on the worktable beside her. He looked up at her with a glint in his coffee-colored eyes. "And you wanted to hear what we were saying."

She squared her shoulders and met his unwavering stare. "Yes, I did. Suffice it to say that I was surprised to see that you and Mrs. DeVault have formed a . . . well, such a . . ."

"Warm friendship?" His eyes sparkled with amusement.

She whisked the eggs with a vengeance. "Well, yes. It's none of my business, of course, but—"

"You are correct. It isn't any of your business." He laughed. "But I do understand your curiosity. After all, she is the mother of your Fred, and you have concern for her welfare. Oui?"

"Yes, of course." She had agreed too hastily. It seemed the chef was enjoying their game of cat and mouse far too much.

"Then I must set your mind at ease. I enjoy Hazel's company. She is a fine lady, and we have much in common."

"Hazel?" The name croaked from deep in her throat.

"Mrs. DeVault," he replied. "Since we have become friends, we agreed to address each other by our given names."

"During working hours?"

He shrugged. "You concern yourself over unimportant details. Other than the kitchen help, who hears our conversations? The maids and kitchen boys are addressed by their first names. Why not the baker?"

"You address me as Miss Mott."

The chef laughed. "Because you English worry over insignificant issues such as using the proper name." He pointed to the bowl. "You should do something with those eggs."

Olivia whisked the eggs one final time and then poured

them into a skillet smeared with melted butter. While she continued the breakfast preparations, Chef René disappeared downstairs. Had she missed all of these signs previously? This relationship couldn't have blossomed overnight, but none of the other staff appeared to be taking note of the chef's behavior. Perhaps she should more closely regard those who surrounded her each day.

She didn't have time to ponder the idea. Mr. Howard entered the kitchen with a determined look that closely resembled a scowl. "Where is Chef René?"

"Good morning, Mr. Howard." The company agent's failure to offer a morning greeting meant he was preoccupied, worried, or angry. Olivia was uncertain which it might be. "He has gone downstairs to the bake kitchen. I expect him to return any moment. May I be of assistance?"

"Tell Chef René there are to be no mushrooms in any of the foods that will be served to the board members. Can you remember that?"

She didn't know whether to laugh or feel insulted, but given Mr. Howard's dour look, she said, "I believe I'm up to the task."

If he thought her remark curt, he made no indication. "We will want our meal served at one o'clock rather than noon. Dinner should be served at six thirty." That said, he turned on his heel and left.

Olivia's shoulders sagged. Since the evening meal would be served later than usual, she'd be expected to work a few extra hours. She silently chided herself. Instead of giving thanks for her employment, she was feeling sorry for herself. She closed her eyes. *Forgive me, Lord,* she silently prayed.

"You now cook with your eyes closed, Miss Mott?"

Chef René was staring at her when Olivia popped her eyes

open. She shook her head. "No. I was simply giving thanks that I have gainful work." She wiped her hands on a towel while relaying Mr. Howard's instructions.

"There are no mushrooms in any of my dishes. He tells me this every time the board members come here for their meetings. I know Mr. Arnold has an allergy to mushrooms. It is imbedded in my brain after all these years."

Olivia didn't respond. The less she said, the more quickly the chef would calm himself. Each time he became distressed, she remembered the doctor's warning that anxiety and turmoil were bad for his heart condition. Unfortunately, Chef René paid little heed to the doctor's advice.

He eventually grew quiet and the two of them worked in silence for the remainder of the morning—except for those times when Chef René disappeared downstairs or when he stood outdoors beside Mrs. DeVault during the morning break from their duties.

Shortly after noon, Chef René sent her to check the dining room. "We are short of help, and I don't trust these new people. Make certain everything is exactly as it should be."

The wait staff was busy in the main dining room when Olivia made her way to the room where the board members would eat. She entered and surveyed each place setting for any missing silverware or dinnerware. The low murmur of men's voices could be heard through a door that stood ajar to help cool the room.

"With the railway convention due to convene, I'd think George would return to town. There are rumors circulating that others may join in the strike."

"Rest assured, Mr. Pullman will return when he's needed."

"He's needed right now. There's enough going on in this

town and in Chicago that warrants his attention. Every time there's a walkout, he hurries out of town with his family in tow and leaves the rest of us to suffer the wrath of the newspapers and answer the difficult questions."

"I don't think that's true, John. Mr. Pullman has his finger on the pulse of this town and his company. He stands to lose more than the rest of us. I don't think he's going to jeopardize this company."

The sounds of scraping chair legs and murmured assents drifted into the room.

Olivia hadn't recognized the voice of the man who'd been upset with Mr. Pullman's absence, but it was Mr. Howard who had offered reassurance regarding the company's owner.

She strained to listen to the ongoing conversation while she circled the table and checked the places. By the time she finished, she'd gained a good deal of insight regarding the directors and managers of the Pullman Car Works. The union's assessment was correct: the primary concern of the stockholders and board members was their dividends. From what Olivia had heard just now, the one thing the men agreed upon was that they wanted to make sure they would receive a substantial dividend. There was no sympathy for the worker, whose rent continued to accumulate at the same high assessment, no mention that the inhabitants of Pullman were paying higher rates for water than residents of Chicago or the surrounding area, and no mention that all credit at the Market had been terminated.

She wondered if Mr. Howard would send word to Mr. Pullman that he should consider a speedy return. Perhaps the convention would accomplish more if the owner of the car works remained at his summer retreat in the Thousand Islands.

Chicago, Illinois
Friday, June 15, 1894

Charlotte lifted Morgan into her arms and stepped off the train in Chicago's bustling Van Buren Street Station. Their journey had been exhausting, though she couldn't complain about her son's behavior. Morgan had performed valiantly—even when he'd become seasick when they'd been barraged by a storm two days out to sea.

A fellow traveler, Mrs. Bancroft, had offered both Charlotte and Morgan assistance. The two women soon developed a friendship. They'd whiled away the hours chatting on the deck while Morgan played nearby. The woman had confided that she hailed from New York and her husband, a banker, had dealings in several large cities, including Chicago.

The news that Charlotte planned to live in Chicago had brought a plethora of negative responses from the New York resident. "Conditions are difficult everywhere, but Chicago isn't the place you want to make your home. What with the Pullman strike, my husband says Chicago is going to face greater difficulties than most cities." She had leaned across her deck chair and quietly confided that the residents of New York were far more sophisticated than those of Chicago. "You'd be much more comfortable mingling with members of the New York Social Register," she had sternly advised.

Although Mrs. Bancroft had been loath to learn Charlotte

didn't plan to heed her advice, the older woman did offer to present Charlotte to all the right people should she decide to make New York her home at some future date. The two women had parted on good terms, but Mrs. Bancroft appeared to believe she had somehow failed the social ranks of New York City when Charlotte and Morgan departed for the train station and their subsequent journey to Chicago.

After making arrangements for the delivery of her trunks, Charlotte balanced her son on one hip and carefully wended her way through the crowded train station. By the time she arrived at the front doors, her face was dotted with perspiration. She hadn't recalled June in Chicago being quite so hot. She reminded herself she'd been traveling for twelve days. No doubt she should have donned a lightweight gown of faille rather than cashmere.

As she hailed a carriage, Charlotte recalled the first time she'd come to Chicago. Instead of Morgan at her side, Olivia had accompanied her. They'd spent their first night in the luxurious Grand Pacific Hotel on LaSalle Street. Tonight would be quite different. Provided there was enough room to accommodate them, Charlotte and Morgan would spend their first night at Priddle House.

Morgan twisted to and fro, his blue eyes taking in the excitement of the city. "We'll soon arrive at our new home," she said. The boy would find it quite different from Lanshire Hall, but he was young and would soon forget the luxuries of nobility. At Priddle House he would learn about Jesus and how to become an independent young man who would help others. That was her hope.

A driver brought his team to a halt in front of her. "Where to, lady?"

Charlotte gave him the address on Ashland Street and settled into the carriage. Morgan squirmed from her arms, eager to look out the window. "Careful," she warned. "If the carriage hits a hole, you'll hit your head."

He turned and grinned, undaunted by the warning. She wrapped him in a protective hold that still permitted a view out the window. "There! Now we'll both be happy."

Charlotte peered over Morgan's shoulders, pointing out familiar stores as they passed by. When they turned on Ashland Street, her heart fluttered. What if something had happened to Mrs. Priddle and Priddle House no longer existed? She should have written a letter before departing England, but she had wanted to surprise the older woman. Now she realized her decision could prove foolish.

She tapped on the carriage window with her parasol to alert the driver. "On the right."

The driver gave her an annoyed look when he helped her out of the carriage. "I know my way about the city, ma'am. I don't need anyone tapping on the window or shouting orders to me."

Charlotte wanted to tell him she hadn't shouted, but she'd already irritated the man enough for one day. She slipped two coins into his hand. He grunted a thank-you and hoisted himself up to the carriage seat. After a slight tip of his hat and a nod, he slapped the reins and was off.

When Charlotte spied the familiar sign over the entrance, she whispered a quick prayer of thanks and made her way to the door. After giving a sharp rap on the front door, she heard the clatter of approaching footsteps and then saw the familiar oval face with hazel eyes staring through the screen door.

"Charlotte! Is it really you?" Fiona pushed open the door

and then squealed in delight. "Mrs. Priddle, come quick and see who's here."

"Land alive, child! How many times must I tell you—" Mrs. Priddle squinted her eyes and hurried forward. "Are my eyes deceiving me?"

Charlotte beamed. "No, they're not. It's me, Mrs. Priddle—and my son."

"Well, don't stand out there on the porch like you're company. Come on in and sit down." After a warm hug, Mrs. Priddle led the way into the parlor, and Fiona held out her arms to Morgan. He lunged toward the eleven-year-old, who immediately carried him into the room and sat down on the floor with him. While Fiona entertained Morgan, Mrs. Priddle settled beside Charlotte on the divan.

"So you've come back to Chicago for a visit. I must say I'm surprised. Though I hoped you would return to see us, I doubted we'd ever lay eyes on you again. It appears young Morgan has accepted you as his mother."

Charlotte nodded. The clopping of horses' hooves on the brick street temporarily captured her attention. "There's something I must ask you, but first, I hope you won't be angry that I didn't write and gain your permission before I arrived on your doorstep."

The older woman's brow furrowed. "What is it, child?"

"Morgan and I need a place to live. We're not here for a visit. I plan to make Chicago my home."

Fiona jumped up from the floor and clapped her hands. "You're truly going to live here? You must mark the page in your Bible, Mrs. Priddle. Jesus answered another prayer."

Charlotte closely watched the older woman's face for any sign of displeasure; however, she saw nothing but kindness in

Mrs. Priddle's clear blue eyes. "You are welcome to share what we have, though I fear you'll find it somewhat meager. I don't suppose that should come as any surprise. I'm certain you realize the economic condition of the country is not at its best."

This didn't seem the time to admit she'd not maintained a close watch on the economy of the United States. There would be sufficient time to discuss unpleasant topics in the days to come. For now, she wanted to hear news of the other Priddle House residents, Fiona's piano lessons, and Mrs. Priddle's vegetable garden.

CHAPTER NINE

Fred's excitement mounted each time he entered Chicago's Uhlich Hall and took his place among the throng of convention delegates. By all accounts, there were more than four hundred men, and a few women, who had come to Chicago to represent their fellow workers at the convention, and he didn't doubt that estimation. The floor had teemed with people and excitement since the first day of the gathering. Hoping to maintain sympathy for the striking workers, Jennie Curtis, a Pullman seamstress who worked in the Embroidery Department, had been called forward to speak to the gathered delegates.

In a choked voice she had explained that her father had worked for the car works for thirteen years, and at the time of his death, he had owed sixty dollars on the flat he rented from the company. The crowd became enraged when she went on to explain that the Pullman Company had deducted the back rent from her five-dollar-a-week paycheck. Bit by bit, they had extracted the back rent from her paltry wages. At the conclusion of her speech, the audience erupted in anger. What kind of a company would charge the dead!

But today was even more exciting, for this was the day that the rest of the Pullman delegation would take their places at the podium. Even Fred would speak to the crowd. His heart thumped like a forge hammer each time he thought of standing before the attendees. Wending his way among the throng, he pushed his way toward the front of the meeting hall. Mr. Debs had sent word they should gather near the steps leading to the stage ten minutes early. Fred didn't want to be late.

"Fred! Good to see you." Matthew Clayborn reached forward and clasped Fred's hand. "I hear you're going to be one of the presenters this morning." He pointed to the pencil and notepad in his left hand. "I plan to take down every word. You may see yourself quoted in the paper tomorrow."

Fred shook his head and laughed. "Now that would be something, wouldn't it?" He ducked his head closer. "To tell you the truth, I'm shaking in my shoes right now. Any advice?"

"I'm afraid not, my friend. I've never spoken to this many people at once. One good thing: you know they're on your side. It's not as though you'll be getting up to speak to a group of capitalists."

While the two of them talked, the other speakers joined Fred, and soon they were standing on the stage in front of the crowd. He looked into the sea of faces and uttered a silent prayer that he would say exactly the right words when his time to speak arrived.

Several men gave impassioned speeches regarding the town and the company for which they'd labored many years, and Thomas Heathcoate told of receiving wages that didn't cover his rental fees while company stockholders continued to receive their tidy dividends like clockwork. "In the dead of winter when ice formed on any standing water inside our homes, these men sat in their warm homes and offices with their hands open to take even more money from us. While our children go without food, they add additional funds to their already bulging bank accounts. I ask each one of you—are we to continue laboring under such conditions? I say no!"

The room echoed with shouts of agreement. After Mr. Heathcoate's impassioned speech, Fred was motioned to the podium. How he wished he could have spoken earlier. He gulped a mouthful of dry air and walked to the dais.

When the room had nearly quieted, he said, "I am Fred DeVault, another Pullman employee." His confidence began to increase as he told of his work with the union and his belief that together they could make a difference for all who would follow in their footsteps. There was a thunder of applause when he finished his speech, yet he couldn't remember all of what he'd said. Like the sea of faces staring at him, his speech had become a blur.

He stepped back with those who had already spoken. There would be one final speaker from the Pullman contingency before Eugene Debs took the podium. The delegates had grown increasingly impassioned, and when Joseph Jensen stood before them and spoke of his son who had frozen to death during the past winter, the room turned eerily silent. Joseph used the moment to advantage and lifted his fist high in the air. "Don't let my son's death be in vain. We call upon all members of the American Railway Union to stand with us at this difficult time. Do not desert us, for we all stand prepared to give our present and future allegiance to the brotherhood."

Then Mr. Jensen and the Pullman employees who had previously spoken descended the stairs and sat down while Mr.

Debs took to the platform. The moment he stepped forward, a hush fell over the room.

He seemed to study the men and women who stood before him. Most worked for western and midwestern railroads, and the majority had been forced to take recent wage cuts. The discontent of the workers had created a sense of sympathy for the plight of the striking Pullman workers.

"Greetings, union members! I'm proud to stand before you this morning. I have listened to those who have made heartfelt pleas for your loyalty to their cause. You all know that I stand against the mistreatment of workers that has occurred in Pullman." He waited until the cheers subsided.

Fred anxiously awaited what would follow. He was certain Mr. Debs would call for an immediate boycott, asking railway workers to refuse to handle Pullman cars, but when the founder of the American Railway Union continued, he called for calm. To those who shouted for a boycott, he countered, "We must proceed with caution. If all else fails, we will consider a boycott, but for now I believe we should make another attempt to negotiate with the Pullman officials."

Murmurs filled the hall, but Mr. Debs silenced the crowd. "We want no one in this great nation ever to say that we failed to explore every possible means of settling our grievances in a conciliatory manner."

The newspaper reporters were gathered at the front of the auditorium, feverishly jotting down each word that was said. Mr. Debs had insisted that all meetings be open to the press and the public, for he wanted the union to escape any hint of conspiracy. He believed citizens would maintain sympathy as long as they were well informed. By permitting entry to reporters, Mr. Debs intended to see that the latest union news was reported.

Under his direction, a committee of six delegates and six Pullman strikers, including Thomas Heathcoate as well as Fred, was sent to meet with Mr. Howard and other members of management.

"You'll give me the scoop once you've met with Mr. Howard and the others, won't you?" Matthew asked immediately following the announcement.

"Yes, of course. You can come along with us and wait outside if you like, but I don't think you'll be getting a scoop." Fred looked above Matthew's head at the group of reporters gathering behind him. "With all these newspapers represented, I doubt any one reporter will gain more information than any other. We committee members will be besieged by reporters the minute we walk out of that room."

Matthew laughed. "Well, *you* must talk to me first."

"I'll try," Fred agreed.

Disappointment abounded when the men returned to meet with Mr. Debs late the following day. Twice they had attempted to meet with Mr. Howard and other members of management; twice they'd been turned away. The second time they were told they should not return. The company would never arbitrate.

"They say there is nothing to negotiate. They've not moved one inch from their original position," Mr. Heathcoate told Mr. Debs. "*Now* what are we to do?"

Mr. Debs rubbed his palm across his balding pate and dropped back in his chair. Distress shone in his eyes. "I feared this would happen, but I had hoped for some sign of capitulation. If the locals agree, we have no choice but to move forward with the boycott." A ripple of excitement permeated the room.

Matthew was standing outside the room when Fred reappeared and gave him the news. After jotting down his notes, Matthew looked at Fred. "When? Do they know when the boycott will take place?"

"Not exactly. Mr. Debs thought we should have a final decision by the twentieth if the local unions are in agreement with the boycott. Then a notice of intention will be served upon Mr. Howard, since he's the spokesman for the company."

"One can only wonder when George Pullman will reappear," Matthew mused.

Though Mr. Pullman's reappearance was of interest to those writing the news, the union members knew it would matter little. Mr. Howard remained at the helm to deliver the company owner's messages for him. Mr. Pullman's return would change nothing.

———

Charlotte had forgotten the challenge of sharing a bedroom; however, since her return to Priddle House, she'd quickly become reacquainted with the inconvenience of cramped quarters and diminished privacy. But adjusting to life in Priddle House hadn't proved as difficult as learning the economy had taken a severe downward plummet since her departure. Mrs. Priddle had been quick to caution Charlotte that life in Chicago would likely prove a challenge.

During the Panic of 1893, the city had been fortunate to have a plethora of tourists attending the World's Columbian Exposition, which helped boost their economy. In fact, for much of Chicago it had appeared as if the economy continued to boom while the rest of the country suffered. However, once the exposition had ended in October of 1893, the depression had crept into the city like an animal stalking fresh prey. At a time when Charlotte had hoped to start a new life, the news disheartened her.

The older woman tapped Charlotte on the shoulder and motioned toward the kitchen. "Come along and have a cup of tea while Morgan is asleep. We need to talk."

The house was unusually quiet, for the other members of the household were either working in the garden or completing household duties upstairs. Charlotte followed along and sat down at the kitchen table. "It seems we've done nothing but talk since my return," she said with a wan smile.

Mrs. Priddle nodded her head. "That's true enough, my dear. We've had much to discuss, but we do need to make plans for the future now that you've been with us for a couple of days."

"I plan to seek work but thought it best to wait until—"

"I didn't expect you to locate employment the moment you arrived, Charlotte." Mrs. Priddle poured the boiling water into the teapot and placed the vessel on the table to steep while she removed cups and saucers from the cupboard. Tucking a wisp of hair behind one ear, she settled in a chair opposite Charlotte. "I wondered if you had stopped by Mr. Ashton's office before you came here."

The question surprised her. She'd given no thought to Mr. Ashton since her departure for England last year. "Why, no, I haven't. Is he no longer sending any funds to assist you?"

"He continues to do so, but he was tardy last month. I imagine he's busy with all this strike business. Still, he shouldn't neglect his other business—don't you agree?"

"Absolutely. I would think he could produce an accounting of the funds. We must find out how much remains in the account since, from all that you've told me, I may discover Mr. Field isn't in need of another employee. I shall pay Mr. Ashton a visit tomorrow." Charlotte poured tea into their cups. "What of my friend Olivia? Has she come to see you?"

"Indeed, she has. Both she and Ellen Ashton have paid us visits. They are lovely young ladies. Miss Mott has been one of the fortunate residents of Pullman. Unlike most of the town's residents, her position in the hotel has remained intact." Mrs. Priddle stirred a dollop of cream into her tea and took a sip.

"I'm pleased to hear Olivia fares well."

"She and Miss Ashton make a point to visit when they know Fiona will be at home. They insist upon hearing the child play a short piano recital each time they arrive. And on one occasion they took Fiona to a restaurant for lunch. She talked about it for days."

"I look forward to seeing Olivia again. However, the first thing on my agenda shall be a visit to Mr. Ashton, followed by a visit to Mr. Field."

Mrs. Priddle nodded. "As usual, it seems we have abundant prayer requests for tonight's Bible study. We must pray that all of the strikers will come to their senses, too. Seems to me these men would help their families more if they simply went back to work. I would think they'd prefer a small amount of money over nothing. They surely know that a strike isn't going to convince Mr. Pullman to raise their wages."

"But you agree they deserve a fair wage, don't you?"

"I do, but I remember the altercations back in 1886 when violence erupted at the McCormick Reaper Works. After that incident, a number of people ended up dead and many more severely injured. I don't want to see that happening again. The men need to sit back and remember God is in control."

"That's true enough, but sometimes God expects His people to take a step forward and help themselves, too, don't you think?" Charlotte took a sip of tea. "Otherwise, we'd all be sitting around waiting for God to take care of us."

"There's truth in what you say, but if they're going to help themselves, they need to do it without weapons in their hands. Killing one another isn't going to resolve their difficulties. It will only create more heartache."

Charlotte removed their cups from the table and placed them in the sink. "You're absolutely correct, Mrs. Priddle. We must add this matter to our prayer list, also."

―――――――

Early the next morning while Charlotte prepared to leave for Mr. Ashton's office, Fiona lifted Morgan from his bed and corralled him into one spot long enough to change him out of his nightshirt. The little boy giggled and twisted a handful of Fiona's light brown hair between his chubby fingers, but his playful antics didn't deter her from the task at hand. She tickled his tummy and laughed along with him while she continued to maneuver him into his clothing.

"You've become quite an expert at handling Morgan in only a few days."

The girl beamed at the compliment. "I've been around other babies. Remember little Sadie, Ruth's girl?"

Charlotte nodded. "Indeed, I do remember."

How could Charlotte forget dear Ruth and Sadie? She and Fiona had shared the same bedroom with Ruth and her little girl during Charlotte's previous stay at Priddle House. Now

Ruth was married and living in California. At least that's what Mrs. Priddle had reported. Unfortunately, Ruth's most recent letter had confirmed there was little work in that part of the country, either. Ruth's name was now on the growing list of names on the Priddle House prayer list.

Morgan squealed with pleasure when Fiona grasped his hand and walked him across the room. "Do you want to eat breakfast, Morgan?"

"Come give me a kiss before you go downstairs, big boy." Charlotte stooped down and held out her arms. Morgan darted toward her on wobbly legs and fell into her arms with a chortle. He planted a slobbery baby kiss on his mother's cheek and then wriggled from her arms.

"Ona," he said, pointing a chubby finger at Fiona.

Fiona offered her hand to Morgan and led him out of the room. The girl had been delighted when Charlotte asked her to care for Morgan during her trip into town. In truth, it had been Mrs. Priddle who had suggested the assignment.

"I'll keep an eye on Morgan, too," Mrs. Priddle had said. "But Fiona will feel grown-up if you ask her to look after the child. She'll relish the responsibility." As usual, she'd been correct.

After a final glance in the mirror, Charlotte retrieved her parasol. Mrs. Priddle was waiting in the downstairs hallway. "Morgan is eating breakfast. No need to upset him with a good-bye. He'll cry and then you'll worry." She escorted Charlotte to the front door. "Let's hope Mr. Ashton will be in his office tending to business instead of stirring up trouble at the convention."

"Yesterday's newspaper said the meetings wouldn't commence until ten o'clock this morning, so he should be at the office."

The older woman followed Charlotte to the front porch. "Do you plan to schedule an appointment to see Mr. Field while you're downtown?"

Charlotte nodded. "Yes, there's no need to delay the process. Even if funds remain in the account with Mr. Ashton, they won't last forever. We will need additional income."

Mrs. Priddle concurred. "Two of the ladies have positions as cleaning maids at Grand Pacific Hotel. Though they work very hard, their pay is minimal. Any additional funds will be a blessing."

Charlotte would do her best, but when she coupled what she'd read in the newspaper with Mrs. Priddle's recent accounts, she worried Mr. Field might not be inclined to rehire her. She offered up a prayer as she hastened toward Mr. Ashton's office.

CHAPTER TEN

Charlotte lowered her parasol as she approached the front door of Montrose Ashton's law office. When she opened the door, a small bell jangled to announce her entry. Ellen Ashton immediately looked up from the papers scattered on her desk.

For a moment, the lawyer's daughter looked as though she'd been struck dumb. "Charlotte? Is it truly you?" She jumped up from her chair and circled around the desk. "I can't believe you are here. What brings you back to Chicago? Has the earl returned on business?"

Charlotte shook her head and informed Ellen of her father's recent death. Without giving further details, she sat down and folded her hands in her lap. "I am hoping that your father is available for a short meeting with me."

"He currently has someone in his office, but I know he'll be delighted to see you when he's completed his appointment. Do you have accommodations here in Chicago?"

Charlotte fidgeted with her gloves. There was no sense in

hiding her living arrangements. "Yes. I'm staying with Mrs. Priddle."

Ellen clasped a hand to her chest. "Oh, how delighted she must be that you elected to reside at the house while you're in town. I'm certain all of the ladies are honored to live with a member of nobility for a short time." Ellen sat down beside Charlotte. "How long will you be visiting?"

Before she could answer, the door to Mr. Ashton's office swung open. "I tell you, Matthew, you always bring a smile to my lips." He clapped a handsome man on the shoulder. Their ensuing laughter stopped short when they caught sight of the two women.

Mr. Ashton bowed his shoulders and squinted his eyes. "Why, isn't this a pleasant surprise! I didn't know you were visiting in our fair city, Lady Charlotte."

The younger man nudged Mr. Ashton. "I believe an introduction is in order, Montrose."

"Indeed. This lovely young lady is Lady Charlotte, daughter of the Earl and Countess of Lanshire. Lady Charlotte, may I present Matthew Clayborn."

The man who'd been introduced as Mr. Clayborn bent over until his fingers touched the floor. She longed to giggle at his attempt to behave in a proper courtly manner. "You need not bow, Mr. Clayborn. While in this country, I avoid the use of my title." He stood upright and she could see the questions in his midnight blue eyes.

"It is an honor to make your acquaintance, Miss . . ."

"Spencer," she replied and then turned her attention to Mr. Ashton. "I do hope you have time for a brief meeting. I've several matters I wish to discuss with you."

"Of course." With a flourish of his arm, Mr. Ashton waved her toward his office door.

Once inside Mr. Ashton's office, Charlotte wasted little time advising the lawyer of the reason for her visit.

He leaned back in his chair and removed a cigar from his pocket. "Had I known Mrs. Priddle was desirous of receiving an accounting, I would have provided one." He wove the unlit cigar up and down between his fingers. "When I met her, she didn't appear reticent to make her views known. I'm rather surprised she didn't pay me a visit herself."

"That fact aside, I would be grateful to receive the information—today, if possible." Charlotte rested her parasol beside her. "Mrs. Priddle mentioned that the payment was late last month."

Before Charlotte had returned to England, she'd insisted her father send funds to help defray monthly expenses at Priddle House. The earl's finances had been stable at that time, and he had willingly complied. Prior to her sailing, Charlotte had charged Mr. Ashton with the responsibility of disbursing the money. She hoped she hadn't misplaced her trust in the man.

He nodded. "I do apologize. I was out of the city on business and should have ordered the draft prior to my departure, an oversight for which I am deeply sorry." He pushed away from his desk. "If you'll give me a moment to retrieve my ledger, we can then go over the account."

Charlotte looked out the window while she waited for him to remove the book from a nearby shelf. He dropped the thick ledger onto his desk and absently flipped through the pages.

"Ah, here we are." He turned the book around and shoved it across the desk in front of her. Using his cigar, he pointed to the column titled *Balance*. "You'll see there isn't a great deal remaining in the account. Mrs. Priddle was in need of a new roof for the house." Sunlight spilled through an adjacent window and accentuated the whiteness of the lawyer's hair. "If the roof had been left in disrepair, those leaks would have caused extensive damage to the house. And then there was—" He stopped midsentence and pushed the ledger a little closer. "Well, you can see for yourself. There were other repairs needed to the house. If you'd like to deposit additional funds at the bank, I know Mrs. Priddle would be thankful."

Charlotte's spirits collapsed like a deflated balloon. She had hoped to see a larger balance, yet the expenses could all be verified. Mr. Ashton produced an envelope containing the receipts, which he promptly offered for her review, but she refused. Mrs. Priddle could easily confirm that the work had been completed.

"I'm certain you have done your best to maintain the house properly while keeping a careful watch on the balance of the account." Charlotte slowly pushed the ledger back to his side of the desk.

"Added to the woes of the depression, Chicago suffered a terrible winter, one of the worst in our history." His low chuckle echoed in the large room. "Of course, folks tend to think that each year, but I'd agree that this was one of Chicago's worst. As you can well imagine, the price of keeping warm increased each time the temperature took another dip. Of course, for those who have adequate financial means, there's no concern over such issues as keeping warm, but those folks are few and far between right now."

"I trust your finances have sustained you, Mr. Ashton."

"I'm getting along better than some, but when there's no money for food, folks aren't going to spend their last few coins on a lawyer." He dropped into his chair and chuckled. "Not that

I blame them." He tapped the ledger book. "Did you plan to donate additional funds to the Priddle House account while you're visiting in Chicago?"

"I do wish that I could." Charlotte pressed her palms together and met Mr. Ashton's inquiring gaze. "May I trust that our conversation will be held in confidence?"

"Why, of course."

Without fanfare, Charlotte revealed the truth to Mr. Ashton. When she'd completed the tale, she sighed. "So you see, I'm in no better financial condition than are most other residents of this fair city. Once our meeting concludes, I will be seeking employment in order to help Mrs. Priddle meet expenses. Otherwise, I have little to offer in the way of financial aid."

Mr. Ashton closed the book's leather cover. "I am sorry to hear of your father's death and of his financial losses. He's not the first man who's succumbed to gambling fever. They all think that with one more roll of the dice they'll regain their losses."

With a rueful smile, Charlotte grasped the handle of her parasol. "So my father told me. I know he regretted his actions. Still . . ."

"Yes, quite difficult for you and your mother. I do hope she has someone to assist her with the creditors who will likely hound her."

Charlotte explained that her father had entrusted his solicitor with that duty and thanked Mr. Ashton for his concern. "I don't suppose there is anything further for us to discuss. If I'm able to locate employment, I'm hopeful we won't need to draw on the account except for emergencies."

"I wish you well in your endeavor, Lady—Miss Spencer. I'd offer my name as a reference, but I fear it would prove a detriment with the Chicago businessmen."

"Especially with Mr. Pullman, I suspect."

He laughed and nodded as he escorted her to the outer office. "Indeed. Give my best to Mrs. Priddle."

Charlotte couldn't guess which one of them was more surprised to see Mr. Clayborn in the reception office visiting with Ellen.

Mr. Ashton arched his bushy brows. "Must be a slow day for news. I didn't expect to see you sitting around all morning, Matthew."

"There's plenty of time before the convention begins. To tell the truth, I hoped Miss Spencer would permit me to escort her to her next appointment." He rested his forearms on his knees as he leaned forward in his chair. "The streets of Chicago can be difficult to navigate."

She offered a stiff smile. "I am familiar with the city, Mr. Clayborn. I don't anticipate any problem arriving at my next appointment."

He snapped his finger and thumb together. "I thought you might like to have news about Olivia Mott and Fred DeVault."

"You know Olivia?" Charlotte glanced at Ellen for affirmation.

"He does. In fact, he sees Fred nearly every day," Ellen said. "You can trust him, Charlotte. He's perfectly harmless. I've known Matthew for years."

Matthew lifted his hat from the hall tree. "You see? I'm harmless."

Mr. Ashton didn't concur that Matthew was harmless but agreed that Charlotte should accept his offer to escort her. "Walking the streets of Chicago isn't quite as safe as when you were last in the city. Dressed in your finery, I fear you'll encounter a few folks along the way who may attempt to snatch your reticule. Poverty does terrible things to people."

Though Charlotte was uncertain whether such precaution was truly necessary, she accepted Mr. Clayborn's offer. After bidding Mr. Ashton and Ellen good-bye, the couple departed.

Charlotte noted that Mr. Clayborn appeared quite pleased with himself when they turned to walk down the street.

"Where would you like to go, Miss Spencer? Would you join me for a cup of coffee—or tea, perhaps? Your wish is my command."

She quickly declined his offer for refreshments. "I have a stop to make at Marshall Field and Company and then have other matters that need my attention." She didn't want to tell him she was residing at Priddle House and that the older woman would worry if she was away longer than anticipated.

Besides, she didn't want to be away from Morgan any longer than necessary. If Mr. Field offered her employment, she'd have little enough time to spend with her son.

"Then perhaps you'll agree to join me for tea another day. When do you plan to return to England?"

"My future remains uncertain, Mr. Clayborn. I believe you mentioned you're acquainted with Olivia. I don't believe I ever heard her speak of you."

"We met when she was traveling the rails. I was writing a story for the newspaper—I work for the *Herald*."

He regaled her with stories of his first encounter with Olivia, their subsequent disagreements, and the friendship that had finally evolved. "Olivia continues to work at Hotel Florence with Chef René, and Fred is a union representative attending the convention on behalf of the Pullman workers."

"So they haven't married?"

"No, but I'd say a proposal is in the offing. There's no doubt Fred loves Olivia, but he's one of those men who needs a push to make those big decisions in life." When they approached the corner near Marshall Field and Company, Matthew came to a halt. "I'll leave you to your shopping, Miss Spencer. May I tell Fred that you've arrived in town, or would you prefer to surprise Olivia?"

"I'd prefer to surprise both of them. Please don't mention you've seen me."

He held a finger to his lips. "Your secret is safe with me. At least for a short time. When do you plan a visit to Pullman?"

The man didn't hesitate to ask questions. She supposed such behavior was second nature to him. "I'm going to arrange a visit next Sunday afternoon. If you'd be so kind as to refrain from mentioning my arrival until after that time, I'd be grateful."

"I'll do my very best. I promise." He tipped his straw hat and offered a charming smile. "Enjoy your shopping."

She nodded. Let him believe whatever he wished. Friend of Olivia or not, she didn't wish to confide her true reason for visiting the emporium. Besides, with his inquisitive nature, it would take Mr. Clayborn only a short time to discover why she'd returned to Chicago, which was one reason why she'd told him to keep her presence a secret. With only a modicum of questioning, Fred would unwittingly divulge every remnant of her past to Matthew Clayborn.

She had accepted the consequences of the poor decisions she'd made in the past, and she'd asked for and received God's forgiveness. But that didn't mean she desired her private life to be discussed with total strangers—especially with someone who made a living writing for newspapers.

An Uncertain Dream

As he had for many years, Joseph Anderson stood sentry at the entrance of the store. He tipped his hat in greeting, but Charlotte could tell the moment he'd remembered her. His eyes shone in recognition, and he revealed a row of uneven teeth when he smiled.

He stepped forward and pulled open the door. A small man with graying hair, he looked like a grandfather who should be surrounded by a roomful of descendants at a family dinner rather than guarding the doors of Marshall Field and Company.

"Miss Spencer. What a special treat to see you. We've missed you here at the store."

"Why, thank you, Joseph. It's good to be back in Chicago." Perhaps it was the warmth of his welcome or the fact that he reminded Charlotte of her father, but she felt as though she wanted to hug the doorman. She stifled the urge and inquired if Mr. Field had arrived.

"He has, ma'am. I'm sure he'll be very pleased to see you."

"Let's hope so, Joseph. And Mrs. Jenkins?"

Joseph shook his head. "She took ill and hasn't been able to return to work. Someone said she went to stay with a relative in Springfield, but I'm not sure."

He turned to greet another customer, and Charlotte entered the main floor of the store. Her stomach knotted with a mixture of fear and excitement. What if Mr. Field didn't remember her? She silently chided herself for her foolish thoughts and strode to the elevator. *I must remain positive*, she told herself while she marched down the hall to Mr. Field's office. If good fortune was with her, she'd discover that Mr. Field had a new clerk managing his appointment calendar.

She tapped on the door and waited, but when no one answered, she turned the knob and peeked inside. The clerk's desk was unoccupied. She tiptoed into the office, feeling like an intruder. "Hello? Is anyone here?"

"Who's out there?"

Mr. Field! She hadn't forgotten his voice. Charlotte tentatively stepped to the doorway and folded her hands like a schoolgirl. "Good morning, Mr. Field." He hadn't changed one iota. His white hair and perfectly trimmed mustache were exactly as she remembered.

He stood and waved her forward. "Miss Spencer! What a delightful surprise. I had no idea you were in Chicago. When did you arrive? Do sit down!"

Charlotte exhaled a sigh of relief. She had crossed her first hurdle. Now she hoped the remainder of the obstacles would prove as painless. Mr. Field occasionally stroked his mustache while she explained her decision to return to Chicago.

"I am aware the economy is not at its best." She twisted her lace gloves between her fingers. "But it's my hope that there is a position available."

He leaned forward and rested his forearms on the desk. "I am delighted to hear you are interested in returning to the store. I would be happy to have you reinstate the personal shopper service to our customers."

"With the downturn in the economy, I was afraid you wouldn't have need of my services. I am most pleased to accept the position."

"Although we've seen less profit than I'd like over the past months, the ladies and gentlemen who will use the services of a personal shopper have not been financially affected like those of lesser means. I believe we will have sufficient customers to keep you busy."

Charlotte could scarcely believe her ears. She would return

to work at the same rate of pay she'd been receiving prior to her departure, and she would be assigned to her previous duties and responsibilities. God had answered her prayer.

"When would you like me to begin?"

"Shall we say a week from today—Monday, June twenty-fifth?" He glanced at his calendar. "That would permit me sufficient time to run ads in the newspaper to announce your return to our employ. I suspect you'll be deluged with customers."

Charlotte was less optimistic, but she didn't question Mr. Field's assessment. He was, after all, the man who had continued to reign as the Merchant Prince.

"Will you be living at Priddle House, Miss Spencer?"

"Yes."

He looked surprised that she would choose to return to the dwelling where she would contribute the majority of her earnings toward the expenses of others. But then, Mr. Field didn't realize how much Charlotte owed Mrs. Priddle. Without the little gray-haired woman's prayer and guidance, she might never have accepted Jesus as her Savior.

"I'm certain Mrs. Priddle is as pleased as I am to have you back in Chicago. Let me escort you downstairs. There are few changes since your departure, but we do have one new supervisor I would like you to meet."

All eyes were upon them as Mr. Field escorted her up and down the aisles of the store while drawing her attention to the latest arrivals. They entered the fabric section, and Charlotte slowed to admire a length of silk.

"Here's Mr. Rehnquist now." Mr. Field beckoned to a beady-eyed man who hastened to Mr. Field's side.

"Mr. Rehnquist, I'd like to introduce you to Miss Charlotte

Spencer. Miss Spencer has recently returned from London, and I've hired her to return to her previous employment here at Marshall Field and Company. You may have heard some of our other employees mention her. Miss Spencer worked as our personal—"

"Shopper," Mr. Rehnquist said and then immediately apologized for the interruption.

"No need for an apology. I'm delighted to know Miss Spencer's abilities haven't been forgotten by my employees." Mr. Field held Charlotte's elbow. "Mr. Rehnquist is supervisor of the lace and fabric section. His predecessor wasn't meeting sales quotas for this department and is no longer with us."

Charlotte recalled the sales quotas. Though she'd never been forced to meet any specific sales numbers, she wondered if that would change. She had always maintained excellent sales, but even so, she found the idea of a quota daunting.

"It's a pleasure to meet you, Miss Spencer. I look forward to working with you." Mr. Rehnquist stared at her with such intensity that she looked away.

After stops at several other sections of the store, Mr. Field bid Charlotte farewell. She passed through the Accessories Department and then back through Lace and Fabric while making her way to the door. A tap on her shoulder caused her to stop and turn.

"Mr. Rehnquist. You startled me."

"I wanted to speak to you before you left. I am a great admirer of the work you performed here at the store." He brazenly reached forward and grasped her wrist. "I wondered if you would join me for supper this evening. I would very much like to become better acquainted."

"Please release me," Charlotte said, twisting her arm from

his hold. "I have no desire for communication outside of the store, Mr. Rehnquist."

He narrowed his eyes and permitted his gaze to travel the length of her body. An involuntary shudder coursed through her body as she turned and walked away. She hoped future contact with Mr. Rehnquist would be nominal.

CHAPTER ELEVEN

Pullman, Illinois
Wednesday, June 20, 1894

Fred waited, his impatience mounting with each tick of his pocket watch. He knew Olivia couldn't join him until ten o'clock. The kitchen staff took their break at the same time every morning—after breakfast had been completed and the kitchen cleaned for preparation of the noonday meal. There had been no reason to arrive early except he hoped that just this once she might complete her tasks early. The two of them had seen little of each other since the convention had begun, and Fred had promised to stop by this morning before leaving for Chicago. His recent days had been filled with meetings in Chicago, but Olivia's—well, hers hadn't changed at all. Few in Pullman had continued to work since the strike. However, the hotel employees and those who worked in the businesses that provided the town with necessary services were among that number.

Although Fred would be late for what was sure to be an inspiring meeting, he missed Olivia and longed to spend at least a few minutes with her this morning. Besides, he'd been one of the few who had remained until eleven o'clock the previous night. A decision had been made to serve notice upon the company. He had been one of the men who had helped draft the notice of intent. In truth, he'd merely watched and listened, but since he and Thomas Heathcoate were the only representatives of their delegation who had stayed behind, Fred's name was among those credited with drafting the important missive. All of the unions had overwhelmingly responded that the boycott of the Pullman railcars was the only avenue left to them. The company had thrown down the gauntlet with its refusal to negotiate.

"There you are. I thought you had decided not to come." Olivia came hurrying toward him, swinging her white toque in one hand. His heart thumped a chaotic rhythm at the sight of her. He loved her, of that there was no doubt. Oh, he'd never actually said the words, but he was certain she knew how he felt. How could she not?

Her eyes shone with a mischievous twinkle. She held one hand behind her back. He tipped his head to the side hoping to see if she held anything in her hand or was merely teasing him.

"What are you hiding?" he asked.

She giggled and extended a folded piece of stationery. "Look inside."

"I don't understand. What is this?"

"My new address. I'm moving."

He stared at her, astonished by the announcement.

"Aren't you going to say anything? I thought you'd be pleased. You're the one who's been after me to move for all these months." Her lips curved into a beguiling smile.

"What about Mrs. Barnes? I thought you worried she would slip into a state of depression if you moved from their home."

Olivia motioned him toward an empty bench. "Lucinda is returning home," she whispered.

"The Barnes's married daughter? Why would they return to Pullman?"

"Not *they*, only Lucinda. It seems there is some marital discord, and she wants to return home for an extended stay. At least that's what Mrs. Barnes told me. I don't think she knows what to expect, but I offered to relocate." A wisp of her brown hair blew across Olivia's forehead and she swiped it into place. "Mrs. Barnes accepted my suggestion. She said Lucinda is distraught over the dissolution of her marriage. Mrs. Barnes believes my presence might cause her daughter undue distress."

He looked at the piece of paper once again. "You won't be living far from us. Isn't that where Jules and Sarah Mayfield live?"

"Yes. They had an extra upstairs bedroom. My accommodations will be somewhat meager, but I know they are in need of the additional income."

Fred tucked the piece of paper into her hand and gave a nod. "And I will be pleased to have you living nearby."

"Your mother and I could walk to work together if I wanted to leave earlier in the morning, though I'm not certain I'll want to do that every day." She chuckled and surveyed the grassy expanse until her attention settled on his mother and Chef René.

Fred turned toward the older couple. His mother was sitting close to the chef and appeared to be whispering in hushed tones. "What is all of that?" Fred nodded toward his mother.

"Your mother and Chef René seem to enjoy keeping company with each other. I thought perhaps she had—"

He shook his head. "No. Nothing at all." The sight was somehow disquieting. His mother involved in a romantic relationship? *No.* Wasn't she beyond an age at which she would care about romance or a husband? Perhaps they had merely formed a friendship. "They have become friends?"

Olivia glanced back at the couple. "I believe they are more than friends. I think they have begun to care for each other in— well, in a romantic fashion. Quite sweet, don't you think? Wouldn't it be wonderful if they should decide they are suited and wed?"

Fred tugged at his shirt collar. "Marriage?"

Olivia giggled. "What's wrong with marriage? They are both alone and have much in common."

"I disagree. They are opposites in most every way." Fred wondered if Olivia had encouraged the relationship.

"You barely know Chef René. I think you're making an unfair assessment, but I certainly don't plan to argue the matter."

Olivia waved to one of the upstairs maids who walked toward the hotel carrying a huge bouquet of fresh flowers. Even if the folks in town didn't have enough to eat, the hotel guests would have fresh flowers in their rooms this morning.

"Have any new decisions been made regarding the strike? I saw Albert for a short time last evening. He said you and Mr. Heathcoate remained at meetings until quite late."

"An ultimatum will be served on the company today. The union locals of the American Railway Union throughout the

United States have voted to give the company until the twenty-sixth of June to address the many grievances of the Pullman employees. If management fails to do so, the union will refuse to handle Pullman cars and equipment. Mr. Debs is afraid Mr. Pullman won't meet our demand." Fred nervously pressed the brim of his cap between his fingers. "So am I. We all believe Mr. Pullman gave Mr. Howard strict orders that no negotiations were to take place—under any circumstances."

"And all of these union members plan to leave the Pullman cars on side tracks and not attach them to the trains? Across the entire country?"

"That is exactly what will happen unless the company will negotiate prior to midnight on the twenty-sixth. We will boycott all Pullman cars and equipment." He spoke with conviction, but his chest tightened at the thought.

There was little doubt Olivia was shocked by the union's decision. He hoped the Pullman officials would react with the same surprise and decide to negotiate.

Olivia glanced over her shoulder. "I have some news to tell you, also. Mr. Pullman has returned to Chicago. I heard Mr. Howard talking to several stockholders at the hotel. They say he returned earlier today. Do you think that may help the cause? Perhaps Mr. Pullman has decided to relent."

The news came as a complete surprise to Fred. No one in Chicago had mentioned the possibility of the company's owner finally making a return to the city. Fred wondered if the newspapers had caught wind of it yet. "The boycott is likely inevitable, though Mr. Pullman may wonder if we'll actually carry through with the threat. I suspect he's returned to see for himself."

"And will you?"

"Of course. We can't give in now."

Fred explained exactly what Mr. Debs had outlined the night before: A boycott would catapult the strike into a matter of national concern. When passengers could no longer avail themselves of the comfort and services of the Pullman railroad cars, the union hoped the public would pressure the company into negotiation. Perhaps the loss of income would change Mr. Pullman's attitude. Never before had the Pullman workers remained so firm in their convictions. Could it be that Mr. Pullman had accepted the depth of dissatisfaction among the workers and was now willing to arbitrate? Fred wanted to think so.

"The stockholders and Mr. Howard are going into Chicago to meet with Mr. Pullman this afternoon. Mr. Howard said there was a plan to rally a group of businessmen to meet later today or tomorrow—at least I think that's what he said."

Her comment set off an alarm. Had Mr. Pullman banded together with supporters beyond those in his own company? There had been talk such a possibility existed, although most of the delegation had chosen to ignore the idea. Now Fred wondered if they should have more fully deliberated the possibility. A bead of perspiration descended from his temple, and he swiped it away, unsure whether the June humidity or his nerves had been the cause.

"Anything else you recall?" A train whistled in the distance, and his anxiety mounted. He must be on the next train to Chicago.

She furrowed her brow. "I don't think so." He scooted forward on the bench, and she grasped his arm. "Oh, wait! I do remember one of the stockholders said an association of some sort had been formed. Does that help?" Her eyes shone with expectancy.

"I don't know what it means, but I'm sure Mr. Debs will have it sorted out in no time. Thank you for your help, Olivia."

They stood and Fred looked across the lawn. His mother and Chef René appeared to be holding hands. Squinting his eyes against the sun's glare, Fred craned his neck forward but jumped back when his mother spotted him. Just as quickly she appeared to yank her hand from the chef's. Fred uttered a hasty good-bye to Olivia, offered a halfhearted wave to his mother, and raced toward the train station as though his life had been threatened. And perhaps it had—at least life as he'd known it all these years.

Fred handed the conductor one of the train passes the union had acquired for delegates to use during the convention. Mr. Debs had made his wishes known: he didn't want delegates hopping trains. Such behavior might bring condemnation upon the union and its representatives.

He dropped into one of the seats and stared out the window. Had the trees been barren of their leaves, he could have probably captured a glimpse of his mother and Chef René. He didn't know which was more worrisome—Mr. Pullman's return or the possibility of a budding relationship between his mother and the chef. Fred leaned back and rested his head against the back of the seat. He closed his eyes and attempted to clear his mind.

Perhaps he'd have time to visit Bill Orland in the next few days. Fred grinned, remembering the first time he and Bill had traveled to Chicago to visit the glass etching shop. Bill had been frightened out of his wits, unable even to remember Mr. Lockabee's name. They had both laughed when Fred pointed to the signage on the window of the shop.

With the owner's blessing, Bill had continued to run the business under the Lockabee name. Bill had proved to be a quick study, learning not only the etching but also how to run a profitable enterprise. Even during this time of depression, he'd managed to convince the wealthy they had need of his etched pieces. Bill Orland was a talented craftsman, of that there was no question. Along with his wife, Ruth, Bill and his three children had carved out a better life in Chicago—one where they weren't required to worry over where their next meal would come from. During the next couple of weeks, Fred would make a point to spend some time with the Orlands.

By the time the train arrived in Chicago, his thoughts had returned to the news of Mr. Pullman's arrival. He moved down the aisle with a determined step, detrained, and hurried toward Uhlich Hall. He must get word to Mr. Debs.

Fred panted as he raced up the front steps of the meeting hall. Matthew stood inside the front door and grasped him by the arm. "Have you heard the news?"

"About Pullman's return?"

Matthew nodded. "We've been notified that the General Managers Association has been contacted. I'm sure it was either Mr. Howard or Mr. Pullman who called on them, but nobody is offering further information. My guess is that they are going to do their best to block the boycott."

Fred silently chided himself. He should have realized the association that Olivia mentioned was the General Managers Association. The group had never amounted to much until last year, when word had leaked out that the association was forming committees to aid railroads in the event of a strike. The management of twenty-four railroads that either centered or terminated in Chicago had banded together; they apparently were going to stand united against the proposed boycott. At least that's how it appeared to Fred. And Matthew quickly concurred.

Matthew patted his jacket pocket. "I received some inside information that the association is setting up a temporary headquarters in the Rookery."

It didn't surprise Fred that management would choose to meet in the architecturally acclaimed building situated in the heart of Chicago rather than in some modest site. The magnificent towering building had replaced a temporary city hall and water tank. A favorite roost for pigeons, the old structures had been dubbed the Rookery, a nickname that had transferred to the new building. Fred doubted pigeons would be welcome to roost on the fine new edifice.

"Obviously Mr. Pullman is taking the union's letter of intent seriously. My guess is that he's going to remain in the background and convince railroad management to wield a heavy hand when the boycott takes effect."

"Is that what Mr. Debs thinks?"

Matthew shrugged. "Haven't heard what he thinks, but I don't know how he could figure any different. Right now, I'm trying to find some way to get the inside scoop on what goes on in the management meetings." He tucked his notebook into his pocket. "Unfortunately, there's no way I can get in there. They've banned reporters from the place."

Fred wasn't surprised. Railroad management would be required to walk a fine line. They wanted to maintain good relations with the public, which continued to sympathize with the workers, yet if they refused to honor their contracts with George Pullman's company, they could be sued for breach of contract. Neither option held much appeal. And they wouldn't want a roomful of news reporters listening as they hammered out their plans.

Matthew rested against the doorjamb, his focus darting about the room. He slapped his hat against the side of his pant leg. "I've got it." He pointed to the messenger boys posted around the meeting hall who were expected to be at the ready when needed to deliver a note, fill water pitchers, or purchase sandwiches at a nearby restaurant. "They'll have messengers in the meetings."

Fred laughed. "And what type of disguise did you have in mind? I don't think they'll be fooled by a pair of knee pants."

"Nor do I, or I'd try it." He thumped Fred on the shoulder. "But there may be a messenger who'd be willing to share some information with me."

"For a price?"

"I can't divulge all my secrets, but I don't usually pay for my information. I think we're in for a hard-fought battle, my friend, and I had better be on my way." With a wave, Matthew hurried out the door and down the front steps.

Fred watched until Matthew was out of sight and then strode into the meeting hall. All of the exciting news he had planned to deliver to Mr. Debs had arrived before him. Probably just as well. This way, there was no possibility he would jeopardize Olivia's position at the hotel. Mr. Heathcoate called Fred's name and waved him forward.

"Didn't take long to gain a reaction to our letter of intent. Have you heard that Mr. Pullman is back in town? He supposedly arrived during the wee hours of the morning. Either he doesn't want us to know he's in Chicago or he's afraid someone's going to do him harm." Mr. Heathcoate lifted his water pitcher in the air and waited until one of the messenger boys hurried toward him to fetch the pitcher. "I figure it's a little of both—and rightfully so."

Fred arched his brows. "I do hope it won't come to that. The members need to mind Mr. Debs's instructions. We don't want the union getting a black eye."

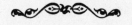

CHAPTER TWELVE

Pullman, Illinois
Sunday, June 24, 1894

Thunder rumbled overhead, and a wall of dark clouds rolled across Lake Calumet, heading directly toward the center of town. Fred glanced heavenward and then picked up his pace.

"Not so fast. My legs aren't nearly as long as yours." His mother tugged on his arm, chiding him.

"I'm sorry. I'm hoping to have you safe inside the church before the rain begins." As if to emphasize his comment, two fat raindrops landed on the sidewalk in front of them.

"You're correct. We need to hurry," she said. His mother now pulled him toward Greenstone Church, obviously concerned the feathers on her hat would be ruined by a downpour. "I understand the church board has decided to offer Reverend Stanhill a permanent position."

"He'd be a good choice. Unlike Reverend Oggel, he doesn't use the church as a place to promote his personal beliefs."

Fred hadn't been the only member of Greenstone who had raised objections to Reverend Oggel's sermons. Days after the preacher's mid-May sermon, the church board suggested he take a vacation. He took their advice, and two weeks later Reverend Oggel sent a letter stating that he didn't plan to return, which was good news so far as Fred and the other workers were concerned. The only ones who lamented the man's decision were Samuel Howard and the other members of management who attended the church.

Hoping to spot Olivia, Fred glanced toward the street corner. He inhaled deeply and unconsciously squeezed his mother's arm.

She followed Fred's gaze, and he watched his mother's features immediately soften with pleasure. "What an unexpected surprise."

Fred arched his brows. "Truly?"

"Yes. Why would you question me? Had I known that René planned to attend church, I would have told you." Without awaiting Fred's response, his mother released her grasp and motioned the rotund chef forward.

As of yet, Fred hadn't had an opportunity to discuss this newly formed friendship with his mother. Each time he had planned to broach the subject, either Paul or Suzanne Quinter had been close at hand, and he didn't want to discuss such a personal matter in front of either of them. Perhaps he should have pushed aside his concerns and spoken up. Likely Suzanne already knew his mother had befriended the chef.

"Why are you standing out here? You're going to get wet."

Olivia's question disrupted Fred's thoughts, and he glanced at the church steps. His mother and Chef René had apparently already gone inside. Olivia clutched his arm in a possessive hold and beamed at him—much the same way his mother had greeted Chef René.

"I do appreciate the fact that you waited, however."

A raindrop plopped onto Olivia's hand, and Fred hurried her up the steps. Once they'd entered the vestibule, he led her to the far end of the foyer. "It'll be a few minutes before services begin. I need to speak with you in private." Fred didn't fail to see the anticipation in her eyes. She likely expected an invitation to dinner. Perhaps he should begin with that. "I thought we might have dinner together today. There are no union meetings this afternoon."

"That would be lovely." She giggled. "Your mother invited me yesterday. I suppose she failed to tell you."

He could feel the heat rise beneath his collar. "We've seen little of each other lately." He nodded toward the sanctuary. "Did my mother know Chef René planned to attend church this morning?"

She shrugged. "When I left work last evening, he didn't mention his plans. And your mother said not a word." Olivia raised up on tiptoe and craned her neck. "Where are they sitting?" She didn't wait for a response. "How exciting!"

"So you didn't know?"

"Of course not." Olivia stepped toward the doors leading into the sanctuary and scanned the crowd. "Oh, there they are!" She pointed toward the right side of the church. "Let's go sit with them."

"I'm certain they'd prefer their privacy," he said.

"Privacy? Don't be silly. This is church." She didn't permit time for further discussion. She tugged on his arm. When he didn't move, she yanked him forward and frowned. "What is the matter with you? If the chef feels unwelcome, he may never return."

Fred didn't comment. It would be improper to say he wasn't

sure he wanted the man to return. His stomach roiled with emotion. Certainly his mother deserved happiness, but he had never considered the possibility that she would remarry after all these years. Any number of men had expressed interest in her since they'd moved to Pullman, but she'd always turned them away. Why this Frenchman? He'd heard that the French were romantic—perhaps that was it. Had the chef beguiled his mother with fancy words and deeds? In Fred's opinion, the chef didn't seem the type who could capture a woman's heart so quickly, especially his sensible mother. Yet he'd long ago won Olivia's allegiance. There must be something of substance beneath the man's hefty exterior; otherwise his mother and Olivia wouldn't be drawn to him. Yet Fred couldn't help but wonder if the chef's appearance in church was merely an effort to impress his mother rather than because he'd developed a sudden desire to worship God.

Charlotte returned to Priddle House after church services but remained only long enough to feed Morgan a quick lunch before heading off with him to the train depot. She wanted to assure herself time for a full afternoon of visiting with Olivia. Mrs. Priddle hadn't hesitated to point out the possibility that Charlotte's surprise visit could very well go amiss. But Charlotte was undeterred. She thought the idea quite fun.

The older woman walked outdoors with them and issued one final warning. "You'll be squandering your money on train fare if Olivia isn't at home."

Charlotte continued toward the front sidewalk carrying Morgan in her arms. "I'll find her. And if I don't, I'll go and visit with Mrs. DeVault." Charlotte pumped Morgan's arm up and down in a wave. "Say good-bye, Morgan."

Though he failed to say good-bye, he squealed and held his arms out toward Fiona when she joined Mrs. Priddle on the front porch. Fiona threw a kiss, and Morgan immediately complied. Charlotte had hoped Fiona could join them on the outing, but the girl had failed to perform all of her chores during the week, and Mrs. Priddle had swiftly denied the request.

Charlotte had urged Mrs. Priddle to change her decision, but the older woman would not relent. Fiona had made a choice and must suffer the consequences. Charlotte couldn't argue with Mrs. Priddle, for she knew the woman was correct. Had her parents been firm with her when she was a child, perhaps she would have made better choices. Like Mrs. Priddle, Charlotte wanted what was best for Fiona. But right now, it was difficult to observe the girl's dejected countenance.

With a sympathetic smile, Charlotte waved to Fiona, walked to the corner with Morgan in her arms, and boarded a cab. Morgan jabbered at the other woman sitting in the carriage. She smiled and talked to him until he attempted to yank the artificial bird from atop her hat. Although Charlotte profusely apologized, the woman moved to the other side of the carriage and glared at them the rest of the drive to the train station.

For an instant Charlotte considered telling the woman that her hat had gone out of style years earlier, and had Morgan removed the bird, it would have been an improvement. But she kept the thought to herself. The moment the carriage came to a halt, the woman stepped out of the conveyance and hurried off as though she couldn't get away quickly enough.

"I don't believe she liked us very well," Charlotte whispered to her son. "You must behave on the train."

He bobbed his head as though he understood. Charlotte

approached the ticket counter, purchased a round-trip ticket, and made her way through the crowd. There was little time to spare before the train arrived.

She pushed open the door leading to the platform and quickly turned when she felt a hand on her elbow.

"May I be of some assistance, Miss Spencer?" Charlotte could see confusion register in Matthew Clayborn's eyes. "And who is this young fellow?" He beamed at Morgan. The child wriggled in her arms and then lunged toward Matthew.

Charlotte gripped the boy around the waist and pulled him back into her arms. She quietly chided her son for his behavior. "This is my son, Morgan." She offered no further explanation. Mr. Clayborn was, in effect, a stranger, and she owed him nothing more. She stepped back and glanced at the railroad tracks. "My train is boarding. If you'll excuse us."

He stepped forward and kept pace as she hurried toward the train. "I'm on my way to Pullman, also—to visit Fred."

She came to a halt and frowned before continuing onward. "Why did you choose this particular time and day for your visit, Mr. Clayborn? I would think you could visit with Fred when he's in town for the convention." Her comment appeared to disarm him, and he hesitated.

"You're quite shrewd, Miss Spencer. You may want to consider news reporting as a career." He reached forward and grasped one of Morgan's pudgy fingers. The boy bounced with delight. "But you have this young fellow to fill your days, don't you?"

"Only until tomorrow." The words slipped out before she could retract them. Charlotte could see the questions forming in Mr. Clayborn's eyes. The man was a newspaper reporter. He would undoubtedly quiz her throughout the train ride to Pull-man.

Hoping to avoid him, she boarded the train and searched for a seat. With all of the empty space, most of the passengers would likely be irritated if she squeezed in beside them with her wiggly child, so she opted for one of the seats away from the majority of the passengers and plopped Morgan beside her.

The boy immediately climbed to his feet and smacked his palms on the train window. "Ope!" His demand was followed by more window smacking.

"I cannot open the window," Charlotte explained, attempting to hold his hands. He struggled against her hold and wiggled out of her grasp. Pressing his foot against her silk gown, he slipped and tumbled forward. With lightning speed, Matthew reached forward and swooped the child into his arms.

He balanced Morgan in one arm and tipped his head toward the seat opposite Charlotte. "Mind if I join you?"

What could she say? She wanted to refuse, but such behavior would be absolutely rude given the circumstances. He had, after all, saved her child from injury, and Morgan was now clinging to the man. She opened her arms to her son, but he twisted and dug his head into Matthew's neck.

"He's fine. I'm quite fond of children."

She arched her brows. "And how many children do you have, Mr. Clayborn?"

"Matthew. Please call me Matthew." He grinned at Morgan. "I don't have any children of my own, but I do have nieces and nephews. My sister thinks I'm quite competent with her children. She tells me I'd make an excellent father. And what of you? Is Morgan your only child?"

His question startled her. "Yes." She hoped her curt

response would put an end to his questions.

He shifted Morgan onto his knee so the boy could watch out the window while the train pulled out of the station. "You mentioned you would be caring for Morgan only until tomorrow?"

She frowned, but he wouldn't be deterred.

"Earlier, when I mentioned news reporting as a possible avocation, but then . . ."

Charlotte shifted in her seat, recalling their previous conversation. "I begin work tomorrow, so my son will be spending his days in someone else's care." She carefully phrased her answer to avoid any reference to Priddle House or where she lived.

He focused his piercing blue eyes upon her. "And who has employed you, Miss Spencer? Everyone I speak to tells me there are no jobs to be had in all of Chicago."

She sighed. The man was relentless. "I have returned to my previous position with Marshall Field and Company." Matthew's eyes shone with surprise. Or was that contempt? "I'm certain Ellen Ashton has provided you with details of my past. We need not continue this cat-and-mouse game."

He bounced his knee, and Morgan giggled with delight. "I won't deny the fact that I attempted to wheedle information from her, but she remained as tight-lipped as a sealed envelope. I hate to admit my efforts were unsuccessful. I wouldn't want my newspaper editor to know I'd been unable to pry information out of an old acquaintance."

"Your secret is safe with me. I promise I won't talk to your editor." Charlotte exhaled and relaxed a degree. It was refreshing to know she could trust Mr. Ashton and his daughter to maintain her confidence.

"Will you be working as a salesclerk in Mr. Field's establishment?"

She decided to repay Matthew's persistence and surprised him with a candid response. After a feeble attempt to hide his distaste for the idea of a personal shopper, he concurred there would be no shortage of customers. "Money abounds in the tight circle of capitalists. And their wives and daughters are more than willing to spend some of it when they're in Chicago. You may see a decrease in sales once the wealthy flee to their summer resorts or sail to Europe in the next few weeks, but Mr. Field knows to expect waning sales in the summer. Such declines shouldn't reflect upon you." He tousled Morgan's shock of fine hair. "What about this young fellow? Who will be seeing to his care?"

"A dear friend."

"A man?"

"No, of course not. I told you I am not married."

"You are a widow, perchance?"

"You are quite forward with your questions, but I'm certain Fred will tell you of my past, should you inquire. And since there is little doubt you *will* inquire, I suppose there's no need to hold back any longer."

While Morgan entertained himself bouncing on Matthew's knee, Charlotte revealed the sad details of the past two years. She ended the tale in a final rush of words. "I'm not proud of my behavior, but I love my son, and I have received God's forgiveness for my sins." She folded her hands in her lap and waited for his condemnation.

"Why would you want to work for Marshall Field?"

She reeled at the question. "Why do I want to work for

Marshall Field? *That's* what you want to know after all that I've told you?"

"None of us can change our past. We can only strive to do better in the future. And it's your future that interests me." He raked one hand through his sandy brown hair while clutching Morgan with the other. "That's why I asked about your choice of Marshall Field as an employer. He is no different from George Pullman or Philip Armour. All these capitalists are cut from the same cloth. Can you not see the similarities? They oppress the rest of the country while they live in the very lap of luxury. It is unconscionable."

The train clanged their arrival in Pullman. "Mr. Field has treated me with utmost respect. He pays me a generous wage—enough for me to help support Priddle House, and I am told he is quite charitable."

"You live at Priddle House? The daughter of the Earl of Lanshire?" His brows furrowed. "Quite a story you're weaving. Perhaps you should consider fiction rather than news reporting."

She shrugged and scooted to the edge of her seat. "What I've told you is true. Whether you choose to believe me makes little difference." Charlotte attempted to lift Morgan from his arms, but the child immediately turned around and clung to Matthew's jacket.

"He's fine. I'll carry him."

She would have preferred to rip her son from his arms but chided herself for her childish thoughts. "As you wish."

They left the train station, looking, to her dismay, like a young family arriving for a visit. Morgan bounced in Matthew's arms and pointed at the ground. "Dow!" Matthew tightened his grip.

"He wants to walk," Charlotte said.

"I know, but I didn't think you wanted . . ." He shrugged and leaned down. Once Morgan had gained his balance, Matthew grasped one hand and Charlotte took the other. The boy giggled and lifted his feet off the ground while the two adults supported his weight. "Typical little boy," Matthew said. "Do you want to accompany me to the DeVaults' and say hello before locating Olivia?"

She nodded. "Yes. I'd enjoy a visit with Mrs. DeVault, and she or Fred should know where I can find Olivia."

They continued down the sidewalk, the scent of roses wafting on the summer breeze. Not much appeared to have changed. Though she had read reports of the strike activities, the town remained well maintained, with children and adults in the park playing games and enjoying a pleasant Sunday afternoon. Morgan attempted to direct them toward a group of youngsters gathered together for a game of ball, but between the two of them, they managed to redirect him.

"I do think this town quite charming, and please don't counter by listing all of Mr. Pullman's faults. You will surely concede he constructed a lovely town. In many respects it reminds me of England."

Matthew grunted and shrugged, apparently unwilling to give a favorable nod to any of the accomplishments created by a capitalist. They turned the corner and walked down Morse Avenue. The front door of the DeVault residence stood open, and sounds of laughter drifted through the screen.

"My reporter instincts tell me that Olivia is inside."

Charlotte chuckled. "I think perhaps it's your excellent hearing rather than your ability to sniff out a story."

Matthew lifted Morgan into his arms and rapped on the door. Charlotte could see Fred striding down the hallway toward the front door. As he drew near, she watched his brow furrow, and then a look of surprise erased his frown. "Charlotte? I don't believe my eyes." He pushed open the door. "It *is* you!" He glanced at Matthew and Morgan and then back at her, his confusion obvious.

"Who is it, Fred? If we have guests, invite them in." Mrs. DeVault stood at the end of the hallway.

Fred waved them inside before turning to his mother. "Come see who's here. And tell Olivia to come, too."

"So that *was* Olivia's voice we heard." Charlotte couldn't believe her good fortune.

"Olivia and Chef René are both here." Fred had barely uttered the words before Charlotte spotted Olivia hurrying toward her.

Olivia stopped midway down the hall. "Charlotte! When did you . . . how did you . . ." she stammered. After a brief moment, she regained her composure and hurried forward to enfold Charlotte in a warm embrace. She leaned back and stared into Charlotte's eyes. "It is so good to see you. I can barely believe my eyes." Morgan chortled and grabbed a handful of Olivia's curls in his chubby fist. "And *this* must be Morgan," she said.

"Morgan!" Charlotte pried his fingers from Olivia's hair. "Do behave, young man. I apologize, Olivia. I fear Morgan has developed quite a penchant for hair pulling."

"No harm done," Olivia said while tucking the curl behind one ear. "I truly cannot wait to hear all that has happened with you and Morgan." She clasped a palm to her chest. "This is such a surprise. I believe my heartbeat has increased tenfold."

Mrs. DeVault extended her arms to Morgan, and the boy dove toward her. The older woman laughed with delight. "You know who has a nice dish of pudding, don't you?" Morgan bobbed his head as though he'd understood every word. "Come along, all of you. We don't need to stand out here in the hall. You're just in time. René is dishing up our dessert."

Charlotte looped arms with Olivia. "René?" she whispered.

"I do believe love has begun to blossom between the two of them." Olivia grinned and tugged on Charlotte's arm. "We have much to talk about. I am eager to hear about your parents. And Ludie—how is she doing? What about the other servants? Is Chef Mallard still in charge of the kitchen? Let's go into the dining room. I can hardly wait to hear all the news." She leaned closer. "And just how do you happen to know Matthew Clayborn?"

CHAPTER THIRTEEN

Fred and Matthew retreated to the parlor while the others gathered in the dining room for dessert.

Matthew dropped onto the divan. "I managed to obtain the services of a messenger boy who is working over at the Rookery. Seems the association has tightened ranks with Mr. Pullman, and they've scheduled another meeting for tomorrow morning. They're permitting Mr. Howard to sit in as an interested party."

"What?" Fred couldn't believe his ears. "That's outrageous. If the company is to have an *interested party* present, it seems the workers should have one, also."

"I couldn't agree more, but we both know that won't happen."

"Did you hear anything else? Any inkling if they're going to persuade Mr. Pullman to negotiate?"

Matthew laughed and shook his head. "Do you truly believe any of those men will convince George Pullman to bow to their wishes? I'm afraid the managers and Mr. Pullman are going to be working hand in glove throughout this strike. Tomorrow they'll decide how they will handle the situation should the workers carry through and refuse to couple the Pullman cars. While you are receiving your final orders from Mr. Debs, the General Managers Association will be finalizing their plans to thwart your efforts."

Fred buried his face in his hands. Could there be no peaceful solution to this matter? Negotiation seemed such a simple remedy. The men weren't asking for outrageous sums. They merely wanted a livable hourly rate and rental fees that were commensurate with their wages.

"From all appearances, we're in this for the long haul. I had prayed that once Mr. Pullman returned, he would see that the men were determined to be heard. I thought he would make some effort to negotiate. Pride and greed—not a pretty picture."

Matthew clapped him on the shoulder. "You're right, but I suppose Mr. Pullman is thinking the same thing about the workers. No doubt he views the workers as unappreciative and greedy. All of us attempt to rationalize from time to time."

"What? You're taking his side now?"

"Of course not. But I'm a journalist. I attempt to look at things from every vantage point. It doesn't mean that I've changed my opinion or that my support has wavered." He turned his palms upward and moved his arms up and down. "I'm weighing the scales, my friend, and they tip heavily in favor of the workers. But that still doesn't mean you'll prevail."

Matthew's warning cast a pall of defeat across the room. If they didn't win this time, the likelihood of future bargaining with the company would probably be forever lost to the workers. And some of the newspapers that favored the Chicago capitalist had been quick to point out that Mr. Pullman had taken on contracts at a loss in order to keep his employees on the job.

Of course, these same newspapers didn't report that the workers' pay had been decreased while their rents remained unchanged. Nor did they tell their readers that the stockholders continued to receive their usual large dividends. Fred had gone over these matters in his mind day after day. Thinking on them any longer would change nothing.

Fred stood and signaled for Matthew to follow him. "Surely the others must be finished with their dessert. Let's see if they would like to go outdoors and enjoy this fine weather."

———

Olivia peeked out the door, concerned the sun might prove too warm for young Morgan. She waved Charlotte forward. "What do you think?"

Charlotte settled Morgan's sailor cap atop his head. "He will be fine. The sun is hidden behind a bank of clouds at the moment, and I'm certain we can find enough shade that I needn't worry over Morgan's fair complexion."

"Can we go, too?" the Quinter girls asked in unison, their pigtails bouncing as they twirled in front of Mrs. DeVault.

"I have no objection, but you must first ask your mother."

Suzanne was quick to agree, but she and Paul declined the invitation, deciding to remain at home while baby Arthur napped.

"The two of them won't know how to act having a bit of free time for themselves," Olivia commented as Mrs. DeVault herded the group out the front door.

The girls immediately appointed themselves Morgan's caretakers, each one grasping one of his chubby hands. He chortled with delight when they pointed out a neighbor's kitten sitting on the porch railing. By the time they arrived at the park, he could say *kitty-cat* with proficiency, and he continued to repeat the words until the Pullman Band struck the first chords of their Sunday afternoon recital. Captivated, Morgan was soon marching in place beside the girls, the kitten now forgotten.

Fred and Matthew took up residence on a grassy spot near the children, but Chef René and Mrs. DeVault continued to meander, obviously seeking a place closer to the bandstand.

Olivia pointed Charlotte to a nearby bench. "Now that we are alone, you must tell me all that has happened since your letter telling me that you had arrived safely in England."

The two of them settled side by side, and Charlotte briefly related all that had occurred since she'd gone home to England. "It wasn't an easy time, but I'm certain I've made the proper decision for Morgan."

Olivia understood Charlotte's reasons for permanently relocating in America. Had she stayed in London, both she and Morgan would have been shunned by the English aristocracy, and her social ranking would descend into the chasm that divided nobility from commoners. She would be accepted by neither and despised by most—and so would her son.

Olivia clasped Charlotte's hand. "I am very sorry to hear of your father's death and the difficult circumstances that beset you and your mother. I prayed you would find happiness upon returning to London, but I understand your desire to give Morgan a different kind of life in a new land."

The music continued in the background, and Charlotte nodded. "Yes, although I must admit that the upheaval I find here is somewhat disconcerting. Mrs. Priddle's account of the poverty that has taken hold here is frightening." She scanned the crowd that continued to gather in the park. "I cling to the fact that I fervently prayed for God's direction and believed I was to return to Chicago."

Olivia brushed a strand of hair from her forehead. "Then you must rest in that decision. God has already provided for you. Didn't you tell me that you have already secured your former position at Marshall Field's?"

"Yes, but—"

"If you believe God directed your path, you must stop questioning your decision. It will only lead to turmoil, and young Morgan is in charge of turmoil," Olivia said, grinning at the little boy, now holding a worm between two fingers. Had it not been for Matthew's quick intervention, the worm would have become Morgan's snack. "Matthew certainly appears to enjoy Morgan."

Charlotte maintained a watchful eye on her son and on Matthew. "Yes. He's almost too helpful."

"How can anyone be too helpful? Most women would be delighted to have a man take interest in their child."

Charlotte waved to her son. "If the interest is genuine. I'm not entirely convinced that's the case with Mr. Clayborn. I worry he's sniffing for information every time he asks me a question."

Olivia giggled. "You're much too suspicious. Matthew is consumed with details of the strike and the American Railway Union convention at the moment. You need not fear that he's planning to splash your picture across the front page of the *Herald*. Besides, you have nothing to hide."

Charlotte arched her brows and fixed Morgan in her sights. "You forget that Randolph Morgan lives in Chicago."

Olivia shook her head. "Oh!" she whispered. "He's dead. I should have written and told you, but I thought it was of little importance since you'd returned to London."

"Randolph? Dead? But how?"

"There were a number of wealthy men who suffered huge financial losses when the depression hit. Some weren't affected much at all. Others, like Randolph, lost a great deal and were unable to face their ruination. From all reports, he took his own life. I saw his obituary in the newspaper and made a few discreet inquiries." She tipped her head closer. "His wife and daughters now live in New York."

"Surely not! Are you certain that isn't malicious gossip?"

"No. I inquired of Ellen Ashton, and she confirmed it's true. His wife's family resides in New York. I suppose that's why she moved there."

"I'm sure that's one of the reasons."

"And so that she and the children wouldn't be subjected to the gossip," Olivia added.

"True, but moving to a different city also helps in other ways. If Randolph's wife had remained in Chicago, each time she heard the front door unlatch, she'd expect to see him walk inside; or when she walked in front of his office building, she'd long to go inside and convince herself he truly wasn't there." She turned her gaze back toward Olivia. "It's difficult to understand, I suppose, but it's easier for me to be here in Chicago where I don't think about my father as being dead—at least not as often."

Olivia scooted closer. "Will Randolph's death be difficult for you to accept in that way?"

"No. Randolph and I didn't make any fond memories in Chicago, but I do regret that Morgan will never have an opportunity to meet his father." Olivia appeared surprised by the remark, and Charlotte hastened to explain. "I didn't return to

Chicago with any intention of making demands upon Randolph, but I had given thought to the fact that perhaps one day, when Morgan is a man, the two of them might meet. Morgan will eventually have questions about his father, and it would have been . . ."

Olivia squeezed Charlotte's hand. "Yes, of course. I'm sorry I had to be the one to deliver the news. It seems you've had more than your share of death to deal with in a short time."

"The two of you appear as though you're preparing for a funeral rather than celebrating a reunion," Matthew observed as he and Fred approached. "Fred and I would be pleased to lend our assistance and help solve any troubles that may be afflicting you lovely ladies."

Charlotte forced a smile. "No difficulties at all. We're merely discussing acquaintances from our past. Nothing that you'd find of interest."

"Well, we've managed to solve the world's problems and thought you ladies might enjoy a walk down to the lake. We might even consider a boat ride. I think Morgan would find that a good deal of fun, don't you?"

Charlotte laughed. "We've just completed quite a boat ride. I don't know if I'm prepared for another just yet."

Matthew joined in her laughter. "I had completely forgotten your recent voyage. Would you prefer to remain here at the park?"

"I'll bow to Olivia's wishes, but I am enjoying the music. The band is even better than when I last heard them play."

"They have continued to win awards and are now considered the finest band in the state," Fred said. "With the strike, they now have more time to perform, and their concerts seem to raise the community spirit."

Morgan toddled toward his mother and extended his arm. He uncurled his tiny fingers to reveal a ladybug cupped in his palm. "Bug."

"Indeed it is. Let's put it on the ground," Charlotte suggested.

Morgan squeezed his fingers together and shook his head. "Mine."

"Come here, Morgan. Let me show you how your bug can fly." Matthew held out his arms, and the boy scampered toward him and opened his hand. With a gentle flick of his finger, Matthew boosted the ladybug into the air. The boy giggled and hurried back to join the girls, who were playing a game of hopscotch.

When the musicians stopped for a brief respite, Olivia glanced toward the bandstand. "Where are your mother and Chef René? I thought they'd taken a bench near the pavilion."

Fred shaded his eyes and scanned the area. "Perhaps we should take a walk and see if we can locate them."

With a loud guffaw, Matthew dropped to the bench alongside Charlotte. "At their age, I don't think we need to worry about their whereabouts. I think they're old enough to take care of themselves. Besides, it's not as though they're going to get lost in Pullman. I'd venture a guess that they're enjoying their time alone."

Olivia noted Fred's frown. "I'd be happy to accompany you, but I tend to agree with Matthew. Your mother is a grown woman. She'd likely think you'd gone daft if you traipsed after her."

Fred folded his arms across his chest and nodded. "You're right, but I plan to speak with her tonight. I'm not certain Chef René is the well-intentioned man you believe him to be."

"Really, Fred, you're acting like an overprotective father rather than an adult son. I think you better change your approach before you speak to your mother, or she may toss you out the front door on your ear." Olivia hoped he would heed her advice. She thought Mrs. DeVault and the chef made a fine match.

A short time later the musicians returned to the bandstand. The group of friends walked to the far side of the park, where several children had set up a lemonade stand. Olivia wondered how long it would take before they were told such activity was not permitted in the parks, or anywhere else in Pullman, for that matter. Charlotte and Matthew hurried after Morgan, who was hurtling toward the stand. It seemed his chubby legs couldn't keep pace with the rest of his body.

"They make an attractive couple, don't you think?" Olivia sat down on a bench a short distance from the lemonade stand.

Fred shook his head. "You do enjoy matching folks into couples, don't you?"

She grinned. "Why not? Isn't that what God intended?"

"For most, but not necessarily everyone."

What was that supposed to mean? Was Fred sending her a hidden message that he wasn't interested in her? She tried to maintain a carefree tone. "And do you include yourself in that number?"

"Me? Of course not. I want to marry one day, but Matthew travels a great deal, and he may never want to settle into the day-to-day life of a married man. As for my mother—she's already been married. Why would she want to do so again?"

Were all men so naïve or only Fred? Attempting to hide her exasperation, she answered, "To have someone with whom she can share her hopes and dreams. Someone who is there for her when she feels alone. Age doesn't erase the need to be loved, Fred."

"I know, I know. But I'd at least appreciate the opportunity to discuss the matter with her before she's ready to accept a marriage proposal."

Olivia squeezed his hand. "I don't think you need worry about a wedding just yet."

"What's this I hear of a wedding? It's about time you asked this girl for her hand in marriage," Matthew chortled. "I thought you'd never get around to it."

Fred swiveled around on the bench. "Where did you come from? I thought you were purchasing lemonade."

Matthew pointed to Morgan, sitting with his mother on a nearby bench and downing a glass of the sweet liquid. "Don't hold back with the news. We'll want to put the special day on our calendars."

Olivia's cheeks burned with embarrassment. She peeked at Fred, hoping to gauge his reaction and silently hoping Matthew's comment would urge him to action.

"We . . . um . . . weren't discussing *our* wedding plans."

"You're not fooling me, Fred. There's no need to keep a secret from us. We're good friends who can maintain a confidence." Matthew turned his attention to Olivia. "You'll tell me, won't you, Olivia?"

Fred jumped up from the bench. "We're not keeping a secret." The band ended their musical selection, but Fred continued to shout. "I didn't propose to Olivia." His voice carried like a rumble of thunder on a quiet morning.

Everyone in the area turned to stare at them. Mortified, Olivia grabbed her reticule and flew from the park. The sounds of laughter and hoots of several young boys mocked her as she continued to run. Her hat tipped askew, and her skirt flapped about her legs as if to trip her, but she continued her flight.

"Olivia!" Fingers tightened around her arm and jerked her to an abrupt halt.

She attempted to shake herself loose, but Fred tightened his grip.

"Don't!" he panted. "I'm so sorry. We need to talk." His breath came in uneven spurts, and though she knew he was tired, his hold remained fast.

Olivia doubled forward to ease the stitch in her side. "There's nothing more to say. You've shouted to the entire town that you don't plan to marry me."

"No! That's not what I said. Please! Let me explain." He gulped a breath of air and swallowed while still clinging to her arm.

"It *is* what you said," she argued, still attempting to wrest her arm free.

"I said I didn't propose to you. I didn't say that I didn't plan to marry you. I *do* want to marry you."

She stared at him in disbelief. His declaration stunned her into a momentary silence, and she took a backward step. "You *do*? Then why didn't you say that to Matthew?"

He nodded toward a large oak a short distance away. "Could we sit down in the shade?"

She matched her step to his, and moments later they settled beneath the tree. Olivia folded her hands in her lap. "You may explain."

He grinned. "I do love you very much, and I want to marry you, but this isn't at all how I had planned to propose. Nor is it the time when I envisioned asking for your hand."

This wasn't the manner in which Olivia had expected to

hear his declaration of love, either, but she couldn't refrain from pressing him further. "If you're certain you love me, exactly how much longer did you intend to wait before you shared your feelings with me?"

Fred raked his fingers through his hair. "When the strike is over, when I could purchase a ring and offer you a proper wedding, when I had work that would pay enough to provide for you in a proper manner. I have nothing to offer right now, yet Matthew has forced my hand." He wrapped his arm around one knee and stared into the distance. "Who knows what will happen with this strike and the depression? I had hoped to wait and speak of marriage when life was more settled." He looked into her eyes and brushed her cheek with his fingertips. "You do know I love you, don't you, Olivia?"

She clasped his fingers in her hand. "A girl likes to hear the words, Fred. You've never before spoken to me of your feelings. As for the ring and a proper wedding—those are of little importance to me. Being certain you truly love me is what matters."

He lifted her fingers to his lips and lightly kissed them. "But surely you knew."

"You can be a puzzling man. One minute I believe I understand you, but the next I'm not sure."

"Then that means I shall keep our life interesting, doesn't it?"

She chuckled. "I suppose that's true enough."

"Then you'll marry me? I don't think we should set a date until the strike is over and I've returned to work. But we can announce that we're engaged if you truly don't care about a ring." He leaned forward and pulled her into an embrace.

Though she knew that she should have been concerned over the impropriety of a public exhibition of affection, she leaned into his arms and accepted the warmth of his kiss.

When their lips parted, Fred traced his thumb across her lips. "I love you, Olivia, and I want you to be my wife. I've wanted to say that for a long time, but fear of the future has kept me from speaking. Yet now that I've asked and you've accepted, I'd like to shout it from the rooftops."

"I don't think we need to go quite that far, but we could at least tell your mother and Charlotte."

"And Matthew," he added, rising. He extended his hands, helped her to her feet, and chuckled. "He'll be delighted to know I'm still speaking to him."

CHAPTER FOURTEEN

Early the next morning, Fred boarded the train for Chicago. His heart thumped beneath his suit jacket in a drumming cadence that seemed to match the rhythm of the train. They traveled the twelve miles in record time. The usual hustle and bustle that passengers had come to expect hadn't changed, and folks continued on with their normal routines—at least those who remained unaffected by the strike in Pullman.

Young boys hawking newspapers in the train station shouted to prospective customers as they forced their way through the station. Fred glanced at one of the headlines, but he didn't purchase a paper. He could hear the news that interested him first-hand once he entered the doors of Uhlich Hall.

Several men greeted him as he bounded up the steps to the building. "Anything taking place yet?" Though he knew it was far too early to expect any action, something may have occurred during his absence on Sunday, and he wanted to carry a full report to the men in Pullman.

They shook their heads. "Mr. Debs is going to address the

delegation in about a half hour. He arrived a few minutes ago."

Once inside the building, Fred spotted Matthew talking to a young messenger boy. He waited until they finished their conversation and then watched the youngster race out of the building before approaching his friend.

Fred glanced toward the front doors. "Your informant?"

"You know I don't divulge my sources." He chuckled and winked. "Want to go for a cup of coffee before the meeting begins?"

"No, thanks. I don't want to take a chance on missing out on anything. It's hard to tell if I'm more concerned about today's meetings or the discovery of what will happen tomorrow if the responses we receive aren't what we're hoping for." Fred tucked his straw hat beneath his arm. "I've been praying about every issue and every vote. We're going to need a miracle to pull us through."

"From all reports, I think you're correct. Guess we'd better get into the auditorium if we're going to find some seats near the front."

The two men made their way down the aisle, stopping here and there along the way to exchange a few words with delegates and spectators. When they finally found two seats in the second row, Mr. Debs had ascended to the stage. Fred dropped into a chair, keeping his sights fixed on their leader and hoping he could gauge something from the older man's appearance. But as usual, Mr. Debs's features portrayed a picture of calm.

When he stepped to the podium, the crowd immediately quieted, the hush palpable. He held a sheet of paper between his thumb and forefinger and waved it for a moment.

"Good morning! We have not yet received any definitive word except that the General Managers Association has banded together. They have declared they have no interest in the Pullman strike per se, only as it may affect the railroads and their existing agreements with the Pullman Company."

The sound of derisive hoots filled the room. Mr. Debs signaled for the crowd to quiet.

"They state they have been placed in a quandary, for if they refuse to connect the Pullman Palace Cars, they could be subjected to litigation for breach of contract."

"So they've thrown in with Mr. Pullman?" one of the men shouted from the back of the room. "I'd say there's no need to wait until tomorrow. We might as well join with the Pullman workers right here and now."

Mr. Debs pounded a gavel and called for order. "No! We have given a certain date, and I intend for the membership of the American Railway Union to honor its word. We are going to conduct ourselves in a manner befitting the membership of this union."

The crowd grew quiet and listened while their leader outlined his expectations and prepared the men for the following day. "If the General Managers Association doesn't change its position by tomorrow, then the switchmen must refuse to couple any Pullman cars, inspectors must not examine them, and engineers and brakemen must refuse to haul any train carrying a Pullman car. If any worker is discharged, all men on the system must immediately walk out."

"*Then* what?" one of the men shouted.

"We will direct further strategy from here at Uhlich Hall. Bear in mind that train service will become nonexistent until either George Pullman negotiates or the railroads drop his cars from their trains." Mr. Debs retrieved a handkerchief from his pocket and wiped his brow. "Let us pray Mr. Pullman or the managers will come to their senses and sit down at the bargaining table with their employees."

Cheers of approval filled the room. For the remainder of the morning, they listened to Mr. Debs and other members of the committee issue their instructions to carry back information to the men they represented. He sent them on their way with the promise that tomorrow would make a mark in history. "Either Mr. Pullman will negotiate or his cars will sit idle."

Matthew's young messenger stood at the back of the hall, and Matthew signaled to him. The boy hurried to Matthew, who, with his head bent low, listened and then spoke to the lad. The youngster held out his hand, and Matthew reached into his pocket.

Fred stepped forward as the boy sprinted out of the auditorium. "Any news?"

"Same as Saturday. Sounds as though they're not going to relent. I'd say the union members should gird themselves for battle. I doubt this will be pretty." Matthew shook Fred's hand and nodded toward the door. "I've got to get over to the paper and write my story. See you later?"

Fred followed along while scanning the crowd. "I'm going to talk to Mr. Heathcoate and see if he wants me to return to Pullman and call a meeting of the workers. He can remain here in Chicago in case anything new should arise."

Matthew donned his hat and stepped toward the front doors. "I'll see you tomorrow, then."

———

Olivia didn't fail to note Mr. Howard's absence in the dining room that morning. He'd stopped by the hotel only long enough to advise Chef René that the board might reconvene their meetings at the hotel on Tuesday evening. In such an event, the chef should be prepared to serve the men his finest offerings.

When they walked outdoors after the noonday meal, Olivia followed the chef. "Will Mr. Howard remain in Chicago tonight?"

"He did not say. I can only guess that his decision will be based upon what occurs today. At least I know the only special guests this evening will be our hotel guests. And they are few in number."

Mrs. DeVault bustled out the door and joined them at the bench beneath a cluster of trees. "My baking duties have lessened since the departure of all those businessmen." She sat down beside the chef. "I can't say that I'm not pleased for a bit of a respite."

Chef René patted her hand. "I have pleaded with Mr. Howard to hire another baker, but he is adamant. He says costs must be kept down until the depression and this strike are resolved."

Mrs. DeVault swiped the back of her hand across her forehead. "It could be several years before the depression ends. I doubt I can keep this pace for so long without help." She flashed him a smile. "But I shall try."

"And I'll lend my assistance whenever possible," Olivia threw in.

"Oui. You must do everything you can to help Hazel. She will soon be your mother-in-law."

Olivia chuckled. "She was my friend before Fred proposed, and I would help her even if he hadn't asked."

One of the kitchen boys stood in the doorway and waved a towel in their direction. "Chef René, you are needed inside."

He pushed his ample body upright. "Now what?" he murmured. "Excuse me, ladies. I must see to this urgent matter for which I am being summoned. No doubt it is *verrry* important."

"I don't think he's particularly happy," Olivia remarked, watching the chef cross the grassy expanse to the kitchen door.

Mrs. DeVault shook her head. "I've talked to him incessantly about remaining calm, but it seems to have little effect. I worry about his heart condition. Do you think his agitation is a characteristic of the French, or is it simply René?"

"Perhaps it is some of both. He does have a flair for the dramatic. You two appear to be getting along quite well. He dotes on your every move."

The color heightened in Mrs. DeVault's cheeks. "I must admit we have formed a fast friendship. But enough about me. I want to once again tell you how pleased I am that one day soon you'll become my daughter." She squeezed Olivia's hand. "Since I don't have any daughters, we can forget that 'in-law' portion, don't you think?"

"I would be honored, but I don't think we'll be making plans in the immediate future. You heard Fred say that he wants to wait until after the strike is settled and he knows what the future holds for him."

"Oh, posh. If we wait until life is in order before making our decisions, we'll never make any," the older woman rebutted. "I believe I'll tell him just that."

"You certainly have my permission," Olivia said with a grin. "Did Fred discuss anything else with you last evening?"

The scent of roses floated on a light breeze drifting from the park, and Mrs. DeVault inhaled deeply. "Lovely, aren't they? The roses, I mean."

Olivia agreed and wondered if the woman planned to avoid her question with talk of the roses, but Mrs. DeVault surprised her.

"After all of our guests departed yesterday, Fred questioned me at length about René. He fears I'm making a fool of myself."

Olivia gasped.

"Oh, not to worry. Fred would never actually say such a thing. But I knew what he was thinking. He is, after all, my son. And he's not the best at hiding his feelings from me. I had been expecting his little talk."

Two of the dishwashers headed back toward the kitchen. Olivia glanced at the tower clock. She hoped she and Mrs. DeVault would have time to complete their talk before they must return to the kitchen.

Olivia leaned forward. "What did he say?"

"He asked if René had made unwelcome advances."

Olivia muffled a laugh. "And what did you tell him?"

"I told him René is a perfect gentleman and he need not worry on that account. However, when he said that women of my age usually preferred needlework to courting, I set him straight." She looked toward the kitchen door. "I'd much rather spend my evenings enjoying a band concert with René or enjoying his company over a cup of tea than sitting alone with my embroidery. I think he was somewhat surprised by that."

"I have no doubt."

"However, I do believe it's good that we openly discussed the matter. René wanted to speak to Fred and explain his intentions are honorable, but I asked him not to. I see no need for him to do that." Mrs. DeVault peeked at her watch. "We'd better get back to work before the chef sends someone to fetch us. I wouldn't want to make him angry."

The two women smiled and walked arm in arm across the lawn. Olivia loved the idea of Mrs. DeVault being her mother one day. She hoped Fred would warm to the idea that Chef René might become his stepfather sometime in the future, too.

———

Matthew stood on the corner and watched the entrance to Marshall Field and Company. His editor had approved the article he'd written; now he hoped to catch a glimpse of Charlotte leaving work. Had he not been banned from the store, he would have gone inside and attempted to secretly watch her as she helped her customers. Matthew didn't know if Mr. Field actually had a list, but he did know the man had no tolerance for anyone who sided with the unions. Matthew's opinions on labor issues were no secret, as his views had been spelled out in newspaper articles carrying his byline.

Matthew tried to picture Charlotte showing the latest fashions from Paris or assisting the likes of Mrs. Pullman or Mrs. Armour with the selection of a new hat or a pair of gloves. Charlotte would know exactly which items would please Chicago's wealthy social set.

The throng of workers emerging from the store meant the emporium was closing for the night. If all went well, Charlotte would be among them. Small groups of employees walked across the street, and he strained to the side to keep his vigil. There! He captured sight of the hat she'd been wearing yesterday and moved in her direction.

She was engrossed in conversation, and it was the older woman walking beside her who finally acknowledged him. "Were you looking for someone?"

Finally Charlotte turned in his direction. "Matthew! What are you doing here?"

"I planned to escort you home from work."

Charlotte returned her attention to the older woman and begrudgingly introduced her as Mrs. Brandt, a fellow employee.

When they reached the opposite side of the street, Mrs. Brandt stopped. "I turn here." The older woman hugged Charlotte and then quickly released her, seemingly embarrassed by her action. "I'm so pleased you've returned to us," she said before hurrying down the street.

Matthew arched his brows. "Returned to us? What exactly does that mean?"

"Mrs. Brandt is a lovely woman who has no family. She considers her friends at the store her family. Thus the reference that I had returned to them." She stepped out of the crowd congregated on the corner, and Matthew followed along. "I don't recall your asking if you could meet me after work."

He grinned. Charlotte apparently was a woman who stood on formality—likely it was her noble English upbringing, he decided. "My apologies. I should have gained your approval beforehand. I thought perhaps I could spend a little time with you and Morgan this evening."

"I will be joining the other residents of Priddle House for dinner. Funds are scarce, and our meals aren't prepared with an eye toward unexpected visitors."

"What about after supper? I'd enjoy spending some time with you. And it would give me an opportunity to meet the young girl you spoke of yesterday—Fiona, wasn't it?"

She nodded. "Yes. Fiona. I suppose if you'd like to join us after supper, I won't object. I'm sure you'll find the evening quite enlightening."

Matthew hailed a carriage, gave the address of Priddle House, and handed the driver several coins. Grasping Charlotte's arm, he assisted her inside. "I'll come by at seven o'clock."

"Don't be late."

He stared after the carriage and reveled in her parting words. Apparently she'd decided a visit would be enjoyable. With a spring in his step, he headed for the Good Eats Café. He'd have time enough for the evening special, a cup of coffee, and a chat with Hank before going to Priddle House.

A short time later, he entered the café and waved at a couple of newsmen seated at a nearby table. He turned down their invitation to join them. He didn't want to get involved in a discussion that might cause him to be late for his visit.

He surveyed the specials written on a board over the counter. When Hank approached, Matthew rattled off his order. "I'll have the chicken potpie, a piece of that chocolate cake, and a cup of coffee."

"Sounds good. Make it two, minus the cake." Matthew turned around to see Ellen Ashton standing next to him.

"How are you, Matthew? You've been a stranger lately. You spending all of your time on the convention floor?" She sat down beside him.

"Either there or at the office writing something my editor will give the nod to. How've you been, Ellen?"

"As good as a person can be with all this commotion swirling through town stronger than the Chicago winds. I'll be pleased when it all comes to an end. Dealing with folks unable to keep life and limb together during this depression is difficult enough. The town is like a pot of water ready to boil over and scald the entire population."

"Care if I use that remark in tomorrow's issue?" Matthew nodded when Hank settled a cup of steaming coffee in front of him.

She grinned. "Tomorrow will be too late. The pot will either have boiled over or returned to a simmer, depending on the circumstances."

"Guess you're right. Too bad—would have made good copy." He gulped a swallow of coffee and returned the cup to the matching green-rimmed saucer with a clank.

Hank brought two broad bowls of potpie and topped off Matthew's coffee. "You two need anything else?"

"Just don't forget that cake," Matthew said. He patted his stomach. "I still consider myself a growing boy."

Ellen shook her head. "If you don't cut down on cake, you'll grow right out of that suit." She took a bite of chicken and vegetables and nodded her approval. "How's Fred holding up?"

Between bites Matthew regaled Ellen with the events of yesterday afternoon. "Can you believe it? Fred finally asked Olivia to marry him."

"That's wonderful news. I'm certain Father will be pleased to know that Fred's not going to move forward with a wedding until after he's completed his duties as a union delegate. You know Father—first things first."

Matthew laughed. "I hate to disappoint your father, but I think Fred's desire to hold off on the wedding has more to do with acquiring a job and supporting his wife than making your father happy."

They continued their conversation until Matthew had finished his cake and downed the last of his coffee. He reached into his pocket and counted out the exact change.

"What's the hurry? You could wait until I finish my meal and come down to the office. Father and several other men are going to have some sort of conclave."

Matthew pushed away from the table. "Any other night you

couldn't keep me away, but I've another engagement this evening."

"There's a glint in your eye, Matthew Clayborn. Who is she?"

He leaned down. "Charlotte Spencer."

"I don't believe you."

He picked up his hat and winked. "Then you can ask her the next time you see her."

A short time later Matthew walked down Ashland Street toward Priddle House and spotted Charlotte standing on the front porch. His heart swelled at the sight. She was waiting for him. As he drew closer, she waved him on. He glanced at his watch. Exactly seven o'clock.

The sound of piano music floated from inside the house. "What's the hurry?" he asked as he bounded up the front steps.

"We begin prayer meeting at seven o'clock sharp each evening. I don't want you to miss a thing."

"Prayer meeting?" His voice cracked. "But . . ."

"Come along. We're eager to have you join us."

Charlotte tugged him forward, and the two of them stepped into the parlor. Matthew peered around the room. With their Bibles already opened and resting on their laps, the women each nodded in turn as the introductions were made.

Then Mrs. Priddle pointed to a chair beside her. "You may sit here beside me, Mr. Clayborn. When we've finished our singing, you may lead us in our first prayer of the evening."

Matthew dropped to the seat and loosened his necktie. He could feel the beads of perspiration beginning to form along his upper lip. The woman wanted him to pray? In front of all these women? His hands trembled at the very idea. He glanced across the room. Charlotte grinned, obviously enjoying every minute of his discomfort.

Well, if this was a test, he planned to pass with flying colors. He was, after all, a wordsmith with at least three minutes to gather his thoughts while the women raised their voices in song. When they'd sung a melodious amen, Mrs. Priddle tapped his hand and gave a nod that nearly sent her gray knot of hair into a downward spiral.

"Dear God, we are all thankful to be here tonight—especially me."

Fiona giggled and Mrs. Priddle shushed her.

"I admit I felt like Jonah walking into the lion's den when I entered the parlor this evening, Lord, but you've given me that same kind of courage tonight, and I'm asking that you shower blessings on the ladies who live in this house." Matthew continued to beseech the Lord for several minutes before ending his prayer with a vigorous amen and a smile at Mrs. Priddle.

"Thank you, Mr. Clayborn. That was lovely." The old woman leaned closer. "For future reference, it was Daniel who walked into the lion's den—not Jonah. A mere slip of the tongue, I'm sure," she whispered while patting his hand in a motherly fashion.

He gulped and swallowed hard. *Did I really say Jonah? I learned those Bible stories as a young boy. How could I possibly make such a mistake?* Suddenly he realized that in his desire to impress Charlotte and Mrs. Priddle, he'd forgotten he should have been talking to God rather than the roomful of women. No wonder he'd made such a foolish error. So much for passing his test. *Forgive me, Lord*, he silently prayed.

CHAPTER FIFTEEN

After his meeting with the Pullman workers at the union head-quarters in Kensington, Fred boarded the last train of the evening into Chicago. He wanted to be in the city early Tuesday morning, and there was nothing further to be accomplished in Pullman. The men of Pullman understood what was expected: maintain order and civility yet remain steadfast in their demand to negotiate. By this time they realized that their strike had been demoted to a secondary position, superseded by the American Railway Union's demands and the conglomerate of railroads that had banded together as the union's adversary.

Returning to Chicago would also provide him with an opportunity to visit Bill Orland. Although Fred had stopped by Lockabee's Design and Glass Etching Shop on several occasions since Bill had begun his tenure there, the visits had been related to Bill's etching questions. Both Bill and his wife had extended offers to come for dinner, but it never seemed to be the right time—until now. When he'd stopped in last week to extend a quick hello and inquire about the business, Bill had offered Fred a place to stay while he acted as a delegate to the convention. Tonight Fred had arranged to take him up on the offer.

Fred climbed the outside steps that led to the upstairs apartment and knocked. The door swung open, and Bill greeted him with a broad smile. "I was beginning to give up on you."

"I hadn't intended to return quite so late. I hope it isn't going to cause you any inconvenience."

Bill shook his head and motioned Fred inside. "The children have gone to bed and my wife is doing her mending, so we'll have a couple of uninterrupted hours to visit. I want to hear an inside view on how things are shaping up with tomorrow's deadline."

"And I want to hear how your business is doing," Fred replied, taking a seat in the kitchen. Mrs. Orland peeked in long enough to say hello and offer a piece of her apple pie but then disappeared as quickly as she'd arrived.

Bill poured each of them a cup of coffee and sat down opposite Fred. "First the strike; then I'll tell you about this place."

Between bites of pie, Fred related the events leading up to their current status. "Tomorrow will tell the tale of whether anyone other than the workers will be willing to sit at the table and negotiate."

Bill took a gulp of the coffee and rested his forearms on the wood table. "I have to tell you, I'm mighty thankful to be sitting in this place right now. I know it's a terrible thing to say to someone who is fighting to help all of the workers in Pullman, but I don't regret for a minute that I've left that place." He shook his head and laced his fingers together. "I thought my wife would never stop crying when she heard about the Jensens' boy. I can't imagine one of my children freezing to death." A tear glistened in his eye, and he downed another mouthful of coffee.

"You're right. It's been a hard-fought battle, but let's hope something good will come from all of this. If we lose, I don't know what will happen—especially to those of us leaders."

"You need not worry. You know I would bring you on as a partner here, Fred. We might struggle earning enough to support two families, but we'd make do."

"Thank you, Bill, but I hope it doesn't come to that. Now, tell me about the business. I want to hear how you've fared and if the locals are appreciative of your artistic abilities."

The two men talked late into the night. Later, when Fred lay down in bed, he remembered how much he missed fashioning the beautiful etched glass that he'd learned to create years ago. The memories combined with thoughts of the strike filtered in and out of his dreams, providing a restless sleep.

When he awakened the next morning, Fred felt as though he'd not been to bed at all. After downing Mrs. Orland's hearty breakfast of bacon, eggs, and thick slices of buttered bread, he offered his thanks and hurried off toward Uhlich Hall. Several delegates had already arrived.

"Any news?" he asked.

"No. So far as we know, the trains are running on schedule, just like always."

Fred could barely believe his ears. After all that had happened, all the planning and the promises that the American Railway Union and Mr. Debs had made, were the trains actually going to continue to run as though an ultimatum had never been issued?

———

Matthew positioned himself among several other reporters at the railroad station. As far as he was concerned, this was the place to be. He wanted to see firsthand whether Pullman cars would continue to be coupled to the trains running in and out of Chicago. After a morning and afternoon of disappointment, he walked across the station and tucked his notepad into his pocket. Thus far, the Illinois Central had kept to its schedule, and there had been no evidence that the boycott of Pullman cars was going to occur. Matthew could only imagine how Fred must feel.

"Hey, Matthew! Did you hear the news?" Hurtling across the depot at a gallop, Sam, a young messenger from the *Herald*, closed the gap between the two of them in no time.

"If there's any news, I sure missed it. Looks as though everything's moving along pretty normally to me. I was just going over to grab a cup of coffee at the shop on the other side of the depot. Want to come along?"

Sam grabbed his sleeve and shook his head. "The president of the Illinois Central has invited George Pullman to come to the station and watch the Diamond Special depart for St. Louis. Since things have been going so well for the railroad today, the company president figures the boycott was merely a threat."

"I'm beginning to wonder the same thing," Matthew said. "So is Pullman planning on making an appearance?"

"No one seems to know yet, but you're supposed to stick around and cover the story—if there is one. That's what the news editor said I should tell you. Want me to wait with you?"

Matthew chuckled. "I think you'll find sitting around here about as boring as watching paint dry, Sam. Besides, you're probably needed at the paper. If you hear anything else, let me know. I'll stick around until nine o'clock, when the Diamond Special leaves the station, but I'm going on home afterward. It won't take long to write this story."

Matthew strolled across the depot and made himself comfortable at one of the tables in the coffee shop. It had already been a long day, and now he'd be there until well into the evening. When six o'clock arrived, Matthew was standing across the street from Marshall Field's. He could walk Charlotte home and be back well before eight thirty. If George Pullman planned to make an appearance, he'd likely wait until close to nine o'clock to make his entrance. He wouldn't want to stand around and face the possibility of reporters asking him questions he didn't want to answer about his model town and the starving workers. In fact, Matthew doubted that he'd appear at all.

After last night's Bible study, Mrs. Priddle had permitted him the opportunity of bidding everyone good-night. She'd then escorted him out the front door while Charlotte retreated upstairs to check on Morgan, so the evening had proved less than exciting.

This evening the same woman he'd met the night before accompanied Charlotte across the street, but this time he didn't reveal himself until Mrs. Brandt had bid Charlotte good-night.

Once the older woman had turned to cross the street, he stepped to Charlotte's side. "May I escort you home, Miss Spencer?"

"Mr. Clayborn, you surprise me. After attending last night's Bible study, I didn't expect to see you again."

"You think I'm so easily deterred that I would permit a group of women and a Bible study to keep me away from you?" He chuckled. "Just proves you don't yet know me."

Charlotte continued onward without slowing her pace. "I truly have no idea what it would take to deter you. However, I'm surprised you're not off gathering news regarding the strike. Wasn't the boycott scheduled to occur today?"

"Yes, but nothing's occurred so far, and I had to while away the entire day at the train depot. Other than thoughts of you, I've had nothing with which to keep my mind occupied. I thought you might agree to be my guest at supper. What do you say?"

"I say that I have a son awaiting my return home and other responsibilities that require my attention. You should find some carefree young lady upon whom you can shower your attention. I have little free time for such things."

"But you must eat supper, and I'd be delighted to have Morgan join us."

Her eyes sparkled, and his heartbeat quickened at the thought that she might accept his offer. Instead, she quickened her pace. "We have the same routine nearly every night at Priddle House. Mrs. Priddle maintains a strict schedule for all of her residents. Had I told you about the Bible study, you would have thought I was merely making an excuse to avoid you."

"So you're *not* attempting to avoid me?"

She sighed. "You are a very nice gentleman, albeit a bit forward and somewhat tenacious. However, I assume that goes hand in hand with your profession."

Matthew laughed and tipped his head as though she'd slapped him. "We reporters aren't such a bad lot."

"I'm sure you're not, but as I said earlier, I have obligations. Between my work, my son, and Priddle House, my days and evenings are full."

"What about your Sunday afternoons? Are they filled, also?

Surely you're entitled to a few hours of leisure each week. If you won't permit me to call on you before then, what about next Sunday afternoon?"

She glanced at him from beneath her wide-brimmed hat. "What about Sunday morning? You could attend church with us."

Another test? If so, he didn't want to fail. "I would be pleased to attend. What time shall I call for you?"

"Nine o'clock would be acceptable. We could visit in Pullman afterward, if you like."

"Perfect." He was already relishing the idea of an entire afternoon with her.

"And perhaps Fiona could join us?"

He nodded. "Yes. Fiona would be most welcome," he said, thankful she hadn't added Mrs. Priddle into the mix.

He hailed a carriage, paid the driver, and tipped his hat. "Until Sunday morning."

She smiled in return. "I shall look forward to your visit."

He watched until the carriage was out of sight. She had said she would look forward to his visit. That must mean she at least *liked* him. He headed down the street. He'd have his supper at the Good Eats, where he could always depend upon seeing a few of his fellow reporters or an acquaintance or two. Maybe he'd even see Ellen again.

Matthew's disappointment mounted when the Diamond Special departed at nine o'clock with Pullman cars in tow. Had he not overheard a surreptitious comment between two of the switchmen, he would have called it a night. Instead, he decided he'd take up residence on one of the benches. He could write his story and catch a short nap in the depot. If anything happened, he'd be on hand to get what every reporter longed for—a scoop.

When the night crew reported for duty at midnight, Matthew received his wish. He was the first reporter to interview one of the switchmen who refused to work the Pullman cars. The other railroad employees arriving for the night shift followed suit. They, too, refused to move any train that carried a Pullman car.

He scribbled his story and raced to the office, shouting the news as he entered the building. His editor, Mr. Baskin, snatched the story from his hand and began to read, signaling for Matthew to join him while he ordered the story sent out to the wire service. "I trust you've corroborated all of this?" The excitement caused Mr. Baskin's florid complexion to take on a purplish hue that emphasized his bulbous nose.

"I was there. I saw it with my own eyes and heard it with my own ears. The quotes from those switchmen and inspectors were made directly to *me*."

Mr. Baskin clapped him on the back. "Good work! You stayed at the depot all night?"

"Isn't that what you instructed?"

"I did." The older man smoothed his palm across his balding pate. "I didn't expect you to follow my orders, but I'm sure glad you did. You can expect something extra in your pay envelope at the end of the week."

"How about something extra on a weekly basis? I could stand a raise."

"Just because you're in the midst of reporting on a strike, don't go getting any ideas." Mr. Baskin leaned back in his chair. "I'll see what I can do, but no promises."

"Good enough." Matthew jumped to his feet, pleased that his request would be considered. Though he hadn't entered the building with a raise in mind, it somehow now seemed important that he have a more substantial income, yet he didn't quite understand why. He didn't have difficulty meeting his week-to-week living expenses. He shrugged the thought from his mind and headed back to the streets to sniff out another story that would please Mr. Baskin.

He decided to check at Uhlich Hall and see if he could get Mr. Debs's take on how the boycott was progressing thus far. When he reached the building, he saw Fred standing out front. "Appears as if the boycott has begun. No word from Mr. Pullman or the General Managers Association that they're now interested in negotiating?"

Fred shook his head.

"Mr. Debs inside? I thought I'd try to get a few remarks from him."

"He handed out a printed statement a short time ago that says he won't be giving any further comments for the time being. I truly believe he's heartbroken that it has come to this. Until the boycott actually began, he held out hope that someone would step forward from the other side and offer to negotiate." Fred pointed to his heart. "But I think deep down inside he knew it wasn't going to happen. I think he fears we'll be unable to hold out long enough to win."

The two of them sat down on the top step, and Matthew shoved his hat to the back of his head. "I hope this doesn't turn violent. Do the men in Pullman appear content to bide their time and wait this out?"

"I carried Mr. Debs's message to them early Monday evening, but I haven't been back since. I'm going to return later this evening and give them a full report. Thomas Heathcoate will accompany me. I'm afraid the men may be receiving conflicting reports from every side. We hope to maintain their confidence."

Matthew rested his forearms across his knees. "I wish you well, my friend. No doubt Chicago will soon be filled with unrest. Let's hope all remains quiet in Pullman."

CHAPTER SIXTEEN

Pullman, Illinois
Friday, June 29, 1894

The sun shone overhead as creamy clouds billowed in a pale blue sky. Except for the depression that firmly gripped the nation and the railroad strike that threatened to bring the country to its knees, it was a perfect day.

Olivia grasped Fred's arm, and the two of them sauntered toward the hotel. "How soon will you return to Chicago?"

"I'll go in this afternoon if there's an available train."

Within two days after the American Railway Union had declared an impasse, fifty thousand railroad workers across the country walked out, and the Illinois Central trains now ran only sporadically. Switchmen, firemen, brakemen, engineers, and other laborers had held fast to their word and joined their fellow workers in the boycott. And those who didn't walk off announced that they would not work on any train that included a Pullman car. The railroad lines that crisscrossed the midwestern states rapidly clogged, and the busy Chicago freight yards fell silent. The Chicago *Times* led with the headline "Not a Wheel Turns in the West."

Fred and Mr. Heathcoate followed Mr. Debs's order and urged the strikers to remain nonviolent. However, tempers mounted as railroad managers soon hired nonunion men who weren't qualified for the railroad jobs but were willing to work as strikebreakers. There was little doubt the railroad managers hoped these scabs would force the union men back to work.

"After last night's incident, I'm not certain what we're going to do to keep tempers in check."

Olivia squeezed his arm. "But you said you didn't believe Pullman workers were involved."

"Yes, but that doesn't mean the rest of the country will believe that. No matter who sabotaged the tracks, it looks bad for the union. We've worked hard to keep sympathy on our side."

Maintaining the country's support would be difficult if some resolution didn't occur soon. Fred didn't have the answers, but he hoped Mr. Debs could provide a reasonable solution, for he feared last night's near derailment of the Diamond Special a few miles south of Chicago would be a black eye for the workers. As the strike gained momentum, the struggle that pitted workers against management could escalate.

"Now that there has been one incidence of violence, I fear more will follow. We don't want mob rule taking hold."

"I've been praying a miracle will occur and all of this will be set aright. The fear in the men and women of this town is palpable." A light breeze ruffled the hem of her skirt. "So much has changed since I arrived here. I wonder if life will ever be the same."

Fred shook his head. "Let's hope not. That's what this strike is about: making life better for the workers and their families."

"Yes, but in the meantime, I wonder how much the people and the town will be damaged. Don't misunderstand me. I know the strike was necessary and the workers were willing to negotiate. Yet the entire country is in an upheaval while nothing has changed for the better here in Pullman."

"Not yet, so we must continue to pray that our efforts aren't in vain." They stopped near the oak tree a short distance from the kitchen entrance. "You do realize what all of this could mean for me if the union doesn't prevail, don't you, Olivia?"

She bowed her head. "I try to push it from my mind and dwell instead on the fact that I will become your wife one day."

He lifted her chin with his thumb. A hint of sadness shone in her eyes, and he forced a smile. "Nothing will change my love for you, Olivia, but you must be prepared for what may happen. If we fail in our efforts, I may be forced to leave Pullman. There is the possibility that the company won't consider rehiring me or anyone else who played a role in unionizing the workers."

"But if we marry, you could still remain in . . ." Her voice trailed off on the wind.

He shook his head. "When we marry, you could lose your employment, too. Mr. Howard would likely enjoy taking revenge. If the strike fails, you may want to reconsider my proposal. It would break my heart, but I would understand."

"Fred DeVault! Do you think me so fickle? If you must leave Pullman, then we will both go."

He leaned against the tree and watched a wren fly into her house. "I don't think you're fickle, but I know you enjoy living in this town. And there's your work. I don't know if I could ask you to give up your position."

"But you already asked me to marry you, and I accepted. It is my choice, isn't it?"

He cupped her chin in his hand. "I suppose it is, but I would never want you to regret the decision to marry me."

She lifted on tiptoe to accept his kiss. "I could never regret that decision. We will be fine. I know we will."

Fred didn't argue, but they would visit this topic again in the future—when the strike ended and he knew what the future held. He didn't expect Olivia to step into an uncertain future with him. She deserved better.

He glanced toward the hotel. His mother and Chef René stood just inside the kitchen door. "I wonder if my mother will as readily accept a move from Pullman."

"You must stop these negative thoughts. Your gloomy attitude will serve no good purpose."

"You're right. We must trust that we will prevail and my mother will not be required to make difficult decisions."

Olivia followed his gaze and grinned. "Perhaps she will choose to remain. As a hotel employee, she will be entitled to live here."

Fred arched his brows. "I hadn't thought of that. But I wonder if Mr. Howard would permit her to remain an employee. She may lose her position because of me."

"I have a feeling that if Mr. Howard ever threatens to fire your mother, the chef will threaten to follow her out the door. I know that neither Mr. Pullman nor Mr. Howard wants to lose Chef René's services."

"Don't be too sure. The Pullman employees thought they could force Mr. Pullman's hand. You see how far it has gotten us."

Olivia squared her shoulders. "I think you have far greater

concerns than what may happen to the kitchen staff in the future."

"You're right." He leaned down and kissed her cheek. "I don't know where I'll be over the next several days, but don't worry. If I'm able to catch a train to Chicago, my return will depend upon where I am most needed."

Chef René stood near the kitchen door and greeted Olivia when she crossed the threshold. "Your Fred does not appear to be in good spirits this morning."

Olivia removed the pins from her hat. "My Fred is worried about what will happen to my position here if management should win this battle. He believes that once we are married, I will be discharged."

"Oui. If they lose, he is most likely correct." He flicked his wrist in a defiant gesture. "But I would fight to keep you on my staff."

"Thank you, Chef René, but I wouldn't ask you to do such a thing. Though I long to continue my work as a chef, I will follow Fred. Who knows where it might lead me?"

"This is true. And if that day should arrive, you may depend upon Chef René for an excellent reference." He leaned across the work table. "One that is genuine!"

Olivia grimaced at his subtle reminder of the falsified letter she'd used to gain employment at the hotel when she and Charlotte had first arrived in Pullman. Those early lies had caused her more problems than she could have possibly envisioned.

"And what would you think if Mrs. DeVault had to leave her position as your baker?"

He scowled at the question. "What you have suggested is not humorous, Miss Mott. I would be outraged by the suggestion." The chef stepped around the worktable. "I am quite fond of Hazel, and I do not wish for that to happen. I suppose I would marry her—*then* what would Mr. Howard do?" His belly jiggled and his laughter echoed off the kitchen walls.

Olivia stared at him, unable to believe her ears. "You've only known her six weeks."

"You are counting?" He motioned for her to hang up her hat. When she returned with her white jacket and toque, he pointed to the eggs. "We don't have many guests. That should be enough."

Once she'd completed the task, she stepped away from the stove and tapped his arm. "Would you truly consider marriage to Mrs. DeVault when you barely know each other?"

"Let me tell you something about love, Miss Mott. It does not take months or years to know when you have found the right person. Hazel brings out the best in me, and I like that. When you reach my age, you can't afford to wait too long with such decisions."

Olivia clasped a hand to the neck of her tunic. "You mean you've already asked her?"

"Non. But only because I fear she will say we must wait. If the strike should cause difficulties with her employment . . ." He shrugged his broad shoulders. "Then I believe she would readily accept my proposal. At least I hope she would."

Even though Olivia had realized early on that the chef and Mrs. DeVault had become fast friends—she had even mentioned to Charlotte the possibility of a romantic link between the pair—Chef René's admission of love and a possible marriage at this early date surprised even her. She wondered what Fred would think.

———

Having once again spent the night at the Orland residence, Fred returned to Uhlich Hall Saturday morning, where the mood remained grim. Anger and frustration oozed through the union hall like a festering wound. Mr. Debs had once again called for nonviolence when he had attended a peaceful rally at Rock Island rail yard in Blue Island, located seven miles southwest of Pullman. But soon after his departure, a group of unidentified men had derailed a locomotive, destroyed the railroad yard, and set numerous fires. No one seemed to know who the men were, but union members were being blamed.

"Look at this." One of the delegates shoved a newspaper into Fred's hand. He shook his head in disbelief as he read the column. The Chicago *Tribune* article referred to the boycott as an insurrection and blamed the strikers for the ensuing food shortages and disruption of mail service.

The man tapped the paper with his index finger. "They don't say nothing in there about the union agreeing to move the trains so long as they didn't try to attach the Pullman cars. How do they get away with pointing a finger at us?"

"Because most of the newspapers are owned and operated by wealthy men just like George Pullman. They protect each other," Fred replied. He glanced around the hall, hoping to spot Matthew and see if the *Herald* had printed anything to repudiate the *Tribune* article. Instead of placing blame on the General Managers Association for insisting upon attaching the Pullman cars, they pointed a finger at the striking workers.

The man's anger continued to escalate, and several other delegates gathered around. "What about the scabs that are arriving here? Word has it the Association has hired Pinkertons to protect them."

"Worse than that, they're deputizing hooligans, calling them marshals, to keep the peace. Those unruly gangs of 'marshals' are stirring up more trouble than all the union members combined."

Another delegate stepped forward and joined the group. "Well, they best be careful. If this keeps up, there's gonna be trouble, and once it gets going, it will spread like wildfire."

Fred spotted Matthew. "I'll be back in a few minutes, fellows. I see someone I need to speak with." Weaving his way through the crowd, Fred waved to Matthew. "Have you seen the article in the *Tribune*?"

His friend nodded. "I'm afraid it's only going to get worse. Public opinion is beginning to turn against the union and the strike. The *Times* is still on the side of the union, and I'm still writing evenhanded articles for the *Herald*. But people quickly tire of rising food costs and the inability to travel or receive their mail. They don't like the inconvenience, and the General Managers Association is going to capitalize on that."

Fred gritted his teeth. "Well, the strike is complicating the lives of union workers, too. The public needs to see beyond the end of their noses. The outcome of this strike will affect workers everywhere."

Matthew raked his hand through his hair. "You don't need to explain that to me, but from what we've received on the wire service and through other sources, it appears the federal government is getting involved. After last night's incident at Blue Island, Attorney General Olney has asked President Cleveland for an injunction."

"No one knows for certain who caused that damage at Blue Island. Involving the federal government is exactly what the General Managers Association wants. The managers have intentionally attached Pullman cars to the trains that carry mail, hoping for that result. Doesn't anyone in Washington realize what management is doing? If federal troops arrive, I'm afraid there will be bloodshed."

"Let's hope it doesn't come to that. Keep a lid on what I've told you about the federal troops. The mayor has ordered the police force to total readiness. There's always a chance the president will reconsider."

Fred nodded his assent. "With each passing hour, the public seems to further align with management. I imagine they will completely desert us if the strike continues into July."

"July arrives tomorrow morning, my friend. The events of the past few days have caused you to forget the date." Matthew clapped him on the shoulder. "I've got to get back to the office."

Fred dropped onto a wooden chair in a far corner of the dank auditorium. Overpowered by the strain of the past two weeks, he covered his face with his palms; the days had melded into one another without beginning or end. Now it seemed the federal government was determined to intervene and take control of what had begun as a simple request to negotiate. He could only imagine what lay in store for the union workers and the residents of Chicago during the next two weeks. Yet they must wait. It was all they could do.

CHAPTER SEVENTEEN

Chicago, Illinois

With a determined step, Matthew strode down the sidewalk toward Priddle House. He'd been perfectly clear with his editor, Mr. Baskin: he would not be available for any breaking news story; not even if the federal troops arrived at the Van Buren station in the middle of the day. Today was Sunday, and he planned to devote the entire day to Charlotte and Morgan. First church, and then an afternoon of relaxation at a nearby park, since there was no guarantee of a train to and from Pullman. Neither he nor Charlotte could take that risk.

At nine o'clock sharp, Matthew knocked on the front door. Mrs. Priddle greeted him with a tight smile and an appraising look. She opened the screen door and motioned him forward. "The knot in your tie is crooked." With a jab of her finger, she pointed toward the hall mirror. "You can see for yourself."

Matthew took a long stride and assessed the tie. With a gentle tug, he adjusted the knot. It had appeared perfectly fine to him, but he wasn't about to argue with Mrs. Priddle. "That better?" He grinned.

"Not the best I've seen, but it will do. You may wait in the parlor. Charlotte will be down in a few minutes. We leave promptly at fifteen minutes past the hour." She furrowed her brows. "And we all walk to the church together."

Hat in hand, Matthew made a right turn into the adjacent room. Mrs. Priddle had no problem making her wishes known. He hadn't planned on group attendance at church, but he wouldn't argue. Mrs. Priddle sat down opposite him, her black straw hat perched atop her gray hair and her hands folded in her lap.

"Exactly what are your intentions, Mr. Clayborn?"

"Intentions? To attend church and escort Charlotte—"

She raised her hand and silenced him. "I *know* your plans for today. I'm speaking of your long-term intentions toward Miss Spencer."

"We've only recently met, Mrs. Priddle. Isn't it a bit early for this discussion?"

"Not so far as I'm concerned. If she were living in England, you'd be required to answer such an inquiry from her parents. Consider me a protective parent, Mr. Clayborn."

Matthew cleared his throat. He knew Priddle House wasn't a normal boardinghouse. Nevertheless, he thought the older woman's question intrusive. "I'd like the opportunity to get to know her better."

"For what purpose?"

Matthew hesitated. *For what purpose?* How did one answer such a question? He had no idea what would satisfy someone like Mrs. Priddle. He could feel the beads of perspiration beginning to form along his upper lip.

"The simple truth will do, Mr. Clayborn. You need not search for the words you think I want to hear."

Could she read his mind, too? "I am attracted to Char—Miss Spencer. I find her company delightful. I enjoy her intelligence and her humor, and I also find Morgan a wonderful little boy. He reminds me a great deal of my sister's young children." He absently removed a speck of lint from his suit pants. "Until we have an opportunity to become further acquainted, I can't speak of my future intentions, Mrs. Priddle. Perhaps one day I will want to marry her. On the other hand, I may find that we are completely unsuited to each other."

When she nodded her head, Mrs. Priddle's hat bobbled like a buoy in rough waters. "Good. An honest answer." She pointed her index finger in his direction. "Do not attempt to take advantage of Miss Spencer, or you will be required to answer to me—and to God, Mr. Clayborn."

The ominous tone of her voice set Matthew's teeth on edge. He hadn't entertained any improper thoughts regarding Charlotte, and Mrs. Priddle's stern warning annoyed him. Did the woman dislike all men or only him? He wondered if a Mr. Priddle had ever existed or if the woman had merely created the title. For a fleeting moment he considered asking but then decided the idea lacked wisdom.

When Charlotte descended the stairs, he stood and hurried to greet her. He was pleased to see her but even more thankful to escape Mrs. Priddle's unyielding appraisal.

"I trust you and Mrs. Priddle have had a nice chat?"

With Mrs. Priddle nearby, he knew he dared not exaggerate the truth. "We've had sufficient time for an informative conversation." He glanced toward the stairway. "Where is Morgan?"

"He'll be down with Fiona. They are like two peas in a pod. One can't go anywhere without the other, it seems. I don't know what he'll do when school resumes in the fall."

Mrs. Priddle thumped the floor with the tip of her parasol—three quick raps. This was apparently the signal for everyone to gather on the front porch, for soon the ladies clattered downstairs in rapid succession, with Fiona and Morgan bringing up the rear. They lined up two by two behind Mrs. Priddle, who led their procession to the church.

Matthew leaned to one side, his lips close to Charlotte's ear. "We look like a brood of chicks following a mother hen."

She giggled and nodded. "I think the very same thing every Sunday."

Morgan soon tired of walking alongside Fiona, so Matthew swooped him up. "Come on, big fellow. You can ride the rest of the way." Morgan insisted that Fiona remain nearby and Charlotte drew closer to make room for the girl. Matthew didn't think Mrs. Priddle would approve. But since they brought up the rear, he doubted the older woman could see them unless she had eyes in the back of her head. He relished Charlotte's propinquity.

Once inside the church, Mrs. Priddle stood at the end of the pew. Using her closed parasol as a baton, she directed the ladies into their assigned spaces. Matthew had intended to take the seat nearest the aisle, with Charlotte to his right, but Mrs. Priddle decided otherwise. She sat to his left with Charlotte to his right. Not a word could pass without a stern look.

At the end of the service, he was uncertain whether he or Morgan had fidgeted more. Mrs. Priddle's constant surveillance had brought out the worst in him. The moment they stepped outdoors, he hoped they could make an escape.

Unfortunately, Mrs. Priddle had other plans. "We will all return to Priddle House. Those of you with plans for this afternoon may then depart."

"Not what I had hoped for," Matthew whispered on the return.

Gracing him with a warm smile, Charlotte grasped his arm. "Mrs. Priddle has a penchant for regulation."

"I've noticed. I hope she doesn't add any further restrictions to our afternoon."

Once they arrived at Priddle House, Charlotte bid Matthew to have a seat in the parlor while she gathered a few necessary items for Morgan.

While he rolled a ball across the floor to Morgan, Mrs. Priddle arrived in the doorway. "I think I remembered everything. I even packed a small jar of my apple butter. You may retrieve the picnic basket from the kitchen before we leave, Mr. Clayborn."

We? Surely the woman had misspoken. He dared not question the remark; he didn't want to give her any idea that she would be welcome to join them. She returned down the hallway, and he sighed with relief. Obviously it had been a simple misunderstanding on his part.

Fiona bounded into the room and joined Matthew on the divan. "I wish we could go to Pullman. I'd like to see Mrs. DeVault and Olivia."

Matthew could see the longing in the girl's eyes. While he knew she understood the reasoning, it didn't erase her desire. "Once the trains are back on schedule, I promise we'll make a trip to Pullman. How's that?"

"What's this about going to Pullman?" There was an undeniable sternness in the older woman's voice. Matthew looked up to see Mrs. Priddle and Charlotte standing in the parlor doorway. "Attempting to take a train nowadays is hazardous and unreliable."

"Yes, I'm aware of that fact. I've been covering the strike for the Chicago *Herald*." He leaned forward, picked up Morgan, and settled the child on his lap. "I explained we wouldn't make the trip until after the strike and the trains were back on schedule."

"Well, I should think so." Mrs. Priddle's lips formed a tight knot. "The basket is waiting in the kitchen."

With Morgan in one arm, Matthew jumped to his feet. Charlotte reached for the boy, but Morgan immediately yelped in protest. "He'll be fine," Matthew said. Moments later he returned with the basket on one arm and Morgan resting on the other. "I believe we're ready."

"I think the park two blocks to the west would be our best choice," the older woman said.

Matthew snapped to attention at Mrs. Priddle's remark. "You plan to join us?"

"Of course. It's a lovely day. What else is an old woman supposed to do with her Sunday afternoon?"

Several suggestions came to mind, but Matthew didn't mention them. He didn't think Mrs. Priddle expected a response, and Charlotte appeared content with the arrangement. He wondered if she would ever permit him to escort her without a chaperone.

Fred rolled up his shirtsleeves and edged along the west wall of the empty auditorium. He silently longed for life to return to some semblance of normalcy. That he missed the daily routine he had taken for granted before the strike had begun surprised him. A year ago he had wanted nothing more than to break out of the mold of plodding to work each day with little hope for anything different. And now? After months of preparing to take their stand against George Pullman, he wondered if it would all be for naught. Days ago, news had filtered down that George Pullman and his family had secretly boarded an unmarked car attached to an eastbound train and departed for their retreat in Long Branch, New Jersey. Robert Todd Lincoln, son of the former president and a member of the Pullman Board of Directors, had been placed in charge. With Pullman's departure from the city, hope for a peaceful resolution diminished in Fred's mind.

He dropped to the floor, back against the wall, and bent his knees. Resting his arms across his knees, he cradled his head and hoped for a few minutes of sleep. The growing frenzy that seemed to be accomplishing little for the Pullman workers had become wearisome. Discouragement took hold of his thoughts, and he wanted only to sleep. Now there was little doubt that Attorney General Olney would have his way and federal troops would arrive in Chicago. Huge crowds of angry men had gathered at the Rock Island yard in Blue Island over the past several days, and the railroad had demanded protection. On Monday afternoon, the federal marshal of Chicago had attempted to disperse a mob of over two thousand men but failed.

Fred hadn't been present at Blue Island, but the results of that incident had been swift: a telegraph requesting the immediate dispatch of federal troops to the city of Chicago. Reactions to Attorney General Olney's request were mixed. The attorney general sat on the board of several affected railroads, and the union thought him tainted by such involvement. Mr. Olney denied his decisions were colored by his ties to the railroad, but along with union leadership, Fred had his doubts. The argument no longer mattered, for on this day of independence, July 4, 1894, a detachment from nearby Fort Sheridan would arrive to take control of the masses.

"What are you doing sleeping when the troops are arriving at the station?"

Fred lifted his head and looked at Matthew through blood-shot eyes. "They'll take control of the town whether I'm present or not."

Matthew nudged him with the toe of his shoe. "Come on, Fred. This isn't like you. Tired or not, this is history in the mak-ing. Nothing like this has ever happened in the United States."

"It shouldn't be happening now, either." The toll of weari-ness echoed in his words.

His friend grasped him beneath one arm and hoisted him upward. "That doesn't change anything. You'll regret it if you don't see it with your own eyes." He pulled Fred down the aisle. "How can you report to the men in Pullman if you sit here sleeping?"

With a hollow grunt, Fred followed behind Matthew, the crowds swelling as they neared the train station. "Has the gov-ernor made an appearance?"

"He sent a telegram to the president and said it was an unconstitutional impingement on states' rights, but Cleveland says the troops are necessary and proper." Matthew continued with a quick stride. "While you were back at Uhlich Hall sleep-ing, Debs issued a statement saying the president's action is yet another confirmation that the federal government has sold out to the capitalists."

"Any rebuttal to that?"

Matthew laughed. "Of course! There are those who assert that both the mayor and the governor are pandering to the locals in order to ensure reelection next term. They say neither of them is capable of restoring stability to our fair city."

As the troops marched through the well-manicured northern limits of the city, children of the well-to-do offered them flowers. But as soldiers continued pouring into the neighborhoods of the workingman and into the slums that surrounded the stockyards, they were greeted with a mixture of angry taunts and the odious stench permeating the area.

"I think President Cleveland is going to be disappointed with the results of his decision," Fred said, observing the anger spreading through the masses.

Instead of a joyous celebration of the holiday, angry chants and threats of violence filled the air.

"They ain't gonna tell us how to run our town!" a man shouted from the crowd.

"Send them soldiers back to Fort Sheridan where they belong!" another man demanded.

Matthew yanked Fred aside as a rotten tomato whizzed by his head.

"Thanks. I'd rather not spend the remainder of the day covered with tomato juice."

For the rest of the day, the two men milled about the city. Fred watched the unfolding scene in dismay while Matthew jotted notes for another column. Fireworks exploded amidst the intermittent clanging of fire wagons dispatched to extinguish the many fires throughout the city. Fred wiped the perspiration from his forehead and wished his prediction hadn't proven true.

Pullman, Illinois

Olivia settled on a blanket next to the bench that Mrs. DeVault and Chef René had chosen. It was one that provided the pair a good view of the bandstand in the park for the July Fourth celebration. With Fred in Chicago, Olivia had insisted the chef join Mrs. DeVault for the beginning of the band concert.

To the casual visitor, Olivia supposed the sight of residents sitting on blankets and benches would offer an appearance of normalcy. But since the outbreak of violence at Blue Island, tension had mounted within the town. The company men, who continued to wear the small American flags pinned to their lapels, now walked in pairs and armed with revolvers. Mr. Howard and other supervisors took turns inspecting the shops for possible intruders who could damage equipment or set fires, and the guards at the factory had been ordered to sleep on the premises.

Only yesterday Mr. Howard had requested that Chicago Mayor Hopkins send additional police reinforcements to Pullman. Much to the pleasure of the town's residents, the mayor had declined and issued a statement that there had been no incidents to warrant such action. Like the other Pullman citizens, Olivia considered the mayor's denial an affirmation of their civility and had celebrated the news as a small victory.

But when word arrived that federal troops had been scattered throughout Chicago only hours earlier, the celebratory mood of the residents waned. Members of the band continued to play their patriotic marches, but a pall of despair now shrouded the park.

The holiday didn't ease the shortage of food or the daily difficulties faced by the families, and with too much time on their hands, many of the men disappeared to the saloons in Kensington. "The holiday celebration isn't the same this year," Mrs. DeVault remarked.

"At least the children can play their games, non? Even now, they are filled with laughter and are creating special memories."

"I suppose that's true. Laughter is good medicine for the soul."

Olivia watched the older couple with a pang of envy. They appeared oblivious to her presence as they spoke in soft words and gazed into each other's eyes. How she wished Fred would return. Her fear had swelled since hearing of the federal troops' arrival in Chicago. With the troops and hundreds of armed security guards hired by the General Managers Association now present, she wondered how long it would be before someone would suffer serious injury. Though the evening was warm, the idea of armed men patrolling the streets of Chicago caused a chill. She feared Fred might be in danger if the strike didn't soon end, yet she understood the need for the union members to remain strong.

An overhead explosion startled her, and Mrs. DeVault leaned over to pat her arm. "You're as excited as the children, aren't you?"

Olivia forced a smile. If someone stepped into town at this very moment and observed the celebratory scene, they would think all was well with the citizens of Pullman. For a short time the turmoil was masked and life placed on hold by the sounds of music and the explosion of fireworks. Independence Day! Olivia wondered if next year the residents of Pullman would look back upon this day with a sense of accomplishment or a sense of defeat.

CHAPTER EIGHTEEN

Chicago, Illinois
July 6, 1894

Strong fingers squeezed Fred's shoulder. He swiveled on his chair and glanced up. "Sit down, Matthew."

After signaling the owner of the Good Eats Café to bring him coffee, Matthew slapped his notebook on the table and dropped onto the chair. "One of the private security guards hired by the General Managers Association tells me they're being paid $2.50 a day. Quite a wage, huh?"

Anger quickened Fred's heartbeat. "That's much more than the railroad pays its laborers. How is it they can find the money to pay men to tote weapons but they can't pay their own workers a livable wage? Who are these men, anyway?"

"Most I talked to are drifters who arrived for the World's Fair and stuck around after the fair ended. I don't think there's a genuine lawman among them. Half of them probably don't even know how to load those guns the association has furnished them." He jabbed Fred in the side. "Maybe I should write a column about them and hope it detracts from last night's mayhem."

Fred slumped in his chair. He had planned to return home this morning, but the events of the previous night made him believe he should reconsider. Thousands had gathered at the union rail yards, many of them petty criminals and hooligans who had no involvement with the railroad or the strike. From all reports, when the soldiers and police became overwhelmed by the size of the crowd, they retreated and never returned to the rail yard.

The mob of vagabonds had succeeded in destroying railroad property valued at over three hundred thousand dollars, and then they'd set fire to buildings in Jackson Park that had been constructed to exhibit the world's latest inventions and wonders during the Chicago World's Fair.

"None of this bodes well for the workers, Fred. Even though a few newspaper reports say the workers weren't involved, the general public thinks otherwise. It makes the strikers appear to be rabble-rousers intent upon destroying the city."

Fred shrugged. "There's little I can do about it. No matter who is at fault, blame will be placed upon the union and the workers. The public has been swayed by slanted news reports and the inconvenience that the strike has inflicted on them." He took a sip of coffee. "It's clear that the arrival of the troops will thwart the boycott—even Mr. Debs has said so. He once again asked Mr. Pullman to arbitrate with the employees, promising to end the boycott in return, but to no avail."

Matthew nodded. "I'm not surprised. Now what?"

Fred pushed away from the table, his decision now firm in his mind. "I'm going to go home for a few days. Mr. Debs has called for a meeting on Sunday night at Uhlich Hall. He's appealing to all organized labor to attend. Until then, I want to return home and see Olivia."

At the moment Fred wanted nothing more than to escape the city now dotted with hundreds of canvas military tents. The area surrounding the Illinois Central rail yard near downtown Chicago had taken on the appearance of a sprawling circus, albeit a tent city with performers carrying loaded rifles.

Pullman, Illinois

Olivia stood in the kitchen doorway and peered outside. The sun blinded her and she squinted, uncertain she could trust her eyes. Was that Fred sitting under the oak tree? She pushed open the screen door and cupped her hand across her forehead. It *was* Fred. Without a word to Chef René, she raced pell-mell across the short distance. He had barely made it to his feet when she raced into his arms. "Why didn't you tell me you were home?"

He didn't answer. Instead, he tightened his embrace, lowered his head, and kissed her soundly. "I've missed you so much." Without giving her time to respond, he again pulled her close and permitted his lips to linger over hers.

She allowed herself the luxury of his embrace for a few moments longer before she gently pushed against his chest. "What will people think?" She glanced over her shoulder. "I'll be considered quite the little tart, don't you think?"

"Is that how you English refer to a woman of questionable conduct? A tart?" He hugged her close. "I rather like tarts— especially the ones you bake," he joked, continuing to hold her in his arms.

She lightly slapped his chest and feigned indignation. "Chef René will probably come looking for me at any moment. I was so excited to see you, I didn't tell him I was going outdoors."

"Let him come looking. I doubt he'll blame me for wanting to spend a few minutes with the woman I love after being in harm's way for the past several days."

She clutched his hand. "The reports we've been hearing have frightened me out of my wits. I don't know what is true and what has been exaggerated. And the newspapers aren't reliable. They seem to contradict each other with every printing."

"In the midst of the turmoil, determining what is true has become nearly impossible. Lies and deceit surround us on every side. The president has succumbed to the wishes of management, claiming the union and the Pullman strikers have formed an illegal trust. The government has joined hands with the capitalists to overthrow our efforts to gain livable wages for the workingman."

Olivia tightened her hold. "You've given in to defeat, then?"

"I don't want to talk of the strike. I want to speak of something pleasant—like us. I want to spend the evening with you, if you don't have other plans."

She chuckled. "And if I did have another engagement, would you not expect me to put it aside for you?"

"I would like to think you would do so, but I would never attempt to force such a headstrong girl as you!" He laughed and kissed her cheek.

"First you think me a tart and now I'm headstrong?"

"I may have called you headstrong, but you're the one who mentioned tarts," he rebutted.

"Miss Mott!" Chef René's voice bellowed across the open expanse.

Olivia took several backward steps. She waved and smiled brightly. "Coming." She grabbed Fred's hand and pulled him along. "Come with me and say hello. I'm certain he won't mind if you go downstairs and greet your mother."

"They are still seeing each other?"

Olivia nodded. "He seems to make your mother very happy."

"And *you* make *me* very happy," he said with a broad smile.

Chef René reached forward to shake Fred's hand. "Fred! It is good to see you have returned. I was worried our Miss Mott was hugging some strange fellow out in the garden. I am pleased to see it is you." His exaggerated wink was accompanied by a grin. "Your mother will be pleased you have come home. With all the reports of violence, she has been worried for your safety."

"I am a grown man, able to attend to my well-being, but it's always good to know I have two women here at home concerned for my welfare."

"You are indeed fortunate. A woman's love is a precious gift." The chef's words were shaded by an undeniable sincerity. All signs of his earlier joviality had disappeared when he suggested Fred go downstairs and greet his mother. "She will, no doubt, be reduced to tears when she sees you have returned to her, safe and sound."

Fred tilted his head to the side. "I've been only twelve miles to the north. The two of you make it sound as though I've been off fighting a war in some distant country."

Chef René gave his jacket sleeve a push toward his elbow. "Yet that's exactly how it seems when we read the newspapers."

Fred gave a quick flip of his hand. "You can't believe everything you read, especially in the newspapers. The majority of men involved in the mayhem aren't union members. Most are vagabonds and hooligans who enjoy brawling and have used our cause as an excuse to create chaos." He glanced toward the steps leading to the lower kitchen.

"My apologies. I am keeping you from your mother, and I have work that must be completed." Chef René immediately turned around and issued several commands to the kitchen boys, who had decided the chef's involvement was an excuse for them to relax. "Like little children you are! The minute I turn my back, you want to play. There are many who would like to have a job in my kitchen." His terse warning sent the youngsters running back to their duties.

Olivia watched Fred cross the kitchen and disappear down the stairs. She patted the chef's arm. "That was very kind of you. I know Mrs. DeVault will be surprised—and pleased."

He glanced over his shoulder and then came close to Olivia's side. "Do you think your Fred approves of me?"

Even though she had great difficulty suppressing a smile, Olivia forced herself to remain solemn. "In what capacity? As my supervisor?"

"Non! I am asking if he has said anything about me with regard to his mother." He emitted an exasperated sigh. "Does he object?"

"I don't know that I should speak for Fred. If you want his opinion, perhaps you should ask him."

"Come, Miss Mott. You can surely give me some inkling."

"I think he has been rather surprised by . . . um . . . the situation. Naturally, he doesn't want his mother to be hurt in any way."

He slapped his palm to his forehead. "He thinks I would do her harm? What kind of man does he think I am?"

Olivia touched her hand to her heart. "Not physical harm.

He worries you may break her heart."

"Oui! He characterizes me as a cad—isn't that the word the Americans use?"

Olivia giggled. "I believe that may be one of them, but you forget, I am English. Perhaps you should ask one of the kitchen boys."

He tightened his lips and gave her a disgusted scowl. "I do not speak of my personal life to the kitchen boys. You know better. And I am not a man who toys with a woman's emotions. I care very much for Hazel, but I don't want to create difficulty between a mother and her son."

"Have you discussed this with her?"

"Oui. She says she is an adult and does not need her son's agreement. Another reason I am concerned your Fred has expressed his disapproval of me."

Olivia motioned him to join her on the other side of the kitchen away from two young dishwashers, who were obviously eavesdropping. She didn't want to mention the discomfort she'd witnessed in Fred's eyes when the two of them had discussed his mother and Chef René shortly after Mrs. DeVault had taken her position at the hotel. Fred had been less than receptive when Olivia had joked about the older couple being suited to each other.

"Unless you have some plan to ask Mrs. DeVault to marry you right away, I don't think you should overly concern yourself with Fred's opinion. With all the tension of the strike and his duties as a delegate to the convention, Fred hasn't been himself."

"So he doesn't approve?"

"I didn't say that." She took a backward step and studied

him. "You aren't planning a wedding in the near future, are you?"

An uncomfortable and prolonged silence pervaded the room. The sparkle in his eyes was now gone. "Non. You may tell your Fred he need not worry. There will be no wedding."

Olivia arched her brows. The chef had misinterpreted her comments. She'd simply wanted him to understand he should proceed slowly before proposing to Mrs. DeVault. There was no doubt Fred would need time to accept the idea of his mother's remarriage. Before she could question him further, shouts erupted in the distance.

The chef signaled one of the kitchen boys. "Go see who's causing all that commotion." The boy scurried outdoors and then returned moments later when the shouting continued to escalate.

"There's about two hundred men trying to force their way into the shop grounds. The watchmen got their riot guns aimed at 'em."

Fred rounded the corner at the top of the stairs. "Any shots fired?"

Wide-eyed, the boy shook his head. "Nope. But the men said they was coming back later and they was gonna burn all them palace cars out in the yard northeast of the factory buildings."

Fred crossed the kitchen and headed toward the door. "I'm going to find out who they are and see if I can talk some sense into them."

Olivia stepped in front of him. "Please don't go out there, Fred. If those men are intent on doing someone harm, you're the one who will be the object of their anger."

Fred motioned to the kitchen boy. "Did you recognize any of them?"

The youngster shrugged. "A few of them, I think, but there's lots of folks who live in Pullman that I don't know."

Taking hold of her shoulders, Fred gently moved Olivia to the side. "I'll be fine. I promise to return once I've talked to them."

The throng of men had turned and were obviously leaving town. Probably going to Kensington, Fred guessed. He recognized Micah Wilson, one of the men who worked in the carpenter shop. After shouting his name, Fred loped toward the crowd, heading directly toward Micah.

Joining the group, Fred matched Micah's stride. "What's going on?"

"We was just trying to put a scare in 'em," he said.

The smell of liquor lingered in the air, and Fred wondered if the men had spent the early part of the afternoon at a saloon in Kensington. "We made a pledge that we wouldn't turn violent. You men remember that, don't you?" Fred raised his voice above the crowd.

"We need some action out of the company. We can't go on like this all summer," one of the men shouted.

"Spending the little money you've got on liquor and threatening the guards at the factory isn't going to bring the results you want. Why don't you all go back home before you regret your actions."

The men briefly discussed his suggestion, but in the end only a few broke away from the crowd. The majority, mostly men he'd never seen before, continued walking toward Kensington. Fred stopped when they crossed the boulevard and then turned back toward the hotel. He'd had little influence, but since they'd done no damage at the car works, Fred hoped their angry behavior would be overlooked by management.

Olivia met Fred outside the kitchen upon his return and told him that Mr. Billings, the hotel manager, had rushed to the car works once the crowd dispersed. When he returned to the hotel, he'd been delighted to report that Mr. Howard had wired a demand for troops and deputies to the governor and the United States marshal in Chicago.

"What? Without even waiting to ascertain the details?" Fred slapped his hat against his leg, his anger rising. "What else did he say?"

"It seems Mr. Howard's clerk, Mr. Mahafferty, panicked when he saw the mob gathering. He locked the company books in the office vault and phoned Mr. Howard, telling him an invasion was taking place."

"Does the man not realize what those exaggerated claims can do? You'd think any intelligent man would use a bit of common sense before making such outrageous statements. An invasion! They didn't even breach the gates."

He could only hope the governor would deny Mr. Howard's request.

CHAPTER NINETEEN

Chicago, Illinois

Matthew watched the smile fade from Charlotte's face as he approached Priddle House the following Sunday. He had attempted to force a cheery look, but apparently his effort had failed.

"Whatever has happened? You appear distraught." She opened the screen door and bid him come inside.

"I'm afraid I'm going to have to cancel our plans for this afternoon unless you're willing to accompany me to Pullman." Morgan toddled toward him, and Matthew lifted the boy into his arms. "Problem is, I don't know if it would be safe to take Morgan along."

Charlotte frowned and motioned him toward the parlor, where Mrs. Priddle had already taken up her post to make certain they wouldn't be late for church services.

"What's this? More trouble brewing?"

Taking a seat opposite Mrs. Priddle, Matthew situated Morgan on his lap. "I'm beginning to wonder if there's going to be any end to all of this. A number of riots have occurred at rail yards throughout the city, and I must travel to Pullman to see Fred. A man Fred is acquainted with was shot last night. I doubt he's aware of the situation."

"A man was shot in one of the protests?" Charlotte clapped a hand to her mouth. "How awful!"

"Unfortunately, several men were shot. The soldiers shot into the crowd, and I understand that innocent bystanders were injured—Fred's acquaintance among them."

"If the shootings occurred in Chicago and you're traveling to Pullman, why are you concerned for Morgan's safety, Mr. Clayborn?"

Mrs. Priddle pursed her lips and folded her hands in her lap while she awaited Matthew's answer. She reminded him of a tutor quizzing a student.

"I simply can't vouch for the safety at the railroad station or in Pullman. I wouldn't want to place a child in harm's way."

"Or a woman?" Mrs. Priddle asked with an appraising look.

"I believe Matthew is merely exercising caution where Morgan is concerned, Mrs. Priddle. However, if you think I should remain at home, I'll bow to your wishes."

The remark appeared to satisfy the woman; she shook her head. "When church services have concluded, you go and make certain your friends in Pullman are faring well. Fiona and I will attend to Morgan."

Once they'd formed their line and were headed toward the church, Matthew leaned close to Charlotte. "Mrs. Priddle makes your decisions for you?"

"Not all of them. However, I do seek her counsel frequently. I find her to be a very wise woman. Does that bother you?"

"No. I was merely surprised. I think of you as being independent, so the notion that you would so quickly submit to someone else's advice surprised me."

"I think of myself as independent, too. But I've learned from past experience that accepting good advice is one way to help avoid tragic consequences."

Matthew grinned. "A lesson we could all take to heart."

The minister had apparently heard of the tragedies that had taken place the previous evening, for he preached about the need for healing and forgiveness. His parting remark was a request for his congregants to do their part in bringing an end to the violence that persisted within the city. Matthew thought the words well-meaning, but he wasn't certain how the members of the small church could help end the mayhem that had spread throughout the city like a deadly disease.

When he said as much to Mrs. Priddle on their return home, she pointed her parasol toward heaven. "We can pray, Mr. Clayborn!"

Charlotte tightened her grasp on Matthew's arm. "You see? She *is* very wise."

Matthew ruffled Morgan's hair. "Take note of how it is, young fellow. To get along well in this world, you must agree with whatever the women in your life say."

Charlotte playfully slapped his arm. "That is not true and you know it! You agree because you know the women are correct." She tipped her head and giggled.

Matthew's heartbeat quickened at the sound of her laughter. To him, Charlotte Spencer was the loveliest creature God had ever created. And her son—well, he thought young Morgan simply delightful. The introspection surprised him. Though he'd spent many hours thinking about Charlotte and Morgan since he'd first met them, he'd never before considered the possibility that he might be falling in love with this enchanting woman and her child. He had thought her stunning from the first time he'd seen her, but he had considered winning her affections a daunting challenge. Only now did he accept the fact that she had won his heart.

———

The arrival and departure of trains on a somewhat regular schedule had been the one positive outcome since the arrival of the federal troops in Chicago. And the bustling train station was proof enough that many were taking full advantage of the partially reinstated schedule. Charlotte waited patiently while Matthew purchased their tickets. He had stepped away from the counter to rejoin her when she felt a tap on her shoulder.

"How pleasant to see you, Miss Spencer."

Charlotte turned and came face-to-face with Herman Rehnquist, the offensive supervisor of the fabric and lace section at Marshall Field's. Her smile faded at the sight of him. He'd proved to be a constant annoyance. Each day he made an excuse to visit her office for some nonsensical reason. When she had consistently refused his invitations to dinner or the theater, he'd made no attempt to hide his irritation. With each rejection, his dark eyes flashed with increasing anger. She was thankful when Matthew returned to her side.

Charlotte clung to Matthew's arm like a lifeline. "Has the train arrived?" She hoped he would hear the urgency in her voice and rush her out of the train station and away from Mr. Rehnquist.

"No. We have twenty minutes or so." He settled his gaze on Mr. Rehnquist and extended his hand. "I'm Matthew Clayborn. I don't believe we've met, have we?"

Charlotte wilted. "I apologize. This is Mr. Rehnquist. He's an employee of the store."

Mr. Rehnquist shot a look of annoyance in Charlotte's direction before he grasped Matthew's hand. "Herman Rehnquist, supervisor of the Lace and Fabric Department at Marshall Field and Company." With an air of pomposity, he extracted a calling card from his pocket and handed it to Matthew.

Charlotte squeezed Matthew's arm with a ferocity that immediately captured his attention. "I believe we need to make some other arrangements before our departure, don't we?" The gentleness of her tone was in direct opposition to her viselike grip, and he stared at her as though she'd lost her mind.

"Yes. If you'll excuse us, Mr. Rehnquist. Pleased to make your acquaintance." Matthew took a backward step, and Mr. Rehnquist touched the brim of his hat in a farewell gesture.

When they'd reached the platform outside the train station, Matthew arched his brows. "What was *that* all about?"

Charlotte quickly detailed Mr. Rehnquist's unwelcome advances. "I've done my best to discourage him, but it's done no good."

Matthew's chest swelled. "Now that he's met me, perhaps he'll stop his advances."

Charlotte wanted to believe that was true, but she didn't think a brief meeting in the train depot would deter Herman Rehnquist. The man simply did not take no for an answer. With a glance over her shoulder as she boarded the train, Charlotte spied Mr. Rehnquist standing on the platform watching after them. One look into his dark, beady eyes and a chill coursed down her spine.

By the time they arrived in Pullman, all thoughts of Mr.

Rehnquist had fled her mind. From the windows of the train, they could see pointed tops and concave drapings of white canvas amidst the thick foliage of the tree-lined streets. They stepped from the train station and Matthew pointed toward the hotel. "Troops have camped on the grounds of the hotel."

Drawing nearer, Charlotte could barely believe her eyes. White military tents like those she'd observed in Chicago now dotted the hotel lawn, and uniformed men were all about. "It appears the military has taken command here in Pullman, also, doesn't it?"

"Yes. And I doubt that's sitting well with the residents of Pullman," Matthew said as the two of them continued onward.

When they walked up the steps of the DeVault row house, Charlotte was pleased to see the front door standing open. She could hear the sound of voices drifting from inside, specifically Olivia's. After seeing the troop encampment, she had wondered if Olivia would be at the hotel. Matthew knocked on the door, and Fred soon greeted them from the hallway.

Dark circles rimmed Fred's eyes, and Charlotte immediately detected a clipped tension in his voice. The strain of the strike had obviously taken a toll on him. Even Mrs. DeVault's normal joviality was absent when she offered them a cup of tea. Charlotte didn't fail to note a look of gloom in the older woman's eyes when the Quinters excused themselves to go outdoors with the children.

Once the Quinters had left, the five of them settled in the parlor. "Where is young Morgan?" Mrs. DeVault inquired.

Charlotte glanced at Matthew, who took her cue. "I was concerned for his safety. There were some disturbing incidents that occurred in Chicago late yesterday afternoon, and I thought it best if he didn't accompany us." Matthew waved in the direction of the hotel. "I didn't stop at the newspaper office before church this morning, so I didn't realize troops were encamped here."

Fred quickly explained the action that had precipitated Mr. Howard's plea for troops. "There was no need, but federal intervention helps bolster the company's position. What happened in Chicago?" Fred leaned forward and rested his forearms atop his thighs. "I was planning to return for tonight's meeting at Uhlich Hall. Has it been called off?"

"Not to my knowledge, but what with the riots that took place yesterday, who can say? As to what happened—I'm guessing hunger and frustration. Residents from throughout the city descended on various railroad yards and broke open doors of freight cars carrying food. They attempted to carry off sacks of potatoes and huge cuts of meat. From what I'm told, fights broke out, boxcars were overturned, fires were set, and shots were fired."

Mrs. DeVault appeared to bow her head in prayer.

"Any railway union members injured?" Fred asked.

Matthew shook his head. "No. From all reports, they continue to heed Mr. Debs's warnings and stay away, but there were people killed and many injured." He looked into Fred's eyes and choked out the bad news. "Your friend Bill Orland was shot."

Fred jumped up and sent his chair teetering on two legs. "*Bill?* He wasn't involved in the strike. He and his family were getting by quite nicely on his income from the etching business. There would be no reason for him to become caught up in an attempt to steal food. You must be mistaken."

Matthew shook his head. "I wish I were, but his wife is the one who asked that I come and tell you. I told her you'd likely be returning this evening, but she feared with all the rioting, you might decide to remain in Pullman."

Although it didn't appear Fred was listening to him, Matthew explained that he'd seen Bill's name on the notes of a fellow reporter who'd been covering the incident in which Bill had been injured. "I recalled you'd stayed with them on occasion since the strike began."

Fred buried his face in his hands and shook his head. "I can't believe this."

"His wife said he'd been asked to come to the Smithton Law Office across town. Someone had recommended Bill's work, and Mr. Smithton asked if Bill could come to his office with some etchings he'd drawn up. Smithton wanted his wife to take a look at them, too. Seems his route to the law office took him directly into the path of danger."

"What a tragedy. Poor Bill was simply in the wrong place at the wrong time," Mrs. DeVault said.

"How serious is the injury?" Olivia asked.

"The doctor stopped by to talk with Ruth. He told her Bill may recover if infection doesn't set in. She didn't appear hopeful. With all the commotion and so many injured in the different skirmishes throughout the city, Mrs. Orland indicated a good deal of time lapsed before Bill finally received medical treatment." Matthew sighed. "Doesn't appear things are much better here in Pullman."

Fred paced in front of the fireplace. "At least nobody's been shot here. But having the troops set up camp on the hotel lawn hasn't set well with the workers."

Matthew understood the strategy of the military commander's choice. The hotel was situated only a short distance from the main entrance of the car works and provided an excellent vantage point. The surrounding lawns permitted adequate space for the tents, and the hotel afforded his men several benefits.

"So that's why Chef René isn't present today. He's helping prepare meals for the soldiers," Charlotte said.

Fred ceased pacing and turned toward his mother. "He's cooking for those men?"

"You need not adopt that disdainful tone with me, Fred." Mrs. DeVault sent a warning look in her son's direction. "I have no idea where René is. I thought he would be at church this morning, but he didn't appear. If he's been ordered to prepare food for the soldiers, I'm certain he will follow instructions. And so will I," she added. "I assume Olivia will do the same."

Olivia nodded her agreement.

"As far as I'm concerned," she continued, "it makes little difference whether we're preparing food for Mr. Pullman and his board of directors, for those soldiers, or for hotel guests. We are paid to perform our assigned duties."

Fred circled around the divan and sat down. "I suppose you're correct, but somehow it seems wrong to prepare food for the enemy."

"Don't forget that we help feed some of the starving people of this town with food from that kitchen," his mother replied. "If it weren't for the leftovers that pass through that door, there would be more hungry children."

"I didn't mean to cause dissension. I merely expected to see Chef René. I was going to tell him about a new recipe being served at the tearoom," Charlotte said.

"I'm the one who's at fault." After making an apology to Charlotte and his mother, Fred turned to Matthew. "Is Bill at home? I should go and see him."

"They took him to Mercy Hospital. If his condition is as bad as Mrs. Orland indicated, I have my doubts whether he's gone home," Matthew said.

"If I return to the city early, I'll have time to stop by the hospital before the meeting at Uhlich Hall. I'd also like to see Mrs. Orland if time permits. As I recall, she doesn't have any family in Illinois." Fred looked at Matthew. "Were you planning to take the three-o'clock train?"

Olivia frowned. "Three o'clock? Surely you needn't leave so early," she told Fred. "I agree you should go see Bill and his wife, but I've barely seen you of late. Can't Mr. Heathcoate handle matters for the union without you?"

As Matthew understood it, tonight's gathering wasn't a meeting where a vote would be required by the membership of the American Railway Union, so he didn't think Fred's presence was an absolute necessity. But he didn't offer an opinion. Charlotte's earlier comment had nearly caused a rift, and he didn't want to cause further disagreement.

"I'm certain Mr. Heathcoate doesn't need me, but the men elected me as their delegate. I feel I should give my best effort on their behalf."

Olivia didn't argue with Fred's reply, but Matthew now wished he had spoken to Fred in private. The entire issue should have been handled with greater diplomacy, and Matthew silently chided himself. He took heart when Olivia and Charlotte excused themselves for a private visit a short time later and hoped their time together would raise Olivia's spirits.

Once the two men were alone, Fred motioned Matthew to join him outside. "I can't tell you the despair I'm feeling right now. Do you realize that Bill would be safe and sound had I not encouraged his move to Chicago?"

Matthew couldn't believe what he was hearing. "Surely

you're not going to hold yourself responsible for Bill's injury. That makes no sense. What if you'd failed to tell him about the opportunity and he was somehow injured here in Pullman? Would that be your fault because you hadn't insisted he move to Chicago? I can't believe you're placing blame upon yourself."

The two men continued their discussion. By the time they departed for Chicago, Matthew had, at least for the most part, convinced Fred that his guilt was misplaced. He hoped Fred would continue to believe that once he visited with Mrs. Orland.

CHAPTER TWENTY

Later that day Fred slowly ascended the stairs leading to the apartment over Lockabee's Design and Glass Etching Shop, each step more difficult than the last. He felt as though heavy weights had been attached to his shoes, yet he continued upward.

The apartment door swung open before he had an opportunity to knock, and Ruth Orland greeted him with a weary smile. "I'm so pleased you've come. I worried the newspaper reporter might not deliver my message and you wouldn't know what had happened to Bill."

She motioned him toward a chair in the large room that served as a parlor by day and a sleeping area for the children by night. Ruth instructed the oldest child to take the other two into the kitchen. "They don't quite understand what's happened to their father." She bowed her head. "I haven't been to the hospital yet. I'm afraid to leave them alone, and after what happened to Bill, I'm afraid to take them out with me. I don't want . . ."

Ruth's words trailed off in choked emotion, but Fred knew what the woman feared. She didn't want to risk the possibility of harm to her children. "Do you want me to remain here with them while you go to the hospital?" He would be late for the meeting, but it was the least he could do.

"The children would be frightened if I left, but I wondered if you would stop by the hospital and then let me know how he's progressing. If he's doing better, you could tell the doctor I can care for him here at home." She glanced toward the door. "You should tell the doctor that Bill will have to be able to climb a flight of stairs."

Fred scooted forward and pushed to his feet. "I need to make a quick stop at Uhlich Hall first, and then I'll head over to the hospital. I'll try to get back here before nightfall, but if I haven't arrived by then, you go on to bed. I'll be staying with Matthew Clayborn. I can stop over here in the morning if necessary."

She walked him to the door and grasped his arm before he departed. "It doesn't matter how late it is; I'll wait up. I need to know how Bill's doing."

"I understand. And don't worry about the business, Ruth. I'll come back and help with the work orders."

"You tell Bill I love him and that I'm praying." A tear appeared in the corner of her eye, and she quickly released Fred's arm and turned away.

His footsteps echoed a series of hollow thunks on the wooden steps as he descended to the street below. The sadness he'd seen in Mrs. Orland's eyes haunted him long after he'd departed. After stopping for a brief conversation with Mr. Heathcoate, he headed for the hospital. He would have preferred to ride the trolley but, after weighing his options, decided to walk instead. Tonight he'd be glad to have the money for a sandwich and a cup of coffee.

Besides, Mr. Heathcoate had assured him his presence at the meeting wasn't a necessity. The men casting the votes would be the officers of nearly a hundred trade unions who would decide if they would join with the American Railway Union in support of the strike. With yet another refusal to arbitrate having been delivered from the Pullman management, the railway union needed the added momentum the other unions could add to their cause.

After walking several blocks, Fred passed a small eatery with a Closed sign prominently displayed across the front door. He wondered if his mother had gone to assist Chef René in the hotel kitchen after his departure. Would the hotel staff be expected to cook for the troops while they remained in Pullman? Surely not. The military had cooks who accompanied them and were responsible for food preparation. After all, soldiers would rarely be able to camp near a hotel or restaurant. But if Mr. Pullman thought it would gain him an advantage, the soldiers would no doubt have their meals catered. Fred could see it now: cloth-draped tables dotting the hotel veranda and lawns. Soldiers in uniform sitting at flower-bedecked tables and eating from fine Pullman china while Olivia and his mother scurried back and forth with tureens and platters of delectable food for the invaders.

Climbing the hospital steps, Fred pushed thoughts of the hotel from his mind. After securing directions to Bill's ward, he ambled down the long corridor, up two flights of steps, and down another hallway. Stenciled numbers on the walls outside each ward led him to 3-B, where he offered a silent prayer before entering. He wasn't good with sick people—never had been. His mother seemed to know exactly how to act and what to say, but Fred fumbled for words. Attempts to squelch his discomfort had always proved futile, and he doubted he'd do any better today.

He forced himself into the room and quickly scanned each bed until he caught sight of Bill. His friend's bed was in the far west corner, which would require walking past rows of ailing men. Fortunately, they didn't pay him much heed.

Fred did his best to appear nonchalant when he came alongside Bill's bed, but he gulped for air when he saw his friend's bandaged hand and arm. "I was told you'd been shot. No one mentioned your . . . your . . ."

"The gunshot was the least of my problems. I lost some blood, but the bullet merely grazed me."

"Then how . . . ?" Fred motioned to Bill's arm.

"When the shot hit me, I fell to the ground beside a wagon. In all the noise and chaos, the horse bolted, and my arm got caught in the wheel spokes. The doctor seems to think I'm lucky to be alive. I told him not to tell Ruth about the arm. No need to worry her."

The doctor entered the room, and once he arrived at Bill's bedside, he began to remove the bandage. A sense of light-headedness nearly overcame Fred, and he turned away. He didn't want to faint and end up in one of the hospital beds. When the doctor had completed his ministrations, he glanced over his shoulder.

"You a member of the family?"

Fred shook his head. "Friend." He didn't look toward the bed.

"I didn't tell Mrs. Orland the seriousness of her husband's injuries when I stopped by the house to speak with her. She thinks he's suffering from the gunshot wound, which, as you can see, is the least of his injuries."

Fred turned his back toward Bill and faced the doctor. "Bill's a craftsman, an artist who designs and creates beautiful etchings. Has he told you that?"

The doctor's features tightened for a moment. "He has. And I've told him that unless he can figure out how to work with his left hand, I think he'll need to find a new trade." When he spoke, the doctor made no attempt to lower his voice. Bill had listened to every word without comment.

"Mrs. Orland asked when she could hope for her husband to return home. She says she's a capable nurse if you'll give her proper instructions."

The doctor offered a sad smile. "I'm certain she'd do her best, but Bill needs to be in the hospital for the time being. We're going to have to see how that arm does. I've got to keep watch for the possibility of—"

"Infection?" Fred arched his brows.

"Gangrene." This time the doctor spoke in a muffled tone. "You can tell Mrs. Orland that her husband will be in the hospital at least another five days and that I'm pleased with his progress." The doctor leaned to one side and looked at Bill. "Does that message meet with your approval, Mr. Orland?"

Bill agreed, and after a promise to see him tomorrow, the doctor moved to his next patient. Fred clasped his hands behind his back and rocked on his heels. "I'll do my best to keep the shop operational during your absence, Bill. I know it won't be the same as having you there, but it's the least I can do."

"Probably would be best if you didn't accept any additional orders until I know what's going to happen with my arm. I know the doctor fears gangrene. He doesn't want to tell me, but I can see it written all over his face. Even if he saves the arm, I'm never going to draw again or manage to operate the business." He settled his head into the pillow and stared overhead. "I need to accept what's happened and prepare for change."

"I don't think you need to make any decisions right this minute. There's always room for one more miracle, don't you think?"

"Right. You have your mother pray for a miracle. In the meantime, I'll try to figure out how I'm going to operate a design and etching business as a one-armed man." Bill's attempt to remain casual failed.

The anger in Bill's words faded into a fear that settled in his eyes. They both knew that nothing short of a miracle was going to restore him to the man he'd been late yesterday afternoon. Certainly nothing Fred could say was going to ease the situation. He wanted to escape from the room and pretend this had never happened.

"Anything I can do or bring to you?"

Bill shook his head. "It's okay for you to go. Tell Ruth not to come down here. I'd rather she stay at home with the children. Besides, there's nothing she can do for me and she's needed at home." He stared out the window. "I appreciate your offer to help out, Fred. It means a lot. You take whatever you need from the business to cover your own expenses. I don't want you working for free, understand?"

Fred didn't argue. It would only prolong his need to remain within the confines of the hospital. He didn't want to appear anxious to leave, but every fiber of his being longed to race for the doorway and inhale a deep breath of fresh air.

"I'll do my best to stop by tomorrow, but with helping at the business and acting as a delegate for the union . . ." His words trailed off as he continued to take backward steps toward the door.

"I understand you have your own obligations. And your help at the business is more important than having you spend time in this hospital." Bill gave a nod, and Fred took it as a signal that he'd been released.

He raced down the street, partly to free his mind from thoughts of Bill's ravaged arm and partly because he wanted to hear the outcome of the union meeting. Unless the discussion went longer than anticipated, the vote would already have been taken. But some of the men would stay afterward to discuss the outcome.

When he rounded the corner, Matthew was standing on the front steps and waved Fred onward. "You missed the vote. Delegates for the trade unions have agreed their membership will join the strike, but rumors already abound that many members won't actually participate." Matthew tucked his notebook into the pocket of his suit jacket. "You need a place to stay tonight?"

"I have to go over and tell Mrs. Orland about Bill's condition. Why don't you walk along with me?" Fred could use the support of another person when he talked to Mrs. Orland. He'd promised Bill that he wouldn't mention his arm. When Ruth finally discovered the full extent of her husband's injuries, she'd likely never forgive him for hiding the truth. But he'd given his word. For now, he hoped Bill's wife wouldn't ask too many questions.

Having Matthew along when he arrived at the Orlands' apartment proved to be a benefit. His presence subdued Ruth's queries, and after she had heard Fred's limited report, she agreed a check of the work invoices was in order. After unlocking the door to the shop, she made a hasty retreat back upstairs with a request that Fred lock the door on leaving. When they finished going through the papers and Fred had placed the most urgent items on top of the stack, the men departed.

"I suppose the time will pass more quickly if I spend a portion of my days here at the shop working. At times I feel I should be in Pullman, especially now that the militia has arrived."

"Once we see what happens with the other unions, I think you'll know where your time and effort will be best utilized. If the trade union members desert the cause, most of us believe the strike will collapse," Matthew said.

Fred didn't comment. He didn't want to think all of this had been in vain. He refused to entertain the idea of defeat—at least for now.

———

Pullman, Illinois

On Monday morning, as Olivia wended her way to the kitchen door, she surveyed the white tents that dotted the hotel lawn. Entering the kitchen, she gave the chef a cheery good-morning and donned her white toque and jacket.

Chef René grunted a halfhearted good-morning and waved his wooden spoon toward the door. "We are to feed the soldiers. Mr. Howard has ordered that we will do so. I want no complaints."

The chef's words were tersely spoken. Olivia wondered if he'd argued with Mr. Howard or if the kitchen boys had grumbled at the news. With a bright smile, she gave a nod and set to work. "If hard work is truly good medicine for the soul, then we should be quite healthy by the time these soldiers depart, don't you think?"

"The menu for the hotel guests will remain the same. According to Mr. Howard, the food for the soldiers should be hearty but not equal to the quality we serve our guests. In other words, half of the food we prepare will be mediocre, and the rest will be our usual fine fare."

He was clearly unhappy. Olivia couldn't decide if she should attempt idle conversation or simply remain silent. Obviously his early morning coffee with Mrs. DeVault hadn't cheered him. In fact, she was surprised the older woman had already gone downstairs. The chef's foul mood had apparently been too much for her, too.

"I missed seeing you at church yesterday," she ventured.

He slapped a whisk on the worktable. "Because I come to church one time does not mean you will see me there again."

His words stung, but Olivia didn't retreat. "I hope you will at least consider the idea." She stepped closer and lowered her voice. "I know Mrs. DeVault was pleased to have you attend. And why weren't the two of you having coffee when I arrived this morning?"

"We have duties that require our attention. I do not wish to continue this discussion, Miss Mott."

Olivia turned her head. "As you wish." For the next couple of hours, she avoided any further discussion with the chef. She spoke only when a comment was needed in order to achieve their culinary goals. And she didn't fail to note that Mrs. DeVault hadn't made an appearance throughout the morning, either. Olivia wondered if the chef had snapped at the older woman, too. When the time for their midmorning break arrived and Mrs. DeVault still hadn't come upstairs, Olivia peeked around the corner. The wonderful scent of baking pies wafted to the upper kitchen, and Olivia knew the older woman was hard at work.

Holding the rail, she walked down several steps and then bent forward. "It's time for a breath of fresh air, Mrs. DeVault. Come up and join the rest of us."

"Thank you, Olivia, but I have additional baking that requires my attention."

Olivia detected a hint of sadness in the reply, so she continued down until she reached the bottom step. "What's this? You don't have even a few minutes to join me for a cup of tea?"

Mrs. DeVault pointed to the crocks of rising dough. "I'm preparing baked goods for the soldiers as well as the guests. My work has increased by leaps and bounds, but I'm not given any additional helpers." She lifted her flour-covered hands above the worktable. "I have only these two hands to accomplish all of this work." She raised her right shoulder and bent her head to wipe a stray tear on her sleeve. "Forgive me. I am acting like a silly schoolgirl."

"It's Chef René who has upset you, isn't it? Don't take his words to heart. He was abrupt with me this morning, too. I think he's annoyed that we must feed the soldiers."

Mrs. DeVault shook her head. "No. It's more than that. I knew when he didn't appear for church yesterday that something was amiss. His behavior this morning only confirmed my feelings." She punched down a bulging heap of dough and began to vigorously knead the mass. "When I arrived this morning, he handed me a list of duties and said we should forgo our practice of taking early morning coffee together."

"I'm sure he means there won't be time until the troops have departed."

An Uncertain Dream

"No. He said he feared he had misrepresented his intentions and that he had overstepped the proper boundaries of a supervisor. He apologized for interfering in my personal life." She shook her head in obvious dismay. "*Interfering!* Is that not the most ludicrous thing you've ever heard? Why would he think he had been interfering? When I asked him to explain further, he declined. I will not embarrass myself by asking any additional questions. Still, I cannot help but wonder what has changed."

Fred! His name popped into Olivia's mind with the speed of lightning flashing through the heavens. The chef's sudden change of heart could be attributed to only one person, and that person was Fred. Mrs. DeVault might be unwilling to pursue the matter, but Olivia was more than anxious to discover exactly what had transpired between the two men. With a quick wave and an offer to send one of the dishwashers to help, Olivia rushed back upstairs to locate Chef René. She wanted answers. And if she must endure the chef's wrath, so be it!

CHAPTER TWENTY-ONE

Chicago, Illinois

Charlotte neared the entrance to her office and grimaced when she caught sight of Herman Rehnquist standing beside the closed door. The man had become a nuisance of the worst sort. Her efforts toward deterring his annoying advances had so far proved futile. She hadn't wanted to report his behavior to Mr. Field. He might believe her an ineffective employee if she couldn't handle such a trifling matter. At least that's what she'd told herself when Mr. Rehnquist had first begun his flirtatious behavior.

She squared her shoulders and leveled a cold stare in his direction. "Are you waiting to speak to me, Mr. Rehnquist?" A dark gleam shone in his eyes and caused an involuntary shudder to course through her body.

His lips curled in an uninviting smile. "Why else would I stand outside your door?"

Charlotte didn't comment upon his insolent tone. Instead, she removed a small appointment book from her reticule. "I don't believe I see your name listed on today's schedule, Mr. Rehnquist."

"This is an *unscheduled* meeting, my dear."

She narrowed her eyes. How dare he speak to her in such a bold manner! "I don't have time for unscheduled meetings, Mr. Rehnquist. My appointment book is full. Now, if you'll excuse me, I have pressing work that I must attend to."

Without waiting for his response, Charlotte reached for the glass doorknob. The sooner she could remove herself from this man's presence, the better.

She'd made only a quarter turn when his hand covered hers in a tight grip. "Please, let me open the door for you—*Charlotte*." His warm breath grazed her ear. She yanked her hand from beneath his fingers.

With a quick sideward step, she moved away from the door. "Your behavior is completely inappropriate, Mr. Rehnquist. If you don't want me to report you to Mr. Field, I suggest you leave immediately. I'm certain there is work awaiting you in your department."

He opened the door and walked into her office. With a half smile, he stood beside the open door. "You *do* want to hear what I have to say, my dear. Your future here at Marshall Field's depends upon it. Why don't you come into your office so we can talk privately? You're not going to want anyone else to hear what I'm going to say."

Charlotte raised her brows. "I don't believe there's anything you can say that will compromise my employment, Mr. Rehnquist. Please leave."

Still standing inside her office with his hand on the doorknob, he bent closer and shook his head. "Dear lady, don't brush me off so quickly. We both know that you are keeping company with a man who is banned from this store. Not only would Mr. Field frown upon such behavior, but he would also fire you—*if he knew*."

The cunning gleam in his eyes seemed to beg a denial, but Charlotte remained silent. Maintaining an aloof bearing, she entered the room and stepped behind the highly polished desk.

With an air of authority, she placed her palms on the desk and leaned slightly forward. "Say what you've come for, Mr. Rehnquist, and then take your leave."

Ignoring proper etiquette, he sat down. "I have discovered that Matthew Clayborn, the man you were with in the train depot, is a reporter for the *Herald*." He leaned back in the chair and gazed up at her. "You may as well sit down, Charlotte. You look like a schoolteacher prepared to reprimand her students."

"You need not concern yourself with my comfort or appearance. This conversation won't take long." Charlotte lifted her palms from the desk and folded her arms across her waist. "I am well aware of Mr. Clayborn's profession and his employer. I am also cognizant of those people who have been banned from entering this store. If you have nothing more to say, you may leave."

"Then that begs the question of whether Mr. Field knows you are romantically involved with Mr. Clayborn." He looked at her from beneath hooded eyes.

"You make many assumptions, Mr. Rehnquist. If I were in your position, I would be extremely careful before I spoke to Mr. Field." She rounded the desk while maintaining a safe distance. "I'm not at liberty to discuss this matter with you. Suffice it to say, you are not aware of all the circumstances involved. I can only say that some things are not what they seem."

His eyebrows dipped, and lines creased his forehead in zigzag fashion. He shifted in the chair, obviously rethinking his position. For the moment, she'd managed to forestall any further onslaught.

Finally he rubbed his jaw and eyed her suspiciously. "I'm not at all sure I believe you."

She lifted her shoulders in what she hoped was a nonchalant shrug. "Then do what you must, Mr. Rehnquist, but I've done my best to forewarn you. Your future with this company is of little consequence to me."

He stiffened at the remark. "I believe Mr. Field values me and my contribution to this company. I have been an employee far longer than you."

"Indeed you have. I'm certain you know Mr. Field quite well. Therefore, you're keenly aware of what you must do if you hope to maintain your employment." With a confident stride, she walked to the door. "I believe we have nothing more to say to each other."

From her vantage point, Charlotte watched Mr. Rehnquist slowly rise from the chair and turn. He walked toward her, his features masked. She couldn't tell if she'd convinced him to remain silent.

His gaze slowly traveled the length of Charlotte's body and stopped when he looked into her eyes. "I don't know if you are quite cunning, very foolish, or extremely bright, Miss Spencer. I can only assume that since Mr. Field has placed you in a position akin to management, he believes you are loyal to him." He leaned in, and she could smell the scent of tobacco on his breath. "Time will tell if he has misplaced his trust."

"That would be true for all of his employees, Mr. Rehnquist." She took a backward step and opened the door. "Even you."

His lips tightened into a thin seam, but he didn't reply. He turned and strutted down the hallway with his head held high. Charlotte watched until he was out of sight, then closed the door and leaned against it. Her hands were clammy and her breathing shallow. She forced herself to inhale a deep breath. He was gone, and if she'd succeeded in her ploy, there was nothing to fear. She knew one thing: her cautionary words wouldn't be enough to stop Mr. Rehnquist. He would continue to dig until he unearthed the truth.

Charlotte circled the desk and dropped into the leather chair. *The truth.* She reconstructed exactly what she'd said to Mr. Rehnquist. Had she lied? When she accepted Jesus as her Savior, she'd asked forgiveness for so many lies and made a vow to tell the truth henceforth. Was she once again reverting to her old ways in order to protect herself? She turned and stared out the windows that overlooked State Street. She had encouraged Mr. Rehnquist to think he was mistaken about her relationship with Matthew, but she hadn't actually lied to him. There appeared to be a very thin line between what she'd done and actually telling a lie. She didn't want to cross that line.

———

After bidding Mrs. Brandt good-night, Charlotte exhaled a sigh of relief, thankful Matthew hadn't been waiting for her when she departed the store. Although she'd attempted to keep a lookout for Mr. Rehnquist, he could be watching from one of the upstairs windows. Or he could have someone else watching her, an unsettling thought that caused her to glance over her shoulder. She silently chided herself for looking. His informant could be any one of the many people who appeared to be heading home for the evening. There would be no way of knowing if someone was following her. She hastened her step, anxious to arrive home safely.

After three blocks at a near run, Charlotte rounded the corner and slowed to catch her breath. She'd gone only a short distance when fingers clamped onto her arm. Her throat constricted. What she had hoped would be a shriek for help was instead a strangled mewl. A knot formed in the pit of her stomach, and she fought to wrestle free of the hold.

"Let go of—" She jerked around and immediately relaxed. "Matthew! I thought it was—"

"With that look of terror in your eyes, I *hope* you didn't think it was me. What's wrong?" He peered behind her as though he expected to see someone menacing there.

She followed his focus, relieved to see nothing appeared out of the ordinary. "I don't think we should be seen together."

"Charlotte, what is this about? Your hands are shaking. Tell me what has happened."

"Let's keep walking. I don't want to attract unnecessary attention." She grasped his arm. A carriage slowed as it passed by, and Charlotte dipped her head.

When she looked up, Matthew was staring at her. "Are you going to explain, or must I resort to my news-reporting techniques and badger you?"

She could overcome this problem if she and Matthew terminated all contact with each other. Mr. Rehnquist would then assume her involvement with Matthew had truly been to serve some surreptitious purpose for Mr. Field. There was no other way around this problem: she must tell Matthew what had occurred and hope that he would cooperate.

When she'd finished the tale, he shook his head. "I'll not

allow you to be bullied by the likes of anyone, especially that man."

"Please, Matthew. I have a son to support, and my income is important to Priddle House, as well. If I'm going to maintain my position at the store, I believe it's the only answer."

"I'm not willing to give in so quickly. There may be some other way. I need time to think on this and develop a plan." Matthew patted her hand. "For the time being, I'll concede to stay away from the store. I won't meet you after work or during your lunch break." His look turned solemn. "You must promise to contact me if Mr. Rehnquist makes any further threats or advances." He placed his index finger beneath her chin and lifted her head until their eyes met. "Do you promise?"

Charlotte felt inexplicably breathless and backed away from him. Something deep within her stirred, and she realized Matthew Clayborn had taken her heart captive with his deep blue eyes, boyish charm, and unsolicited promises of protection. The silent admission caused a stir of fear and excitement to mount within her chest. She inhaled a ragged breath, thankful he couldn't read her thoughts.

"Charlotte?"

Forcing herself from the self-induced fog, she became aware of the tiny creases that pinched between his eyebrows. She gave fleeting thought to pressing the pad of her thumb against the worry lines. "Yes."

"Yes, you promise you'll contact me if there's any problem with Mr. Rehnquist?" Matthew bobbed his head as though coaching a young child for the sought-after response. She repeated the phrase for him, and he gave a final nod. "Good. Then the matter is settled."

At Mr. Heathcoate's request, Fred boarded a train in Chicago on Thursday morning. The union membership had anxiously awaited the arrival of Wednesday, July 11, the agreed-upon date of the general strike. The day had come and gone, and so had their hopes for a nationwide walkout by the trade unions. There had been a smattering of support, but it was mostly from unions with their own grievances to settle.

Instead of first stopping in Pullman for a brief visit with Olivia, Fred followed Mr. Heathcoate's instruction and went directly to Kensington, where the workers would gather to discuss this latest development. Fred had argued that Mr. Heathcoate should be the one to deliver the news, but Mr. Heathcoate had disagreed and countered that his presence was required in Chicago to attend meetings with other members of leadership.

The unrelenting sun beat down across Fred's shoulders. He removed his hat and wiped the perspiration from his forehead. A group of men were sitting on the grass along the east side of the building, and Fred waved his hat in greeting.

"Hope you've come to give us some good news for a change!" one of the men hollered.

Fred forced a half smile to mask the truth. Just once, he'd like to be the bearer of glad tidings. "Round up as many of the members as you can find, and let's go inside."

A short time later he stood in front of a large group of men who represented most of the departments in their membership. "Mr. Heathcoate asked me to advise you that, from all reports, the national strike is considered a failure." Before a reaction could erupt, Fred signaled for quiet. "Please remain calm. If there is shouting and mayhem, we'll accomplish nothing. I will stay and answer your questions, but you must maintain order here and when you leave this meeting hall."

One of the men raised his hand, and Fred acknowledged him. "I thought the newspapers said Mr. Gompers met with Mr. Debs and they were in agreement about the trade unions and the AFL joining us in the strike."

Nods and a hum of agreement filled the room.

"As president of the American Federation of Labor, Mr. Gompers came here at the request of the Chicago membership. He didn't appear to be strongly aligned with the concept of a nationwide strike and didn't think a walkout would be good for his trade union members."

Angry murmurs rose from the crowd, and Fred pounded the gavel on the podium numerous times before regaining control of the meeting. He understood the frustration. The men had expected a quick solution when they'd walked out in May, but with dwindling resources with which to provide for their families and little hope of resolution, their dissatisfaction and anger continued to mount. Now Fred had arrived and dashed their remaining hopes.

"You've got to put yourself in his position. I'm not certain Mr. Debs would want to thrust the American Railway Union into a fray that had begun with the American Federation of Labor. You must think about whether *you* would be willing to walk out of *your* job in support of a trade union strike in New York or California." He looked out over the crowd. "We had hoped these other unions would join us and support our cause, but we must be realistic. After all, we can't ask them to do more than we would be willing to do ourselves. If the AFL calls a strike next year, will you be willing to walk out to support them?"

"We're concerned about what's happening in the here and

now," one of the men called, and several others murmured agreement.

A Paint Department representative stepped forward. "You haven't been around much, Fred, so you may not know that the Relief Committee is in dire straits. We're told they're desperately low on supplies, and all other help has dwindled to nothing."

"My wife tells me the committee has already announced there's going to be another reduction in aid unless someone gives a generous donation," another man shouted.

"How much less can we get by on?"

The men waited. Expectation shone in their eyes. They wanted answers, but Fred didn't have any. "I can't answer your questions. All I can tell you is that we must remain steadfast and continue to maintain the peace. Once we have word from Mr. Debs and the other leadership, either Thomas Heathcoate or I will report back to you."

He could have told them that the lack of support from the AFL was the final straw and their fate was sealed, but he withheld that disclosure. Instead, he mentioned the financial contributions made by the membership of the Chicago Knights of Labor and a few other trade unions. Money to assuage the guilt they harbored over failure to join the strike—at least that's what Fred thought. Hardship won over pride, and the donation had been accepted, although it was a mere pittance compared to the daily needs of the Pullman citizens.

"What about Mr. Pullman? Any word that he'll reconsider and negotiate?"

Once again, the company's founder had fled the city while others were left to enforce his orders, but Fred knew such a comment would further inflame the men. "Management continues to refuse to meet with us, and we don't expect that to change."

After answering several additional questions, Fred left the meeting with a list of grievances in his pocket—mostly regarding the lack of available aid, but a few men wanted Fred to convey their ongoing anger over the presence of armed troops. Beyond the pleas that had been made by Mr. Heathcoate, Mr. Debs, and the governor, Fred advised there was little more that could be done to remove the soldiers. But he had dutifully jotted down the message.

For days rumors had spread throughout Chicago that an invasion of more than ten thousand men was being organized to march into Pullman and set the factories ablaze. Each time the union attempted to dampen the fiery rumor, the tale was exaggerated with fresh gossip. Mr. Debs surmised that the troops would remain as long as rumors abounded, and he believed the rumors would continue until the General Managers Association put a stop to such talk. The leaders of the American Railway Union were convinced the association would use its resources to turn the country completely against the railway union. They had already blamed the railway union membership for horrendous acts of violence in the past. What better way to seal the fate of the striking workers than to spread rumors that their union members planned to set the town and factories afire? There was no foundation for such rumors, but it was excuse enough to keep the military in Pullman.

CHAPTER TWENTY-TWO

Pullman, Illinois

Ignoring the presence of the white military tents that dotted the lawn of Hotel Florence, Fred lengthened his stride and skirted the outer edge of the encampment. The tower clock chimed the hour. He would have at least two hours before he must return to Chicago. He hoped Chef René would be willing to release Olivia from her duties for the remainder of the morning. With the troops bivouacked on the front lawn, Fred doubted there were many guests at the hotel. Surely the chef could manage without Olivia for an hour or two.

The scent of roasting meat wafted through the hot air, and Fred's stomach growled. He had considered stopping for breakfast before leaving Kensington but decided against the idea at the last minute. He hadn't eaten since last night and hoped Olivia would offer him some leftovers from breakfast.

Above the rattle of pots and pans, Fred heard Chef René shouting orders to the kitchen staff. From the tone of his voice, the chef was unhappy. Moving close to the door, Fred strained to capture a glimpse of Olivia. Instead, Chef René spotted him.

255

With several heavy steps, the rotund man approached the door. "You are eavesdropping, or do you have business with me, Mr. DeVault?"

Fred retreated as though he'd been singed by an open flame. "I'm in town for union business and hoped to visit with Olivia— if she's not too busy, that is."

The chef slapped his palm across his forehead. "Not too busy?" His beefy hand remained on his forehead as he gazed heavenward. "Not too busy? Non, of course not, Mr. DeVault. I have only all these soldiers expecting one meal after another. How could we be too busy?"

"Why are you cooking for *them*?" Fred asked with a quick glance over his shoulder.

"Because that is what I've been told to do, Mr. DeVault. Just like the soldiers out there in the yard, I follow orders. Miss Mott will join you when she has a few free moments. Who can know when that will be." He pointed toward the tree where the staff gathered for their midmorning breaks. "Wait over there. It is one place the soldiers haven't occupied."

Fred didn't argue. He located a spot beneath the oak tree and dropped down onto the grass where he could watch the entrance. Moments later Olivia opened the door, flashed a smile, and quickly disappeared from sight. He would wait no longer than an hour. If she didn't come outside by then, he would return to Chicago. He closed his eyes and leaned back against the sturdy tree trunk.

"Fred."

He forced his eyes open. Olivia was standing over him, smiling. He pushed himself upright and pulled her into a warm embrace. "I was beginning to wonder if Chef René was going to hold you hostage the entire day."

She leaned away from him and shook her head. "You didn't seem to be missing me overly much. In fact, you appeared to be asleep."

He laughed and held her close, enjoying the scent of her hair. "I've missed you."

"I've missed you, also. I was beginning to wonder if you were ever going to return."

He caught the hint of accusation in her voice. "When I haven't been attending to union duties, I've been doing my best to keep Bill's business running smoothly or visiting him at the hospital."

At the mention of Bill and his family, Olivia's features softened. "How is he progressing?"

"He should be released from the hospital next week, but his future is bleak." Fred explained the extent of Bill's injuries. "I don't know what he'll decide regarding the business, but Bill and his family will need our continued prayers."

Olivia nodded. "So much sadness surrounds us. Sometimes it's difficult to believe God hears my prayers."

Fred understood, for he'd had those same feelings ever since the strike began. It seemed God had aligned with the men who embraced capitalistic greed rather than the poor man trying to eke out a living for his family. But he didn't want his time with Olivia embroiled in a discussion of good versus evil or unanswered prayer. He wanted to forget the turmoil and concentrate on her.

She sat down beside him and withdrew something wrapped in a linen napkin from the pocket of her chef's jacket. "When Chef René told me you were here, I asked your mother to place one of the beef pasties in the oven with her pies. We're serving them today for the noonday meal, although Chef René says they aren't fancy enough." She giggled. "He expects complaints."

"Let's hope the soldiers don't eat them. The Pullman residents would consider them quite a treat." He took a bite and nodded his approval. "Tell Chef René I doubt he'll hear any grumbling once the soldiers have tasted them." After devouring the beef pie, he wiped his hands and mouth on the napkin. "Does my mother continue to enjoy working with Chef René?"

"I don't think you need worry that Chef René is going to steal your mother away from you."

"What is that supposed to mean?"

Olivia tugged at a clump of weeds near the base of the tree. "Are you going to play naïve with me after your obvious objection to his interest in your mother?"

Fred grasped her hand. "I didn't object. I merely wondered at his intent."

Her brows lifted in two perfect arcs. "Fred! You were obviously upset by the idea your mother might consider marriage."

"She barely knows him. I don't dislike him or even object to him as a person. I said they were complete opposites. And they are."

"How can you say they are opposites? You don't even know him. Your mother is a good judge of character, and she enjoyed his company. He made her laugh and brought joy to her life."

Fred waited until a group of soldiers passed by. "You make it sound as though he's dead."

"Oh, he's very much alive. Didn't you hear the anger in his voice when you arrived? He's been sullen and angry ever since he accepted the fact that you didn't want him to court your mother."

"Since the strike began, I've been involved in nothing but

union business, yet now I'm blamed for my mother's unhappiness and Chef René's anger. I had hoped to spend a peaceful hour or two enjoying your company. Instead, I'm confronted with accusations that I've ruined my mother's future."

She tipped her head to the side and offered a winsome smile. "You could set things aright easily enough, you know."

"And how do you propose I do that?"

"Tell Chef René that you would be pleased to have him court your mother."

"*What*? My mother would be appalled. That would sound as though I've decided to marry her off to the first eligible man."

A light breeze rippled through the tree, and a leaf floated to the ground near Olivia's skirt. She folded the leaf in half and pressed it between her fingers. "They are two halves that make a whole." She opened the leaf. "Don't make excuses. Simply find the proper words and speak to him. You'll be glad you did. And so will your mother."

"Now?" He didn't want to spend this short window of time apologizing to Chef René and fumbling for the proper words to give the man permission to court his mother. The idea seemed ludicrous. He'd come here to deliver a message for Mr. Heathcoate and to enjoy a brief time of relaxation with Olivia. But he knew she'd not relent until he'd spoken with the chef. He pushed to his feet. "Wait here," he said and strode toward the kitchen.

Once inside, he waited. The chef didn't like to be interrupted while working. Fred had learned that much from Olivia. When the rotund man turned to retrieve a large crock from the shelf, his thick brows lifted. "There is a problem, Mr. DeVault?"

Fred took a tentative step closer. "When you have a moment, could we speak in private?"

Fred detected what appeared to be a hint of suspicion in the chef's eyes, or perhaps it was merely apprehension. He couldn't be certain. Unlike Olivia, he barely knew the man. Chef René slid the bowl onto the worktable. It skated across the wooden surface, and Fred waited, expecting it to drop to the floor and break. Though it wobbled several times, the crock finally came to rest at the edge of the table without incident. With a wave, Chef René beckoned him forward. They must be heading for the office Olivia had described to him on several occasions.

The chef's body swayed with each footstep, the shoulders of his white jacket dipping in a rhythmic motion until he came to an abrupt halt. "We will talk in my office." He turned the doorknob and walked inside. "Come in," he said without fanfare. "Close the door behind you." He maneuvered around the desk and wedged himself into the chair. "Sit down."

Fred dropped into the chair. He pressed his sweating palms on the chair arms and attempted to swallow the cottony dryness that constricted his throat. The chef shrugged his shoulders and arched his brows, obviously Fred's signal to speak. "I . . . uh . . . asked to speak to you," his voice cracked, and he coughed.

The chef turned and poured a glass of water from a pitcher sitting on his desk. He reached across the expanse. "See if this helps."

Fred gulped the contents and gave a quick nod. "Thanks. About my mother."

Chef René held up his palm. "You need not concern yourself, Mr. DeVault. I have bowed to your opposition, but I hope you have not come to tell me she must now quit her job in the hotel. You have my word that I will not pursue her affections."

"I don't know how you came to the conclusion that I would oppose my mother's decisions about her own future. Because she has been without a husband for so many years, my mother is more independent than most ladies. And I truly find no objection to you. I barely know you. Any concern is based upon the fact that I didn't think she knew you well enough to consider marriage."

The chef arched his back and straightened his shoulders. "But I have not yet proposed."

"Well, no, but I thought you might, and I suppose I gave the appearance of being less than pleased my mother was keeping company with you." He shrugged. "I want you to know that if you make her happy, then that's all that is important to me."

The chef's eyes glistened. "And that is what is important to me, also. I find your mother a lovely woman. We are somewhat different, yet we seem to balance each other. She has great joy—though not so much lately. I miss seeing her smile."

Fred surmised that his mother's smile had disappeared when the chef had withdrawn his attention. That issue could be set aright easily enough, but Fred braced himself before asking one final question. "What about my mother's faith?"

"Her beliefs are not so different from my own. Do you think me a heathen?" Chef René's lips curved in a lopsided grin that reminded Fred of a question mark.

"No, no," he stammered. "I have no idea what you do or don't believe, but I would like to know." Summoning his courage, Fred leaned forward and rested his arms on the desk. "Are you a Christian?"

"Oui. I believe Jesus is the Son of God and that He died for my sins. Is that what you want to know?"

Fred gave a hesitant nod. "But you don't attend church regularly?"

He laughed. "Attending church does not make one a

believer. This much I know for sure." He patted his heart. "Attending church strengthens faith and teaches, and sometimes those who don't believe learn the truth in church." He wagged his index finger. "And sometimes the people who attend church turn people away from God, too. Not a pleasant thought but true nonetheless." He pointed to his eye. "People watch how you churchgoers act, you know. Sometimes they don't like what they see and decide Jesus isn't the answer for them."

Fred leaned back in the chair as though he'd been slapped. "Is that how you perceive me? Have I turned you against the church?"

"I am not blaming you, Fred, but I must say that I didn't approve of the way you treated Olivia after you discovered she'd been telling lies about her past. Of course, all is now well between the two of you, but you were less than forgiving when she attempted to make amends for what she had done. I thought your mother behaved in a kind and forgiving manner toward Olivia while you . . . you didn't inspire me to attend church on Sunday mornings."

Fred knew he was correct. His behavior had been less than praiseworthy during that period of his life. He'd asked God's forgiveness and Olivia's, as well. "Is that why you attended church only once? Because of my behavior?"

The chef chuckled. "I don't mean to heap blame upon you, Fred. I have my own past that has contributed to what I believe and how I conduct myself. It would have made the situation more difficult between your mother and me if I had continued to attend the same church these last two weeks after we ceased seeing each other."

Fred didn't know what else to say. The conversation had veered off into an entirely different direction than he had anticipated. Their talk was supposed to resolve matters rather than intensify them. "I plan to speak to my mother before I return to Chicago. May I mention our discussion and tell her that you and I have come to an understanding of sorts?"

"Exactly what would that understanding be? I want to be entirely certain before we part company."

"That I have no objection should you decide to court my mother and that whatever she may decide for her future will be acceptable to me." He met the chef's intense stare. "Is that satisfactory?"

"If that is truly how you feel, then it is completely satisfactory."

"And you will reestablish your relationship with her?"

"If she is disposed to the arrangement, I will be delighted." He leaned across the desk and extended his hand. "We are agreed. And you have my word that I will do everything in my power to make your mother happy."

The men retraced their footsteps to the kitchen, and Fred glanced toward the stairs leading to the bakery. "May I go down and speak with my mother now?"

Chef René clapped him on the shoulder. "But of course. And I must see to preparing food for the soldiers."

Fred's shoes clattered on the steps as he descended the stairs into the baking kitchen. He smiled at his mother when she saw him, pleased at the surprise that shone in her eyes. "You're the last person I expected to see coming down those stairs," she said. "Are you hoping for a piece of pie?"

He shook his head. "Nothing as simple as that."

"Has something happened?"

The tremor in her voice startled him. He hadn't intended to frighten her. "No, nothing has happened. I have come to offer an apology for my childish behavior."

She wiped the flour from her hands and pointed to a stool near her worktable. "What are you referring to, Fred?"

"I have already apologized to Chef René and asked his forgiveness. He is a good man, and I have judged him harshly, I fear. I hope that the two of you will reestablish your . . . your . . . companionship," he stammered.

"Exactly how did René respond to all of this?"

Tears gathered in his mother's eyes as Fred recounted the discussion. "I believe you'll once again have your companion back by your side."

"Thank you, Fred." She kissed his cheek. "You are a good son."

He laughed and shook his head. "I wish I could take full credit, but it is Olivia who you have to thank. She convinced me that I needed to set this aright. And I'm glad she did."

"Didn't I tell you? Olivia is a fine girl. You are very fortunate to have her in your life."

"You're right. I'm a very lucky man," he agreed before bounding up the stairs. And he was. It had taken Fred a good while to come to that conclusion, but he now realized that he was indeed most fortunate.

———————

The train left the station on time. Fred peered out the window and waved to Olivia as the locomotive slowly gained speed. Chef René had sent Olivia along to bid him good-bye. It was a tribute of thanks, Fred suspected. He leaned against the seat and closed his eyes. Except for the news he'd been forced to deliver to the workers, the day had gone well.

The train passed through the grassy expanse between Pullman and Chicago. As he stared through the window, Fred decided that once the strike ended and he was back to work, he and Olivia would have a fine wedding. He recalled Martha and Albert's wedding, which Olivia had helped to plan. A ceremony and reception such as theirs would be good. Then again, with the growing deficit in his savings, Fred didn't know how he could possibly pay for anything as nice as Albert's wedding.

He wondered if Olivia would settle for a small private ceremony instead. Even more, he wondered if he would have a job once the strike ended. If their efforts failed, management might not see fit to hire him back. He'd realized that when he'd agreed to become a delegate, but he hadn't considered the long-term consequences at the time. He'd been certain they would win. Olivia wouldn't want to quit her job at the hotel, and if he wasn't permitted to work in Pullman, he couldn't live in Pullman. Had his involvement in the union jeopardized their future together?

Perhaps it was time to resume their earlier conversation about his future in Pullman, which daily became increasingly bleak.

CHAPTER TWENTY-THREE

Chicago, Illinois

Charlotte, Morgan, and Fiona were the last of their group to enter the church on Sunday morning. Charlotte preferred to sit near the end of the pew in case Morgan became restless during the sermon and she needed to step to the rear of the church. They had settled themselves when Morgan let out an excited squeal and raised his arms. Charlotte looked up to see Matthew standing at the end of their pew.

He reached forward, lifted Morgan into his arms, and then squeezed into the small space beside Charlotte. "Good morning," he said with a broad grin.

"You promised you would stay away," she hissed while glancing toward the rear of the church. "What if Mr. Rehnquist sees you?"

"He lives on the other side of town. Besides, I was careful to make sure nobody followed me." He tipped his head and his lips grazed her ear. "I'm a reporter, remember?"

"That doesn't make you infallible," she whispered.

Mrs. Priddle cleared her throat with a shrill rattle that left

266

no doubt she expected their whispering to cease.

Pressing an index finger to her pursed lips, Charlotte signaled Matthew to refrain from further comment.

When the voices of the congregation melded into the stirring second stanza of "Revive Us Again," Matthew sang along until they began the chorus. He nudged Charlotte, and when she looked at him he said, "I may not be infallible, but I know it's safe for me to be here."

He'd barely uttered the final word when Charlotte saw the end of Mrs. Priddle's parasol jab Matthew in the arm with a fierceness that made him jump. Matthew's brows furrowed into a tight frown, but his talking ceased and his singing began. Mrs. Priddle appeared pleased by the result.

When they walked out of the church and into the warm July sunshine an hour later, Mrs. Priddle motioned them to wait beside her while she directed the other Priddle House ladies to form their line and begin the walk toward home. Fiona carried Morgan. Mrs. Priddle expressed her dissatisfaction over Matthew's recent behavior.

"We teach by example, Mr. Clayborn. How can we expect children to behave in church if the adults around them won't follow the rules?"

"My apologies, Mrs. Priddle. I will do my very best to see that it doesn't happen again."

She opened her parasol, a large black contraption that defied the sun's rays. "I don't believe Charlotte mentioned you would be calling on her today."

Matthew ducked his head to avoid the umbrella's pointed spoke. "A surprise. She didn't know I was going to meet her in church. I do hope you don't have any objection. I had hoped she would permit me to escort her to the park this afternoon."

The older woman tipped the parasol and looked at Charlotte. "Well? Do you want to invite Mr. Clayborn to join us for lunch, or shall I send him on his way?"

Charlotte turned toward Matthew and lowered her voice to a whisper. "Are you certain you weren't followed?"

"Positive," he whispered.

Charlotte glanced over her shoulder toward the older woman. "Mr. Clayborn would be pleased to accept an invitation to dine with us."

Instead of leading the way, Mrs. Priddle took a position directly behind Matthew and Charlotte. They hadn't gone far when the older woman tapped Matthew on the shoulder. "Is the news in yesterday's *Tribune* correct? Has the strike ended?"

"Not exactly. While the defeat of the national strike is a blow to the Pullman workers, the strike can't be considered over. There's no doubt the American Railway Union is in grave danger. There are many who believe this latest defeat may signal the end of the union's battle. But who can tell? They may still rally and prevail. Stranger things have happened."

Charlotte had read the newspaper article with interest. The story indicated the majority of the Pullman residents were eager to return to work on any terms. She'd found that statement difficult to believe. News in the *Tribune* generally aligned with management. The workers had given up so much in order to wage their battle. Would they now simply return to work without having gained anything? She couldn't imagine Fred would be willing to accept such terms. On the other hand, men with wives and children—men such as Olivia's cousin Albert, or Mr. Quinter, who lived with the DeVaults—might consider decreased wages better than no income at all.

Morgan insisted upon walking, and Charlotte leaned down

to capture his hand in her own. She turned to Matthew. "You're not required to attend today's parade and write about it?" In the same news report, Charlotte had read that a parade was planned to honor the National Guard, and the uniformed guardsmen were going to perform drills for those in attendance.

"One of the other reporters agreed to write the story. Unless another battle occurs, I don't think there will be much to report." He grasped Morgan's other hand. "Besides, I'd much rather spend my day with you and Morgan."

Morgan tugged on his mother's hand, and Charlotte looked down at her son, who had planted his feet firmly. He pointed to a rock that sparkled in the sunlight. "Woc," the toddler announced before he stooped down to pick up the shiny object.

"That's dirty, Morgan." Charlotte attempted to remove the item from the boy's hand, but the more she insisted, the tighter he clutched the object.

"It's only a rock. If you don't make such a fuss, he'll soon forget about it," Matthew said.

"Or he'll stick it in his mouth and choke," Charlotte rebutted.

"I suppose that is a possibility, but why don't you trust me on this? Little boys like to pick up rocks and sticks—it's what they do. At the moment that rock is his treasure. Let him enjoy it."

"Matthew's correct, Charlotte."

Mrs. Priddle had agreed with Matthew, and it appeared he could hardly believe his ears. He grinned at Charlotte.

She playfully squeezed his arm. "You don't have to look so pleased with yourself," she whispered with a mock frown. "Don't forget that I can still withdraw your invitation to dinner."

He chuckled. "Please don't. I promise I'll behave."

The group turned to go up the front walk leading to Priddle House. Charlotte refrained from asking any question about Mr. Rehnquist or discussing her employment until they were alone after dinner. With a promise they would go to the park after his nap, Morgan willingly permitted Fiona to take him upstairs.

Charlotte joined Matthew on the front porch and sat down beside him. "Perhaps you'll tell me exactly why you decided it was safe to come here after agreeing we shouldn't be seen together."

"Mr. Rehnquist hasn't made any effort to follow you except on two occasions when you left work during your lunch break."

She clasped her palm to her bodice. "How do you know that Mr. Rehnquist followed me?"

"I have someone watching—a friend who works as an investigator. He used to be a policeman. I trust him. And it wasn't Rehnquist who followed you. It was one of the cash boys. No doubt Rehnquist paid him and figured no one would be the wiser."

Charlotte did recall seeing Douglas, one of the cash boys who worked in Mr. Rehnquist's department, while she was out during her midday break on Wednesday. She'd gone to the bank for Mrs. Priddle. The idea that the boy had been persuaded to follow her was disquieting.

"You're certain he wasn't merely walking in the same direction? A coincidence?"

Matthew shook his head. "No. Each time he waited out of sight while you completed your errand and then followed you back to the store. Mr. Rehnquist observes your arrival and departure from a corner window on the top floor. He takes up his sentry post each morning and evening with precise regularity."

"Your friend has told you this, also?"

Matthew nodded.

"How can he imagine he would ever win my affection or even my friendship by threatening to go to Mr. Field? He must realize that even if he should thwart our relationship, it will not help his cause. I am baffled by his frightening actions. I've even considered going to Mr. Field myself."

Matthew straightened his shoulders. "But what if he immediately terminated your employment? I thought that was your fear—the reason you told me to stay away."

She nodded. "It is, but Mr. Rehnquist's behavior is more offensive than anything I am doing. Union supporters are banned from the store, but I've never been told I could not associate with anyone on that list. Employees assume that is true, but Fred and Olivia support the union, and I don't hesitate to visit them or Mrs. DeVault."

"I doubt if Olivia or Mrs. DeVault is on Mr. Field's list of names, although Fred may be. Unless you're certain you are willing to suffer the consequences of losing your job, I wouldn't talk to Mr. Field."

A mother pushing a carriage strolled down the sidewalk, the warm breeze tugging at her bonnet ribbons. The woman's carefree countenance served to underscore Charlotte's situation. Did she want a stranger dictating whom she could or couldn't visit? The idea that her every move was under scrutiny caused both fear and anger; she didn't want to live a life filled with either. She must decide upon a plan.

———————

After Morgan awakened from his nap, the three of them spent several hours at the park before returning to Priddle

House. When they arrived in front of the house, Morgan insisted upon clinging to Matthew's neck. "Since Morgan doesn't want to turn me loose, I'd be more than pleased to stay longer," he said with what he hoped was a charming smile.

"It's kind of you to offer, but Morgan needs to learn he isn't in charge. Besides, I must write a letter to my mother. I've been negligent in keeping her posted of Morgan's latest antics. A fact she pointed out to me in her latest missive."

Morgan planted a sloppy kiss on Matthew's cheek before finally permitting Fiona to escort him indoors. He waved enthusiastically and called good-bye until they were well inside the house.

"Unless you send word to the contrary, I won't plan to see you except on Sundays," he said.

She grinned. "You could always come by in the evenings for Bible study. I'm certain Mrs. Priddle wouldn't mind an extra student."

"Did I hear my name?" Mrs. Priddle opened the screen door and walked onto the porch.

"You did. Charlotte was inviting me to attend the weeknight Bible study and prayer meetings. She said she didn't think you would object."

Mrs. Priddle glanced back and forth between them. "I don't want visitors at the house every night, but once a week would be fine. Wednesdays."

Charlotte giggled. "There you have it. Come prepared with your Bible on Wednesday night."

"If I don't have a work assignment, I'll be here." Matthew waved and strode down the sidewalk, wishing he'd had a few minutes to tell Charlotte good-bye in private. He figured that was exactly why the older woman had joined them. He smiled at the thought of Mrs. Priddle protecting her brood of chicks like a mother hen. She was a fine woman.

After a late supper at the Good Eats restaurant and a visit with several patrons of the establishment, Matthew headed off for Uhlich Hall. The lights were still ablaze when Matthew approached the meeting hall, and he instinctively jogged up the steps. He might discover some new item that could be developed into a story for the paper. After a quick scan of the room, he spotted Fred. He waved and threaded his way through the crowd until he arrived at Fred's side. "I'm surprised to see so many men here this evening." He glanced over his shoulder. "Is it because of the parade, or is something else happening?"

"Partially because of the parade, but also because we've received word that the chaplain and officers of the First Regiment have called a meeting of the Pullman strikers at the Market Building tomorrow evening at eight o'clock."

"Is that as much as you know?"

Fred raked his hand through his hair and gave a nod. "I'm certain rumors abound in Pullman, but all I know is what's written in this message that was delivered to me a short time ago." He handed the note to Matthew. "Has Mr. Pullman returned to Chicago?"

Matthew shook his head. "Not to my knowledge, but he manages to slip in and out of town in secret. He could have come in last night or early this morning without anyone knowing."

"Or even during the parade and drills. No one would have noticed. They were too busy watching the exhibition."

"Quite a show, I take it?"

A hint of irritation shone in Fred's eyes. "The public appeared in droves. I'd guess there were at least five thousand spectators. People in Pullman are starving, yet the children here were offering the soldiers baskets of fruit and bouquets of flowers. I was disgusted that the soldiers accepted the gifts."

Matthew nodded toward a couple of chairs along the outer perimeter of the room. "You have to accept the fact that the people of Chicago don't have a stake in this strike like those who live and work in Pullman. I fear they're ready to move on, and the newspapers aren't helping. They're fueling that attitude."

"Believe it or not, there were a number of Pullman residents among the spectators. I personally saw at least thirty or forty scattered throughout the crowd, so you know there were even more. Seeing them truly disappointed me."

The two men sat down, and Matthew more closely perused the message Fred had handed him. Looking up, Matthew saw a couple of reporters from the *Tribune*. "Let me go talk to those fellows. I'll see if there's anything new to report."

Matthew ambled toward his two colleagues with an air of disinterest. He didn't want to appear greedy for news or they'd lock their lips tighter than a clam's shell. With a light slap on the shoulder, he greeted first one of the men and then the other. "You're keeping late hours, aren't you?"

They glanced at each other, and Julius shrugged. "Not too bad. With the picture our photographer got, the parade and the meeting scheduled in Pullman should give me enough for a front-page story."

"I saw one of the other reporters for the *Herald* at the parade, and he said you had taken the day off," the other man said. He appeared to be eyeing Matthew with a degree of misgiving.

"I was on my way home after supper at the Good Eats, and

I saw the lights on in here. Reporters—we're all the same. I couldn't go home without checking to see if there was something going on." He gave an exaggerated hike of his shoulders. "You heading to Pullman tomorrow evening?" he asked.

"Just me," Julius said. "No need for two reporters when everyone already knows the scoop. I'm just going to check out the employees' response when Mr. Howard asks for authority to go to Mr. Pullman."

Matthew did his best to remain nonchalant. "I didn't know Mr. Pullman was back in Chicago."

"Oh, he's not, but my sources tell me Robert Lincoln went to Long Branch, New Jersey, to visit with him. Rumor has it they've reached a decision to reopen the car works." Julius frowned. "Surely you heard?"

Matthew deflected his question with another one of his own. "So the meeting is to determine whether the Pullman workers will end their strike?"

Julius shook his head. "No. Only to give the chaplain authority to speak with Mr. Pullman and to get his assurance that all strikers will be rehired if the union pledges to call a halt to the strike. Tomorrow night they will vote on whether to give the chaplain authority to wire Mr. Pullman on their behalf. If they agree, I'd say the strike is over."

Matthew glanced toward the other side of the room and then extended his hand to Julius. "If you'll excuse me, I see an acquaintance I'd like to speak to."

"Sure. We were leaving anyway. I think the janitors are trying to get everyone cleared out so they can sweep up and lock the doors for the night."

Taking long deliberate strides, Matthew returned to the other side of the room and motioned for Fred to join him. "I don't know what you've got scheduled for tomorrow, but you might want to return to Pullman. Sounds as though things are coming to a head. Do you think the men will want the chaplain to deliver a message to management?"

"Who can say? I didn't expect to see any Pullman workers at today's parade, but I did. There's no way I can leave before tomorrow afternoon. Bill's supposed to be released from the hospital in the morning. I promised Ruth I'd take him home." Fred glanced at the clock at the rear of the hall. "It's not too late to stop and talk to Mr. Heathcoate. I can let him know what you've told me. If he thinks the matter warrants immediate attention, he'll have time to catch the last train to Pullman tonight."

The two men walked into the warmth of the summer evening. Children played in the waning light, catching fireflies and calling to one another with each successful capture.

Matthew spied a little boy sitting on his mother's lap on a front porch. "I spent the day with Charlotte and Morgan," he told Fred.

"You've taken a liking to her, haven't you?" Fred asked.

Matthew nodded. "I care for her very much, and little Morgan, too."

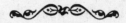

CHAPTER TWENTY-FOUR

Pullman, Illinois
Tuesday, August 7, 1894

The final weeks of July had passed in a turmoil that melted into the heat of long August days. The residents of Pullman had been shocked when a notice was posted on the main gates of the car works on July 18 stating management was now hiring new workers. By early August hundreds of new employees from Chicago had been hired, and several hundred Dutch workers who had initially walked out with the strikers returned to work. The Hollanders had broken with the union early on and expressed no regret for their decision. Fred imagined they hadn't felt any remorse over returning to work, either. Management reported that they had received numerous applicants from among Chicago's unemployed and would soon fill three thousand positions.

A stir of restlessness and discontent spread among the workers. In a move that stunned the union membership, Thomas Heathcoate told reporters his men could no longer continue and he desired a peaceful cessation of the strike. The Pullman

Strike Committee called for an immediate meeting, and with swift accord they issued a statement that repudiated Heathcoate's comments to the press. They also removed him as chairman.

The discussions that day were as heated as the summer temperatures. A caucus had approached Fred with a proposal to elect him to the chairmanship, but he quickly declined. He thought the responsibility far too difficult for anyone who lacked the experience and temperament of Mr. Heathcoate. The conclave had expressed disappointment, but they quickly moved along to another possible candidate. Now Fred wondered if he'd made a mistake, for control of the strike had slackened under the leadership of men even younger and less experienced than Fred.

The daily meetings once held at the union hall in Kensington were now a random happenstance. Assignments to help accomplish union business were no longer issued, and the men found themselves with little to occupy their time. Fred's mother had warned that idle hands were the devil's workshop—one of her favorite sayings—and in this case, she'd been correct. Even Matthew had mentioned the prevailing atmosphere of hopelessness and lack of discipline exhibited by the men. Yet there seemed little Fred could do. Many of his days were occupied helping at Bill's shop in Chicago. He'd given his word to help the Orlands until they arrived at some decision about their future, and Bill insisted upon paying him for his work. Fred had agreed to accept the money and had donated every bit of it to the relief fund, hoping the money would assist in some small way. Yet it wasn't enough; nothing seemed to be enough. Only one thing remained unchanged in Pullman: the desperate circumstances of the town's residents.

An Uncertain Dream

Fred stepped off the train in Pullman, weary from another day of working and managing Bill's business. He was thankful for the busyness the work provided, and he'd even become accustomed to handling the orders and keeping financial records. What he hadn't been able to endure was Bill's anger. Not that the man wasn't entitled to a period of reflection and even self-pity, but Bill's rage continued to simmer beneath the surface. Both Fred and Ruth tiptoed around him, careful of every word they spoke. And the children maintained a safe distance from their father. If they weren't needed to help with chores, they played outdoors until bedtime each night.

Late in the afternoon when Bill had exploded over a mistake in the bookkeeping figures, Fred had pulled him aside for a talk. He knew he would miss his usual train home because of their lengthy discussion. Fred didn't know if anything he said would help, but he hoped Bill would read the Bible passages he suggested and prayerfully consider the future of his family. The admonition he delivered to his friend was harsh, but strong words were needed if Bill was going to change his attitude and dispel the anger he directed at those attempting to help him. Before Fred had finally departed, he'd suggested Bill read the book of Job and reconsider the fairness of his circumstances. Perhaps God's Word would soften Bill's heart, and he would then be able to make a decision about the future.

As Fred approached his house, he spotted Lydia and Hannah Quinter playing hopscotch in the waning daylight. Lydia waved in greeting. "You're late. We've already finished supper."

Hannah offered a half grin, her attempt to hide the gaping hole that had been filled by her front teeth not long ago. "We get in trouble if we're late. You think your momma will send you to bed early?"

"I can only hope so."

The girl's smile was replaced by a look of utter confusion. "My daddy's unhappy, but I don't think it's 'cause you were late to supper."

Fred tousled the girl's blond curls and proceeded up the steps. Paul Quinter was unhappy a great deal of the time, and he didn't fail to make his discontent known at every opportunity. Fred hoped he wouldn't be subjected to hearing about it this evening. His talk with Bill was enough for one day.

"Finally home! Come and have your supper," his mother called from the kitchen when he entered the front door.

Both Paul and Suzanne were in the kitchen, Paul drinking a cup of coffee while Suzanne and Fred's mother washed the supper dishes, a task generally assigned to Lydia and Hannah.

"I fixed you a plate and put it on the stove. Chicken potpie. It should still be warm." His mother turned her cheek for a kiss. "Did you have a good day? I didn't know you would be late."

He lifted the plate from the stove, picked up a fork and knife, and joined Paul at the table. "I apologize. Bill and I needed to have a talk, and it took longer than expected. His business is growing."

"Business must be on the upswing for Mr. Pullman, too," Paul said.

Fred shoved a forkful of the potpie into his mouth. There was a distinct absence of chicken in the dish, but he didn't comment. His mother and Suzanne did their best to stretch the household allowance. "How so?" Fred asked once he'd swallowed the food.

"They hired between two and four hundred men today, all for the Construction Department."

Fred arched his brows. "But the Construction Department hasn't reopened."

"That's just it—they're going to reopen as soon as they hire enough men. They announced they'll fill all vacancies by the fourteenth and start work on the sixteenth. There's a rally scheduled to begin in half an hour. If you hurry and eat, we can get there before it begins."

Fred glanced at the clock. He wished he could simply complete his supper and go to bed. His entire day had been filled with pressure and strain. Now he must gobble down his supper and rush to a meeting that would probably last until late into the night. The men cared little about the lateness of the hour. Unlike him, they could sleep late tomorrow or rest during the heat of the afternoon. Free time was in abundant supply in Pullman.

Paul gulped the remainder of his coffee and soon was tapping his spoon on the table in an annoying rhythmic click while Fred continued with his supper.

When he could bear the sound no longer, Fred pointed toward the door with his thumb. "Why don't you go ahead to the rally? I'll meet you there once I've finished my supper."

Paul pushed away from the table and jumped to his feet. "I'll tell the men you're coming. They'll be pleased to see you."

Though Fred should have been flattered by the remark, there was an undercurrent to the words. Paul was forcing Fred's attendance with that statement to the men. He could have stopped him, but it would have given Fred even less time to complete his meal. Once Suzanne followed her husband down the hall, Fred motioned for his mother to sit down with him.

"We've had little time to talk these past weeks. Have you been busy at the hotel?"

A hint of amusement played at the corner of her lips. "Are you seeking information about the hotel kitchen or about René?"

His mother knew him well. He hadn't fooled her for even a minute. "I have more interest in you and Chef René than in discovering how many pies or rolls you prepared this week."

She leaned across the table and squeezed his hand. "I thought so. We have become very good friends. Does that news distress you, Fred?"

He scooped the last of the potpie onto his fork and shook his head. "No. If you enjoy his company and he treats you with the kindness and dignity you deserve, then I am pleased." He grinned and carried his plate to the sink. I believe he's an honorable man who has good intentions. I did note that he hasn't been at church lately. Is that not a problem for you?"

"His lack of attendance is not of his own doing—at least not entirely. With the troops to feed, he agreed to work in order to permit others an opportunity to worship. He enlisted the help of soldiers to assist him in the kitchen."

"That's generous of him."

"I think so, too. I've done my best to prepare the bread and desserts in sufficient quantities to help ease the burden, but it's been difficult. Since management's fear of any further uprising has now subsided and the troops have been ordered to leave the city, I believe the worst is over. In fact, I've heard that the balance of the militia is scheduled to depart before week's end."

"Let's hope so. I thought the troops would all be gone by now."

His mother stood and met Fred's gaze with a look of anticipation. "So you truly have no objection to René?"

"No." He hesitated and turned. "Is there something more you wish to tell me?"

A blush colored her cheeks, and she shook her head. "Not at the moment, but you should bear in mind that neither of us is as young as we used to be. We will likely make a decision more quickly than some would consider prudent."

He wrapped her in a fleeting hug. "I know you will give great thought and much prayer to any decision. It goes without saying that I would not want you to suffer a broken heart. If that should happen, I would be forced to take the chef to task."

"You may set your mind at ease. I will carefully weigh any decisions about the future. And you must do the same." She looked toward the street. "I know you have always supported the union, and I have done my best to remain silent. But you need to give thought to your own future. You've asked Olivia to marry you. Keep that thought in mind as the men gather to bolster their morale and commitment to the strike. Sometimes it is best to give in to defeat."

There wasn't time to discuss the merits of her warning. He knew she spoke the truth, yet he couldn't initiate such a discussion with the strikers. They already believed Mr. Heathcoate had betrayed them. If other members of leadership did the same, they would be completely disheartened. He could only hope that a contingent would broach the topic and an honest debate would ensue. Armed with facts, the men could then make rational decisions.

Many union members greeted him with loud cheers when he arrived at the rally, and Fred could smell the odor of beer and whiskey on the breath of some. He wondered where they found money to spend in the local saloons when most couldn't afford to put bread on the table. He waved to several of the men and was surprised when Bernie Dunphy, a man younger than Fred by several years, took to the stage to lead the rally.

Fred sat down and tipped his head toward Paul. "When was Bernie elected to office?" Fred had missed several union meetings during the past weeks, but he hadn't heard about any elections.

Paul shrugged. "I don't think he was ever formally voted upon. One night when none of the elected officers appeared, he took over. Since then, he's been taking charge more and more. Nobody seems to care enough to question him." He nudged Fred in the side. "You could go up there and take his place. I'm sure he'd relinquish the podium and gavel."

One of the other men leaned forward and rested his arms on his knees. "I'm not so sure of that. Bernie enjoys his new-found importance, especially after he's tipped a few—like tonight."

"Then I don't believe I'll attempt to challenge him." Fred leaned back in his chair, content to relinquish leadership. Heathcoate's dismissal as their spokesman and Fred's long hours working for Bill Orland in Chicago had combined to prevent his constant participation. He'd been present back in mid-July when the men gathered in a show of solidarity for Eugene Debs after his indictment and arrest for contempt. But Fred's attendance had waned after that, and he'd slowly begun to accept that the workers might lose their battle with management.

Although their gathering tonight had been touted as a rally, the meeting eventually turned into a debate between those who favored accepting defeat and returning to work and those who wanted to emphasize their determination by entering the car works and removing their personal tool chests. "They'll know we mean business if we remove all of our belongings!" Bernie shouted from the podium.

John Harkins waved and stood up. "They don't care if we come back or not, Bernie. There's plenty of out-of-work men willing to take the jobs we left without the company making any concessions. Either we go back to our jobs now or we pack up and leave town. The men they hire to take our jobs are gonna have the right to rent the houses. They ain't gonna let us live in company housing forever."

The validity of John's statement struck a chord. Beyond the ramifications of losing their jobs, these men needed to consider where they would live, and so did he. They would all need to make serious choices in the days to come.

During a brief recess in the meeting, Fred slipped out the back door. The rally would change nothing, for the union had lost its power when President Cleveland ended the boycott. Facts were facts, and whether or not the members wanted to admit defeat, there was little to be gained by sitting in the union hall arguing. Instead, he would put his time to better use. Or at least he hoped so.

The tower clock struck a solitary chime marking the half hour. Nine thirty. Rather late to call on Olivia, but they could walk the short distance to the house he shared with his mother and the Quinters, where they would be properly chaperoned. Many things had changed in Pullman, but gossip remained a constant. Receiving a gentleman caller without a chaperone would provide sufficient fodder for the rumor mill, even for an independent young lady such as Olivia. Would she choose to remain an unwed, self-reliant woman when he explained his earlier fears were now coming true? Granted, she had chided him for considering her fickle. But that was earlier, when they both had thought the union would prevail. Now faced with the probability rather than the possibility of failure, he wondered if she would remain so certain they should wed.

He stopped in front of the redbrick row house, but the only lights that shone from within were on the third floor rented by the Marley sisters, who worked in the laundry. Obviously Olivia hadn't expected him. He'd write a note to her when he got home and invite her to spend the afternoon with him on Sunday. They would go to the lake, and he would rent a rowboat. They would have a perfect afternoon together; at least he hoped it would be perfect.

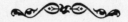

CHAPTER TWENTY-FIVE

Fred's invitation delighted Olivia. His mother had delivered it with great ceremony on Wednesday morning. The message explained he would be working late for several days, but a request that she reserve Sunday afternoon for him immediately followed. The invitation had been scribbled on a remnant of brown wrapping paper, then folded and glued at one end. Though the paper and penmanship lacked beauty, Olivia tucked it away as though it had been written on fine stationery. She took pleasure in the fact that Fred had written a personal note. For the rest of the week, she wondered if he had a special plan in mind. She imagined several possibilities, and by Sunday morning her thoughts were clear: he was going to ask her to set a date for their wedding. Her heart quickened at the thought.

While she waited for Fred to appear and escort her to church, she gave careful thought to what she must accomplish before their wedding could take place. It would be small, of course. She would ask Martha if she could borrow her wedding gown, but she would purchase lace to fashion her own headpiece. She would bake and decorate their wedding cake, just as she had done for Martha and Albert. She would want Chef René to prepare the wedding breakfast. Would Fred ask Albert to stand with him as his best man? The two no longer shared the same close friendship they had in the past.

Albert didn't attend union meetings, and he'd been one of the first in line to apply for his old job when the company began rehiring in his shop. Fred had commented on her cousin's lack of loyalty, but Olivia defended Albert's decision. Albert must think of Martha and the baby. Their child was due to be born at the end of the month, and Albert's sense of responsibility was greater than his concern over what others would think of him. Olivia refused to be counted among those who criticized Albert and the other men who had returned to their employment at the car works.

How could she find fault with them? The strike had never placed her employment in jeopardy. None of the hotel employees had been criticized for retaining their employment, nor had they been frowned upon when they hadn't suffered the same wage decreases as those employed in the car works. They were never told they should quit their jobs and support the union. Guilt had never been heaped upon her, but Olivia suffered from guilt of her own making.

It seemed improper that her life should continue normally while entire families were thrust into turmoil. Mr. Pullman had said the situation was of the workers' making, yet Olivia didn't entirely agree. Were the men to silently accept the continual decrease of their wages? Surely Mr. Pullman would not do so—especially if his wages were reduced until they no longer equaled his living expenses.

The desperation of the Relief Committee had become a

dilemma of growing proportions. Pleas for help continued to go forth with regularity, but with the defeat of the boycott and the reopening of many shops within the car works, most of the country appeared to consider the battle over. And since the union meeting earlier in the week, rumors were running rampant that many of the men would reapply for their jobs come Monday morning. She doubted Fred would be among them. Though he'd not been at the forefront of union activity of late, Olivia knew his dedication to the union remained steadfast. After church they would have time to discuss this and much more.

With a glance at the clock, she deftly pinned her hat into place and stepped outside.

Fred waved his hat as he approached. He appeared surprised to see her waiting for him. "Am I late?"

"No, but it's a beautiful Sunday morning, and I decided I'd rather spend a few minutes outdoors." She met him on the front sidewalk and immediately grasped his arm. "It's good to see you. I'm looking forward to our afternoon together."

"I'm pleased the weather cooperated."

His words had a formality and an uncommon stiffness that troubled her. Had she completely misinterpreted his invitation? Perhaps he was rethinking his decision to marry her. Is that why he asked her to go to the lake? He wanted to ensure they would have privacy when he told her of his decision?

A neutral question might help her discover the cause of his solemn demeanor. "How is Bill's health?"

He pointed to his heart. "I worry more about what's going on inside of him than about his physical condition. He's become bitter and angry. Poor Ruth. It seems she can do nothing to please him, and he has no patience with the children.

I've tried to talk to him, but he'll hear nothing I have to say. Each day he finds someone new to blame for his condition— the wagon driver, the horse, the strike, and even God."

"Does he condemn you, also? You've supported the strike from the very beginning."

"To some extent I think he does, yet he treats me with more civility. Most likely because he needs my help operating the business."

"No doubt he lashes out at his wife because he knows she'll love him in spite of the way he's treating her." Olivia collapsed her parasol as they neared the church.

"That's true, I believe. We take those we love for granted and expect them to love us in spite of our poor behavior. Ruth is a good woman, and I know she understands Bill is suffering. I've been praying he will accept his circumstances and seek a meaningful future rather than dwell in self-pity."

"I'm certain he is thankful to have you there to help him."

"I know he is, but that doesn't lessen the depth of his pain. When Mr. Lockabee agreed to sell the business to Bill, he thought his prayers had been answered. Now he feels as though God has deserted him."

"If he'd push aside his bitterness, perhaps he'd see God has another plan for him."

Fred nodded as they walked inside the church vestibule. "That's not always easy. Think how you would feel if you were injured and could no longer work as a chef."

There was no simple response when she equated Bill's loss to a corresponding change in her own life. Olivia clamped her lips together and said nothing further. The church service was a blur. She didn't listen to the sermon. Instead, she weighed Fred's words during the hour. How easy it had become to expect others to accept difficulties when her own life remained unchanged. What would she want if she suffered tragic injuries? She didn't discover the answer to her question, but she knew she would want more than simple platitudes. She would want a plan, someone to help her decide how she could piece her life back together.

"There needs to be a plan for him," she said as they departed the church.

Fred looked at her as though she'd gone daft. "What are you talking about?"

"Bill. I think if we could come up with a plan to help him rebuild his life, he'd more readily accept what has happened. He needs purpose. Right now he's defeated with thoughts that he'll never be able to provide for his family. He believes he's useless."

Fred smiled down at her. "I can see that the sermon had an impact upon you. We'll see if we can come up with some ideas this afternoon."

———

They decided to row to a lovely spot Fred had discovered when he'd been a part of the rowing club last year. The warmth of the day ensured the picnic area near the lake would be crowded, and Fred said he wanted a quiet place where they could visit. The statement seemed to carry an ominous tone, and Olivia wondered if he feared she would create a scene. All concern for Bill vanished, and her thoughts returned to her earlier worries—the ones that would affect her life.

The sound of the oars slapping the water and distant shouts of young children along the shore mingled with the music of twittering birds and humming insects. Olivia closed her eyes and dipped her hand in the water, allowing the flow to cascade between her fingers.

A short time later, Fred's cautionary words caused Olivia to withdraw her hand from the lake. They were nearing shore. He carefully guided the boat toward land, removed his shoes and socks, rolled up his trousers, and then jumped out and pulled the boat to a spot where Olivia could step onto dry ground.

He offered his hand to assist her. "Thank you, kind sir." She giggled when he offered a formal bow in response. While he secured the boat, she spread a quilt on the ground and unpacked the chicken sandwiches. A twinge of guilt assailed her as she thought of the hungry families in Pullman. "The Relief Committee continues to struggle to help all those without enough to eat. Help from Chicago has dwindled, and there seems to be little interest in their plight."

He leaned against the thick trunk of a maple. "A citizens' committee is going to write to the governor and see if he will help. I don't know how much good it will do, but at least it's an attempt to find some means of assistance. The residents of the town have been forgotten."

Olivia handed him a sandwich. "Tomorrow morning many more strikers are expected to reapply for their positions."

He nodded. "So I've heard. Each man must decide what is best for him."

"And you?" Olivia waited, knowing he wasn't prepared to admit defeat just yet.

His gaze remained fixed upon the sandwich he held in his hand. "That time will never arrive for me. Even if I wanted to return to work, they wouldn't hire me."

"You can't be certain of—"

"Oh, but I *am* certain. They've established their list, and my name is on it. Even if it weren't, I couldn't return to this place. Too much has happened for me to consider Pullman my home any longer. Like those who have already departed, I know I must start over. I must begin a new life somewhere else."

She swallowed hard, forcing herself to hold back threatening tears.

Fred gently cupped her hand in his own. "I know we discussed this before, but now that the reality of failure is at hand, I must be honest with you. I fear that if I took you away from Pullman, you would forever regret the decision. Should that happen, our marriage would be doomed to failure."

"I've already told you I'm willing to move from Pullman."

"And give up your position as an assistant chef? Our marriage would seal your future, and there is no guarantee you could find work elsewhere. At least not as a chef. I doubt the chefs in Chicago restaurants would welcome a woman into their fold."

"I think I could find at least one who would, and I'm willing to marry you based on that belief."

He placed the sandwich on his napkin and grasped her hands in his. "I think the best idea would be for you to discover whether that belief is realistic. Explain my thoughts to Chef René and ask him to write you a letter of recommendation. Armed with his letter, I'd like you to apply for positions in Chicago and see if anyone will offer you a job. Not as a dishwasher—as an assistant chef." He released her hands and leaned back against the ancient tree. "What do you think?"

She hesitated. If she refused, it would appear as if she lacked confidence in her own ability to locate a new position, but if she accepted and failed—what then?

Gathering her courage, she met Fred's gaze. "If I'm unable

to locate a position, are you going to withdraw your proposal of marriage?"

"No. But why don't we see what happens and then decide? Nothing has changed in regard to my love for you, but I think it's unwise to move forward until we know what hurdles we will have to overcome—and if we possess the strength to conquer them."

She was already certain they could overcome any obstacle if they worked together, but if it would set Fred's mind at ease, she would agree to his request. "First thing tomorrow I'll ask Chef René to write a letter."

"Good. Now, what ideas do you have that might help Bill and his family?"

Olivia stared at him, dumbfounded by the sudden shift of topic. "Ideas for Bill?"

"Yes. You mentioned helping him find ways to rebuild his life."

"I did say that." Fred obviously thought she'd had some perfect solution at the ready. She floundered, still trying to settle her scattered thoughts. "Did you speak to his physician about what type of work he might be able to perform?"

"Bill isn't interested in any other type of work. The doctor attempted to speak to him, but he brushed aside any suggestions. He wants only to draw and etch. Until he accepts he can no longer do either, he'll not embrace any other work."

"If that is his attitude, then he must learn to draw with his other hand. Have you suggested that to him? Has he made any attempt?"

"I think he would scoff at such a suggestion," Fred replied.

"Let him scoff, but force him to try, unless he's willing to seek some other form of employment. You're his friend. Force him to listen and take action; that's what friends do, isn't it?"

"You're right, but I doubt—"

"Don't doubt until you've tried. You're certainly willing to issue challenges to me. Perhaps you need to do the same with Bill. Tell him that he must do one or the other: either make a considerable effort to draw with his uninjured hand or determine what other employment is available for him. Tell him to compile a list of ideas."

Fred chuckled. "I doubt he'll come up with a list. He'll probably consider himself fortunate if he's able to conjure up one or two ideas."

Olivia knew Fred was correct. Locating jobs was difficult enough for able-bodied men. But Bill still possessed talent and intelligence. He should not waste either.

———————

When she approached the hotel the following morning, Olivia couldn't believe her eyes. There appeared to be more than a thousand strikers outside the main gate of the car works. They had formed orderly rows while they awaited a signal from one of the clerks or supervisors. Benjamin Guilfoyle, one of the men who had worked with Fred, stood in line.

He waved in recognition as Olivia approached. "Good morning, Benjamin. You're going back to work?"

"Yes. My wife insisted that I reapply while the company is giving preference to former employees. I didn't want to resign my membership in the union, but it's the only way they'll agree to hire us back." He shook his head. "It seems our strike was for naught. We go back to the same job for the same wage, and our rent remains as high as ever."

Olivia watched one of the men step forward, sign his name

in the ledger book, and add his tattered union card to the mounting pile.

"What about Fred?" Benjamin asked. "I heard the union organizers won't be considered."

"He's helping Bill Orland with his business in Chicago. I don't know what the future holds, but he won't be able to return to Pullman." She nodded toward the hotel. "I had better get to work. Give my regards to your wife."

"I'll do that. Tell Fred I hope he won't hold it against any of us for going back to work."

Olivia reassured Benjamin before she hurried back across the street to the hotel. Now she must face Chef René. She had considered waiting until later in the day, but she feared she would lose her courage. After donning her white jacket, she quietly made her request.

"You want *what*?" The chef rested his beefy hands on his hips and stared into her eyes.

Olivia forced a feeble smile. "A letter of recommendation," she whispered.

He pointed to the hallway. "Into my office, Miss Mott!"

Every member of the staff had turned to look at her when he bellowed his command. She followed behind the chef, feeling like a disobedient child. He proceeded into the office and waited until she sat down before closing the door and wedging himself into the chair across from her.

"I would like an explanation for this sudden request of yours." He folded his arms across his chest and waited. She explained her conversation with Fred, and when she'd finished, he slowly shook his head. "Your Fred is an intelligent man." The chef pointed to his head. "He knows how much the cooking means to you, and I can understand why he worries you will become a disgruntled wife. If you cannot continue to work and develop your cooking skills, I, too, worry you will be most unhappy. This would not be good."

"Then since you agree with Fred, you'll write a letter?"

He shrugged his broad shoulders. "A letter will serve no purpose for you. The chefs in Chicago's fine hotels will not hire you."

"Why not?"

He held up his thumb. "One, because you are a woman." He extended his index finger. "Two, because you are a woman who will soon be married." With his next finger extended, he said, "Three, because there are many men seeking work right now, and you are a woman."

Olivia scooted forward and leaned across the desk. "I know I am a woman, but I am a fine chef—you've said so yourself. I don't think it will matter once they taste my food."

"I will write the letter, but you will see I am correct. You can go and ask those Chicago chefs to hire you; then you will return to my kitchen. There is no reason why you can't work here and be married to your Fred. Once you are married, I will not discharge you." His chest puffed like a giant balloon. He acted as though he were the only man who would do such a thing.

Obviously he didn't understand the full depth of their situation. "If I marry Fred, do you truly believe Mr. Howard and Mr. Pullman will permit me to remain an employee of the hotel—or to work anywhere in Pullman? My Fred, as you call him, was a union leader. He helped organize and encourage the men to strike. Do you think they would permit Thomas Heathcoate—or his wife—to work for the company?"

"Did she work for them before the strike?"

Olivia rested her forehead in her palm. The man simply did

not understand the complexities of this situation. "No, she didn't work for them, and they have moved from Pullman."

"Then I don't see the problem."

There was no use continuing this discussion. She doubted whether anything she said would clarify the issue. "You will write the letter?"

"I will write the letter, *if* you will agree to continue to work for me when you do not find other employment, and if I can convince Mr. Howard you should not be discharged when you and your Fred are married." He offered an exaggerated wink. "He has not forced me to discharge Hazel."

Of course he hadn't. Unlike Olivia, Mrs. DeVault had never rebuffed Mr. Howard's advances or manipulated him to secure her position at the hotel. The chef was comparing apples with oranges and expected Olivia to consider his conclusion an unshakable truth.

She scooted her chair back and stood. "If I cannot secure employment elsewhere, and—"

He held up his hand and interrupted. "Employment as a chef."

Olivia sighed. "If I cannot secure employment elsewhere as a *chef*, and if Mr. Howard agrees I may continue to work in Hotel Florence as a *chef*, then I will do so." She turned and took the few steps to the door. With her hand on the glass doorknob, she glanced over her shoulder. "*If* you write a suitable recommendation." That said, she hastened from the room.

"Do not tell me what I must write, Miss Mott!"

She hurried down the hallway with his declaration ringing in her ears. For a moment she considered returning to ask if he would prepare the letter by noonday. Her lips curved in a faint smile. No. She dared not push him too far.

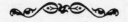

CHAPTER TWENTY-SIX

Chicago, Illinois
Wednesday, August 22, 1894

A chair scraped across the wooden floor of the café, but Fred didn't turn away from his meal until a chair clunked down beside him. "Mind if I join you?"

He smiled up at Matthew and pointed to the plate of food. "Sit down. Hash is the special—not pretty but tasty and filling."

Matthew waved at the owner. Hank's wide girth was covered with a stained white dish towel. No chef's jacket or apron for him. He tucked a towel around his waist, and when it got too dirty, he yanked it off and replaced it with another. Hank said his business was about efficiency and good food. If people were looking for more, he sent them to the fancy hotel restaurants, where they could spend a week's wages on their meal.

"I'll take the special and coffee," Matthew shouted over the din of lunching patrons. Hank waved in recognition, and Matthew sat down. "Didn't expect to see you, my friend. Business slow over at Bill's place?"

Fred shook his head. "No. It's on the upswing." He rubbed

his midsection. "They do give me time to eat."

Hank ambled across the crowded room with Matthew's order. A buttered roll divided the hash from a serving of cottage cheese. Matthew turned up his nose at the sight. "Cottage cheese? Can't stand the stuff."

Fred held out his plate, and Matthew quickly scooped the unwanted food onto his plate. "What's today's story? Are you sitting in on more of the Strike Commission hearings?"

President Cleveland had ordered the hearings, using the Arbitration Act as his basis of authority. One portion of the legislation provided that a fact-finding commission could be set up for labor-management disputes if a governor or the president requested such a commission. The commission was meeting at the main Chicago post office and taking testimony from anyone who wished to come before them.

Matthew shoved a forkful of the hash into his mouth before removing several folded pieces of paper from his pocket. "No. I'll not be attending the strike hearings today. From all appearances, the commission is going to have at least another full week of testimony."

Fred hadn't attended any of the hearings, and he didn't intend to, for he thought it would do little good at this juncture. However, when the commission said it would accept written statements from those who could not attend, he'd written a lengthy report. He had nothing more to lose, though the commission would undoubtedly consider his remarks tainted by his American Railway Union affiliation.

"I'll return to the hearings tomorrow," Matthew continued. "At the moment I have a more interesting story to write. This should interest you." He shoved the pages toward Fred. "I copied these word for word. Don't ask how I gained access to them."

"I wouldn't think of it." Fred unfolded the pages and took a sip of his coffee. The first page, dated August 19, and addressed to George M. Pullman as president of the Pullman Palace Car Company, was from Governor Altgeld. Fred glanced over the rim of his cup.

"Go ahead. Read them. You'll find each one quite interesting. If my editor won't let me print them word for word, I plan to at least give readers the primary message each letter contains."

The first letter mentioned that the governor had received a formal appeal for aid from the residents of Pullman, stating that sixteen hundred families were starving and they could not get work because the car works was bringing in men from all over the country to take their places. The letter avowed that the governor had no wish to interfere in the company's business but asked Mr. Pullman to consider the fact that the state was without sufficient resources to further aid the town's residents. The governor went on to say that he would travel to Chicago that night to make a personal investigation before taking official action. He requested that Mr. Pullman call on him at ten o'clock the next morning.

Matthew held his cup overhead and caught Hank's eye. "After receiving that letter, you'd think any man would bow to the governor's request, wouldn't you?"

"Any *reasonable* man. We must remember we're speaking of George Pullman."

Matthew thanked Hank for the coffee and tapped the papers. "Read the next one."

The second sheet was a subsequent letter from the governor

to Mr. Pullman dated August 21. The letter had been written after Governor Altgeld's inspection of Pullman and stated two representatives of management had accompanied the governor on the visit. The letter confirmed the suffering and waning charity for the town's residents. Fred was pleased to see that the governor had managed to review the records listing employee names and the number of those who remained unemployed.

While management touted they were hiring any man who had previously worked for the company, Fred knew that assertion to be false. And these numbers proved that fact. Prior to the strike, there had been over three thousand employees, but on August 20 there were only two thousand, and of that number over six hundred were new employees. Only fourteen hundred of the old employees had been taken back, leaving over sixteen hundred out of work. Altgeld went on to state the men verified they had applied for work but were told they were not needed.

The governor suggested that Pullman cancel rental fees for the town's residents until the first of October to give families an opportunity to use their wages for food and other urgent needs. And Altgeld recommended that the company hire as many people as possible on at least a half-time basis.

Matthew tapped the page. "What do you think of the governor's proposed solution?"

"It might work, but I have no doubt Mr. Pullman will throw the letter in the trash—if he even bothers to read it."

"I think he's a fool if he doesn't make some attempt. He's part of the problem, so he should help with the solution." Matthew swallowed another gulp of coffee.

Fred didn't disagree. But he also didn't believe that George Pullman would let any other man dictate how he should address the problems within his company.

At the end of his letter, once again the governor requested a response or personal meeting with Mr. Pullman. This time Mr. Pullman replied. A missive was hand-delivered to the governor while he was still in Chicago. The third sheet was the governor's response to Mr. Pullman's letter.

Fred riffled through the pages. "You don't have a copy of the letter Mr. Pullman wrote the governor?"

Matthew shook his head. "No. But there's enough in that last letter from the governor to let you know exactly what was written."

Apparently Mr. Pullman had attempted to place the moral responsibility for the strike upon the workers and had alleged that the men and their families were not suffering. However, Altgeld's response chastised the company owner for permitting the starvation of former employees, many of whom had been in his employ for more than ten years.

Fred pointed to a sentence near the end of the letter. "I must say, the governor's words should have given Mr. Pullman pause. But it doesn't appear he's going to shoulder any of the responsibility. He's going to leave it to the state of Illinois and its citizenry."

"I wonder if he'll be embarrassed when people discover the governor has upbraided him for asking the state to expend large sums of money to protect his property while he will do nothing to help the starving residents of his town."

Fred wiped up the remnants of his hash with a bite of roll and popped it into his mouth. "Little seems to bother Mr. Pullman's conscience. And it appears there is nothing that will convince him to spend any of his profits to help the residents of his town, either." Fred swiped his napkin across his mouth and dropped it onto the table. "Good food. Glad you told me about this place."

"Not as good as the food Olivia prepares, I'm sure. And what of Olivia? Have the two of you set your wedding date? I've not received an invitation."

"We've come to an impasse, and I'm not certain if or when we will wed."

"If? Now that sounds serious." Matthew rested his forearms on the table. "What's happened? Another man? Please don't tell me Samuel Howard has managed to win her affections."

Fred quickly recounted their recent agreement. "Olivia wasn't in favor of the idea, but she finally accepted. She spoke to Chef René the very next day, and he agreed to give her a letter of reference, though he hasn't yet given it to her. The last I heard, he told her ten days was a reasonable amount of time, and he would do his best to have it to her by tomorrow."

"Wouldn't it be easier to simply marry her and hope for the best? That's what most folks do. If she locates work, fine. If not, she'll learn to be content."

"Or be unhappy. That's not what I want in my marriage. I don't want to come home to a wife who will grow to resent me and spend her days and nights longing for another life, or the life she had before she married me. It would be unfair to Olivia. She deserves happiness, and much of what makes her happy is working as a chef."

"It's true she's accomplished something few women have achieved, yet if she says—"

Fred grasped Matthew's arm. "No. First she must realize the depth of what she might be required to sacrifice before she can begin to make a clear decision. She says she wants to marry me even if she can't work." Fred tapped his index finger to his temple. "But up here she believes she will have no difficulty locating a position in Chicago."

Matthew shook his head. "I admire your desire to ensure Olivia's happiness, but life is full of unplanned circumstances that can send even the best of plans awry. Look at Bill Orland. Who would have ever thought he'd made a poor choice by moving to Chicago and purchasing the etching business? Now he's at your mercy."

"I hope that's not how Bill looks at it," Fred said as he picked up his hat. "After all, he's paying me a small wage and providing me with a place to live. And most days I take my meals with them."

Matthew stood and the two of them walked to the counter to pay their bill. "I know you've been an immense help, and I'm sure Bill is grateful, but if he'd known what lay in store for him, he probably wouldn't have accepted Mr. Lockabee's offer to purchase his business."

As the two men walked out of the restaurant, Fred donned his cap. "This isn't the same as what happened to Bill. But since you've mentioned him, I'm trying to develop a plan to help him sort out his future. He's not himself, and his behavior makes life difficult for Ruth and the children." The two men continued down the street and stopped at the corner as they prepared to part ways. "You're in contact with a lot of people. Maybe you could help me come up with a strategy for him."

"I can't think of anything right off, but I'll give it some thought. Lunch again tomorrow?"

"How about Friday? I'm not a newspaper reporter. I can't afford to eat at a restaurant every day." He slapped Matthew on the shoulder. "By the way, how is Charlotte? I haven't seen her for quite a while."

"We don't have time to discuss both Charlotte and Olivia in one day." He chuckled. "We'll save that conversation for Friday." With a wave he headed across the street.

Fred waited until a fancy carriage pulled by two sleek black steeds passed by before he continued on his way. He should have cautioned Matthew against mentioning their conversation to Charlotte, for Olivia would surely disapprove.

After tucking Morgan into bed for the night, Charlotte went downstairs. The house seemed unusually quiet. Had it not been for the dim light in the parlor, she would have returned to her room. Charlotte entered the sitting room and circled the wing chair to find Mrs. Priddle with her head bowed. The older woman's open Bible rested in her lap, and the familiar white bun sat atop her head in perfect symmetry. Keeping her knobby index finger pointed to her place on the page, Mrs. Priddle looked up, her eyes shining with expectancy.

"Did you wish to speak to me?" the older woman asked.

The endearing tone was as inviting as a warm embrace, so Charlotte sat down in the nearby chair. "I have a problem. Together I hope we can arrive at a suitable solution."

Mrs. Priddle placed a crocheted bookmark in her Bible and closed the worn leather cover. "I'm listening."

The older woman was attentive while Charlotte described Mr. Rehnquist's indecorous advances and his subsequent threat. "I'm uncertain how to handle this situation. I can't afford to lose my employment with Mr. Field, yet I refuse to succumb to Mr. Rehnquist's menacing behavior."

"I agree that Mr. Rehnquist's actions are abhorrent. And I now see why you've been so reluctant to go outdoors of late."

She patted Charlotte's hand. "As you said, your wages are important to you and Morgan—and to Priddle House, as well." She massaged her forehead with the tips of her fingers. "Can you possibly wait a day or two longer before taking any further action? I need time to think."

"Yes, of course. I didn't expect you would have an answer at the ready." Charlotte nodded toward the kitchen. "Would you care to join me for a cup of tea?"

Mrs. Priddle shook her head. "No. I believe I'll go upstairs, but you go right ahead. Make certain the door is locked when you come up."

———

When Charlotte prepared to depart the store on Thursday, Joseph Anderson pulled her aside outside the front door. "That Mrs. Priddle is quite a little lady, isn't she?"

"Indeed she is. I didn't know you were acquainted with her, Joseph."

He glanced up at Charlotte. Even with his shoulders squared at full attention, Joseph was at least three inches shorter than Charlotte. "Until she arrived at the store this morning, I wasn't, but she—"

"Mrs. Priddle was here? This morning?"

He tilted his head to the side and met Charlotte's gaze. "That's right. She came to see Mr. Field." He chuckled. "She didn't have an appointment. When Mr. Sturgeon told her he couldn't fit her in the schedule until next week, she returned downstairs and talked to me."

Charlotte was becoming more confused by the moment. "About what?"

"This and that . . . nothing of any importance. She asked me if I liked working at the store and if Mr. Field treated me well, did he speak to me when he arrived in the morning or did he come and go through another entrance. She was very attentive when I explained how he visits each department on a daily basis just to see if everything is in proper order. When I finished, she even asked a few more questions," he proudly announced.

"What questions?"

"Oh, she inquired if he followed a certain routine each day or if he merely made random visits to the departments. She was curious how long it took him to check each area." He grinned. "After we finished our talk, she went back inside the store for a while. I have to say that she was far more interested in the store's operation than any of the other customers I greet each day. Nice lady."

"Did she say if she happened to come upon Mr. Field during her final excursion through the store?"

Joseph's brow wrinkled as he contemplated her question. "No, I believe I'd remember if she told me she'd spoken to Mr. Field." He brightened and his eyebrows rose high on his forehead. "She did tell me it had been a successful venture. Yes—those were her exact words: 'a successful venture.'" He waved his gloved hand and hurried to open the door for a departing employee.

Charlotte walked across the street and stopped at the corner. She lifted on tiptoe while pretending to look at something in the distance. She glanced toward the upper windows of the store and spotted Mr. Rehnquist as he watched the unfolding scene below him. Forcing herself to turn away, Charlotte headed toward home. Although she hadn't seen him yesterday, the department manager was clearly visible this evening. Despite the warmth of the day, she shivered.

There would be little time to speak to Mrs. Priddle about her visit to the store until later in the evening, for she was busy overseeing preparation of the evening meal. While two of the ladies dished up the food, Mrs. Priddle and Fiona carried it to the table. Charlotte corralled Morgan and attempted to entertain him with a game of peek-a-boo, but he was more interested in the bowls of food being carried to the table.

"Eat!" he said, tugging his mother's hands away from her eyes.

"We'll eat in a minute," Charlotte said. Holding each arm, she bent his chubby elbows and positioned his hands over his eyes. "Now you say *peek-a-boo*."

"Eat!" Morgan shouted, pointing a finger toward the dining room.

Fiona laughed and motioned him forward. "We're ready for you now, Morgan."

He ran toward her on chubby legs and crawled onto his chair with only a little assistance from Fiona. Charlotte marveled at his antics. He was growing up so rapidly. It didn't seem possible he would turn two in a matter of a few days. One part of her was amazed at each of his new accomplishments, while the other longed for him to slow down and remain her baby. All mothers must possess mixed emotions as their children grew and matured, she decided.

He pointed to the chair beside his own. "Sit!" Morgan's command carried undeniable enthusiasm.

Charlotte removed the spoon from his fist and clasped his hands while Mrs. Priddle prayed. After thanks had been given for their meal, Charlotte helped herself to a serving of potatoes and spooned a small amount onto Morgan's dish. "Did you have a good day?" she inquired, handing the bowl to Mrs. Priddle.

The older woman grasped the serving dish. "Yes. Very good, thank you."

She'd need to be more succinct with her questions if she expected Mrs. Priddle to divulge where she'd spent a portion of the day. "What did you do?"

"Housework, shopping, and visiting." She pointed to the bowl in front of Charlotte. "Please pass the green beans. We'll talk later."

Their conversation ceased as quickly as it had begun.

———

After they'd completed the evening meal and Morgan was asleep, Charlotte joined Mrs. Priddle on the front porch. "Joseph Anderson, the doorman at the store, said you were at the store today and he'd had a nice conversation with you."

Mrs. Priddle wrinkled her nose. "He should be more tight-lipped. I'll have to tell him that the next time I see him."

Charlotte chuckled. "I don't think he considered your shopping to be a matter that required great secrecy."

Mrs. Priddle continued her knitting, the needles clicking in a quiet rhythm. "Well, he *should*! I don't like anyone discussing my business. And I'd venture a guess that there are women shopping in that store who don't want their husbands to know they're out spending money. How does Mr. Anderson know that I'm not one of those women?"

"Mr. Anderson doesn't know, and I will speak to him tomorrow morning. Why were you at the store?"

The clicking of needles and chirping of crickets were the only response. Charlotte decided the woman was attempting to circumvent any questions about her visit to Marshall Field's, but she didn't intend to allow that to happen again. Mrs.

Priddle had silenced her questions during supper, and Charlotte had acquiesced, but she now wanted answers.

"Mrs. Priddle?" Charlotte arched her brows.

"I purchased a spool of thread for Fiona's dress."

"A spool of thread doesn't require a visit to Marshall Field's. There's more to the visit than you're admitting."

"I stopped to have a chat with Mr. Field."

"With Mr. Field?" Charlotte choked out the words. "How did you manage an appointment on such short notice?"

"My visit with Mr. Anderson proved beneficial. He explained Mr. Field's route through the store, and I managed to locate him without a great deal of difficulty. He was pleased to see me and even had tea delivered to his office." She grinned and a sparkle of mischief shone in her eyes. "I believe Mr. Sturgeon was annoyed by my reappearance."

Charlotte didn't doubt that fact in the least. Mr. Sturgeon had likely considered Mrs. Priddle an interloper of the worst sort.

"I gave him an update on Priddle House and thanked him for his continuing kindness in hiring my girls when he had openings." She pointed her knitting needles in Charlotte's direction. "He immediately mentioned how pleased he'd been with all you'd accomplished in the store. His comment gave me the proper opportunity to tell him that he had a less than upstanding employee working for him. I knew he would be pleased to receive the information."

Charlotte gasped. "You told him about Mr. Rehnquist?"

"Of course. I knew you wouldn't do anything other than worry over the situation. I thought it best to take matters into my own hands."

"You're only going to succeed in making the situation worse.

Once Mr. Rehnquist discovers Mr. Field knows, he'll retaliate. You mark my words: this isn't a good thing you've done."

"Have a little faith, Charlotte. I think you'll find that the three of us have the situation under control."

"Three? You've told someone else?"

She placed her knitting in her lap. "Me, Mr. Field, and God. I wouldn't leave God out of the equation."

Charlotte sighed. "No. Of course you wouldn't."

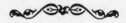

CHAPTER TWENTY-SEVEN

Armed with Chef René's letter, Olivia boarded the train Friday morning for Chicago. Her request for a day away from her kitchen duties had met with the chef's resistance, but after much cajoling and checking of schedules, she'd finally convinced him. There were few guests registered at the hotel this week, and no special luncheons or dinners had been scheduled. Moreover, the board members and Mr. Howard had been spending most of their days at the commission hearings in Chicago. They didn't hide the fact that they wanted firsthand reports of any information furnished to the Strike Commission.

Her departure had been delayed until later than expected. Although she'd agreed to help with breakfast, each time she removed her toque, Chef René requested assistance with just one more item. When Olivia finally removed her white jacket and hurried toward the door at ten thirty, he made one final attempt to waylay her, but she successfully resisted.

The train was scheduled to arrive in Chicago at eleven o'clock. Nearly half the day had already passed, and she'd accomplished nothing. Olivia had hoped to see both Fred and Charlotte while in the city, but now she wondered if that would be possible. She should have insisted upon leaving immediately after breakfast.

She leaned her head against the cushioned seat and willed the train to move faster. Although she'd made a list of a few places where she could apply, she hoped Charlotte would provide her with further assistance before beginning her job search.

Leaving the train station in Chicago, she hailed a carriage. "Marshall Field and Company," she told the driver and braced herself for the ride. The mere remembrance of most of her previous carriage trips through Chicago was enough to set her on edge. It seemed as if the drivers took great pleasure in traveling at breakneck speed.

The driver reined the horses to an abrupt stop that caused her head to tip forward and back in a snapping lunge. She clasped a hand to her bodice, pleased to have arrived at the department store without major injury. The doorman hurried forward to assist her from the carriage, and she grasped his hand in a tight grip while she attempted to gain her balance.

He offered a broad smile and tip of his hat. "Are you new to our store, ma'am? I don't believe I recognize you."

Olivia tipped her head close. "I live in Pullman and don't normally shop in Chicago."

"Ah, I see. Well, you're in for a real treat. I hope you'll enjoy yourself and come back again and again."

His kindness set Olivia at ease. "I am a friend of Miss Charlotte Spencer. She works for Mr. Field. Might you know her?"

"Indeed I do. A lovely lady. She holds an important position, you know. Even has her own office." The man pointed toward the upper floors of the building and grinned like a proud parent. "Up there."

A wave of fear washed over Olivia as she stared through the glass doors. How could she possibly locate Charlotte's office? "Perhaps you could direct me. I tend to get lost easily, even after visiting the same location several times. And this store, well, it's enormous, isn't it?"

The man squared his shoulders and gave a nod. "Indeed it is. The finest in all of Chicago—or anywhere else, so far as I'm concerned." He chuckled and stepped closer. "Of course I've never been anywhere but Chicago, but I still think I'm correct." He opened the door and waved Olivia forward. "Come along. I'll take you to Miss Spencer's office."

The doorman signaled to another uniformed man to take his place at the front door, and Olivia followed him through the maze of aisles. "Miss Spencer should be in her office, but if she's not, you rest easy. We'll find her. By the way, I'm Joseph Anderson."

"I'm Olivia Mott. Miss Spencer and I were traveling companions two years ago when we relocated from London to Chicago."

"I did notice you and Miss Spencer share a similar accent. Always nice to have friends living nearby. Now me, I've got all my friends and family right here in Chicago—sometimes too many of them," he said and then chortled. "My wife says you can never have too many relatives, but I'm not sure I agree." He pointed toward the elevator. "We're going to Miss Spencer's office," he told the elevator operator.

The operator closed the folding metal gate with great precision, rotated the dial to the proper position, and then pulled a lever that propelled them upward. The same queasiness she'd experienced while riding the giant Ferris wheel at the Colum-bian Exposition assailed her. She grasped a thin iron rail along the side of the car.

Mr. Anderson grinned. "You'll become accustomed to it after a few times."

Olivia didn't reply. She feared the slightest movement might cause her to lose her breakfast. She'd felt somewhat queasy ear-lier in the morning, and the carriage ride hadn't helped. Mr. Anderson cautioned her to wait for a moment after stepping off the elevator so she wouldn't experience any dizziness. She didn't tell him she might have need of more than a few moments before she regained her sense of well-being.

He took hold of her arm. "Right this way."

Mr. Anderson didn't seem to notice her woozy state as he continued to chatter while they walked down the hallway. He knocked on a beautiful carved door. Olivia remembered nothing more until she awakened. Charlotte was staring down at her while holding a wet cloth on her forehead.

"I cannot believe that I swooned in the middle of Marshall Field's store." Olivia strained to see if anyone else was in the room. "Mr. Anderson?"

"He's returned to his duties at the front door. I told him I was more than able to care for you, although he did want to fetch a doctor."

"Did he say if anyone saw me? I am terribly embarrassed. My first visit to your office and I make a fool of myself." Olivia pushed up on her elbows and took in her surroundings. "And it's such a beautiful office."

Charlotte chuckled. "You didn't make a fool of yourself. There were no customers in the area, and Joseph helped me move you to the settee."

"This room is as finely furnished as any of the sitting rooms in the Pullman mansion." Olivia recalled the fashionable décor she'd observed while helping plan for one of Mrs. Pullman's social gatherings two years ago.

"Yes, it's lovely, but the furnishings belong to Mr. Field, not to me." Charlotte opened the clasp on the watch pinned to her bodice and checked the time. "Are you feeling well enough to sit up? Once you're stronger, we should get you something to eat. I don't want you to faint again. I could have a tray sent up here if you'd rather not visit the tearoom."

Olivia removed the cloth from her forehead. "I'm feeling much better. My stomach wasn't quite right when I woke up this morning, but I believe I'm fine. I would prefer a visit to the tearoom—if it isn't outrageously expensive, and if I'm not required to ride the elevator."

Charlotte chuckled. "We can use the stairway instead of the elevator. And your meal will be my treat. I'm entitled to a discount on any purchases. The tearoom shouldn't be overly crowded at this hour. It's a bit late for luncheon and early for tea."

Olivia's pulse quickened and she shifted to an upright position. "What time is it?"

"There's no need to shout." Charlotte patted her hand. "It's only a little after one o'clock."

"One o'clock!" Olivia jumped to her feet and then dropped down just as quickly when once again assaulted by her earlier dizziness. "What is wrong with me? I wonder if I have contracted some sort of illness."

"In all likelihood you merely jumped to your feet too quickly after suffering the fainting spell. Take a moment and then try standing again more slowly."

Olivia did as Charlotte suggested. With slow, even steps they crossed the distance to the door. When they stepped outside the office, Olivia giggled. "If anyone saw us, they'd think we were ninety years old. What women our age totter across a room in such a dawdling fashion?"

"Only those who have suffered a fainting spell prior to attempting to navigate two lengthy staircases." Charlotte tightened her hold on Olivia's arm when they began their descent. "Hold the railing with your other hand. If you're injured, I'll be taken to task for not insisting on another person to help you."

Olivia clutched the rail and focused upon each step. Although she would have much preferred to take in the sights, she feared the slightest glance at the floors below might cause another fainting spell. She inhaled a deep breath when Charlotte announced they had only one additional hallway to traverse before they would arrive at their destination. Charlotte continued to watch her closely until they'd been seated and served their tea. Olivia was struck by how their lives had changed since arriving in this country. She would never have imagined the Lady Charlotte of old lending a helping hand or worried over the welfare of a scullery maid.

"I'm feeling much better now. Thank you for your kindness."

"Well, of course. That's what friends do for one another, isn't it?" Charlotte took a sip of her tea. "I haven't yet heard why you happen to be in Chicago on a workday. All of this strike business hasn't caused you to lose your position at the hotel, has it?"

"No, but I am seeking other employment."

Charlotte arched her brows. "Why? What's happened?"

While Olivia explained Fred's concerns and his request that she seek employment in Chicago before they set their wedding date, a uniform-clad waiter delivered their food. The china placed in front of her rivaled anything used in Hotel Florence, as did the food. At Charlotte's suggestion, she'd ordered chicken potpie, a tearoom specialty. The flaky crust equaled the best she had ever tasted.

"Delicious!" She dabbed the corner of her mouth with the embroidered linen napkin. "Perhaps I was simply hungry. I didn't eat much for breakfast this morning. I wonder if the chef would consider sharing the recipe with me."

Charlotte chuckled. "I think you need to expend your energies on seeking employment rather than a recipe for potpie. Have you developed a plan? Where do you intend to apply? It's going to be extremely difficult, you know."

"Why? I have an excellent letter of reference." She grinned. "And this one is genuine."

The two of them laughed, but Charlotte soon turned sober. "Even if a position is available in one of the finer restaurants, I'm afraid you'll meet with resistance."

"Once they taste my food and learn of my varied culinary abilities, I hope they will all want to hire me."

Charlotte folded her hands together and rested them atop the table. "You're deluding yourself if you truly believe what you're saying. First of all, few women are hired into positions of authority."

"But you've attained an impressive position. Why should it be any more difficult for me?"

"This position is one that was created after I had been employed as a clerk in the Accessories Department. I didn't carry a letter of reference, but even if I had, I don't believe Mr. Field would have hired me for my current position." Charlotte reached for her cup and took a sip of tea.

"Chef René hired me with no more than a letter—and I couldn't even cook back then."

"Women aren't easily accepted, especially in positions generally given to men. Granted, folks appear to think it's acceptable for women to work as maids and housekeepers, or as teachers and the like, but opportunities are few for other positions—especially for married women."

Olivia remained silent until the waiter had removed their plates. "But Chef René hired me!"

"Of course he did—because the letter I wrote bore the Lanshire seal. Mr. Pullman didn't want to insult my father. Otherwise, do you truly believe you would have been selected to work in the hotel? They hadn't even advertised for an employee. You're deceiving yourself if you believe otherwise."

"Then you're unwilling to help me?" Olivia rested her elbow on the table and propped her chin in her palm.

Concern shone in Charlotte's eyes as she leaned across the small table. "Are you going to swoon again?"

"No, of course not, but I need to prepare a list of restaurants where I can apply. I had hoped for your help since I'm unfamiliar with the city."

"I didn't mean to indicate I would not help you. I merely want you to understand the difficulties so that you will be forearmed and won't be overly disappointed when you are faced with opposition." Charlotte signaled to the waiter and requested a pencil and paper. "We'll make a list, and you may still have time to make one or two calls today."

Olivia glanced at the clock. Charlotte was correct. No chef would want to be interrupted during the busiest portion of his day. Such a disruption would identify her as a novice of the worst sort. Unfortunately, valuable time had already been frittered away. The likelihood that she would find employment on this day appeared bleak. And how many days would pass before Chef René would agree to another day away from the hotel kitchen? Perhaps if she agreed to work extra hours, he might consider her request.

"These are the two hotels I suggest you visit today. They are the finest hotels and boast exceptional restaurants. You will at least be able to form some idea as to how you will be received." Charlotte jotted down the names and addresses. "Afterward, come back to the store and we'll formulate a plan for your next visit." She handed Olivia the paper and grinned. "Do avoid the elevator upon your return."

"I don't need a warning about that!"

Moments later the waiter appeared with their bill, and soon Olivia was on her way. She did her best to remain calm. Charlotte had suggested the Grand Pacific Hotel and Palmer House for Olivia's first attempts. Because she and Charlotte had stayed at the Grand Pacific when they had first arrived in Chicago, Olivia decided she would begin there. She would at least have a small sense of familiarity when walking into the establishment.

Following Charlotte's instructions to keep her shoulders squared and head held high, Olivia stopped outside the entrance to the Grand Pacific and asked the uniformed doorman for directions to the manager's office. He was extremely helpful and gave her detailed directions. In her concern to remember all that he'd told her, she'd forgotten to give him a tip and wondered if he would still be on duty when she left. If so, she would slip him a coin on her way out of the hotel.

OFFICE was stenciled in large gold letters on the door.

Below, in slightly smaller letters, was the word *Manager*. She knocked lightly and gulped.

A voice from within bid her enter. Olivia had hoped to hear a woman's voice, but upon entering was instead greeted by an austere man who appeared old enough to be her grandfather. His look of disdain was enough to cause her voice to tremble.

"Good afternoon. I am Miss Olivia Mott of Pullman."

"And you have entered my office for what reason, Miss Mott?"

She fumbled in her purse and removed the letter of recommendation. "I have come to apply for a position as a chef in your restaurant. Well, an *assistant* chef—not the head chef, of course."

His disdain was replaced by a smirk. "*You* wish to apply to work in this hotel as a chef?"

"Assistant chef," she corrected. "Yes, I would very much like to do so. Is there an application form, or do I make an appointment to be interviewed? I'm not familiar with the process utilized by your establishment."

He tipped his chair back and stared up at her. "There *is* no process for a woman to apply for such a position. Our kitchen is fully staffed by professional chefs."

"I am a professional chef. I work at Mr. Pullman's Hotel Florence. I'm certain you've heard of Mr. Pullman."

"Who in all of Chicago has not heard of Mr. Pullman?" The man looked down his long, thin nose. "Your employment in his hotel is of little import to management here at Grand Pacific. We have standards for our employees, and you, Miss Mott, do not meet those standards." He returned to his paper work. She didn't move a muscle, and he finally looked up from his desk.

An Uncertain Dream

With a wave toward the door, he said, "Please close the door on your way out."

"You won't even look at my recommendation? It is written by Chef René, the executive chef of Hotel Florence. I may be more qualified than some of the men who are currently employed by you."

"I doubt that possibility exists, but I do not have time to argue with you." He tapped his desk. "I have work that requires my attention. You are dismissed."

At the door she cast a final glance over her shoulder, hoping he would stop her and say he'd made a terrible mistake. When that didn't occur, she stepped into the hallway and waited beside the door. Perhaps he needed a few minutes to realize the error of his ways. But when he didn't appear after five minutes had passed, Olivia slowly returned to the lobby and left. She arrived at the corner before she remembered the tip for the doorman, but her earlier feelings of generosity had already evaporated, and she trudged on toward the corner of State and Monroe.

She forced her shoulders straight and walked down Monroe Street. As she approached Palmer House, a doorman stepped forward and tipped his hat. "The ladies' entrance is off of State Street."

"And where do I enter if I want to apply for a position with the hotel?"

"I'd still suggest the ladies' entrance." Like the earlier doorman, he explained the path she should follow to arrive at the office where applications were accepted. She handed him a coin for his trouble, and he thanked her. "I don't think you'll find any opportunities, miss. There are lots of men looking for jobs."

Yet another reason she'd likely be passed over if a position existed. She continued down the street and rounded the corner, her confidence waning. With a forced smile, she entered the building and stepped down the hallway with what she hoped was an air of confidence. At the end of the tiled hallway, she made a sharp turn to the right and entered the office. Obviously stunned by her air of authority and uncertain what to do, the clerk summoned the manager. But when the older man appeared, her excitement fizzled. Like the manager of the Grand Pacific, he refused to accept an application from her.

Disheartened, she rushed from the office and collided with a man in a navy blue business suit. Her hat dipped over her eye and her purse fell to the floor.

"Let me retrieve that for you. My apologies, miss—" He stopped midsentence and stared at her.

Olivia couldn't guess which of them was more stunned. "Mr. Howard." She spoke his name like a breathy prayer.

He retrieved her purse while she hurriedly shoved her hat back into place. "Exactly why are you away from Hotel Florence during your working hours, Miss Mott?" The coldness of his voice matched his icy stare.

CHAPTER TWENTY-EIGHT

Anxiously watching for any sign of Olivia, Charlotte paced outside the store. Unless she'd been asked to prepare some dish and prove her talents as a chef, Olivia should have returned by now. Surely she would have asked someone for directions if she'd lost her way. Charlotte attempted to push aside thoughts of Matthew's many warnings to be careful of the vagrants and troublemakers wandering the streets. Had one of them taken advantage of Olivia? Could she be lying in an alleyway, battered and bleeding? Soon all of the employees would exit the building, and even Joseph, the trusty doorman who waited until the doors were locked each evening, would depart for home.

With silent determination, Charlotte paced back and forth until a carriage approached and came to a halt in front of the store. Joseph hurried to advise the passenger that the store had closed for the evening while Charlotte continued her vigil.

Then Joseph waved to Charlotte. "Your friend is inside the carriage, Miss Spencer."

Charlotte hurried forward. Inside, Olivia sat huddled with

her head resting on the velvet interior of the carriage. Joseph opened the door, and Charlotte glanced toward the man who sat opposite Olivia. She clasped her palm to her bodice, unable to conceal her astonishment. "Mr. Howard!"

Charlotte hadn't failed to note his look of surprise, either. Obviously, no one had mentioned her return to Chicago, or if they had, Mr. Howard had forgotten.

"Olivia is unwell. I offered to escort her back to Pullman, but she insisted upon coming here. She has experienced several fainting spells since we first encountered each other at Palmer House." He glanced at Olivia. "Except to direct me to this location, she seems unable to converse. I've not succeeded in extracting any additional information from her. I suppose there's nothing left to do but leave her in your care. Would you like the carriage?"

"Yes. That's most kind of you. I'll take Olivia home with me. I do appreciate your assistance."

Mr. Howard climbed out of the carriage.

"Although Olivia swooned earlier in the day, I thought she had returned to full health or I wouldn't have permitted her to walk about the city in this heat."

Mr. Howard touched his finger to the brim of his hat and turned to leave.

Charlotte stepped forward to block his path. "Will you be returning to Pullman this evening, sir?"

"Yes, but I'll return to Chicago in the morning. Is there something you require?"

"I wonder if you could advise Chef René of Miss Mott's condition and that she will not return home until tomorrow. I believe he is expecting her this evening."

Mr. Howard folded his arms across his chest. "I have no

idea what Chef René expects. I still do not know why Miss Mott is in Chicago when she should be at the hotel. Each time I broached the topic, she swooned. Perhaps the chef will have some answers."

Charlotte stared after him until he turned the corner and disappeared. Joseph assisted her into the carriage, and she bid him good-night before turning her attention to Olivia. "How do you happen to be keeping company with Mr. Howard?"

Once the carriage lurched forward, Olivia sat upright. "I wasn't keeping company with him. We collided in Palmer House. He's in town to attend the Strike Commission hearings. From what I gather, he had been at Palmer House to visit with several acquaintances before returning to Pullman." Olivia explained how she'd literally walked into him after attempting to apply for a position at the hotel. "He asked why I was there, and I felt a wave of panic when I could think of nothing to say, so I pretended to swoon. I didn't know what else to do. It seemed quite natural after my experience earlier in the day."

Charlotte giggled. "I'm sorry, but it's so dramatic. I can see it all as clearly as if I'd been there with you. Mr. Howard must have been very surprised to see you."

Olivia's eyes sparkled and a hint of pink tinged her cheeks. "I don't think his astonishment was any match for my own. However, I believe my performance would make me an excellent candidate for the stage."

Charlotte laughed until several tears trickled down her cheeks. "We must regain our composure before we arrive at Priddle House or the ladies will think we've taken leave of our senses."

The mention of Priddle House was enough to silence Olivia's laughter. "Will Mrs. Priddle object to my sudden appearance? I don't even have a nightgown with me."

"Mrs. Priddle is accustomed to emergencies of every sort. As for clothing, you need not worry. We have a closet filled with different styles and sizes, all donations from various churches and charities. If you stay for more than a day, you'll be expected to perform assigned chores. And everyone must attend the evening Bible study and prayer time after supper."

Charlotte tapped on the window to signal the driver. When he had brought the carriage to a halt, Charlotte turned the handle and pushed open the door. She attempted to pay the driver, but he shook his head. "The gentleman already paid me, ma'am."

Olivia shrugged. "I didn't know or I would have reimbursed him. I don't want to be obligated."

"You're already obligated—you work for him."

"Only indirectly," Olivia argued.

"He has the power to discharge you, so you work for him whether you care to admit it or not. I'm certain he's going to ply you for answers. And poor Chef René will be forced to endure arduous questioning this evening. I do wonder what he'll say."

"He may avoid a response, but I know he won't lie. I'll likely be unemployed come morning."

Their conversation was cut short when Fiona carried Morgan outside to greet his mother. After she set him on his feet, he toddled toward his mother with his arms outstretched. She lifted him into the air and laughed when he squealed with delight. "Look who I brought home with me, Fiona."

"Welcome to Priddle House, Miss Mott. It's very nice to see you again. Will you be joining us for supper?"

Charlotte gave an approving nod to the girl. "Fiona has been practicing her manners. What do you think, Olivia?"

"I believe your manners are impeccable, Fiona. At Miss

Spencer's invitation, I plan to join you for supper, thank you."

Fiona burst into a girlish giggle. "I'll inform Mrs. Priddle that we will be entertaining a guest this evening." She offered a slight curtsy and hurried back inside.

Morgan tugged at his mother's hat. "Hat off," he demanded.

Charlotte nuzzled his neck. "Let me get inside the house and put you down, and then I'll remove my hat." She turned toward Olivia. "He's learned that my hat means I'm going to leave," she explained. "Let's go in and I'll explain your circumstances to Mrs. Priddle and see if she needs any assistance before supper."

Olivia rolled a ball across the floor to Morgan while Charlotte hurried off to speak with the older woman. When she returned, she stooped down and retrieved the ball from beneath the sofa and handed it to her son. Cradling it in both arms, he scurried to the kitchen.

"Mrs. Priddle is pleased to have you stay with us."

"That's very kind of her."

"You were feeling fine when you departed the store. Did you go to the Grand Pacific?"

Olivia nodded. "Yes. I went there first." She described the disastrous results of her meeting with the manager and sighed as she leaned back in her chair. "He wouldn't even look at my letter of recommendation."

"I fear you're going to meet with those same results at all of the restaurants. Remind me again why you can't remain at Hotel Florence?"

"If I marry Fred, I will be considered an unacceptable employee because of his leadership position within the union."

"And what of Mrs. DeVault? I'm surprised Mr. Howard hired her."

"Chef René hired her without his approval. I think Mr. Howard decided with all of the strike activity and upheaval in the town, Mrs. DeVault was the least of his problems. He knows she poses no threat to the company."

"If you go to Mr. Howard, perhaps he would—"

Olivia shook her head. "Mr. Howard will not break the rules—especially for me. He's still angry that I chose Fred over him. He won't accept the fact that I would never have chosen to marry him."

"There's no doubt you're in the center of a difficult predicament."

Morgan toddled into the room and pointed toward the dining room. "Eat!"

Mrs. Priddle appeared and confirmed the boy's announcement. They gathered around the table, and after Mrs. Priddle's lengthy prayer of thanks, the bowls and platters were passed.

"I'm afraid this won't compare to your offerings at the hotel, Miss Mott, but it is substantial food, and I believe you'll find it palatable. I trust you are feeling better?"

Olivia smiled. "Yes, thank you. I've been plagued by waves of dizziness throughout the day, but I do hope they'll disappear completely soon. I plan to return to Pullman in the morning."

"If your health improves, perhaps you should apply at the DeJonghe Hotel. It's directly across the street from the main entrance of Palmer House. The DeJonghe has a fine restaurant."

"Early morning is a busy time in hotel kitchens. I don't think a visit would be appreciated at that time."

Charlotte spooned a small helping of noodles into Morgan's bowl. "I don't think you need worry on that account. You'll be fortunate if the manager permits you to complete an application, but it's important at least to make the attempt. That way Fred will know you're doing what he asked. Perhaps he'll retract his requirement."

"What kind of requirement?" Mrs. Priddle inquired.

Charlotte explained while the other ladies listened with interest. Morgan occasionally banged his spoon on his dish. He'd obviously learned the noisy activity would capture attention.

"I don't understand why he wants you to work. Most men prefer their wives remain at home. Sounds strange to me." Mrs. Priddle took a bite of her green beans. "Times are changing, I suppose, but it's never been the way of things for women to work outside the home. That's what the man does."

"Fred wants me to be happy. He thinks I'll grow to resent him if I must give up my duties as a chef."

"Fiddlesticks! You can cook for your husband and children. With your other household duties, that will keep you busy enough to ward off any bitterness. And you can tell him I said so."

Charlotte nudged Olivia. "You'll recall Mrs. Priddle isn't one to keep her opinions to herself."

Olivia nodded. "I agree with what you've said, but I don't think Fred will marry me unless I've found employment. I would be happy to remain at home and care for him, but how do I convince him?"

Mrs. Priddle shrugged her shoulders. "Men can be an ornery lot. Even when they have it wrong, they often think they know best. If it's God's plan for you to marry this young man, then it will happen. Otherwise, you must serve God without him. I wanted more years with Mr. Priddle, but God didn't see fit to leave him on earth with me." The old woman glanced around the table. "But look at the fine family He gave me to fill the void of not having Mr. Priddle with me. God's plan for you may be entirely different from anything you ever imagined."

Olivia didn't respond to Mrs. Priddle's comment about God's plan for her life, but she considered the older woman's words while she finished supper. Although there was truth in what Mrs. Priddle had said, Olivia didn't want a life without Fred. Even if God had some other plan, she wasn't interested. She simply had to make Fred understand that marriage to him was all she needed to make her happy.

The group gathered in the parlor after supper for Mrs. Priddle's Bible lesson. She opened her Bible and turned the whisper-thin pages. Apparently arriving at the page she wanted, she looked up. "Turn to the book of Ruth. It isn't long, so we'll read all four chapters."

The older woman waited while they thumbed through their Bibles and then nodded her approval when they all reached the proper place. She read with a serene countenance and strong voice while they followed along. When she completed the final verse, she gazed at each of them.

"Who would like to explain what we can learn from Ruth and Naomi?"

Fiona waved her hand in the air and waited until the older woman gave a nod. "That we should always be nice to old ladies and make sure they have enough to eat."

"Yes, that's certainly true. Thank you, Fiona. Anyone else?" She pinned Olivia with a probing stare. "What about you, Olivia? What can you learn from the story of Ruth and Naomi?"

"Naomi was very bitter about her husband and sons dying, but Ruth stayed with her. Later, Ruth married Boaz," Olivia replied.

Mrs. Priddle's lips curved in a soft smile. "I *know* the story, but there is a lesson to be learned if you'll open your heart to what is written."

Olivia squirmed in her chair. She'd understood the lesson, but she wasn't certain it applied to her life. Naomi might have been bitter about her circumstances and believed God had deserted her, but in the end He'd had a wonderful plan for both Naomi and Ruth. But Olivia didn't need another plan.

In fact, she had no desire for any plan other than the one she had in mind for her life. Quite frankly, she didn't believe God could improve upon it one bit. If He would merely melt the cold heart of a hotel manager so she could secure employment in Chicago, she'd be content.

When she didn't respond, one of the other ladies raised her hand. "I think the story shows us that what God allows in our lives will eventually bring good to us or teach us an important lesson so that we may help others."

Olivia sighed, thankful she hadn't been forced to say anything further, but she saw the disappointment that shone in Mrs. Priddle's eyes.

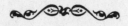

CHAPTER TWENTY-NINE

Olivia followed Charlotte downstairs Saturday morning. Except for dreams of being chased through the streets of Chicago by an angry chef, she'd slept well, with no remaining signs of yesterday's malady.

Mrs. Priddle stood near the front door while Olivia and Charlotte prepared to depart. "Will you be returning to Pullman, Miss Mott?"

"Once I've stopped at the hotel and completed my application." She forced a smile. "If I'm permitted to submit one, that is."

"Just remember what the Bible says." She patted Olivia's arm. "And if you begin to feel unwell, you must promise to return."

"Thank you for the generous offer, Mrs. Priddle."

Charlotte chuckled and looped arms with Olivia. "Mrs. Priddle says *men* think they always know best, but she's only a step or two behind them. She does mean well."

"I know she does. I think she's disappointed I'm going to

apply at the other hotel. She probably believes she failed in making her point, but she didn't. I understood every word she said, but I'm not ready to simply sit back and wait for Fred to change his mind." She looked at Charlotte. "Do you think I'm wrong?"

"I can't make your decisions for you, Olivia. I have enough trouble with my own dilemmas. And Mrs. Priddle inserts herself in those, too," she said with a faint smile.

When they arrived at the DeJonghe Hotel, Olivia grasped Charlotte's hand. "Do wish me well."

"You know I do. I want nothing but the best for you." Charlotte pulled her into a warm embrace.

"Tomorrow is Sunday. Why don't you and Morgan come for a visit? Matthew, too, if you'd like."

"Matthew meets me at church every Sunday. I'll ask if he'd like to spend the afternoon in Pullman. With the Strike Commission meetings, I can't say if he'll be working. He tells me the committee meets even on Sunday afternoons to permit testimony from those unable to attend during the workweek."

"If you decide you'd like to come, we'll be at Fred's house after church. I'm certain Morgan would enjoy himself."

The two of them parted, and Olivia entered the DeJonghe. With the help of a doorman, she located the manager's office and knocked on the door. A gentleman bid her come in. Remembering Charlotte's caution to stand tall, she squared her shoulders before entering the room.

The manager sat with his hands folded atop the desk as though he had expected her arrival. "Yes?" His eyebrows arched high on his forehead. "How may I be of assistance?" he inquired without offering her a chair.

"I am Olivia Mott—Miss Olivia Mott, assistant chef at

Hotel Florence in Pullman. I've come to apply for a position in your restaurant as an assistant chef." She watched his eyebrows coil into a scowl.

"I don't have time for nonsense. Who encouraged this hoax?"

"This is no prank, sir." She nodded toward the chair. "May I sit down for a moment?"

"I see no need, Miss Mott. Our kitchen is fully staffed"—he leaned across the desk—"by men!"

She hastily dug inside her purse. "I have a letter of recommendation from Chef René of Hotel Florence. If you'll read—"

"We have no need of you in our establishment." He stood and walked to the door. "If you'll excuse me, I have work to do." He opened the door.

She took his cue and left. "Well, that didn't take long," she murmured as she exited the hotel. She permitted the doorman to hail a carriage. There was no need to make any further attempts to find work in Chicago. None of these men were going to hire her as a chef. She would make a speedy return to Pullman.

———

The clock chimed ten o'clock when she walked across the street from the Pullman train depot. The kitchen staff would be enjoying their midmorning break. Chef René and Mrs. DeVault were sitting together on one of the benches when she arrived.

"Ah, Miss Mott, I see you have decided to grace us with an appearance. How kind of you. Your visit to Chicago provided you with some surprises, oui?"

"Yes. Several surprises and none of them pleasant. I trust Mr. Howard advised you of my infirmity?"

"Oui. He demanded to know why you were away in Chicago on a workday."

Olivia dropped to the bench beside Mrs. DeVault.

"I was sorry to learn of your illness, but I was pleased Charlotte and Mrs. Priddle offered their hospitality." The older woman patted her hand. "Did you see Fred?"

"No. There wasn't time." She bowed her head. "I accomplished nothing."

She detailed the three visits she'd made and then shrugged her shoulders. "I don't think I'm going to meet with any success in Chicago, so Fred won't marry me. I'll never marry and will grow old working in the kitchen of Hotel Florence."

"I wouldn't count on that chicken," Chef René replied.

Mrs. DeVault grinned. "He means don't count your chickens before they hatch."

"Oui! Don't count on the chicken you don't have. Mr. Howard is most unhappy. I cannot say how much longer you will have a position here." He pointed at the tower clock. "It is time we return to work."

Chef René and Mrs. DeVault walked side by side toward the hotel while Olivia trailed behind them. She would question him further regarding his conversation with Mr. Howard later.

After donning her jacket and toque, Olivia read the menu for the noonday meal. "What would you like me to do? Begin the veal or the vegetables?"

Chef René crooked his index finger. "To my office, Miss Mott."

She followed him and took her customary chair while he edged behind the desk.

"Since we did not consider the fact that you might see Mr. Howard while in Chicago, we now have a problem."

Although she heard no accusation in his voice, she felt as though she must defend herself. "Thousands of people live in Chicago, and the possibility that I would come face-to-face with Mr. Howard never entered my mind." She removed a handkerchief from her pocket and wiped her perspiring palms. "Tell me what he said."

"He interrupted me during preparations for the evening meal, and although I explained I didn't have time for a meeting, he insisted upon joining me here in my office. He asked if I had given you permission to be in Chicago on a workday."

"What did you say?"

"I said I had granted your request to leave and that you were not being paid for the time you were away from work." The chef rested his arms on the desk. "He asked why you were in Palmer House."

Olivia's breath caught in her throat. "And?"

"I told him you could better answer his question than I."

"If he doesn't know, then why do you think I'll be discharged?"

"He said if you are able to spend your days in Chicago, then perhaps we have no need of an assistant chef. I attempted to convince him otherwise, but who knows with that man? One minute he is angry; the next he appears calm. I tell you this only so that you may be prepared for your meeting with him."

"Thank you for keeping my confidence. I know you didn't want to lie."

"I did not lie, Miss Mott. I told him to seek his answer from you. Now you must decide how you will weave this story of yours. I hope you will remember that no matter how painful, the truth will be the best way to go. I'm certain you haven't forgotten the terrible results that occurred . . ."

She nodded. "I don't need a reminder of what happened when I first arrived here."

He stood up and stepped toward the door. "You might want to consider prayer, Miss Mott. I don't think you will easily extract yourself from this situation."

"*You're* advising me to pray? Mrs. DeVault seems to have worked wonders in your life."

"Hazel says it is God that has worked wonders, not her. As for me? I think it was both of them." He waved her toward the kitchen.

Later that night after she had returned home, Olivia considered the chef's words. She would do everything in her power to avoid Mr. Howard, but he knew exactly where to find her during working hours. There was little doubt she would eventually be forced to answer his questions. It seemed prayer was the only answer. Yet she still didn't want to succumb to the possibility that God might have a plan that differed from her own.

———————

Olivia sat upright in bed. The loud knocking on the Mayfields' front door was insistent and sent her heart pounding. Who would be at the door in the middle of the night? Mrs. Mayfield knocked on her bedroom door and announced her cousin Albert was downstairs. Olivia slipped into her robe and clutched it tightly around her waist while she hurried downstairs.

She'd seen little of her cousin since Martha had made known his desire to distance himself from union members and strike sympathizers. But from Albert's frantic appearance, she knew something was amiss.

"Albert! What's happened?"

"Hurry and get dressed! Martha's having the baby, and she wants you to come."

"She needs a doctor, not me. Just because I was with Charlotte when Morgan was born doesn't mean I know how to deliver a baby. Mrs. DeVault did the difficult part of that birthing."

"The doctor is already there. She wants you there because . . ." He hesitated. "Well, because you're her friend, and you're family. Please come with me."

Olivia didn't miss the longing in his plea. "Give me a minute to make myself presentable."

Olivia could hear Albert's footsteps pacing the narrow hallway as she quickly donned a skirt and shirtwaist. She wouldn't take time to style her hair. Better to be disheveled than have Albert miss the birth of his first child. Moments later, the two of them hurried along the quiet darkened streets, the only light provided by shimmering stars and a half moon.

"Thank you for coming, Olivia. I was afraid you might turn me away."

She tucked her hand into the crook of his arm and leaned a little closer. "It's you who turned me away, Albert. I bear no grudge against either you or Martha. I understand your fears." Patting his hand, she smiled up at him. "I'm pleased you came to fetch me. It will give me great joy to welcome a new member into our family."

———

Fred arrived on the last train from Chicago to Pullman on Saturday night. He wanted to surprise Olivia and attend church with her on Sunday morning. They'd had little time together now that he'd convinced Bill they must continue to build the etching business. Although Bill had resisted at first, Fred had been persistent, explaining that if Bill decided to sell, he'd want to show a prospective buyer that the business had grown, even in the midst of an economic depression. Fred attributed the increase to Bill's innovative design and artwork, but Bill ignored the accolades. It no longer mattered whether anyone thought him talented. He wallowed in the belief he would never again be of use to himself or his family. Fred had to agree that Bill could no longer draw designs, yet he still had a vision for beauty whenever he pushed aside his resentment and shared his ideas.

Though Bill's physical wounds had healed, leaving him without the use of his right hand, Fred worried his friend's spiritual wounds might never heal. Each time something went amiss, Bill railed against God. He believed nothing in his life to be acceptable. He refrained from criticizing Fred but found fault with Ruth on a daily basis, and Fred wondered how much longer she would silently forbear her husband's verbal assaults. On several occasions Fred had broached the subject, but Bill had made it abundantly clear he did not want Fred's interference. If only he could think of some meaningful work that would permit Bill the opportunity to use the talents God had given him.

The house was dark when Fred arrived home. He entered quietly and slipped upstairs and into bed. Before he drifted off to sleep, he prayed for an answer to Bill's dilemma, but mostly he prayed for Ruth and the children.

The following morning he hurried downstairs, and after a hearty breakfast with his mother, he strode toward the Mayfields' flat. His mother had assured him Olivia would be delighted by his unannounced visit. However, when he'd inquired about Olivia's success with her search for a position in

Chicago, his mother had been less forthcoming. He didn't pursue the topic; he'd see Olivia soon enough.

He spotted Olivia on the front porch and quickened his gait. She turned and her face split in a smile when she saw him.

He panted for breath as he reached her side. "Did I manage to surprise you?"

"Yes. It's wonderful to see you."

Fred touched his thumb to the hollow beneath her eye. "Are you not sleeping well?"

"I was with Martha and Albert most of the night. I've been home only long enough to change clothes." She clutched his arm. "They have a wonderful baby boy. I couldn't believe how big he is. They've named him Alexander; he is a handsome little man." She babbled on and on, her excitement mounting as she told him about the child. "I do believe Albert is going to prove an excellent father. He couldn't wait to hold his son."

"I'm pleased all went well, and I'm glad Martha wanted you present for the birth. I know it's been difficult not seeing much of her these past weeks."

"I've missed both of them, but it was their desire that I stay away. And I don't want Albert to think his association with either of us has harmed his future at the car works."

Fred grasped her elbow and escorted her down the front steps. "I'd like to see all of them, but it's probably best I don't."

Olivia nodded. "You're likely correct. Besides, I doubt there will be time this afternoon, for I've invited Charlotte and Matthew to come for a visit. I'm not certain they'll accept my invitation, but it would be great fun for all of us to enjoy a picnic and go boating, don't you think?"

He tucked her hand into the crook of his arm. The softness of her skin never ceased to surprise him. "Yes, a picnic would be wonderful. You look especially lovely today. Is that a new dress?"

She laughed and shook her head. "No. A very old dress that I've refurbished with a bit of ribbon and lace, but I'm pleased you like it."

A group of parishioners had gathered outside the church to visit prior to the service. Several greeted Fred as they approached and then told him the latest facts and figures: how many men had now returned to work and how many families had left in search of employment elsewhere. Those who had left the town had departed owing large sums of rent, but thus far the company had made no effort to collect from them. Fred imagined the effort to locate the former employees would prove difficult. At least those who moved on would begin their new lives afresh. Unless Fred missed his guess, those who remained would be paying off their rental debt for years to come.

Benjamin Guilfoyle clapped Fred on the shoulder. "I hope you don't hold any ill will against those of us who have returned to work at the factory."

Fred extended his arm and shook hands with Benjamin. "Of course not. You have to do what's best for you and your family. I can't fault a man for wanting to put food on his table."

"What about you, Fred? Olivia tells us you're helping Bill Orland with his business. You thinking of throwing in with him on a permanent basis?"

Fred motioned toward the church entrance. "Not sure what the future holds just yet, Benjamin. We best get inside before the services begin." He grasped Olivia's hand and escorted her up the steps before Benjamin could question him any further. Today he wanted to enjoy his time with Olivia and discover what progress she'd made with her job search.

CHAPTER THIRTY

Pullman, Illinois
Sunday, August 26, 1894

At the touch of his fingers on her elbow, Olivia looked at Fred as they descended the steps after church.

Fred nodded toward the grassy expanse down the street. "Why don't we sit in the park for a few minutes before returning home? I want to talk to you in private, and if Charlotte and Matthew arrive, I doubt we'll have much time to ourselves." Lydia and Hannah Quinter raced down the church steps toward Olivia, their pigtails bouncing on their shoulders with each step. Fred grinned at the girls. "And there's certainly no privacy at home."

After they explained their plans to Fred's mother, the older woman and Chef René headed off in the opposite direction. Olivia marveled at the sight of the chef without his white jacket and toque. Seeing him in a dark suit with a crisp white shirt and perfectly knotted tie still seemed strange. He appeared a different man. And in some respects he was. The chef had always treated her with fairness and a greater kindness than she had, at times, deserved. But since he'd been courting Mrs. DeVault, Olivia had observed a more tender nature evolving. He no longer permitted his anger to boil over like a bubbling pot of water, even when the kitchen boys tried his patience. Mrs. DeVault's character had influenced Olivia for the good; now it appeared she was doing the same for Chef René.

She truly wondered what the future held in store for the older couple. There had been several occasions when her curiosity had nearly bested her, but she'd withheld her questions.

"Has your mother mentioned any plans for the future?" Olivia asked as she and Fred walked across the street.

He shook his head. "I've seen as little of her as I have of you. Right now I'm more interested in discussing your progress in locating a new job. That will affect my future much more than any plans of my mother's making."

"Searching for a position is very difficult. There is little time to do so."

"Chef René refuses to assist you?"

She didn't want to cast blame on the chef, for her failure didn't rest with him. He had permitted her time away from work for her venture into Chicago. But she worried that admitting her defeat would confirm Fred's fears and seal her fate. Instead of recounting her failure at the hotels she'd visited, she told him about becoming ill in Chicago and the subsequent need to remain overnight.

"I didn't even have the opportunity to visit you. I had hoped to surprise you with a visit to Bill's glass etching business."

He clasped her hand. "But you're feeling better now?"

"Oh yes. I still don't know what came over me. Charlotte thinks it was a case of nerves over the thought of losing you if I don't find employment."

Fred's upper body jerked as though she'd slapped him. "My intention is to create a solid marriage for us, not to cause distress." He quickly clasped her hand in his. "You explained my reasoning to her, didn't you?"

"Well yes, but I also told her I would happily marry you even if I couldn't secure employment."

For a brief time Olivia successfully steered the conversation away from her failures in Chicago, but after Fred offered sympathy and expressed gratitude for Charlotte's willingness to lend her assistance, he returned to the topic. "Did you have any time at all to place an application?"

She bowed her head. "No, I haven't filled out any applications." That much was the truth.

Using a gentle touch, he lifted her chin. "Did you visit any hotels or restaurants?"

"Yes." She decided a game of cat and mouse would prove dangerous, and she didn't want Fred ever again to accuse her of lying to him. "They wouldn't even look at my letter of recommendation or permit me to apply."

"None of them?" He appeared even more surprised by the turn of events than she had been.

"I had time enough to visit only three hotels. I hope to meet with more success on my next visit."

"When do you plan to return?"

"The opportunity may present itself more quickly than I anticipated." She twisted her handkerchief between her fingers while she described her unexpected encounter with Mr. Howard in Chicago. "I don't know if he plans to discharge me or not. I know he was angry that Chef René permitted me time away from the hotel, but he's said nothing more to either of us. My hope is that he's forgotten the incident."

Fred shook his head. "He's been busy with the commission meetings in Chicago, but when they're completed on Wednesday, you can be certain he'll return and address the matter."

Olivia gulped. "Do you think he will discharge me?"

Fred raked his hand through his hair. "Who's to say what that man will do? If he threatens your discharge, we can only hope that Chef René will come to your defense."

Her spirits plummeted. She had hoped Fred would say that none of it mattered and they would wed in spite of all that had occurred. But he didn't. He remained steadfast in his conviction that she would become restless and unhappy in their marriage without suitable employment.

Before she could wage further argument, Fred spotted Matthew, Charlotte, and Morgan crossing the boulevard from the train depot. Olivia now wished she hadn't invited them. She needed more time alone with Fred—time in which to change his mind about their future—but it didn't appear that would happen this afternoon.

Fred jumped to his feet and waved at Matthew. "Come along, Olivia."

Olivia watched the approaching threesome. They appeared a perfect family. Once they came alongside, Olivia looped arms with Charlotte, and the group headed toward the DeVaults' home. "It's good to see the three of you."

They walked up the front steps, and Morgan waved at a butterfly that swooped on the breeze and came to rest on the porch railing. He giggled and leaned to the side, delight shining in his eyes.

"Butterfly," Charlotte explained as she followed Olivia into the house.

Olivia was happy to discover Mrs. DeVault had returned

home with Chef René and they had prepared and packed the picnic lunch. Even Chef René had agreed to attend, but not without Mrs. DeVault's urging. At first he'd declared that only those who wished to share their food with ants and bugs ate on the ground, but after a few whispered words and an enchanting smile from Mrs. DeVault, he agreed a picnic would prove a fine diversion for the afternoon.

When they arrived at a particularly picturesque spot near Lake Calumet, they spread their blankets beneath a canopy of tree branches, and the women unpacked the baskets. Morgan plopped down beside Chef René and promptly pulled a clump of grass and examined the thin green blades for a moment before rolling to his hands and knees and pushing himself back up to a standing position.

The child grinned and toddled toward a clump of nearby bushes. The chef watched and then saw what had attracted the boy. Two young girls were partially hidden behind the greenery. Ragged and thin, they watched every move with a longing that tugged at the man's heart. Hunger was a terrible thing. He whispered to Hazel, who nodded. Then he beckoned to the little girls.

When they didn't move, he called, "Do you want something to eat, girls?" One of them peeked through the branches and bobbed her head. "Then you must come here, and we will give you some food."

Mrs. DeVault held up a sandwich, and the girls edged toward them with outstretched hands. Their ragged dresses hung from their bony frames, and their hair hung limp around their shoulders. Like young animals fearful of taking food from a stronger creature, they approached with guarded caution, their eyes widening at the food spread on the cloth. They accepted the sandwiches Mrs. DeVault offered and stood by quietly, as if hoping for more.

"Where did they come from?" Charlotte whispered.

"They probably live in the shanties by the brickyards, but you can see children in the same condition living all over Pullman," Fred replied. "Seeing them makes me feel guilty for enjoying a picnic lunch."

"Oui. But we are doing our best to help as many as we can," the chef said, handing each of the girls an apple. They turned and raced off as quickly as they'd appeared.

"Since the letters the governor sent to Mr. Pullman didn't have any effect, I wonder if seeing some of these children would turn his heart," Matthew said while watching the girls disappear. "Perhaps I should write an article about the children and their desperate need for sustenance."

Fred lightly clapped Matthew on the shoulder. "I commend you for all you've attempted to do through your news reporting, but I don't think there's anything that will convince George Pullman he bears any responsibility."

"Unfortunately, you're probably correct. The men continue to resent him, but most were willing to give up their union affiliation and go back to work for him."

Fred shrugged. "If I had starving children, I'd likely do the same."

Morgan toddled toward the bushes where he'd seen the two girls, but his mother scooped him onto her lap to prevent his escape. With a boisterous yelp, he struggled to free himself.

"I'll take him for you," Matthew offered, extending his arms to the child. "Look at the boats on the water. We'll go watch them after you eat your lunch."

"Eat!"

"In a minute, young man. You must learn a little patience." Matthew lifted the boy onto his shoulders and pointed at a boat. While the child watched the water, Matthew inched closer to Fred. "How's Bill been doing of late?"

"Yes, I've been wondering that myself," Mrs. DeVault said.

"He seems to have lost his way, and nothing I say or do seems to help. I worry about Ruth and the children. Bill's hard on himself, but he's hard on them, too."

"Has he come up with any ideas for his future?" Matthew asked.

Fred shook his head. "I've attempted to include him in portions of the business where he could help, but he says he doesn't need my pity. There's no talking to him."

"I think I may have come upon something that would interest him," Matthew said. "I talked to an old friend who teaches at the Art Institute and explained a little about Bill and his work. They have an opening for an instructor who would work with both their architectural and art students. He thought Bill's talents sounded like a perfect fit." Matthew lifted Morgan down from his shoulders as they all gathered to fill their plates. "What do you think? Would he be interested?"

"He would be foolish to pass up such a wonderful prospect," Mrs. DeVault said as she handed René a plate.

Fred shrugged. "Passing up the opportunity might be foolish, but that doesn't guarantee he won't do so. Like I said, he's not himself, Mother."

"Does your friend realize Bill's limitations?" Olivia inquired.

"Yes. I explained in detail, but he doesn't believe it would hamper Bill's ability to teach. However, much would depend upon what Bill thinks. If he isn't enthusiastic and positive, he won't win the confidence of his students. Much would depend upon his interview, I suspect."

Olivia picked up a sandwich and handed it to Fred. "I'm certain you can find the proper method to encourage him, Fred. You seem to have a knack for persuading others to search for employment."

"Only when I deem it absolutely necessary."

Olivia refrained from saying anything further regarding their personal disagreement.

Fred turned to Matthew. "I'll discuss this opportunity with Bill when I return to Chicago this evening. In fact, if you have time, perhaps we could return on the same train and you could come with me. You'd be better equipped to answer his questions."

When Matthew quickly agreed, Olivia leaned close to Fred. "You're not planning an early departure, are you? I had hoped we could continue our conversation from before."

"Have you decided what train you'll be taking back to the city, Matthew?" Fred asked.

Matthew glanced at Charlotte. "The six o'clock. Charlotte doesn't want to disrupt Morgan's bedtime schedule."

Olivia was disappointed, even though she realized the job was an excellent opportunity for Bill.

"I'll do my best to come back during the week. And if you're able to come to Chicago again, there may be time for a visit."

She pulled her lips into a narrow seam at his final remark and leaned close to whisper her response. "I told you Mr. Howard is unhappy with me. I doubt it would be wise to attempt another visit so soon."

As promised, Matthew accompanied Fred back to Locka-bee's. It had taken Fred several attempts and a good fifteen minutes before Bill would even agree to meet Matthew. After crossing the first hurdle, Fred tentatively suggested Bill take a few minutes to prepare for the meeting. But when Bill walked downstairs to meet Matthew, his hair was unkempt and his face unshaven. He'd not even bothered to tuck in his wrinkled shirt. Fred inwardly cringed. It seemed Bill was intent upon self-defeat and failure. For the life of him, Fred couldn't figure out how to reach the man. He hoped Matthew would find the words Bill needed to hear.

When Bill approached, Matthew stood and extended his hand. "I'm Matthew Clayborn."

"I'm afraid I can't properly shake hands." With his left hand, he pointed at his injured right hand.

Fred cringed at Bill's obvious attempt to embarrass Matthew. However, his friend appeared undeterred. "My apologies, Bill. Hope you don't consider me thoughtless, but in my days of reporting I've come across a number of men with injuries such as your own. They simply offer the other hand."

Bill grunted. "Fred said you have some kind of job offer."

"Oh, it's not an offer, but there's an opening at the Chicago Art Institute," he said as they sat down. "Fred has told me about your talent, and I mentioned your name to the man in charge of a new program they're developing." Matthew explained the position more thoroughly, and as he talked, Bill began to ask questions.

Finally Matthew shook his head. "To tell you the truth, I've given you about as much information as I have about the job. However, I'm not certain you're the right man for the position. They need someone with vision and excitement."

An Uncertain Dream

Matthew didn't mince words. He leaned back in his chair, folded his arms across his chest, and told Bill why he would be a poor choice. Soon Bill was arguing and telling Matthew exactly why he'd be the perfect candidate for the position. With each volley, Bill fired back a response until Matthew finally called a truce. "Enough! I think you've finally convinced me you're at least worthy of an interview, but you'll have to give me your word you'll improve your appearance."

"You've got a deal," Bill replied and extended his left hand.

A short time later Fred walked Matthew to the door. "I don't know how you managed that, but I'm certainly thankful."

Matthew chuckled. "He isn't my friend, so I didn't have to worry about hurting his feelings. Since sympathy hadn't been working for you, I figured I should attempt the opposite. I thought he'd walk out on me, but when he started to ask questions, I figured I'd won him over. I'll let you know once his appointment is scheduled."

CHAPTER THIRTY-ONE

Chicago, Illinois

The next morning Charlotte had not yet entered the business district when broad fingers circled her wrist in a tight grasp. Startled, she turned and attempted to yank her arm away. She'd not even heard the sound of approaching footsteps. "Mr. Rehnquist! What are you doing?" She twisted her arm, still trying to wrest it free.

"Quit struggling, Miss Spencer. I won't hurt you. I simply wish to have a talk about what you've done."

She took stock of her surroundings, wishing she had taken a carriage to work. There were few buildings on the street and only one was occupied; the rest were in dilapidated condition, obviously deserted by the owners. Vandals had broken windows, and likely the only inhabitants were occasional transients seeking a place out of the weather.

"Please release my arm, Mr. Rehnquist." Her heart thumped in an erratic cadence, but her tone had been forceful. "We have nothing to discuss."

"Your arm will be bruised if you continue to fight against my hold, Miss Spencer. I will not release you until we have talked. I've waited all these days for this exact moment."

She frowned. "I don't know what you're talking about."

"A time when I could find you alone in a place where we wouldn't attract attention, where we could discuss your behavior."

His stare was cold and aloof. If he'd hoped to frighten her, he'd succeeded, yet she dare not let him know. She steeled herself to remain calm.

"I don't believe there is anything we need to discuss, but say what you've come to say so that I may be off to work. If I'm late, there will be questions."

"You've placed my position at Marshall Field and Company in jeopardy, Miss Spencer. You women want to have a man's job, but the moment you can't handle matters, you use your womanly wiles to aid your cause. I know you and your kind very well."

"If your position is in jeopardy, it is of your own doing, not mine. Have you considered it is this same unsuitable behavior that is the cause of your undoing? Yet you make the situation worse by detaining me." His menacing look was enough to send a shiver coursing through her body.

"I want you to go to Mr. Field and tell him you misspoke and that everything you said about me was a lie."

"I have never spoken to Mr. Field about your behavior. If he has discovered your shoddy actions, it has been through some other person."

Her response appeared to confuse him. A wagon appeared down the street, and Charlotte used the moment to advantage. Forcing her soprano voice to an ear-shattering pitch, she screamed for help. Startled, Mr. Rehnquist dropped his hold.

Hiking her skirt above her ankles, Charlotte raced toward the wagon. The driver reined the horses to a stop, jumped from the wagon, and threw Mr. Rehnquist to the ground. He instructed Charlotte to retrieve rope from his wagon, and soon he'd hogtied Mr. Rehnquist and deposited him into the back of the wagon.

"I'll take him to the police station downtown, where my brother works. You can be sure they won't turn him loose. You might have to come down and sign some papers or talk to my brother, but I doubt it. I'm an eyewitness to everything, so he's sure to take my word that this fellow was holding you against your will." He glanced at Charlotte's wrist. "That's likely going to turn black and blue come morning. It isn't broken, is it?"

"I don't think so." She extended her arm and wiggled her wrist. "See?"

He gave a firm nod. "Try putting some cold cloths on it soon as you can."

A short time later they arrived at Marshall Field's, and he pulled the horses to a halt in front of the store. Charlotte offered her thanks and a promise to come to the police station if needed. Joseph greeted her with a quizzical look, but she offered him only a forced good morning. It was the best she could do.

Taking a deep breath, she hurried up to her office and sat down at her desk to gather her wits. The altercation with Mr. Rehnquist had rattled her, and there was only one thing to do. Though she disliked going to Mr. Field, she must. Mrs. Priddle had already involved him in the situation, and when Mr. Rehnquist didn't appear for work, there would be questions. And she certainly didn't want Mrs. Priddle making another visit to the store when she learned of today's incident with Mr. Rehnquist.

Better to take care of the situation herself.

Mr. Sturgeon looked down his nose when she entered the office and appeared pleased to inform her that Mr. Field had a full schedule. The man's behavior was tiresome. Palms flat on his desk, she met his cold stare. "You go in there and tell him I have a matter of urgency to discuss. We'll then see if he has a few minutes in his schedule."

Mr. Sturgeon sniffed and slapped his pencil on the desk. He didn't look at her when he returned to his desk. "You may go in."

Their meeting didn't take long. Mr. Field expressed his regret and concern and said he would personally visit the police station to ensure all was in order. "I don't want that man accosting you in the future. I treated him fairly and permitted him to remain on my staff, albeit in a different position. I knew he was unhappy that I transferred him to the warehouse store. Give this matter no further thought."

She thanked him for his promised help, but there would be no easy way to cast aside all thought of the assault. Her aching wrist was proof enough of that.

He walked around the desk and escorted her to the door. "You may trust that Mr. Rehnquist will never again accost you in any manner. He will be leaving the city once he is released from jail. You have my word."

———

Late Monday afternoon Matthew had appeared to announce he'd secured an appointment for Bill the following morning at nine o'clock. He'd encouraged Bill to make a good impression. Fred had been pleased when Bill arrived downstairs on Tuesday morning freshly shaved and wearing a suit and tie.

He'd obviously taken Matthew's advice to heart and hoped to secure the position.

Fred sent him on his way with a promise that he'd be praying all would go according to God's plan for Bill's life. Probably not the words Bill wanted to hear, for he continued to hold God accountable for his injury. Still, Fred had seen tremendous signs of progress with his friend over the past twenty-four hours. He prayed it would continue.

Fred looked up from his work when Ruth entered the shop early in the afternoon. "Still no sign of Bill?" she asked.

"Not yet." Fred continued to sift through several orders and jot notes, a job he usually completed late in the afternoon. He didn't want to admit he'd moved to the front of the shop in order to speak with Bill the minute he returned.

"I thought he'd be back before noon." Ruth paced across the wood floor while gazing out the front windows. "You think something terrible has happened to him?"

"What could possibly happen, Ruth?"

She folded her arms across her chest and stepped close to the counter. "The day he injured his arm I never considered anything could happen. I no longer make that assumption."

He observed the pain that shone in her eyes and immediately regretted his casual remark. "Interviews can take a long time, and there's always the possibility he had to speak to more than one person. If so, he may have been required to wait." Fred forced a smile. "Who knows? Maybe they took him to lunch at some fancy restaurant."

Ruth shook her head. "I doubt Bill would want to join them for a meal. He still has too much difficulty cutting his food and handling utensils. He'd be embarrassed and likely not order anything but coffee."

While they continued to discuss the possibilities, the door opened and Bill greeted the two of them. He carried a folder containing his drawings beneath his arm. "They liked these and said I had a natural gift," he said, dropping the folder onto the counter. "I told them I'd produced the last of my designs when I'd been injured, so they'd see no more art from me."

"They didn't offer you the job?" Ruth asked.

Bill shook his head. "Quite the contrary. They said my art would continue so long as I was willing to teach others. They talked to me at length about their hopes to expand this new program at the institute." He enthusiastically explained the details while Fred and Ruth listened. "They offered me the position, but there's still one problem."

"What's that?" Fred asked.

"I'm obligated to Mrs. Lockabee. Since Jacob's death, she's dependent on the money I pay her each month. I can't cancel the contract unless I have someone willing to take over the business."

Fred didn't fail to note the expectant look in Bill's eyes. "Are you asking me to take over the business?"

"Could you? I know you can't move back to Pullman, but I don't know if you want to stay in Chicago. I haven't had the place long enough to acquire much interest in it, so I wouldn't expect you to pay me anything—just take over the monthly payments to Mrs. Lockabee. What do you think?"

Ruth grasped his arm. "Wait! Where will we live if Fred takes over your contract?"

"The institute provides housing for its instructors. Much nicer than what we have here." He grinned. "I've already had a tour. You won't believe our good fortune."

Fred leaned across the counter. "Good fortune? This isn't

good fortune, Bill. It's answered prayer. Let's give God His due. You never said bad luck caused your accident. You blamed God. How come this turn of events is now good fortune rather than the hand of God?"

Bill appeared shamefaced for a moment. "You're right, Fred. I need to have a long talk with God. My behavior has been less than admirable, and I owe apologies to both of you and to the children, as well. I'm surprised you were able to tolerate me."

Fred chuckled. "I don't know about Ruth, but there were several times when I considered using some mighty strong words to gain your attention. However, now that you've offered to let me buy into this business, I may have to forgive you."

Bill's smile spread wide. "You'd be willing?"

Fred nodded. "I'd be more than willing. I'd be delighted. If I can take over the contract, what's happened today would be the answer to more than just one prayer."

"Then let's talk to Mrs. Lockabee and see if we can find a lawyer who will draw up the papers."

By the following morning Fred was the owner of Lockabee's Design and Glass Etching Shop.

He had little doubt Olivia would be surprised by this turn of events.

———

When Charlotte arrived at work on Wednesday morning, Joseph greeted her with a cheery hello. He crooked his index finger, and she stepped to the side of the entrance. "Have you heard the latest news, Miss Spencer?"

She tipped her head to one side. "How would I know if anything I'd heard was the latest news, Joseph?"

His brow furrowed and he hesitated for a moment. "That's

a good point, Miss Spencer. I guess I never thought of that." Then he grinned. "Seems Mr. Rehnquist is off to England on a ship early this morning. Mr. Sturgeon told me. We've become good friends."

"Is that right? I wonder why Mr. Rehnquist is traveling to England."

Joseph leaned closer. "Don't repeat this, but he got in some kind of trouble with the law. Mr. Field didn't want any bad publicity for the store, so he sent him to England to work with his brother. Mr. Sturgeon said he doubted Mr. Rehnquist would last very long at his new position. He said Mr. Field's brother can be very difficult."

"Goodness, but Mr. Sturgeon certainly is a fount of information, isn't he?"

Joseph squared his shoulders. "He only talks to me because he knows I can keep a secret."

"Truly?" Charlotte grinned and stepped toward the door. "I hope you soon learn." She didn't wait for a response. Poor Joseph didn't realize the contradiction of his words and deeds. That fact aside, Charlotte was pleased to know Mr. Rehnquist was on his way out of the country. She hoped he hadn't spoken to Mr. Field of her relationship with Matthew prior to his departure. If so, her discharge would be Joseph's next tidbit of "latest" news.

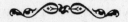

CHAPTER THIRTY-TWO

Pullman, Illinois
Friday, August 31, 1894

Olivia's heart thumped as loud as the drums in the Pullman Band. The summons to Mr. Howard's office had been completely unexpected. He'd arrived back in town on Wednesday morning, and with each passing hour she'd become more confident that he had forgotten her visit to Chicago. He had spoken to Chef René on two occasions since his return, and her presence in Chicago had not been mentioned. He'd merely discussed minor changes he expected to occur now that the car works was returning to full operation. The city agent expected the hotel would once again be filled to capacity and people would soon forget the blemish caused by the strikers.

However, Olivia knew Mr. Howard didn't plan to discuss such matters with her. She crossed the street and passed between the open iron gates. The journey seemed reminiscent of her first visit to the administration office when she'd hurried behind Chef René. How much had changed since then. She inhaled a deep breath before entering the building.

Mr. Mahafferty sat behind his desk bearing the same gloomy countenance he'd worn when Olivia first met him. At least one thing hadn't changed. The clerk signaled for her to have a seat before he returned to his ledgers. Olivia counted the leaves in the wallpaper, thinking it an odd choice for the city agent's office. Strange that she'd never noticed it before. When she'd counted nearly a thousand leaves, Mr. Howard opened the door to his office.

Her heart resumed the jarring cadence she'd experienced earlier. She automatically stood when he appeared, but he waved her back into her chair.

"I have several other matters that require my attention. You'll have to wait." He pinned her with a cold stare before motioning Mr. Mahafferty into his office.

He likely hoped the additional wait would either try her patience or create fear. He had succeeded on both accounts. He'd summoned her to his office while supper preparations were in progress, a time when he knew her absence would cause a hardship. Once again she counted leaves on the wallpaper and hoped Chef René didn't think she was dawdling on her way back to the kitchen.

She tapped her shoes, crossed her legs, folded her hands, and longed to rush out of the office. When she thought she could no longer sit in the chair, Mr. Mahafferty reappeared and bid her go in to meet with Mr. Howard. Now that she'd been granted entrance, she felt as though she'd been permanently affixed to the chair. Her arms didn't seem to have the strength to push her upright.

Mr. Mahafferty glowered and pointed his index finger toward the door. "I suggest you go in there posthaste."

They both knew it was more than a suggestion, and his searing command was enough to propel her upright. She forced one foot in front of the other. The door creaked and Mr. Howard looked up from his desk.

"Close the door after you." He didn't look up but focused on the ledger resting atop his desk.

After doing his bidding, she walked as far as the chairs sitting opposite his desk and clutched the cold wood for support. She selected a spot directly above his head and stared straight ahead.

"Do sit down, Olivia. I don't want you fainting during my questions."

So this *was* going to be about her day in Chicago. Why else would he make reference to her fainting spell? She circled the chair, sat down, and folded her hands in her lap. One thing was certain: he'd have to question her, for she would volunteer nothing.

He placed his pen in the holder and leaned back in his chair. "I've been extremely busy over the past week. I tell you that only to explain why I have waited to speak with you. During the course of my meetings in Chicago, I had an opportunity to visit with the manager of Palmer House. I'm sure you remember him."

Her palms perspired and the air felt heavy. She couldn't seem to breathe, and she tugged at the collar of her tunic.

"Please don't faint again, Miss Mott. I'm truly not up to your theatrics today." He strode to the window and opened it several inches.

A slight breeze wafted across the room. Olivia inhaled deeply and waited. He'd need to pursue her answers with greater vigor if he expected her to respond.

He tapped his fingers on the desk. "Well, Miss Mott? Are you going to answer me?"

She tipped her head to the side. "I didn't realize you'd asked a question."

"If you don't wish to discuss the matter, then I'll simply tell you what I now know. You have been attempting to place applications for employment at hotel restaurants in the city. The managers of Palmer House and Grand Pacific both confirmed you had visited them." He leaned across the desk. "They also stated you had a letter of recommendation from Chef René in your possession."

Olivia didn't respond, but her stomach roiled. She feared that if she didn't faint, she might disgorge her meal on the oriental carpet beneath her feet. She took a deep breath again and swallowed.

"You are discharged, Miss Mott. You have until Sunday night at midnight to remove yourself and your belongings from Pullman."

"But Chef René needs time to—"

"You weren't worried about him when you were seeking employment in Chicago. And Chef René was not overly worried, or he wouldn't have agreed to assist you."

"I haven't yet secured another job."

"That, Miss Mott, is not my problem. You obviously are unhappy working in Pullman. Had you checked with me, I would have told you that you'll not find another restaurant that will hire you as a chef. They hire men to work in their kitchens. You'll be fortunate to find employment washing dishes." He waved at her as though swatting a fly. "This discussion is over. And tell Chef René I will be dining in the hotel for supper. I want to speak with him in his office once the restaurant closes for the evening."

She'd reached the door when he called her name. Olivia glanced over her shoulder.

"It could have been different if you'd have chosen the right man."

"I *did* choose the right man."

She turned the doorknob and walked out of his office, glad that she would never again have to listen to Samuel Howard's hurtful words yet frightened about her future. Where would she go? She couldn't move in with Mrs. DeVault. In fact, after Sunday, she couldn't live anywhere in Pullman.

The tower clock struck the hour, and she hastened her step. She would be needed in the kitchen to help with supper preparations. After tomorrow, she would never again step into the kitchen of Hotel Florence. A knot settled in her stomach. If only she hadn't collided with Mr. Howard at Palmer House. How could a simple incident result in such upheaval? She censured herself. Such thoughts were useless. For now, she must forget the conversation and assist Chef René.

The chef motioned toward the stove. "Did you go home for a nap, Miss Mott?"

She shook her head. "No. Even though Mr. Howard had scheduled a specific time for our appointment, he made me wait a long time before he would see me."

"The man is a nuisance. Does he not realize we have guests expecting a fine dinner?" Chef René stood near the sink and sharpened his carving knife.

Olivia removed the trussed chickens from the oven and set them on the cutting board to rest before carving. "He said he will meet with you in your office after supper."

He twisted around. "You are having fun with me, non?"

"No."

The chef pointed the knife toward the car works. "What happened over there at your meeting?"

Olivia had intended to wait to tell him, but the words spilled out before she could stop them. "He has discharged me. Tomorrow is my last day in the kitchen, and I must move out of Pullman by midnight on Sunday."

The chef's knife clattered as it fell into the sink. "This is a cruel joke, Miss Mott."

She stepped closer and related the full content of their conversation. "I fear he will take you to task for writing that letter of recommendation. You're going to suffer retribution because of me."

He picked up the knife. "Mr. Howard will have his say, and I will have mine. But for now, the poultry must be carved."

Olivia had wanted to wait to go home until after the chef's meeting with Mr. Howard, but he had insisted that she leave after the meal preparation was completed. Now she would have to wait until morning to hear a full disclosure of their discussion. She should go home and begin to sort through her belongings and pack for her move—but move to *where*?

Olivia wished Fred were here so they could discuss what had happened. She had celebrated with him only a couple of days ago the good news regarding the purchase of the etching business and believed God was providing a path for them to eventually begin their life together. All that remained was locating a position for her in a Chicago restaurant. Now she found herself without a job in Pullman or Chicago. And with no place to live, either. Perhaps Mrs. DeVault could offer some sage advice.

Instead of stopping at home, she continued down the street and waved at Lydia and Hannah Quinter, who were enjoying their usual game of hopscotch during the final hour of waning daylight. A pang of envy struck her as she watched them in their carefree play. Even her childhood had been plagued with hardships similar to those she'd experienced as an adult. "No need for self-pity," she muttered while climbing the steps and knocking on the door.

Mrs. DeVault greeted her with her usual good cheer and affection. "Come have a cup of tea with me where we can visit in private."

Paul and Suzanne were in the parlor with baby Arthur. Olivia visited with them for a few minutes before joining Mrs. DeVault in the kitchen.

"I must admit I expected to see René standing at my door, but I'm happy you've stopped by to see me."

While Mrs. DeVault prepared tea, Olivia explained the chef was to meet with Mr. Howard. "I don't know how long he will be detained." She then recounted her own disturbing news.

"It appears Fred's determination for you to locate a job in Chicago has had quite a devastating result." The older woman sat down opposite Olivia. "There is so little time. Have you arrived at any decisions?"

Olivia wagged her head. "I thought about Priddle House. Not a pleasant idea, but I could certainly cook for the residents if I can't find work elsewhere, and I would at least enjoy being around Charlotte and Morgan."

"Do you think Mrs. Priddle would accept you?"

Olivia shrugged. "I don't know if there is adequate space at the moment. There's little time for me to make arrangements, but Mr. Howard cared not a whit. If Chef René will grant me permission, I may go into Chicago after breakfast tomorrow. I could be back in plenty of time to help with the evening meal. It would also give me an opportunity to visit with Fred."

Mrs. DeVault poured a cup of tea for each of them. "I think that's a sound idea. And I'm certain René will permit your absence for a few hours." She stirred a dollop of cream into her tea. "Just between us, I don't think he's overly intimidated by Mr. Howard."

Olivia didn't comment. She didn't want to alarm the older woman. She had avoided mentioning that Mr. Howard had been extremely angry that the chef had penned a letter of recommendation for her. Of course, Mr. Howard could ill afford to discharge the chef. Who would take charge of the kitchen? Only a fool would do such a thing.

Mrs. DeVault offered Olivia one of Suzanne's hot cross buns. "Suzanne prepares these buns at least once a week, and if she attempts to forgo the practice, Hannah and Lydia don't fail to remind her."

"Speaking of the Quinters, has Paul applied for work? Surely he can get back on with the car works."

Mrs. DeVault nodded. "Yes. He begins next week. They're already making plans to rent their own place. Now that Fred has taken over the business in Chicago and will be living in the upstairs rooms there, I've decided to move into a small set of rooms in the hotel. René tells me there is adequate space on the third floor for a small apartment." She chuckled. "I know he disliked discussing the matter with Mr. Billings, but the hotel manager advised him that I could rent the space at a nominal rate—no more than I'd pay for room and board with another family."

The arrangement sounded perfect. It seemed life was on the upward turn for everyone—everyone except her. But perhaps all of that would change once she spoke to Fred. She forced herself not to become overly optimistic, but secretly she hoped her lack of employment would be the impetus Fred needed to move forward with their marriage. She didn't require a large wedding. A simple ceremony performed before a minister with only their closest friends and family present would suit.

Olivia hadn't been listening to Mrs. DeVault's chatter, but when the older woman squeezed her hand, she looked up. "I'm sorry. I was lost in my own thoughts."

The older woman chuckled. "So I noticed. Why don't we spend some time in prayer? I believe we should ask God to give you peace and understanding during this difficult time of indecision."

"And if He'd provide a place to live, that would be good, too," Olivia added.

Chef René's arrival at the front door a short time later ended their prayer session. "Ah! Here you are, Miss Mott. I stopped at the Mayfields', but was told you hadn't come home. I was worried. I am glad you decided to seek solace among friends."

"Your meeting with Mr. Howard—how did it go?" Olivia asked.

The chef shook his head and curled his lip in disgust. "The man tried my patience to the fullest extent, and I was forced to quit."

Olivia jumped up from her chair and sent it plummeting to the floor in a loud crash. "*What?* Why would you *do* such a thing?"

He shrugged. "Why not? Let Mr. Howard see how it feels to be left in the lurch. He seems to have no trouble imposing difficult circumstances upon others."

Mrs. DeVault's eyes were alight with uncertainty. "Don't you think it would have been best to make your decision based upon thought and prayer rather than emotion? I'm not certain this is wise, René."

"Do not worry, Hazel. My decision is not so impulsive as you think. All these years I have been saving money, thinking that one day I would open a restaurant of my own. A place where no one else would tell me what I must serve or who could or could not eat in my establishment. I think that the time has arrived. Tomorrow I will go into Chicago and see what opportunities I can discover."

Mrs. DeVault's jaw went slack. "You're going to purchase a restaurant?"

He gave an emphatic nod. "And you and Olivia will come to work for me, oui? All our problems, they will be solved. Fred will marry Olivia, you will marry me, and we will all live very happily."

Olivia had righted her chair and dropped onto the seat. She didn't know if the chef's pronouncement had come as more of a surprise to Mrs. DeVault or to her.

Mrs. DeVault's cup rattled when she replaced it on the saucer. "Married?" She pointed back and forth between them. "Us?"

"But of course. We love each other. Why should we wait?" He tapped Olivia's arm. "We will have two weddings at the same time. What do you think?"

Olivia clasped her hand to her chest. "I don't know what to

say. I think it's a grand idea if you want to open a restaurant, but such a venture takes time."

"Not when we have Hazel offering up her prayers. It will all work out; you will see. Have faith, Olivia."

Olivia thought he needed to utter the same admonition to Mrs. DeVault, for she didn't appear any more convinced than Olivia. "I think I should go home and permit the two of you time to discuss this matter more fully in private." She patted Chef René's hand. "Marriage proposals usually take place without a third party present."

"Then I shall remain and beg Hazel's forgiveness. And you, Miss Mott, will spend your final day in charge of the Hotel Florence kitchen." He grinned. "I wish you well."

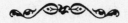

CHAPTER THIRTY-THREE

While she prepared omelets for the hotel guests on Saturday, Olivia considered when she might have time to visit with Fred. Probably not until the next morning, since the chef's announcement had curtailed her plans to visit Chicago. There would be little time for them to formulate a plan. She waved to one of the kitchen boys to pick up the serving dishes and take them to the hot closet.

They'd completed the supper service when Olivia caught sight of a woman loitering near the back door. Olivia recognized her as one of the women who occasionally visited church with her three children. She stepped outside the door. "Mrs. Beacon, isn't it?"

"That's right," the woman mumbled. "I was wondering . . . I mean one of the ladies told me . . ." She twisted a loose thread around her fingers. "My children are hungry. My husband hasn't a job yet, and I thought maybe you'd help." She gazed longingly at the kitchen door. "Do you have any leftovers in there?"

"Wait here and I'll see what I can do," Olivia said.

She packed a basket with leftover chicken, dinner rolls, several pieces of fresh fruit, and the remnants of a coconut cake Mr. Billings had been eyeing earlier in the day. On her way toward the door, she spied carrots that had been purchased from the market yesterday. They'll be wilted by tomorrow, she decided, and she tucked them beside the fruit, not caring if any of the staff might see her actions. When Olivia returned outside, two of Mrs. Beacon's children had joined her near the kitchen entrance. Her young son leaned against his mother's side, his body so frail that Olivia wondered if he had the strength to walk home.

"I hope this will help." Olivia's voice cracked with emotion. Unfortunately, the Beacons were only one family among hundreds who continued to suffer.

Even for those who had returned to work, life remained tough. The strike had not accomplished what any of the workers had hoped. Their wages remained the same, their rent remained the same, they continued to sink further into debt, and the company still controlled life in the town of Pullman. Bitterness had taken root in the hearts of some, but most simply accepted the lack of change and returned to their lot in life. Olivia stared after the young family. Perhaps one day change would occur in this town. She hoped that a seed had been planted in the hearts of the men who maintained power and control. She prayed that one day it would sprout and take root.

Except for the fearful thoughts about her future, this day had passed like most. In truth, she had anticipated a visit from Mr. Howard. She had hoped he would appear and beg her to remain until he could find a replacement. But he'd not even taken his meals in the dining room.

Shortly after she'd given the basket of food to the woman and her children, Mr. Billings came into the kitchen and announced the dining room would not be open on Sunday. Those scheduled to work would have the day off—without pay, of course.

Before he left he beckoned to Olivia. She wondered if he planned to bid her a special farewell. Instead, he pointed at the pantry shelf. "Where is the leftover coconut cake, Miss Mott? I saw several pieces only a short time ago." He glanced around the room.

Olivia smiled sweetly. "Gone. And isn't that a good thing? Our coconut cake won't add to your expanding waistline."

Mr. Billings frowned from the doorway while she bid the remaining staff farewell and hung her white jacket and toque in the closet. Fear and sadness assailed her as she pinned her hat atop her chestnut curls and handed Mr. Billings her key. She descended the steps and inhaled deeply, hoping to carry the scent of this place with her awhile longer. The sound of the key turning in the lock sealed her fate. She'd been cast adrift in turbulent waters.

As she trudged toward home, Fred appeared from behind the trees where the staff gathered for their midmorning breaks. "May I walk you home, Miss Mott?"

She couldn't believe her eyes! Merely seeing him brightened her spirits. He bowed from the waist, and in spite of her sadness, she giggled at his behavior.

He kissed her on the cheek and tucked her hand into the crook of his arm. "I've made a mess of things for you, haven't I?" She attempted to object, but he didn't let her finish. "Chef René stopped to see me late this afternoon. He explained all that happened. I'm truly sorry, Olivia."

"Did he have any success in his search for a restaurant?"

"Indeed. He's found a place he thinks will be perfect. The bank foreclosed on the business several years ago, but it remains fully equipped. The chef isn't overly fond of the china and silver, but he says it will do until the business is in full operation. From his assessment, it will take several days of cleaning, but he signed papers only a short time ago."

"So soon? He should take more time with such a big decision."

"It doesn't seem he took much time before deciding to propose to my mother, either."

Olivia squeezed his arm. "So he told you? I'm pleased for them. They will make a fine couple."

"And so will we." He stopped beside one of the park benches. "I've been a fool making silly demands of you, Olivia. I love you, and that's what's important. Whether you go to work for Chef René when he opens his restaurant or stay at home, it will be your choice. Just tell me that my foolishness hasn't caused me to lose you."

"You could never lose me, Fred. I love only you."

He lifted her chin and kissed her full on the lips, the warmth of his embrace enfolding her with a love she knew would last forever. Together they would form a perfect union.

Recipes

Olivia's Cornish Pasties

Pastry:
4 cups flour
1/8 tsp. salt
1 1/2 cups shortening, chilled
1/2 cup + 2 Tbsp. ice water
1 egg, beaten (for egg wash)

Filling:
1 cup coarsely chopped turnips or rutabagas
2 cups finely diced lean boneless beef—top round or skirt steak
1 cup coarsely chopped onions
2 cups finely diced potatoes
1 1/2 tsp. salt
1 tsp. pepper

Preheat oven to 400°. To make pastry, fork together flour and salt with shortening to make a coarse meal. Add 1/2 cup ice water and mix. If dough crumbles, add 1 or 2 tablespoons more water. Refrigerate for one hour before rolling out.

Roll dough to a circle 1/4-inch thick and cut into six to eight 6-inch rounds. Re-roll the scraps and cut into additional circles. To prepare filling, cut ingredients into uniformly small pieces. The meat and potatoes cook together, so cut to appropriately sized cubes so that everything will get fully cooked in the same time period. Combine filling ingredients in a bowl and mix evenly.

Put ¼ cup of the mixture in the center of a rolled-out pastry. Moisten pastry edges, fold in half like a turnover, and crimp to seal. Place on a greased baking sheet and brush the pastries lightly with egg wash. Make 2 slits in each pasty to allow steam to escape.

Bake at 400° for 15 minutes and then reduce heat and continue at 350° until golden—approximately 45 minutes more. Serve hot or cold. They also freeze well. Makes 6–8.

Apple Butter

3 lbs. Macintosh apples, cored, peeled, and sliced
3 cups cider
¼ cup honey
¼ cup brown sugar, packed
1 tsp. cinnamon
¼ tsp. allspice
⅛ tsp. ground cloves

Bring apples and cider to a boil in a large heavy saucepan; reduce heat and simmer approximately 20 minutes or until apples are soft. Stir in remaining ingredients; mix well. Simmer an additional 45–60 minutes until apples break down into a very thick sauce. Cool just until warm; puree in food processor or blender. If consistency is too watery, return to saucepan and simmer until thickened. Cover and refrigerate. Will keep up to two months in refrigerator. Makes about 2 pints.

Suzanne Quinter's Hot Cross Buns

1 cup milk
2 packages (or 4½ tsp.) yeast
5 cups flour
½ cup sugar
2 tsp. salt
1½ tsp. cinnamon
½ tsp. nutmeg
⅓ cup butter, softened
2 eggs, lightly beaten
1⅓ cups raisins
1 egg white, beaten

Glaze:
1⅓ cups confectioners' sugar
1½ tsp. finely chopped lemon zest
½ tsp. lemon extract
1–2 Tbsp. milk

In a small saucepan, heat the milk until it's very warm but not hot (110°). Pour warm milk into a large mixing bowl. Stir in the yeast and let sit for 5 minutes.

In a separate bowl, mix together flour, sugar, salt, cinnamon, and nutmeg. Add flour mixture to milk and yeast and stir well. Stir in the butter and 2 eggs. Stir in raisins. Turn dough out onto a lightly floured surface. Knead until smooth and elastic, adding more flour if necessary, about 5 minutes. Place dough in a greased bowl, turning the dough once to grease the top. Cover bowl with plastic wrap and let rise in a warm place until doubled, about 1 to 1½ hours.

Line two large baking pans with parchment paper or lightly grease the pans. Turn the dough out onto a lightly floured surface and knead briefly. Shape into two 12-inch logs. Cut each log into 12 equal pieces and shape each into a smooth ball. Place the rolls on the baking sheets, about an inch apart. Cover with a clean kitchen towel and let rise in a warm place until doubled, about 1 to 1 1/2 hours.

Preheat oven to 350°. When buns have risen, use a sharp knife to cut a shallow cross on the top of each bun. Brush buns with beaten egg white. Bake for 30–35 minutes or until golden brown. Transfer to a wire rack. Cool slightly.

Whisk together glaze ingredients and drizzle over buns in a cross pattern. Serve warm. Makes 24.

Chef René's Cheese Soufflé

4 eggs
2 Tbsp. butter
2 Tbsp. flour
3/4 tsp. salt
1/8 tsp. pepper
Grated nutmeg (to taste)
1 1/4 cups milk
3/4 cup finely shredded Swiss cheese

Preheat oven to 350°. Generously butter 4 individual soufflé dishes. Separate the egg whites from yolks. Stir the yolks until they are creamy and set aside.

Prepare the white sauce: melt the butter in a saucepan over medium heat. Add the flour, salt, pepper, and nutmeg, and stir with a wooden spoon until well blended. Cook for 2 minutes. Gradually add the milk; continue stirring and adding milk until all the milk is incorporated and the sauce thickens. Remove from heat. Stir in the cheese. Add the egg yolks, a small amount at a time, stirring vigorously.

Beat the egg whites with an electric mixer until they are thick and frothy. Gently fold the egg whites into the cheese mixture with a rubber spatula. Spoon the soufflé into the 4 dishes, filling each about three-quarters full. Bake for about 25 minutes or until the soufflés are golden brown. Do not open the oven door while they are cooking. Serve immediately.

ACKNOWLEDGMENTS

As this series comes to an end, I want to especially thank the staff of Bethany House Publishers. No book is the simple act of an author tapping words into a computer, and each member of the Bethany House team who worked on this series contributed mightily to its success. I am most grateful.

Thanks also to:

Linda Beierle Bullen and Mike Wagenbach of the Pullman State Historic Site, who answered my many questions and provided me with their excellent insights as well as tours of the hotel, car works, and the town of Pullman.

Tony Dzik for his outstanding photographic services while I visited in Pullman.

Members of the Historic Pullman Garden Club, who hosted a tea and book signing at Hotel Florence to celebrate the release of this series, and to Linda Beierle Bullen for her excellent promotional efforts for the event.

Mary Greb-Hall for her insights and unfailing assistance.

My sister and prayer warrior, Mary Kay Woodford.

Jim, my husband and faithful encourager.

A MESSAGE TO MY READERS

Dear Reader,

I hope this series whets your appetite for further exploration into the life and times of the residents and community of Pullman, Illinois. As you complete this series, you may want to visit the town or check some Web sites to learn more. If you have the opportunity to visit the town, I would encourage you to do so. The residents of the town are proud of their community, and restoration is an ongoing process.

I would particularly suggest you consider visiting during the second weekend of October, when the Historic Pullman Foundation and the Pullman Civic Organization cosponsor the annual Historic Pullman House Tour. The Pullman State Historic Site, which includes the Hotel Florence and the Pullman Factory, is open that weekend for tours. In addition, tours of the Greenstone Church are available. You may learn more about events scheduled throughout each year by going to *www.pullman-museum.org* and clicking on "Current Events" or *www.pullmanil.org* and clicking on "Visiting Pullman" and then "Calendar." Walking tours of the town are conducted on the first Sunday of the month from May through October.

More information on the Pullman era is available at the following Web sites: *www.pullman-museum.org* and *www.chipublib.org/008subject/012special/hpc.html.*

There are also numerous books of interest regarding both Mr. Pullman and his community.

While researching for this series, I visited Pullman and developed a deep love for the history of the town and its people. I hope you will experience the same pleasure.

Judy